The Poor Preachers

Portrait of John Wycliffe

The Poor Preachers

THE ADVENTURES OF THE FIRST LOLLARDS

- **Part 1: The Commission**
- **Part 2: The Missions Go Forth**

By

ARTHUR D BARDSWELL

Edited by

- **James Kochenburger**
  Konsensus, LLC.

- **Deborah Porter**
  Finesse Writing and Editing Services

WESTBOW
PRESS
A DIVISION OF THOMAS NELSON

WestBow Press books may be ordered through booksellers or by contacting:

WestBow Press
A Division of Thomas Nelson
1663 Liberty Drive
Bloomington, IN 47403
www.westbowpress.com
1-(866) 928-1240

Because of the dynamic nature of the Internet, any web addresses or links contained in this book may have changed since publication and may no longer be valid. The views expressed in this work are solely those of the author and do not necessarily reflect the views of the publisher, and the publisher hereby disclaims any responsibility for them.

Any people depicted in stock imagery provided by Thinkstock are models, and such images are being used for illustrative purposes only.

Certain stock imagery © Thinkstock.

ISBN: 978-1-4497-2953-0 (sc)
ISBN: 978-1-4497-2954-7 (hc)
ISBN: 978-1-4497-2952-3 (e)

Library of Congress Control Number: 2011919647

Printed in the United States of America

WestBow Press rev. date: 11/8/2011

To the Great Shepherd,
the Lord of the Harvest

Table of Contents

Preface

This story is based on historical events of reformer John Wycliffe's time, when he launched a special society of 'Poor Preachers', later known as 'Lollards'.

Why do I attempt such a task?

I have read historical accounts of John Wycliffe and his followers. The more I read, the more I became intrigued and inspired by their convictions and labours.

What courage that man possessed! What compassion for the poor he must have had, that he was willing to sacrifice his high position as possibly the most brilliant academic of his day, for the sake of getting the scriptures into the hands of the common folk.

How did his followers spread his message so quickly? Why did it have such a powerful effect, so much so that it was said even by a hostile chronicler that 'almost every second man in England is a Lollard'?

Being of a romantic disposition, my imagination was fired by the spectacle of men in russet-coloured habits walking barefoot throughout England, defying impossible odds to bring a message of hope in the midst of the terrible darkness of those days. Therefore, I began using my sanctified imagination and started to piece together the lives of a few of these followers, and those with whom they came in contact.

This is not meant to be another *Foxe's Martyrs*, even though it is obviously from a Protestant platform. Persecution of 'heretics' was admittedly cruel and brutal at times, but history records brutal acts by Protestants toward those of Roman persuasion and other branches of the Christian church also. Sectarianism is not quite dead, but it is dying, thank God! That is not what this is about.

This work is meant to concentrate on the move of the Holy Spirit and God's work of Grace amongst those who were seeking a real relationship with God, rather than merely an ecclesiastical reformation or a political movement to reduce the power of the rich prelates of the church.

I have the personal conviction that within the most powerful and beneficial ecclesiastical movements throughout the church age (often called 'Revivals') there has been a central core of believers with hearts on fire with a passion for God and for His people. These revivalists and their disciples were basically untouched by political agendas or personal gain, although a few did fall by the wayside. They were characterised by an uncompromising stand for Truth, even in the face of persecution and death. They made no secret of the motivating force that drove them, that is, a personal encounter with God, which owed nothing to established religious practice or socially acceptable 'piety'. These firebrands were the real movers and shakers that launched the greatest ecclesiastical movements, many of which have formed the major denominations or ecclesiastical categories we see today.

Some of these main players, such as John Wycliffe, are recognised in the annals of great historical change agents because of their prominent position and political impact. Many, however, are lost in obscurity because they took Wycliffe's message to the common folk; therefore, their stories were probably not considered worth recording at that time. These are the people I wish to focus on, by creating fictional characters based on my observation of the unsung heroes in more recent times, my research in scripture and the biographies of dedicated servants of God throughout history. Although some recorded historical figures have a look in occasionally, they mainly serve as a background to help me capture the atmosphere of the times in which the story is set.

Some of the historical accounts disagree, even in some important events; so please don't get up in arms if any historical event I mention does not agree with what they taught you at school. At times I have given up on these squabbling historians altogether, and created my own historical events to suit my undergirding convictions and the story's plot. I am a novel writer, not a professional literary archaeologist.

Many secular historians and modern historical documentaries like to look for the human element, often with a cynical focus on the supposed personal ambitions, ideological inconsistencies and weakness of character displayed (or assumed to have been displayed) by the chief players. Although these may have occurred in varying degrees, these mostly sincere scholars of history never see, or totally ignore, what I call the 'God Factor'. By this I mean the phenomena that occur in individual people's lives by the dynamic influence of a personal, compassionate, loving, yet all-powerful and uncompromisingly holy God. He is not particularly interested in our approval or tidy man-made world-views. He simply wants to redeem miserable mankind from the mess they have gotten themselves into.

Often, God's work of grace can only occur after tragedy and shattering events that shake us out of our complacency and comfort, forcing us to listen and give voice to the often stifled cry of our own hearts for the security and love that only God can give—and He is more than ready to give it, if we let Him.

We must remember that historians frequently have their own human frailties and prejudices that colour and even alter the facts. These are based on their own world-view, philosophy, convictions and theology, which drive their motivation and their thinking.

'But,' you may ask, 'aren't you doing the same thing in this story? Physician, heal thyself!'

Well, to begin with, this is not an historical document, and I do not presume to view myself as a qualified historian. There are gaps in my knowledge and research in this subject, so I am filling these gaps with conjectural hypotheses, and I do it without apology. There is only one piece of historical literature that has been proved to be absolutely accurate and has survived the test of time, the most thorough scrutiny and even attempts to discredit and destroy it.

This does not merely reflect my own personal experience and encounter with God. I have heard and read many, many testimonies of people who have experienced the power and the grace of God. These strongly documented experiences have had the same common threads running through them; threads that are also found when you read the Gospels and the Book of Acts.

I am convinced that God has been active in the lives of countless numbers of people throughout history, with the same common principles in operation, often with supernatural 'signs following'. Secular media has largely ignored most of these, which is to be expected. All journalists write from their own world-view, as explained earlier.

I understand, of course, that such phenomena are strongly disapproved of by many modern, western minds, who have never experienced anything supernatural themselves. Hence the focus on the Human Factor, and disregard for the God Factor, in secular history.

Others may look for the supernatural in unhealthy and even dangerous ways, such as in the occult and the New Age movement. The number of shipwrecked lives from this deception is phenomenal and tragic, but if the established church will not recognise the supernatural that our hearts secretly yearn for, people will look for it in unhealthy places. Such was the case in the 14th century.

This story suggests both the God factor and human frailty in the events of the Lollard awakening in 14th century Britain.

Regarding the use of archaic language in dialogue, this is not to be taken as strictly authentic language of the time. After reading, or attempting to read, the works of Geoffrey Chaucer, I considered it impossible to reproduce Middle English exactly as it was in the period. I have settled for a compromise, where I have tried to capture some of the quaint feel of the language and terminology of the period, but balanced it with readability. At times it becomes very Chaucer-ish, and I have thrown in some occasional Middle English words from my reading and research, but I don't claim any expertise in medieval language.

You will also notice the quotations at the beginning of the chapters. These are taken from works that the real-life contemporary historical characters either wrote or read in their day. My intention was to add to the authentic feel of the story, to give examples of the literary genius of the writers/translators, and to help set the theme of the chapter.

My prayer is that you will be as inspired by the courage and the efforts of John Wycliffe and his followers as I was.

Acknowledgements

- My mother, known by her penname: Russel Bavinton. She was the writer who first inspired me and guided me through my very early attempts at writing. It's in the blood.

- My wife, Anne, my kids and my extended family, for their support, enthusiasm, valuable feedback and encouragement.

- My spiritual family at CityLife Church, with a special mention to Jane Gunn, who especially encouraged me to think this whole project might work after all.

- My fellow-writers at FaithWriters.com, who gave me encouragement, good feedback and excellent mentoring.

- The Lollard Society, and other sources of information online, too numerous to mention here.

Part 1:

The Commission

Prologue

'...He was emaciated in body and well-nigh destitute of strength, and in conduct most innocent. Very many of the chief men of England conferred with him, loved him dearly, wrote down his sayings and followed his manner of life.'

(William Thorpe, commentary on John Wycliffe)

'Thou'rt a fool, John Wycliffe! Thou'rt wood wild!' shouted Doctor William Wadeford as he exploded to his feet, red-faced and furious.

Master Molesby, the convener of the debate, nervously hammered twice with his gavel. 'Doctor Wadeford, I beg of thee! This is unmannerly!'

The intervention was totally ignored by the irate and chagrined combatant. The rules of debate now went by the board.

Wadeford had challenged Doctor John Wycliffe to a public debate in order to put him in his place and silence his outspoken criticisms of the hierarchy of the church. Wycliffe had readily taken up the challenge, and every carefully prepared argument William Wadeford had dramatically presented was totally demolished by Wycliffe's forceful and very scholarly use of the scriptures.

Wadeford knew he had lost the debate by fair means, but he was determined to intimidate his enemy by any other means at his disposal. How dare he contradict the great Doctor Wadeford, Head of Merton College, Master Orator and Defender of the Faith, with the use of Holy Scripture! Beside, if this rebellion against Holy Church's iron grip spread any further, the inevitable backlash may affect the whole university faculty staff, and even upset his own comfortable situation and ambitions.

The fact that he could not answer Wycliffe's theological challenges was irrelevant. With a terrible voice of doom and a pointing finger shaking with righteous indignation, he thundered forth, 'Beware! Beware! Dost thou bite thy glove at Holy Church? Wist thou not that thou hast put a noose around thy neck? Dost thou think that thy heresies shall pass unpunished?

Dost thou, a mere mortal, presume to stand against the Holy Father of Rome?'

The object of this invective, wholly undaunted, turned his sardonic gaze upon his opponent. 'Is't the Holy Father of Rome? Or Avignon?' he asked dryly.

The audience, or most thereof, shouted with laughter at this masterly piece of sarcasm.

It had already become a joke around Oxford University that there were now two Popes, one in Rome and another in Avignon, both claiming the full authority of St Peter, and both excommunicating each other with unholy rage.

If Doctor Wadeford was chagrined and offended at his defeat before, he was absolutely furious at his humiliating embarrassment now. His face turned the colour of beetroot.

'That shall be resolved!' he almost screamed in his rage. 'Righteousness shall triumph e'er long, and Holy Church shall arise again and wreak terrible vengeance on them that fleer at her! Beware! Beware, John Wycliffe! Thine evil tongue shall be thy downfall! Repent of thine heresies and seek the pardon of the Holy Pontiff of...'

He broke off and grimaced as he realised that he had once again fallen into his own trap. A few mischievous students cried out, 'Rome? Avignon?'

At this, the great Doctor Wadeford almost had an apoplexy. He turned on the audience in panting fury. 'Scullions! Jack-Rakers! Imbeciles! Ye shall be damned unto perdition! Do ye dare fleer upon the Kingdom of Heaven?'

One powerfully built student with sandy hair rose to his feet and called out, 'The Kingdom of Heaven? Never! But hath not the little Kingdoms of Rome and Avignon poured scorn on their own heads?'

More derisive laughter applauded this comment.

The august Doctor Wadeford was not accustomed to being made to look ridiculous. He was losing control of the situation, which did not suit his dignity at all. The thing that made him the most furious was the suspicion that he had brought it all upon himself.

Master Molesby, in despair of recovering any semblance of order, hammered his gavel again and declared the debate closed. But William

Wadeford was not going to concede defeat that easily. He tried to recover, as Doctor Wycliffe rose to leave, apparently the victor of this engagement. It would be talked of for many a day.

'Heresy! Sacrilege! The hallowed portals of Oxenford are polluted by sin and rebellion!' he pursued desperately. 'And thou, John Wycliffe, art at the root of it!'

He then tried a different tack, appealing to his opponent's status and privileged position.

'Doctor Wycliffe!' He called out his warning to the tall, gaunt figure walking slowly down toward the entrance. 'Dost thou think that the Reverent Father of Canterbury shall suffer thine insolence to pass? Thou shalt lose thy position and privileges, nay, haply worse! Shalt bring shame on us all!'

Then, as Wycliffe turned to answer, another thought occurred to him. 'This also I would demand of thee, John Wycliffe. Thou hast the Gaunt[1] himself to shield thee – for the moment, yea! – but for the moment. But what if that shield forsake thee, or be take from thee? Was not the arrogance of King John himself humbled before the legate from…?'

A shade of annoyance crossed his face. He had nearly embarrassed himself again, but made a swift recovery in the face of his opponent's derisive smile. Summoning up his most persuasive and dramatic oratory, he tried his last throw.

'Answer then me this, John Wycliffe. How many of the great and noble bishops and prelates of England hath taken thy part? Wherewithal doth thy tracts and writings avail thee anon? Yea, even though thou movest them against the glory of the pontificate with thy cautelous and venomous quill!' He was careful not to be specific this time. 'Do those in the high places of Holy Church follow thy lead? Answer me that, John Wycliffe!'

Wrath flashed in the sunken eyes of the other man. 'Nay! They do not so!' he roared in return, breathing heavily in his anger. 'Long have I laboured and in vain, that ye all would hearken – not indeed unto me – but to the warnings of Holy Writ and the doom and reproach that hath come upon this land for its iniquity! The poor become poorer! Many lords of the realm do oppress them and the profligate and orgulous[2] princelings of Holy

---

1   John of Gaunt, Duke of Lancaster, regent for the crown
2   Crafty, cunning

Church do *naught* but bathe in her riches! Indeed, more oppressive yokes they lay upon the backs of the people also! Methought that either pontiff – *whosoe'er* he be – mayhap would right the gross sin that aboundeth within the church! But nay! Rather do they embolden their bishops to bleed dry the people, whilst they themselves live in profligacy! So be it, then. If the guests invited be obdurate[3] and cometh not to the feast of the King of Kings, then *go we forth into the highways and byways and bring in the poor!'*

The students were on their feet applauding thunderously, and cheers broke forth. There were repeated shouts of 'Amen!' and 'God save thee, Doctor Evangelicus!' Many of them were poor students that Wycliffe and his followers had sponsored from their own pockets.

Wycliffe staggered a little, for the intensity of debate and his outburst had wearied him. He caught the arms of his closest friends and supporters, Doctors Hereford and Purvey, and made his slow progress back to his own quarters, nodding and waving his acknowledgement of the enthusiastic crowd's applause.

Wadeford was taken aback by his enemy's tirade and the audience's response, but not for long. Pride and self-satisfaction had always been his mainstay.

Master Gatsby, one of the most sycophantic of Wadeford's followers, picked up his cloak and wrapped it around his shoulders.

'Heed him not, good Doctor!' he said consolingly. 'He and his gokey crew of babbling heretics are but lollards all! They shall fall, but *Thy* Sayings, and Truth and Holy Church will live on when these Jack Mullocks all be suffering the torments of Hell!'

Wadeford gathered his robes and his bruised dignity around him and scornfully watched Wycliffe's departure.

'Lo!' he sneered to the rest of his followers as they gathered at his side. 'He hath won the hearts of the lewd borel-folk. Much may it avail him. Well, there is no ho with him, indurate, heretical fool. Render him no force. And all those low-born Jacks that do fawn upon him? What can they do? It shall come to naught.'

---

3   Stubborn

Chapter 1: The Two Shepherds

'What seemeth to you? If there were to a man an hundred sheep,
and one of them hath erred,
whether he shall not leave ninety and nine in desert
[whether he shall not leave ninety and nine in the hills],
and shall go to seek that that erred?
And if it fall that he find it, truly I say to you,
that he shall have joy thereof more than on ninety and nine that erred not.
[And if it befall that he find it, truly I say to you,
for he shall joy thereon more than of ninety and nine that erred not.]'

(Gospel of Matthew 18:12&13 Wycliffe-Purvey Translation/Revisions.)

Master Alfred Shephard gathered in and stored his final haul of fish for the day and straightened his aching back. He and his colleagues chuckled as they watched the valiant but unavailing efforts of his little son, doing his best to emulate the strength of his tall, gaunt father.

'By the Rood, William!' called another crewman from the other side of the boat, 'Art better with staff and crook, minding the sheep, than casting forth the fisherman's net. Thus fated art thou in thy name.' He gave Alfred a broad wink.

'Heed not the jobbard's tongue, Will,' said the tall fisherman, gathering the embarrassed little boy in his arm and striding homeward. 'Take thou pride in thy name, lad. Forget not that thou'st the blood of King Alfred the Great a-flowing in thy veins. Yon Nicolas sayeth sooth in that thou't a good shepherd boy, natheless – yea – the best in all Dorsetshire. Art as kind of heart as thy sweet mother and twice as canny as Father Giles, if I err not.'

He laughed, tossed the child up in the air and put him down.

Little Will turned his back on the bustling port of Bournemouth, his birthplace, and pointed excitedly up the hill. Four sheep, nonchalantly chewing their cud, were watching them with mild interest. One seemed to recognise him and bleated with pleasure, as though inviting him to play.

'Lo, Fa-fa! It be Matthew, Mark and Luke, and my good co'panion John. Prithee to greet them, Fa-fa? Prithee?'

'On the morrow, my son, for much toil there is still for me to do. From whence these names o' yon lamblings?'

'Father Giles telleth a tale o' them, Fa-fa, as they be the great apposseless as a-preacheth the Gossapel. I will preach the Gossapel someday.'

His father chuckled, but said seriously, 'Many a year must pass and much fish must be netted ere thou canst walk that road, my son. But if that still be thine heart's desire, thy Fa-fa shall not turn thee from it.'

Alfred marvelled once again at the brightness and intelligence of this affectionate little lad, barely six summers. There was something special about him, as his wife often pointed out. He took delight in doing good to others in the village, young or old. He gleefully ran messages, and particularly loved bringing gifts or good news. He would intervene in many of his peer's quarrels and often restored harmony. Smaller children followed him around, and so did his four-legged friends. The ducks and geese would often follow him if he passed by, and his mother called him her 'little Saint Francis of Assisi'. Needless to say, the whole of Bournemouth doted on him.

No. He was not destined to be a poor fisherman. Perhaps his mother was right, mused his father proudly. He had a special calling from God after all.

He also had a strong scholarly bent for so young a child.

The family kept small copied portions of the Anglo-Saxon scriptures in a special clay jar in a corner of their cottage. It was an heirloom, secretly and faithfully passed down from generation to generation. Alfred claimed that these were documents that the greater Alfred himself had translated.

Little William would often peep at these portions with a sense of awe. He was not yet able to read properly, let alone understand the strange hieroglyphics of that ancient tongue, but just to feel that link with his illustrious ancestor, and his faith, inspired him.

He pestered the parson to teach him to read and write, as it was his ambition to read the Holy Scriptures to his friends.

'Read Holy Writ, my son?' Father Giles said, surprised but not displeased. "Tis surely a long road, for the Vulgate is but for the learned holy priests that are schooled in that tongue. Even I wist but little o' that sacred tongue.'

He taught him a little of what he knew, and William showed such aptitude and intelligence that Father Giles thought he would make an excellent scholar, if only he could get him to Oxford or Cambridge Universities when he turned fourteen. But his family barely made ends meet. It would be a miracle if the young man ever went beyond the borders of Dorsetshire.

His scholarly potential notwithstanding, William loved people and he loved animals. Though a quiet lad, he had the knack of making friends, and many would come to him and talk out their woes. Then he would go off and tell his own sorrows to the horses in the town stables, or even to the pigs.

All this changed suddenly and tragically when William turned seven. Once again, the horror of the Black Death raised its ugly head, especially in the poorer, rat-infested quarters of the towns. Bournemouth was a busy port, and it wasn't the first time plague had been borne in on foreign ships.

William watched in grief as one funeral procession after another made its sombre way down the streets, destined for the burial sites reserved for the poorest folk.

One evening, when the epidemic was at its most rampant, his father staggered home, coughing and bearing ugly, black sores, only to find his wife was the same, lying on her bed.

When little William came in from visiting friends at the end of town, he was faced with a horrible nightmare that scarred him for much of his life.

'Nay! Will, liefest! Come thou not nigh!' his mother screamed.

Alfred dragged himself from the bed to find his last remaining coins, threw the bag to William and, before collapsing, gasped, 'Go, son! May God go with thee and bring thee better fortune than ours!'

'Yea, go, my darling boy!' wept his dying mother. 'Go to thine uncle in Abbotsbury! With our last breath our prayers go with thee!'

Grieving, barefoot, hungry and frightened, he walked the many miles from Bournemouth town to find his uncle and aunt in Abbotsbury.

The couple were poor themselves and barely had enough to feed their nephew. So they took William to the local monastery, hoping the brothers would keep him amongst the other orphans.

William was agreeable, for he had been told that holy men were meant to be like the good saints of old – holy and compassionate. He could get the education that his soul craved for, and maybe become a holy man himself.

The rather portly and forbidding-looking brother who received them peered indifferently down at the scruffy piece of humanity looking pleadingly up at him.

'Nay, it cannot be done,' he said brusquely, without any sign of compassion. 'Stay thou with thine uncle and aunt. We have no room for dirty waifs that cannot give aid unto the abbey, in especial they that come of plague-ridden huts. Begone! Ye waste our time.' With that, he stalked out of the room, forgetting how, ten years earlier, the Black Death had laid low many of his fellows.

William was stunned, feeling rejected as though he was an abandoned child. He henceforth made a vow never to become a holy man, even if he died of hunger.

'Come, boy.' His uncle heaved himself to his feet and sighed as though he had expected this.

So his uncle, also a poor fisherman, and his aunt reluctantly adopted him, but seven years later, before William was fully grown, they also died in a recurrence of the plague.

The boy was then looked after by a friend of the family – a gruff, drunken herdsman, who had noticed that young William showed some ability with animals.

William could not love the old man, but he did his best to learn as much of the trade from him as possible. He worked at it so hard that he managed to escape many of the clouts old Toothless Tom used to deal out when he was half sober.

When the old man died a few years later, poisoned by the cheap wood-ale he brewed in the forest, William began to wonder if he brought ill fortune on all those who raised him.

Eventually William became a shepherd and sty keeper for the local monastery, the Abbey of St Bartholomew.

Although most of the brothers treated him like dirt, there were a few that helped to make his life tolerable, especially Brother Joseph. It was largely thanks to him that William obtained employment there at all, even though it was barely enough to feed him.

The brothers had gone beyond the need to humble themselves enough to get their hands dirty and share in the duties of mere peasants – so said my lord abbot. They had 'holier', though unspecified, duties to attend to.

Times had changed since St Benedict introduced the Rule, with its lofty ideals and Spartan lifestyle.

Driven to despair, William turned to wood-ale to ease the pain he felt at the state of his world, his need for acceptance and the aching emptiness he had within. A few times he had to be rescued from the ditch by his fellow labourers after a drunken rout.

He was a personable young man, and occasionally a few of the village girls ran off with him into the woods. Having lost all sense of purpose, William was quite willing and found a tiny degree of temporary comfort in their arms. But the sense of guilt that came from each of these romps drove him further into drink.

In some cases he stole food and drink from the monastery's buttery, to help feed himself and other poor folk. The poor folk accepted him readily, a kindness which he never forgot. In his turn, William looked for ways to ease their sufferings.

It was through the hard times of those days that he learned how to survive. He and his younger friend, Wilfred, another shepherd boy, became skilled in poaching, as many poor folk did, especially with the winter's lean times. However, they never stole from the monastery's flock, for they were William's charge, and they trusted him.

Another survival skill was taught to him by old Dick Little, a soldier discharged from the army due to a lull in French war. He was one of the last surviving bowmen that covered themselves in glory and won victory for the English at the battle of Grécy. But old Dick never spoke of that. His pride was in his lineage, for he claimed to be descended from John Little, the famed outlaw and right-hand man to the legendary Saxon rebel Robin of Locksley. His great grandsire had fled from the avenging arm of the law in Nottinghamshire and settled in Dorsetshire. Old Dick belligerently challenged any scoffers to a fight if they scoffed at his claim. Not many accepted his challenge because he was a giant of a man, an accurate marksman with the bow and also master of the art of quarterstaff combat.

William caught his attention when old Dick witnessed the lad stand up to a couple of poachers who were about to run off with a lamb from the monastery's flock. They fled empty-handed when they saw old Dick Little approaching.

The big man roared with laughter, clapped the grateful William on his shoulder and wheezed, 'By Saint George, thou'rt a flightsome lad, then! Come thou into the wood, and we shall a-striken us a stout staff for thee to swing, so shall we.'

He then proceeded to teach William some useful strokes with the quarterstaff. The lad became so skilled at this, he was able to stand his ground against a group of bullies who had terrorised him and his friends in the past. This resulted in a few of these gentry staggering home with bruises and cracked heads. They never bothered him again.

During one long, bitterly cold winter's night, William stood in the entrance of the sheep-pen and beat off a small pack of wolves that tried to attack the sheep. With a number of well-aimed blows, he cracked the skull of the pack leader. The others gave up and retreated.

He cut up the beast, giving the meat to his friends, the monastery dogs, and making a fine coat of the skin.

'Art thou not full courageous!' cried an admiring scullery maid when he came in late that night wearing the wolf skin.

'Nay! Say rather I be full drunken,' he replied, his voice somewhat slurred.

She giggled and pulled him into a dark corner.

The wolf skin helped to keep him warm for many a cold night, until a generous impulse moved him to give it to a thin peasant child he found shivering, sniffling and coughing one exceptionally cold night.

Sadly, the child died of malnutrition and consumption, but his last few nights were warmer. The child's mother never forgot William's kindness.

William never lost his desire to learn and would occasionally sneak in at the back of some of the orphan's classes at St Bartholomew's to listen. The orphans liked him and pretended not to notice, for his sake. They even let him read some of their books.

Eventually, he found the ways and means of sneaking into the monastery archives when none but Brother Joseph was there. He would find one of the old tomes and read it in some quiet corner. Brother Joseph noticed him, but did not have the heart to expel him. So in this clandestine manner, his education progressed to a reasonably advanced state.

William grew to be a man – tall, thin, hardened of muscle, but not hardened in heart. Nonetheless, his future seemed rather bleak. Was there anything beyond his purposeless existence? He loved his sheep and his friends, but would he be a shepherd forever?

Because of the bitter disappointment in his youth, he had set his face against the church as a profession – the only avenue of success open to intelligent young men and women amongst the lower classes in those days.

He had to admit, however, that among the clergy there were a few good men and women who had a genuine love for God and for people. Brother Joseph was such a man, for all his struggles with his vows of celibacy. William had once seen him in the woods with one of the loose village girls, but he thought nothing of it. Brother Joseph was a kindly man, in spite of it all, and would often stop and talk to William when he could. If the village gossipers were right, there was hardly a brother at St Bartholomew's that had not either had secret affairs or even a concubine in keeping.

William shrugged his shoulders and accepted the situation. After all, he was far from guiltless himself and had the common English resentment for the imposition of the foreign Norman-Romish rules, such as mandatory celibacy for the clergy. It was only when the same lecherous brothers spoke scathingly of the decaying morals of the poor laity, while doing little to relieve their sufferings, that his old resentment surfaced.

So he pondered and he thought deeply about the world around him.

Sometimes despair drove him to drink, but he began to see that it did him no good at all. Realising this, he turned instead to the only one who could really help – God Almighty.

He began to pray as his godly mother had taught him, pleading for relief from the hardships he and the poor people faced.

And God heard his prayer.

While out in the fields minding the flocks one day, he cried out to God for the miseries of his life and the poor of his world.

'O Great God in Heaven!' he cried. 'Thou knowest all things! Wherefore then is this curse upon our land? Have we sinned so grievous that we must be struck down with sword, famine and plague?'

Then he pondered on his own situation. Raising his face to the skies, he wondered aloud, 'And wherefore was I not slain as were my mother and my father, yea as also were my kinsfolk by the Black Plague? For what reason am I thus preserved?'

He heard a voice from behind him saying in a gentle yet strong voice, ''Tis the calling upon thy life. Thou shalt indeed be a tool fashioned of God to ease the sufferings of many in this generation.'

Embarrassed at being overheard in his private soliloquy, yet not alarmed, William turned in surprise to see one who seemed like a travelling friar, seated behind him. He wore a plain, russet-coloured clerical gown with his hood up. His face was in shadow.

William normally had little respect for the wandering friars, many of whom were living immoral and profligate lives, often favoured by the rich, and lately having little regard for the poor. But there was something so mysterious yet wholesome about this man, that William somehow felt drawn to him. He wore no jewellery, his habit was plain, his shoulders were broad from heavy toil and he looked all muscle, with little spare flesh. Although he kept his head bowed, the hint of a beard showed. An indefinable air of kindness mixed with sorrow hung about him.

'Wherewithal knowest thou this, good brother friar?' asked William, looking at the stranger with nervous respect. 'Art thou a prophet?'

'So some hath said,' replied the stranger. There was a quality in his gentle voice that yet had the power to shake mountains. But what William noticed most were the dried bloodstains on the strong, work-calloused hand that held his staff. The back of his habit was also stained with dried blood.

'Art thou a flagellant, then?' He had heard of the groups of fanatical folk that wandered the countryside, publicly lashing themselves with whips in an attempt to earn their salvation, never satisfied until they drew blood.

'Nay, for these wounds were delivered unto me in the house of my friends,' came the strange answer. 'Once was I an artisan, a carpenter, but now am I a shepherd, like as thou art. But my sheep I would raise up as shepherds also. Wilt thou also shepherd the flock of God?'

'I understand thee, good friar,' said William, wondering whether he really did understand. 'But in my youth, I swore never would I be a holy man. For such as I have seen oft have seemed unholy indeed, saving thy presence.'

A hint of anger came into the tone of the stranger's voice.

'Verily thou hast said, for many that be called shepherds are no shepherds. Rather are they as wolves, sparing not the flock. But God looketh upon the heart, not the outward piety, and whatsoever God maketh holy, call thou not unholy. For He hath seen thine heart, William the Shepherd, and so thou hast been named. He hath seen thy pain and sorrow, for so also His great Heart hath been broken for the sorrows of His people. Therefore he seeketh for them that will stand with Him to slay the demon-wolves of evil that would devour the flock. This desire is hidden within thine heart, for so hath God formed thee. 'Tis thy destiny, William the Shepherd, if thou wilt so choose!'

Astonished that the stranger knew so much about him, and spoke with such authority and power, William gaped at him, deeply moved and overwhelmed. Had God sent one of the Holy Saints to speak to him? Or an Holy Angel? But who was he, a lecherous drunkard and a thief, to be spoken to so graciously by this truly holy Man of God? He was so used to being treated with contempt by supposed holy men. He sat down and hid his face in his hands, shaking. It all seemed like a dream.

'Nor angel nor saint of old am I, William the Shepherd,' said the stranger, answering his unspoken thought. ''Tis sooth that thine heart doth need cleansing e'er thou dost pursue thy calling, but abundant cleansing there be in God if thou wilt turn unto Him. But mark: 'Tis cleansing *without* mediation of unholy priests. Think well on this thy choice.' And his voice faded into the distance.

William turned around too late. The stranger had gone.

He ran into the wood behind the man calling, 'Good Stranger! Holy Friar! Await me, I beg of thee!'

Then he stopped. Where had he gone so quickly? It was impossible for him to have melted into the woods without a trace. But at that moment, the mysterious disappearance didn't seem as important as the stirrings of his heart that the stranger had begun to stir.

He knew God had spoken of his future, for it had fanned the sparks of something that had lain dormant in his heart ever since his parents had prayed with him in his youth. Yes, this was his destiny, and it seemed as though the stranger was giving him time to count the cost.

But who? Who? Who was the stranger?

He walked slowly back to his flock, his mind in turmoil. How could God use him, only half educated, on the lowest rung of the social ladder, a sinner of sinners?

But did not Brother Joseph speak of the disciples that came from humble beginnings? Was not Christ Himself born in a manger?

He could not sleep that night. So many thoughts went through his mind. If he did follow this amazing new path that had been opened up to him, he would have to leave the life he was used to. He would leave his lowly friends, including his beloved animals that gave him so much unconditional devotion.

And where to begin? Must he become like those fat priests that had no interest in serving the people? Never! Yet the stranger called himself a shepherd of the flock of God, and William knew instinctively, though irrationally, that he could trust him with his life and follow him to the ends of the earth.

But who, and where, was he?

If a shepherd of the flock of God he must be, he would model himself on that humble, gently-spoken stranger, whoever he was. Surely, if he had given him such a challenge, he would return to hear his answer. William prayed fervently that he would find the man again. It felt as though he had known him all his life. No, he was no stranger. He personified that whispering voice in his heart that had pursued him from his earliest memories.

Yes! He would do whatever it took to become like that man.

He rose early the next morning to tend to his sheep. One quick count and he let out an oath of exasperation. The most wayward of his young lambs, which he had named 'Prodigal', had wandered off again.

Leaving the others in a safe place, William went off in the direction of Prodigal's favourite haunt, the woods, calling the lamb's name as he went.

He had not gone far into the wood when he came into a small clearing and cried out, 'Oh, My God, I thank Thee!'

There sat the stranger, cross-legged, with young Prodigal curled up asleep in his lap.

Forgetting all about the lamb, William knelt by the stranger.

'Father! Good friar!' he panted. 'Whoever thou be. Wilt thou have a poor sinner as thy disciple?'

Laying the sleeping lamb gently aside, the stranger stood to his feet.

'Gladly do I receive thee as my disciple, yea, as my friend, William, thou good shepherd. Thou wert a wandering lamb, but now thou'rt found! Behold the face of thy new master!'

He threw back his hood, and what William saw stayed with him for the rest of his days, and beyond.

Pure, unconditional love shone like sunshine from the eyes of the man, almost blinding him. Pure, unadulterated, unconditional love personified. Yet also there was an uncompromising holiness, strong and powerful, that shone from his face. It was both glorious and terrifying.

William fell forward on his face. He lay there quivering for a moment, dread – and yet a strange joy – coursing through his being. He wondered if he would die, yet hoped the sensation would never leave him.

How could he have been so blind not to know Who the stranger was? But it never occurred to Him that the Lamb of God Himself would come down to commune with the scum of the earth. The King of Kings! The Great Shepherd Himself! The Lord of the Universe! And He called him His friend!

All the hurt and bitterness was being washed out of William's soul as he wept and renounced all his sin, his past life. He became a total slave of his Redeemer. This commitment gave him much of the strength for all the tasks he was called to for the rest of his life.

Presently, the Great Shepherd touched him, bidding him rise. There was healing and strength imparted in that touch.

'Fear not, William the Shepherd. Arise! Old things have passed away. Behold! Now thou'rt a new man. I am sending thee to gather and feed my sheep.'

William lifted his head, but did not dare to do more than kneel and fix his gaze on the sandalled feet before him. He was sure that if he looked into that Face again, he would fall down once more. But again the gentle thunder addressed him.

'Go thou north unto Oxenford, and seek thou for my servant, a man called Nicolas Hereford, a disciple of one John Wycliffe. He will care for thee and thou shalt be instructed and shalt feed upon My Word for a season. Then thou shalt go forth and preach the gospel to many in this land, making them My disciples. Go forth! And I shall ever be with thee....'

Then He faded away from William's sight.

Chapter 2: Oxford

'... and God chose the unnoble things and despisable things of the world,
and those things that be not, to destroy those things that be;
that each man have not glory in his sight.
[that each flesh, or man, glory not in his sight.]'

(First Epistle of Paul to the Corinthians 1:18,29
Wycliffe-Purvey Translation/Revisions)

William had to sit for a while, still cradling the sleeping lamb. An immense lightness and sense of freedom, unlike anything he had ever experienced before, flooded his being. He felt clean. He felt more alive than he had ever been. The greatest Being of the Universe loved him.

He jumped to his feet and gave a loud laugh of pure joy, much to Prodigal's startled annoyance, which he vehemently expressed as he tumbled off William's lap.

Lifting the protesting wanderer, William ran back to his flock, laughing and weeping. There he put the lamb down so it could run to its relieved mother for a long overdue feed.

But would he ever see that blessed face in this life again?

He continued his duties for the next day, and the next, still in his exalted state, wondering what his next step would be. Could he just abandon his post and head north? Surely not. The Great Shepherd Himself would have forbidden it.

William was thinking on this when none other than Brother Joseph approached him. The good brother was looking a little bemused, for some reason, but gave him a kindly greeting.

Brother Joseph was not like his fellow Brethren of St Bartholomew's. With all his faults, he had a heart for people, especially the younger ones.

'Well met, and God save thee, William Shephard! Many a time and oft have I seen thee at the back of the schooling room and the vault of archives, but thou wert a student at heart, I trow, so I minded it not.'

'And so do I thank thee of thy kindness, Brother Joseph.' William responded, touching his forelock respectfully.

The brother looked keenly at the young man before him.

'Wherefore this glow that is upon thee? Almost it would seem thou'st seen heavenly visions.'

William wasn't sure how even this kind brother would take the news of his calling, so he just smiled and said, 'I but rejoice in the goodness of God, Brother Joseph!'

Recalling his errand, Brother Joseph knit his brows and looked down thoughtfully.

'Ferly[4] days of wonders these be,' he uttered cryptically, and William only just stopped himself from saying, 'Amen!'

'Strange dreams and portents came to me a' nightertale last,' continued the brother. 'I saw thy face, William, glowing as I see it now. Thou didst mind the sheep and thou didst hold a common shepherd's crook in thine hand. Then a great hand stretched forth from the heavens toward thee. Thou gavest thy crook into the hand and, in return, received a rod of authority. Simple in fashion it was, but held great power. Yea, even infinite more powerful than the crozier of the Pontiff himself. With that staff, I saw thee go north to a great place of learning, like unto the great University in Oxenford, of which I once beheld in my youth. Then thou didst go forth westward and south. Whithersoever thou goest, and didst raise that staff, many sheep gathered unto thee.'

He paused, looking at the young man before him, who was nearly bursting with excitement.

'So clear was this dream, it hath haunted me sorely since. What sayest thou to this?'

'Indeed, this be my calling Brother Joseph!' William burst forth eagerly. Then he stopped and thought a moment. 'But wherewithal can I forsake the animals if none else care for them? Young Wilfred, perchance?'

Pleased with the responsible answer, the brother smiled and said, 'Thou hast learned thy lessons well, William. I will see they are cared for.

---

4   Strange

Go forth! And take this with thee.' He handed him a small purse with jingling coins.

William's eyes glinted when he felt the riches in his grasp, but then he realised that many things that would have seemed acceptable two days ago now seemed vain and worthless. He looked guiltily at the generous gift, then shook his head.

'Mine hearty thanks, Brother Joseph, but I confess that I owe somewhat unto the Abbey. I pray ye that it should pay for what hath been already eaten. Let it be my penance if thou wilt. I will henceforth earn my bread by the labour of mine hands.'

Impressed by the young man's honesty and integrity, the brother was moved to say, 'I perceive that God hath His hand upon thee, William! Honesty and wisdom beyond thy years sitteth upon thy brow. Would that there were others of higher estate that had such goodness! Wherefore needest thou to tarry then? Go forth, my son, and God speed thee!'

This was how William found himself setting forth to Oxford, forsaking everything he had known and stepping into the unknown. But he was embarking on a new life, a quest and a God-given mission. As he shouldered his very few possessions and took to the road, it felt as though he was walking into a dream.

But even newborn believers need food in their stomachs, so he began looking for work along the way, and God provided for him at each turn.

The Black Death had decimated so much of the rural labour force that farmers and landlord's stewards were now thankful to find a willing and honest worker, even if he was only passing through. The old feudal system was passing away, and the age of the paid itinerant worker was dawning. Some of the stewards even offered him a well-paid post, but although this was very attractive to a man who had been paid next to nothing, the vision and call on his life made him politely decline. Later, he realized it was the enemy of his soul trying to distract him from his destiny.

He harboured enough of his earnings to keep him in health and strength, but gave liberally to destitute widows and other poor folk along the way. God rewarded his giving many times over. William felt like a wealthy man.

It occurred to him that many of the survival skills he had learned were no longer needed. He was a servant of the Most High, and in His service there was no need to merely survive. This faith in God's provision helped him many times when food or money became scarce. God always provided for him just in time.

On his journeys William learned to pray, in his own fashion. Rightly disregarding the pious ostentation that Friar Harding displayed in his style of prayer, he spoke from his heart. He had learnt that these were the prayers the Lord loved the most, and often answered in quite remarkable ways. After all, this was how he had come face to face with the Great Shepherd Himself. Often his prayer was a simple, 'O Father God, aid Thou me!'

The most remarkable instance of God's answers to prayer was on the road to Hungerford. William saw a hooded leper sitting cross-legged at the side of the road, ringing his clapper and crying, 'Alms! Alms! Will ye not aid a stricken and weary pilgrim? I die ere I find an almshouse nor hospice!'

William was ashamed of all the times he had indulged in self-pity over his own situation. Here was one cursed with a living death that made his own sufferings pale in significance.

But what could William do? He had spent his last coin at the previous village, to fill his belly and give him a bed for the night. He had just eaten his last apple and was hoping to find a farmer who could give him half a day's work, feed or pay him and send him on his way. This poor wretch did not have that kind of freedom.

William instinctively walked up to the poor man, who saw him and cried out, 'Unclean! Unclean! Good master come not nigh! If thou'st a coin, prithee cast it forth at my feet and I will pray thee God's blessing upon thy head!'

Moved even more with compassion, William ignored the warning and touched the startled beggar's hood, praying aloud, 'O God, would that I had a pocketful of coins I would give it him. Have mercy O God! Yet I would that Thou didst heal the leper, even as Thou didst in the days Thou dwelt amongst us. Art Thou not the same God?'

He spoke out of the promptings of his heart, but he cursed himself for the inadequacy and apparent futility of his words. Was he giving the poor man false hope?

The beggar held out his withered hand to keep William from coming too close, but suddenly gave a shout and leapt to his feet. "Tis a fire upon mine head! A fire in my limbs! By all the holy saints! Mine hand is whole!' He began to inspect all his limbs, looking for the familiar scars and missing digits he had learned to live without, but he was completely made whole, with even the toes and fingers that had fallen or broken off restored. Sensation was returning to his extremities also.

So stunned was William by the result of his spontaneous prayer, he stepped back unwarily, tripped and sat down hard.

The ex-leper jumped for joy. His hood fell back, revealing a young face with thinning hair on top and a wispy beard. He had burning, intense eyes, now filled with almost incredulous joy at his change of fortunes.

'O blessings abundant be upon thine head! Sickerly thou'rt a holy saint, good master. Yea, God verily be the same God, as thou hast said.'

He was so overwhelmed, he sat down and wept.

Still overcome, William came and knelt next to him, since his posterior was too sore to sit upon.

'Nay, I be no saint. A sinner that hath found cleansing for his sin be I. But God can send his blessing through the vilest and dirtiest of vessels. William am I called, and Shephard also, although a shepherd of the flock of God do I hope to be. What be thy name, my friend?'

'Good humble shepherd, when a man of worth I was, Richard Rolleton was my name,' he said, overcoming his emotions. 'Of a good family came I, until this curse came upon me, and my family cast me forth. Long have I contemplated my life if ever I returned from this living death. How vain are riches! How vain is fame! How vain is life indeed!'

The intensity of his eyes shone out strongly with a fanatical brilliance.

'Well then, good Master Richard Rolleton,' said William, warily observing the fanatical look, 'a happy chance or the Hand of God it be that we have met. And whither away anon? Wilt thou return unto the house of thy kinsfolk?'

'Never!' swore Richard. 'God, Mother Mary and thyself alone hath been my friends and my kinsfolk. I curse them not that they cannot come nigh and suffer like fate as I. But to cast me ever forth and speak to me no more? Nay! I have vowed me a vow before God, the Blessed Virgin and the Holy Angels that if ever I returned to the land of the living again, I shall ever live as a hermit – even as I have been these last seven years. A life of contemplation, where I seek the blessed Face and the Grace of the Holy Virgin Mother Mary!'

He turned to William, grabbed him by both shoulders and stared at him compellingly. 'Had I not so vowed, good Father Shephard, mayhap I would become thy disciple and follow thee whithersoever thou leadest!'

William began to feel a little uncomfortable about his new friend, even though he honoured his devotion.

'Nay, my friend, thou must follow thy calling.' he assured him hastily. 'What canst thou learn of a common shepherd and herdsman as I? I have mine own calling to follow.'

William instinctively felt in his pocket to give the man a few coins to help him on his way, forgetting that he had spent his last coin. To his surprise, he found his pocket was filled with money. Had he earned it all and forgotten that particular pocket? Then he remembered his prayer over Richard. He picked up the man's alms bowl and, before he changed his mind, quickly emptied his pocket into it. Then he leapt to his feet, gave a parting benediction to Richard, who sat there gaping at his newfound wealth, and walked on.

The intensity of the young man had been a little suffocating to him, so William thought it was just as well they parted company. But he would sadly miss those coins, wherever they came from.

He sighed, but still felt very happy. He had seen the mighty power of God in response to his simple and foolish prayers. He was learning many things, and learning fast.

William was not comfortable with the notion of being thought a holy saint, however, since he had heard these saints lived impossibly ascetic lifestyles. William was fond of a good meal, when he could get it, and shuddered at the very thought of voluntary fasting. He struggled with his libido as much as any other man, having had the odd fling in the woods with loose women. He did not consider celibacy was the calling for him, unless the Great Shepherd insisted upon it.

He had very little time to ponder over the miracles that had just occurred, for down the road from Hungerford rode a company of men. William stepped off the road and watched as they passed by. He enjoyed observing the colourful variety of humanity going about its business.

This group was interesting, for at its head was a man richly clad, probably a merchant. He was followed and flanked by three huge men-at-arms on magnificent white horses, which cast the merchant's dappled palfrey in the shade. The soldiers themselves made their charge look insignificant, for they were all abnormally large, handsome, strong and well-disciplined. Their armour reflected the sun like a mirror. The merchant himself looked nothing out of the ordinary, except he had a crooked nose in the midst of a kindly face.

The group drew nearly abreast with William, when one soldier reached over, touched the merchant's shoulder and muttered something. The man raised his head and pulled up his horse. His guard did the same in perfect precision.

Looking around in a puzzled way, it was as if the merchant was unaware of his cortège. Then the soldier leaned over and muttered something again. The merchant sat up straight in his saddle and looked in William's direction.

William bowed respectfully and made as if to pass on, but the merchant called out to him in a friendly manner. 'Hail, good fellow! Whither away? To Hungerford?'

'Verily do I, good sir,' replied William, feeling surprise at being noticed by a wealthy man, many rungs up the social ladder than he. 'But I journey beyond and beyond for many a league yet.'

He came closer, encouraged by the stranger's friendly manner.

'I perceive thou'rt a goodly man, for I see it in thy demeanour,' said the kindly merchant, 'and also that thou'rt in great need, if thy raiment speaks sooth! Thy name?'

'William Shephard am I, kind sir,' William replied. 'Great has been my need, but God hath been bountiful unto me, therefore I beg not for my living. He hath strengthened mine hands for honest toil.'

William was anxious to show the worthy man that he was not hoping for largesse. He had a certain measure of pride, without arrogance, after all.

The other man appeared pleased with his answer.

'Then my heart hath not misled me! God hath prospered me greatly and given me His protection where're I go. Hence, I fear not to journey alone, nor to address strangers. Wilt thou receive of a fellow servant of

God a gift? 'Tis my joy to give when the good Lord doth so prompt mine heart.'

He reached into his saddlebag and brought out a purse full of money.

'A worthy man thou art, Master Shephard. Pray receive this small gift of the good Lord and so fulfil the joy o' this fat chapman. Never do I feel so rich as when I give. In return, pray thou a blessing upon mine head and upon mine house, for God heareth the prayers of the lowly in heart.'

William was overwhelmed.

'Churlish would I be to refuse such a gift from such a generous heart, kind sir. And may God's richest blessings be upon thee and thine house. For God's blessings maketh rich and doth add no sorrow to it.'

'Ha! 'Tis the very words that good young Master Ashton uttered at Mass yestermorn,' said the good man, bridling with pleasure. 'Now wist I that God hath given me the gift of giving. Go forth unto good fortune and thy destiny, whatever it be, good William the Shepherd, and God speed!'

He threw the bag to William, waved farewell and passed on.

His escort bowed their heads toward William in respect, something that men-at-arms normally did not do to common folk. They also smiled at each other in deep satisfaction.

William watched the retinue trotting down the road, his mind in a whirl over the accumulated wonders he had experienced that day. But there was yet one more.

As he watched, the three soldiers faded into thin air, leaving one solitary rider diminishing into the horizon.

'Holy angels! A day of miracles has this been, O Lord, and I thank Thee for this grace,' he breathed. He looked down at the purse and counted out the golden coins. It was more than twice the amount he had found in his pocket and emptied into the aspiring young hermit's bowl one hour earlier.

'And thou didst not fear to ride alone, nor to accost strange men?' he muttered to the tiny dot disappearing over the horizon. 'Yet thou wert not alone, master chapman. May God keep His warrior angels guard over thee alway, that thou mayest ever be a ready vessel of His bounty.'

Pocketing his wealth, William strode on to Hungerford, rejoicing.

Now his resources could be stretched comfortably through Marlborough, Wantage and Abingdon, without the need to stop and work for his faire.

Occasionally, he even indulged himself by sleeping on a real bed, rather than a pile of hay, as was his wont. He made rapid progress, which was fortunate – or God's provision – for winter was rapidly approaching.

Finally, he saw the towers of Oxford in the distance. Oxford – the greatest centre of learning in his day, and he was to study there!

He crossed the little bridge over the river Cherwell, passed through the neglected and crumbling stone walls, and walked along the streets of Oxford town, barefoot and weary, but happy. He had no idea where he would find Nicolas Hereford, but he was sure that God would show him the way. His faith had been strengthened by the events of the week before, which still sent a tingling feeling down his spine when he thought about them.

That faith was about to be tested.

Walking up St Aldate's Street, William saw the sign of a cosy-looking tavern called the Bull and Book, reflecting both the rural and academic nature of the town. He walked in, hoping to find information concerning his quest as well as sustenance.

Looking around, he saw two groups of men, sitting at opposite ends of the main taproom. One group, dressed in clerical garb, was obviously made up of students. They drank, chatted and laughed cheerily, heedless of the dark looks thrown at them by the townsmen at the other table.

William had heard rumours of the recent riots and fighting between the students and townsfolk before Merton College, and there were still simmering tensions between both parties. However, these did not concern William personally, so he bought his tankard of ale from the gruff draper and approached the student group. Surely intelligent young scholars would befriend and guide him to his goal.

'Good morrow, good sires,' he said, as they turned to look askance at this ragged commoner coming boldly into their midst. 'Prithee tell me, if ye will, whither can one find Master Nicolas Hereford?'

The supposedly good sires exchanged derisive glances with each other. One bold-faced fellow, who appeared to be the peer-leader, sat back and stared at him in an insolent manner. '*Eheu, condiscipuli,*[5]' he drawled at last, addressing his grinning comrades. 'This poor specimen of *Homo sinsapiens* [6] hath mislaid the good Doctor Hereford. 'Twas careless of him, dreadless.'

Laughter greeted this sally, and also William's confusion and embarrassment. He was made to feel rustic, uncouth and unlettered. Nevertheless, he was used to put-downs, so he stood his ground.

One of the students, a lively yet tolerant fellow sitting on the outside of the group, took pity on him and said, 'Good fellow, one doth not *find* Doctor Hereford. He hath much to do with weighty affairs and abideth not for any save the King's messengers. A man of his position findeth thee, if he hath occasion thereto. If thou'rt a message-bearer, leave it with the porter at University College in Logic Lane.'

'But it would avail thee not, Master Ragamuffin,' piped in the bold-faced student. 'The good Master left for his home in Leicester, yea, even yester-eve. Alas and alack! Build thou thy mud-hovel 'gainst his return in the spring, but not inside the town walls, I beg of thee.'

More laughter and they all turned away from him, considering the interview over. They had little time for ignorant peasants in rags.

Bowing his thanks to the more helpful of his informants, William retired to an empty table, crestfallen and discouraged. God had led him this far. How could it end in apparent futility like this?

Then he remembered the other seemingly impossible situations where God had miraculously intervened. He breathed his favourite prayer, 'Lord, aid Thou me,' and felt peace settle on his heart. If he had to find shelter over the winter on short commons, so be it. But God may work another miracle yet.

And God did.

A short while later, the door of the tavern opened and three men in academic gowns, proclaiming the distinction of Masterhood, strode inside.

With one glance at the newcomers, the students jumped to their feet, respect and astonishment written all over their faces. Even the townsmen at the other table turned and bowed in respect at the three men.

---

5   Alas, fellow-students!

6   Man without wisdom

The tavern-keeper bustled forward obsequiously, wishing to know their Worships' pleasure. It was seldom that such great dignitaries honoured his hovel with their presence.

The foremost Master held up his hand and looked around the room. He had an air of authority as a leader among men and accustomed to commanding respect, yet flattery was wasted on him. Although only five summers older than William, his responsibilities made him look older. He had fine features, a broad brow and intelligent, piercing, grey eyes.

With a clear and cultured voice, accustomed to addressing crowds, he addressed the room in general.

'Pray tell me, gentlemen all, is there one William Shephard in your midst?'

He brought his gaze around to where William hesitantly rose to his feet, and a kind of strange recognition flashed in his eyes. For a few heartbeats, there was a pregnant silence in the room.

'Indeed, Doctor, I be that same,' William said quietly at last, feeling humbled in the presence of the great man and astonished that he was so looked for.

The great man turned around to his colleagues with a look of triumph.

'Ha! Thanks be to God! Said I not so? "Follow thine heart's still small voice, liefer than thine head," quoth Doctor Ashton. Thy wager is lost, Master Parker.'

He was apparently continuing an ongoing debate with his colleague, and Master Parker smiled, bowed his head and lifted his hands in a good-natured gesture of defeat. A true scholar admits it when he is proved wrong, and he was such a man.

The great man turned back to William and offered his hand.

'Thou'rt right welcome to Oxenford, Master William Shephard. Strange dreams and portents have I received concerning thee, but more of this when thou hast supped with us, if thou wilt. Is the name of Nicolas Hereford aught of significance unto thee? For so I am.'

Grasping his hand gratefully, William replied, 'Of great signification indeed, Doctor Hereford, for so have I been sent, and a strange tale do I tell, and a strange road have I walked to meet with thee.'

'Thou'st the manner of a natural scholar, Master Shephard, rough though be thy raiment. Haply we can amend the latter.'

Turning, Hereford noticed the stupefied group of students.

'And I trust that this good man hath been comely welcomed to Oxenford, as becometh worthy clerics and gentlemen?'

He looked sternly across the group, and many of them paled and quailed, the bold-faced one not the least. A flogging for grossly unscholarly behaviour was still in force – also expulsion, which was a worse punishment for many impoverished students.

They waited, quaking, for William's inevitable condemnation of his recent treatment at their hands, but it never came. William remembered how much God had forgiven him and felt, instinctively, that he had no right to condemn. He was human enough to enjoy their discomfiture, but would not take advantage of it.

'Indeed, indebted am I to this gentleman for information, Doctor!' he said, bowing toward the tolerant youth. That worthy flushed with gratitude and smiled; the rest breathed an almost audible sigh of relief.

'But no joyous feastings at thy coming, methinks,' said Hereford dryly. 'Very well. Be ye seated gentlemen, and be thankful for one that cometh amongst us who hath natural chivalry. Learn ye from such an one.'

He spread his arm out invitingly to William, and smiled.

'Come and sup with us at our board. There is much we would speak on with thee.'

So saying, he shepherded William into his capacious carriage with the other masters.

Chapter 3: The Making of a Shepherd

'A good man was there of religioun
That was a pore Persone of a town;
But rich he was of holy thought and werk;
He was also a lerned man, a clerk,
That Christes gospel trewly wolde preche.

This noble ensample to his shepe he gaf,
That first he wrought and after that he taught.

A better priest I trow that nowhere non is,
He waited after no pompe ne reverence;
Ne maked him no spiced conscience,
But Christes lore and his apostles twelve
He taught, but first he folwed it himselve.'

(From Canterbury Tales – Geoffrey Chaucer)

Soon William found himself in almost luxurious circumstances, partaking of good tender venison, fresh bread that melted in his mouth, butter, cheese and sweetmeats. He had never been treated as an honoured guest like this before, and once again, he felt overwhelmed. God was treating him right royally, as a king's son.

At first, he felt rustic and uncomfortable, not knowing how he should conduct himself amongst such exalted men, but their geniality and genuine interest in what he had to say set him at his ease. They were far more interested in William's intellect and spiritual state than his social graces, status and appearance.

Hereford introduced the two other masters.

Master John Parker, the eldest among them, was the one who had lost the wager, and Hereford made a little merriment over this, calling him the 'Doubting Thomas' among them. But, as Hereford explained to William,

Master Parker was valued for his gift of objectivity, which kept their feet on *Terra firma*. He was once a professor of Mathematics at New College, and dealt only in facts – a characteristic of which he constantly boasted. He had studied further in Theology and joined the Wycliffite Masters.

The other, Master William Smith, was a quiet man with dreamy eyes. A lecturer in Theology at University College, where Hereford was based, he favoured the devotional side of Christianity, strongly advocating the doctrine of the Priesthood of Believers and a personal experience of God. Some dismissed him as strangely mystical, but the dreams and visions he experienced were of far more practical use than most mystics of his day. He was in constant, good-humoured conflict with John Parker over spiritual matters, and had won that last wager.

Once they had assuaged the first pangs of hunger, Doctor Hereford asked William to tell his story, and not to hurry.

As William spoke, Hereford bent his powerful mind to what was being said, occasionally stopping him to ask very insightful questions.

Every now and then, especially when William hesitantly came to describe his vision of the Great Shepherd, the men looked at each other in wonder. When William described Brother Joseph's dream, Smith's eyes grew wide, and he interjected, "'Tis the same! The memory cometh again unto me. In mine own vision I saw thy face with the Rod of Authority given from heaven!'

Looking toward his colleagues, he said with great conviction, 'Gentlemen, let none further doubt this man's credentials.'

'Not indeed!' agreed Doctor Hereford. 'But pray continue, Master Shephard.'

Emboldened by this confirmation given, William was able to tell them of his experiences with the miraculous, without hesitation.

They listened intently and sat silently for a moment when William finished his tale. Then Master Smith commented to his colleagues, 'Doctor Ashton had a like call, had he not? Yet he hath not wrought the miraculous that here we have heard. Even without them, I would give my "yea" for this man's admittance to our league of disciples. What sayest thou, John?'

'Amen! So I do, and thy pardon I beg that I doubted thee, Nicolas,' said the other. 'Thomas the Doubter hath been schooled. But what sayeth this godly man? Will he join us indeed?'

'Well, so we must ask it of him. And our tale we must tell also, that he may choose aright with understanding,' declared Nicolas.

He began by speaking glowingly about Doctor John Wycliffe, Head of Balliol College, the greatest mind in the whole of England, and a personal friend and mentor. They shared the same concern for the deterioration of morals, the poor morale throughout the land, the despair and suffering of the common people, and the profligacy of many of the hierarchy of Holy Church. Wycliffe and his men had become more and more impatient with the established church hierarchy, its arrogance and failure to address the 'manifold iniquities' within herself, while ignoring the sufferings of the people.

The Wycliffites had begun to pray earnestly and study the Latin Scriptures to find answers. Wycliffe had pointed out that the church in the apostolic age was so much simpler in her lifestyle, yet far more powerful and effective than the complicated and corrupt system of the present day.

He had become more and more outspoken in his criticism of the bloated and ungodly princes of the church, who demanded tithes and sold indulgences to build both their own wealth and huge cathedrals, while common people starved.

The eyes of the three men kindled as Hereford spoke of Doctor Wycliffe's vision for the church and the nation, where the church functioned as God intended and the common folk found hope and comfort in the scriptures, in the same way as they had.

Master Nicolas spoke of the labours that Doctors John Wycliffe, John Purvey and himself had done over the years, translating the scriptures into the common tongue.

God had stirred the hearts of many of the Masters, students and even some Doctors who heard John Wycliffe proclaiming the Word of God in their own tongue, for they felt as though God was speaking directly into their hearts.

Master Nicolas went on to describe how a great movement had begun amongst these academics to study the scriptures more closely. Many 'disciple gatherings' came together to study copied portions of Wycliffe's scriptures, and in doing so, had discovered wonderful truths that had been hidden or ignored for many years.

'In very sooth,' said Master Smith fervently, '"Tis a wondrous journey of discovery into the very heart of God! The love of God is, at last, clearly revealed in the Blessed Pages of Holy Writ. To feel Him come nigh and quench the thirsty soul when thou dost read the Psalms thou hast translated into the mother tongue, Hereford, my friend, what a priceless gift!'

For a moment he forgot where he was; it was as though he was back in his own daily devotions in his study.

'"They that dwelleth in the secret place of the Most High shall dwell under the shadow of the Almighty,"' he quoted with a rapt look on his face.

Parker smiled as he turned his grizzled, bearded face to William to add his own perspective.

'A time there was when I would have mocked them in like manner to my mystical comrade here, Master Shephard. But I have beheld with mine own eyes the power of God at work in the lives of those who have found God through the Holy Scriptures. 'Twas not the traditions of men that turned loose-living profligates into humble, generous, holy men. Many of them that be drunken, or went a-whoring or fought in the riots at Merton Square, now find hope and instruction in the scriptures read at the disciple gatherings. Long have I observed the lives of them like to Doctors Wycliffe and Hereford here also, and seen the truth take root and bear fruit mightily. Logic alone brought me unto conviction that them that studieth the Living Word with their whole heart findeth the life-changing power of God. When one hath seen the results thereof, how can one think other?"

He shrugged his shoulders and added, *'Quod est Demonstratum*[7]*!'*

Hereford smiled at how the two men approached the truth in different ways.

'Much more could we speak of all that God hath done in our midst, but we must now turn to thine own calling, Master Shephard, for it concerneth us also. Of late, the name of William Shephard hath come to mine heart when I have sought the face of God in my times of devotion. Then Master Smith received that self-same message as did that the holy brother at the Abbey of St Bartholomew did dream. But winter cometh

---

7   "So it is proved." Often used in mathematical calculations, abbreviated to QED.

on a-pace, and as our office here be in abeyance for this season, my friends and I sallied forth to our havens at Leicester. But this morning at prayers, Master Smith and I felt in our heart to tarry – yea – against reason!'

'*Mea culpa*[8]!' interjected Master Parker ruefully. 'Mine was the reasoning to continue our journey north, and so I persuaded them. But even in mine own heart was there the still, small voice – but I heeded it not. The call of the hearth, the fire and the feast of mine own hovel was stronger, I confess. But the conviction to turn back could not be stayed in my colleagues. They resolved to turn back and seek thee at the Bull and Book, for so did they feel it in their hearts. In mine unbelief, I fleered and I challenged them, wagering my copy of Hereford's works against Smith's copy of the New Testament that thou wouldst not so be found thither. But the scorn hath come upon mine own head, and much to learn have I. Strange doth it seem, that the more one learneth, the less doth one understand!'

'*Credo ut Intelligam,*' quoted Hereford, and as William looked mystified, he translated, '"I believe in order that I may understand."'

He looked at his colleague and friend with approval.

'But thus do we have deep respect unto thy scholarship and humility, Master John, that thou hast so learned of God cheerily and hardened not thine heart, as have many a proud master.'

He clapped his friend on the shoulder, then turned once again to William.

'And so merrily do we meet, Master Shephard. Students all in the School of God are we all, not exalted fonts of wisdom. We would also learn of thee, for thy schooling hath been both stern and harsh, yet hath God spoken unto thee face-to-face.'

Impressed by the wisdom and humility of the men before him, William said, 'Hither have I come to learn what I must to fulfil my calling, good masters. Proud would I be to be schooled of such men as ye be. But I wot not whither nor what I must do to be enrolled as clerk[9], neither do I have the means anon. Also if classes be in recess for Yule-tide, I must winter me somewhither. I will not beg for my meat, but have resolved me to work for it, or starve. Wilt thou give me good rede[10] in these matters?'

---

8   It's my fault.

9   Student

10   Advice

Doctor Hereford turned his keen gaze upon him and appeared to come to a decision.

'I perceive that the hand of God is upon thee, Master Shephard!'

He leaned forward and put his goblet aside.

'Thou'rt a lettered man, if I err not. It is custom and privilege for a Doctor of College to take unto himself a novice clerk that sheweth good promise as intern of his household. There that clerk doth assist the master in his labours and will, in turn, eat at his patron's board and find shelter, hearth and bed until he complete his studies. I am in need of a skilled scribe, one who will copy and aid in my translations and lectures, yet with spiritual understanding. But a man of character and godliness he must be. What sayest thou? Wilt thou be Nicolas Hereford's apprentice?'

The other two men nodded in complete approval.

William's voice was suspended as a lump formed in his throat. God had more than supplied his needs. This was a dream come true.

Finally, he mastered his emotions enough to say huskily, 'Can any man refuse such generosity, such an honour? But is there none other more worthy amongst the body of clerks in Oxenford that....'

'If there were such a one, Hereford would have chosen him anon,' smiled Master Smith. 'And methinks thou hast begun thine apprenticeship already, from thine history that thou hast related.'

'But art thou soothly of a mind and hardihood that thou wouldst serve such an hard taskmaster?' quipped Master Parker jovially. 'He would of a certes make thee to pour his wine and scour his floors, and if thou leeren not thy Latin, he would scourge thee sore!'

They all laughed. Hereford protested that his stomach could not handle wine and opted for ale instead. Then they made plans to leave for Leicester, with William, the next day.

So William began his academic studies under the aegis of one of the greatest translators of his time. Being both intelligent and diligent, he progressed rapidly through his studies, and Hereford encouraged him to complete his Bachelor of Theology over the years that followed.

There was much to do in between his studies. Hereford had a large capacity for work himself, for he was translating the whole of the Old Testament, and more. But William felt like he was in heaven.

From Hereford himself he learned principles of translation and hermeneutics. But more than that, he absorbed much from the spirit of the man and his vision to reach the poor with the gospel.

From Master Parker he learned the principles of exegesis, systematic study and logical thought.

From Master Smith he learned to develop his devotional life and prayer.

From Master Ashton he learned much of the dynamics of homily, although his confidence took a while to build, and it was not until his encounter with the Spirit of God in Master Smith's office that he truly began to preach with power and authority.

He threw himself into his studies and college life, but he avoided much of the trivialities that students often indulged in. His escape from the trammels of daily life was to walk out into the countryside he loved and chat to the villagers nearby, sometimes rolling up his sleeves, girding himself with a labourer's smock and helping with the work.

Villagers got to know and love him. He still retained all of the animal lore he had learned in his previous vocations, and the local herdsmen and animal keepers frequently asked his advice or shared their own experiences with him.

William was of invaluable help to his mentor. He was quick with the quill and an excellent listener when Hereford needed a sounding board for his translations or when preparing his lectures or sermons. Eventually, Hereford began to ask William's opinion on points of doctrine, exegesis and exposition of the scriptures.

Hereford and other preachers of Wycliffe's persuasion occasionally travelled around Gloucestershire, Berkshire and Leicestershire proclaiming Wycliffe's message of the gospel. A few of Hereford's most telling lectures included some of William's input.

Once the people realised that Wycliffe and his party truly had their interests at heart, they had invitations and acclaim wherever they went.

With William's help, Nicolas Hereford worked tirelessly to spread the Word of God, and people wondered greatly to hear the scriptures in their own language. After their lectures and homilies, folk from all walks of life would approach them to ask questions.

Many of the common folk, that were able to hear him, found new hope, and this rejoiced William's heart. Often he would chat outside the church with those who were interested, giving them portions of scripture he had copied – often in his own time. He encouraged them to form discipleship groups that followed the same model as those at Oxford, and he occasionally attended the groups to instruct and shepherd them.

Doctor Hereford commended him for this innovation, noting that he was developing his calling quite rapidly.

William drank in every word that Wycliffe, Hereford, Ashton and others spoke in their lectures, and his diligence, devotion, insights and wisdom soon made him top student whichever class he attended.

He attended Wycliffe and Hereford's disciple gatherings to discuss the deeper and more controversial matters of scripture as it was read in English. They would often follow this with prayer. Chiefly, they prayed for the nation – that God would reach the people with His healing hand and open the floodgates of Truth.

William avoided some of the more extreme and political disciple gatherings, such as the fanatical Master Swynderby's, although he admired the man's courage and bold, outspoken railings against the abuses in the church and state.

He once heard Swynderby's intern, the fiery Father John Ball, deliver a tirade against the rich aristocracy, both secular and the church. He stridently advocated equality of classes and had, more than once, aroused the wrath of the authorities against himself for it. His imprisonments and floggings only made him more embittered and determined. His battle cry was:

'When Adam delved and Eve span,
Who was then the gentleman?'

William preferred to see social change by the power of God, than by the violent arm of the flesh.

Master William Smith never forgot William and invited him along to his own prayer gathering. Here William encountered the power of the Holy Spirit in a powerful way.

The first glow of joy had begun to fade in William's experience, since his encounter with the Great Shepherd. The enemy of his soul began to 'remind' him of his past sins and lowly beginnings, playing on his natural sense of inadequacy.

He was able to pour out his troubles to Master Smith, who was a gifted prophetic counsellor. After prayer and laying on of hands, William felt the presence of God come upon him in waves of joy and power, and he received what Master Smith called 'his language of heaven'. This totally transformed his times of devotion and was, in the days ahead, of tremendous help to him in his remarkable calling.

A day came when Hereford approached him at the gate of University College, in the company of a tall, gaunt, slightly frail figure William knew well.

'I bid you good den, William!' cried Nicolas cheerfully. 'Here is one who is desirous of thine acquaintance. Should I so introduce?'

'Doctor Wycliffe!' exclaimed William, a little overcome as he took hold of the thin hand stretched toward him. 'This is an honour indeed.'

'Well, well,' replied the great man genially, 'the honour of the honourable is honour indeed, so quoth Master Okham, my mentor.'

His voice, oddly at variance to his frailty, had the resonance of one who was accustomed to lecturing to great crowds.

For a moment, he studied William with his hawk-like, sunken eyes.

'Hereford speaketh highly of thee, my son. Thou'st excelled in thy studies, thou'st a heart for the common folk and....' his voice dropped a little, '...thou didst behold the face of the Lord Himself in vision.'

'He hath revealed Himself as the Great Shepherd, Doctor,' responded William, with a slight tremor in his voice. Even after all this time, he felt his visitation as deeply as though it was but yesterday. 'By His abundant grace, He hath called me from my flock to shepherd the flock of God.'

'And by God, there is an abundant need for it!' exclaimed Wycliffe, looking beyond them both, even beyond the walls of the university town to see the poor, wandering flock throughout the land. 'In our generation, there is despair in the land, like to which we have never seen afortime. War, famine, pestilence, gross injustice and worse: gross darkness on the hearts of the people. God have mercy upon England!'

He gripped Hereford's shoulder to steady himself, as if overwhelmed by the grief he felt. Bringing his gaze back to the two men with him, he invited them both to dine with him at his quarters.

Once alone, he didn't waste time in getting to the point he wanted to make.

'My calling is to sound the trumpet in the land, but the great ones will not hearken to it, but for a few. I cannot shelter behind the shield of Gaunt of Lancaster forever, though he stood with me before Courtenay, Bishop of London.'

He gave a loud crack of derisive laughter as he remembered the fiasco in St. Paul's cathedral.

'John of Gaunt is but a reed, for he is moved by politic expediency alone, and that worketh for our cause for the nonce. Yea. But for the nonce. For how long I wist not. We must use the door that God hath opened unto us whilst we can.

'I have surrendered my post at Balliol that I may be free so to finish this work. We have proclaimed the Word of God in the churches in London and many a town in the heart of England, but we must go beyond and into the highways, byways and villages. The poor peasant folk and townsfolk hath as much right to hear the Word preached unto them as we.'

His face hardened as he continued grimly, 'But many of these fat begging friars hath poisoned the minds of many against us, keeping the people in bondage unto fear and superstition in the guise of piety. Piety? Pish!'

He looked challengingly at William.

'My dream is to raise up preachers from among the poorest – them that will go among the poor, as poor preachers, but not to beg. If the people will accept them, and reject the papelardy of these begging friars and their heresies, we can foil the works of the Devil. But whom can we send?'

'It seemeth that Master Shephard hath already gone forth amongst them, Doctor,' interpolated Hereford. 'Throughout Leicestershire, Gloucestershire and Berkshire have we laboured together, I in the pulpit, but Master William outside the door thereof. He hath begun many a disciple gathering from them that have hearkened unto the Word. Many a time hath he gone into the local villages to work with his own hands that he may come alongside the most wretched of the poor. In this way hath he shared the gospel and gathered many unto the fold.'

William coloured and bowed his head.

'To gather the sheep is my calling, Doctor. I cannot stand aside and see them wander away again.'

'Good! Very good!' said Wycliffe, with strong approval. 'O, that we had more of thy spirit, Master William Shephard! God send us more shepherds and evangels.'

In a little while that prayer would be answered.

Before they parted, the great man fixed his gaze on William with a strange, curious gleam. His voice lost its customary touch of oratory.

'Of what like was the Great Shepherd of thy vision, my son? Of what manner of raiment did he wear? His blessed face – what likeness was He?'

William took his time answering, to keep mastery of his own emotions. Wycliffe nodded at each point of description, as if it confirmed his own convictions.

After William had gone, Hereford exclaimed, 'Is it not thine own meeting in dreams of the night, Doctor John!'

'The very same, my friend,' Wycliffe agreed. He sat back in his chair by the fire and closed his eyes in reminiscence. 'Whether in wisdom or in folly, I wear the same russet habit, as His disciple, for many a day thereafter.'

'So then do we!'

Wycliffe gave his customary barking laugh and shook his head. His oratory mode returned, and he opened his eyes with, 'Rather, it is for the new order of friar brethren that we must – nay – whom we *shall* send forth! Disciples of the Great Shepherd Himself, and William Shephard shall be the eldermost, I deem.'

William finally completed his Bachelor Degree, and with it came a new sense of confidence. He had made many friends at University College, and they all came and cheered him at his graduation and then his ordination as a priest of Holy Church.

But now it was decision time. He was in the position to choose from a number of comfortable livings, for highly qualified priests were scarce and in high demand. He could also further his studies, if he wished.

After the ordination ceremony, Master John Parker clapped him on the shoulder and genially said, 'Well, well, Father William Shephard. Thy fame hath gone forth throughout the faculty, and many agree that thou'rt ready and indeed able to undertake a Master's Degree in Theology. Thou'rt a good scholar, Father William. Indeed, if thou will do so, my friend Doctor Ashton is desirous to take thee as intern, so saith he yestereve. What sayest thou?'

William still could not get used to all the honour and kindness heaped upon him by the great men of Oxford. It sat uncomfortably upon his shoulders. He had visualised the dizzy heights to which he could go if he was ambitious, but decided it was not for him. He felt far more comfortable working amongst the poor folk, especially the folk of the villages.

Even in his studies, he had avoided many of the purely academic doctrinal debates in which many of his fellow students loved to become involved. Instead, he looked more for principles of living, helpful scriptures to strengthen his faith and comforting words of hope that could be shared with those that had lost hope.

Therefore he smiled back at his well-wisher and said, 'I thank thee for thy kindness, thy continued kindness, Master Parker. Had I not this calling to shepherd the poor folk upon mine heart, sickerly would I walk through this door that thou openest for me. Pray, think me not ungrateful.'

Master Parker did not seem too surprised, but looked approvingly upon him.

'Well, it seemed that thou wert the logical man to fill the post, for thou hast a great mind. But I also perceive that thou hast a great heart withal. I have observed thy progress and that thou art free of selfish ambition, neither dost thou desire fame nor fortune. God speed thee whithersoever thy destiny lieth! But forget not the principles of logic, my son. If the premise be strong, as the Word of God be, logic shall fail thee not.'

Doctor Hereford was relieved to hear that William would remain with him for the present, and laughed over Parker's parting admonition.

Master Richard Waystract, another of Wycliffe's party, also befriended William. Master Richard was a brilliant organiser and had conceived the idea of the disciple gatherings. He instructed theology students in the principles and practice of pastoring a local gathering, and in helping to get people's lives in order.

Master James Crompe, yet another Wycliffite, was strong in the area of counselling, especially for the broken. He could sense a kindred spirit in William and took him aside to give him special tuition.

Even Master Philip Repton, 'the roiler' as his colleagues jovially called him, returned from his wanderings to coach William in all the considerations of itinerant preaching. Of all Wycliffe's henchmen, Repton travelled the furthest and preached most frequently in his preaching rounds, bringing back news and local information that William would, one day, find very useful. He poured over Repton's hand-made map of southern England, studying the southwest in particular.

So William grew strong through all he had learned, and a desire to go out and share these new truths grew in him. He would fall into conversation with strangers in the streets of Oxford, sharing his findings in ways they could understand. As a result, new disciple gatherings were formed.

One day, as he was walking back toward Hereford's quarters, William heard his name called. It was the same young student who had befriended William on his first day in Oxford. Because of William's graciousness toward him before the three great men in the tavern, he had become a disciple.

Although graduating in his Degree in Natural History a year before William, he now wanted to complete a Theology Degree. He had become fast friends with William and looked up to him. This day he had a stranger with him – a powerfully built young man with intensely blue and laughing eyes in a broad face that resembled that of a friendly lion.

'Benjamin Abyngdon!' William cried gladly as they approached. 'Well met and God save thee, my friend. Whither away? To the tavern again, thou wine-bibber?'

'*Eheu, Padre, peccavi*[11]*!*' answered Abyngdon, in mock contrition. 'Thither have I been. Wist thou that young Holloway hath indeed withered away. Mindest thou when he called thee Master Ragamuffin? He is expelled, alas and alack! But I bring thee one who hath asked of thee by name.'

William turned his attention to the stranger, ready to welcome any friend of his friend. He noticed that this young man had long sandy-golden hair which combined with his beard to form a lion-like mane. He

---

11   Alas, father, for I have sinned.

had a prominent jaw and a smile that outshone the sun. Everything about him proclaimed a successful young farmer, positively bursting with life, strength, health and joy.

But what chiefly struck William was the look of eternity in his eyes, which William had noticed in many of Wycliffe's followers.

And God spoke to William's heart concerning the stranger.

Holding out his hand and warmly welcoming the young man, it was gripped firmly by a huge paw that seemed to seal a permanent friendship. It was as though a spark of kinship recognition flashed between them; a bond strengthened with the joining of their hands.

'I thank thee for thy welcome, Father William,' he said in a strong, husky tenor voice. 'Thomas Plowman be my name.'

Chapter 4: The Laughing Lion

'Do not ye err, God is not scorned;
for those things that a man soweth,
those things he shall reap.'

(Galatians 6:7 Wycliffe-Purvey Translation.)

Master Harold Plowman looked with pride upon his son.

'Verily, he be as Harold Godwinsson reborn, my love,' he said to his wife, as they watched the young man work the team of oxen, singing in his fine, lusty tenor.

'So 'tis said,' smiled the lady, 'but though the Golden Warrior's blood floweth in his veins, yet his fate shall be otherwise.'

Her husband glanced down at her with uneasy respect. She was a godly woman and had developed some reputation as having a prophetic gift. Not without reason. But her pride was more in the sunny temper and endearing smile of her son, and in the generous heart that reminded her so much of his father.

She looked up at the strong, hardworking man at her side, and her smile faded.

'Yet mine heart tells me that thine is the fate of King Harold also, my love,' she added softly and sadly. 'So be it. Then so also shall my fate be. Harold fell, that England may rise again. So we shall fall that our children may rise from our ashes.'

Hal's attention was on his children, and he did not hear the strange prophecy. He waved to his daughter Mary, who divided her time between coaxing the striving oxen onwards and engaging in lighthearted banter with her older brother, sweating happily at the plough.

Hal and Tom Plowman had worked themselves up through hard times to a more comfortable existence than most Dorsetshire peasant farmers could boast. They had recently obtained some land closer to the village

45

of Gillingham, where Hal hoped to build a bigger and more comfortable dwelling, away from the growing danger of outlaws in Gillingham wood.

Lawlessness had been increasing of late, partly from the oppression of greedy landlords driving some poor men mad with despair. But moral laxity was everywhere, even rampant in the Church.

Many of the local parsons, such as Father James, were decent men. They were often poorly paid by their bishops, and only stayed at their posts because they had a heart to serve God and the people. In contrast, the hierarchy, by and large, lived lives of profligacy, ignoring the poorer classes.

But Hal Plowman never let the tragedies of his day affect his attitude to life. His parents had died during the Black Plague, his grandfather in the Great Famine, but that was in the past. He was a free man, with the woman he wanted, children to be proud of, meat on his table and a roof over his head. He felt like a rich man and loudly asserted to his neighbours and friends that God had been good to him.

Everyone loved and respected the Plowman family, whose home was ever open to visitors. They threw themselves into helping their neighbours, even giving sacrificially to the poorer folk. They worshipped God with their whole heart during mass and often in between.

Tom especially endeared himself to everyone, with his cheeriness and enthusiasm for life, and smile that shone like the sun. He could lift the spirits of anyone, wherever he went.

His prowess at the games at Dorchester Fair was proverbial, and he was as strong as an ox. Thus he became very popular, especially amongst the village girls. They would sigh over his blue eyes and rippling muscles, calling him 'The Laughing Young Lion', and gather at their gates to blow him kisses whenever they heard him passing, his voice lifted in song.

He was not considered handsome, in the classical sense, for his prominent chin, sandy-golden beard and wild mane-like hair made him look too much like a wild and wilful beast to pass as an object of portraiture. However, he had rustic masculine charm, together with a sense of honour, a sense of humour, a generous spirit and a joie-de-vive that drew people to him. Many a village girl would almost swoon over his sparkling blue eyes, and longed to run her hands through his wild mane.

Unfortunately, and almost inevitably, his popularity and *joie de vivre* did make it easy for him to be led astray, and he allowed himself to be seduced by wild company, wild wood-ale (strong and heady liquor, forest-brewed in secret) and wild women.

Being godly folk, his parents grieved over this. His father firmly, but kindly, confronted him, but Tom was unrepentant, carelessly insisting that he could easily get absolution and would cheerfully do penance for his illicit good times.

His father responded sternly, 'Hast thou laboured so long in the fields, my son, and wot not that whatsoever a man soweth, that also shall he reap?'

Hal spoke from instinct and natural wisdom gained from observations of his world, not from any knowledge of the scriptures.

'And this shall be thy watchword and thy song for aye, my son,' his mother added prophetically.

Tom turned pale. For the first time he felt healthy fear and a sense of conviction over his loose living. He had too much respect and affection for his parents to go against their wishes in this matter, and he also had a deep respect for his mother's wisdom and mysteriously prophetic insight, sensing a response to her words in his own heart. So, from that day, he gave away the worst of his bad habits.

His father and mother's words were to haunt him for the rest of his life, both in good times and in bad, and he pondered on them often.

Tom had the knack of excelling in almost everything he turned his hand to. His thirst for knowledge led him to learn his letters.

Father James, the parson at St Barnabas' church in Gillingham, liked the lad. He took him under his wing and taught him as much as he knew, finding him quick and exceptionally intelligent.

Tom would drive Father James almost insane with his constant, 'Wherefore...?' The intelligent questions he asked were often disturbing, for Father James could not answer them with the limited and tidy theology he had been taught, and it flustered him a little.

One fateful day, Tom's life totally changed. Without any warning, a large gang of outlaws attacked his parents' outlying farm.

Tom was away in the farthest field at the time, singing lustily as he worked, and he didn't hear the faint shouts and screams in the far distance, until he saw smoke arising in the direction of his home.

With dread in his heart, he cut the oxen loose to graze, and then ran like the wind. The shouting had ceased, and he ran through a copse of trees to be greeted by a horrific sight.

The outlaws had fought and shot both his parents with arrows. Even their bodies had been dishonoured, with the best of their clothing ripped off and taken.

Tom ran, panting, up to his mother, then his father, trying to rouse them in vain. He then ran in among the ashes of his home, and found a third body which appeared to be that of a young woman, burnt way beyond recognition. His beloved sister Mary? The charred, unrecognisable remains were the only precious thing that remained of his home, now burnt to the ground.

A few dead men lying around his father and mother's dead bodies bore witness to a brave last stand, but everything he and his father had worked so hard for was either burnt or gone forever.

And he was too late!

He raised his fists to heaven and cried, 'God! Hast Thou no mercy?!' Then he fell on his knees and wept.

Tom undertook the heartbreaking labour of demolishing the pathetic remnants of the house, an easy task since the fire had done its work too well. Nothing of value remained – the outlaws had made sure of that. He buried his family where their home once stood.

Devastated and seething with bitter hatred, he looked darkly towards Gillingham Wood. 'Someone shall answer for this in blood this night!' he vowed.

After following tracks and the rumour of the passing of the murderers, he crept stealthily into the woods until finally hearing the distant sound of drunken revelling in a forest clearing.

Creeping cautiously under cover, he saw a bandit sentry sitting up in the trees, but not very vigilant. He had a skin of ale in one hand, his bow in the other, and was yawning and belching prodigiously. The bandits had become overconfident, and thinking they were invincible, became rather careless.

Singing drunkenly to himself, the sentry didn't hear Tom climb stealthily up behind him until it was too late. An iron hand clamped over his mouth, and his head was bashed hard against the trunk of the tree, knocking him senseless.

Tom was almost ready to cut his throat, but he was no murderer, and couldn't kill a man in cold blood. His father had instilled a rustic code of chivalry in him that, even now, he could not contravene. If he killed at all, it would be face-to-face, toe-to-toe, fist against fist, knife-to-knife, or arrow-to-arrow.

So he trussed and gagged the man to the branch on which he sat, took his weapons and crept up to where the bandits were feasting and making merry – with his father's ale, meal and meat.

Swaggering with confidence that none would dare follow them into the woods, they laughed, drank, swore and jested about the prizes they had won, especially the prize inside the cave. They did not elaborate, but Tom guessed it was some object of especial value belonging to his mother or father.

Fuming, Tom lay low and waited until they separated.

The loudest, largest and coarsest of them all stood in the centre of the group. He was the toast of his comrades and they drank to the health of 'Baldrick the Boar'.

Tom had heard fearful whispers about such a man, who had terrorized many a village right across Wessex. He ruthlessly slew or maimed anyone who stood in his way and eluded the hunting authorities like a cunning fox.

Finally, Tom saw his chance as the Boar wandered out into the woods to relieve himself. Tom quietly followed, and coming closer, discovered the huge beast of a man was wearing his father's leather sleeveless vest.

That was enough to thoroughly enrage Tom. He threw all caution to the wind and leapt upon the outlaw before he was aware, arm around his throat, nearly choking him.

But none had ever beaten Baldrick the Boar. The big bandit had been fighting all his life. His throat was crushed so he couldn't call his comrades, but though he gagged and coughed, he recovered quick enough to pick himself up and fight. Gasping for air, he charged in with a strangled cry of fury. But though he was named the Boar, he had never confronted Thomas Plowman, the Raging Lion.

Strong as an ox, quick as lightning and lithe as a snake, Tom was a skilled wrestler. As the Boar came for him, Tom threw him on his hip, sending the man crashing to the ground, winded. The Boar staggered to his feet, but a swinging blow to the jaw felled him so hard he bashed his head on a rock, where he lay motionless, blood streaming from a gash behind his head.

Tom ripped the vest off him and disappeared into the trees before anyone could discover what had happened.

The others were used to the Boar regularly getting into fights with his own men, and so they had no idea that an intruder had penetrated their hideaway, let alone beaten him in a fight. But finally, after a long wait, they went looking for him, cursing him for keeping them from their feast.

Furore erupted when they found their chief apparently dead. Who could have done it? Surely no one could have come alone. The sheriff and his hunters thought them miles away.

'The woods be accursed!' one cried. 'Wood-elves a-done this!'

'Nay, it be the Judgment of God!' cried another and crossed himself.

Others demanded that the woods be searched and called out all the men.

But Tom had already gone.

Meanwhile, Tom brooded on his misfortunes, torturing himself over his past life of dissipation, and thinking God had brought judgment upon him. In his bitterness, he knelt by his family's grave and swore a terrible oath:

'Upon the bones of my father, mother and sister, I swear that avenged I shall be on all of those hell-born scoundrels, though I perish in performing this oath! God aiding me or no!'

He crossed himself, stood up and went off in the direction of Shaftesbury.

The sunlight of his eyes was quenched and, from that day, a dark mood took hold of him.

The sergeant of my lord Sheriff's band knew Tom well, but didn't at first recognise the grim young man standing in the doorway that evening. He was not the same happy-go-lucky lad who had often visited Dorchester and occasionally gotten into drunken mischief. Tom had always taken his punishment cheerfully, and the sheriff, like many other men, could not help liking and admiring him for it.

'Thomas Plowman, lad! What be this?' he cried, starting from his chair. 'Come thou in. Wherefore comest thou so blackened and bloodied, lad? Thou hast the look of one that hath fought wild beasts!'

'Aye, that I have done,' said Tom, his brow darkening. 'But the selfsame beasts hath had the best of it. But not for long, God aiding us.'

In a few trenchant and grim words, he told the startled sergeant what had happened to his family.

'My God! Ben Baldrick the Boar? The black scoundrel hath slipped our net once again. Whither he be now? Gillingham forest?' demanded the soldier urgently, buckling on his hauberk.

'In Hell, if there be any justice!' growled the young man, and he spat in that direction. 'He hath not escaped the net.'

Tom went on to tell the amazed sergeant how he hunted down the Boar and fought him with his own hands, and how he had sworn to hunt down the rest of them. He then offered himself as a soldier in my lord Sheriff of Dorsetshire's service.

The sergeant looked at him a moment. He had told Tom, on more than one occasion, that he would make an excellent soldier. If he had truly killed the notorious bandit in hand-to-hand battle, in the midst of his own hideaway, then Tom would be a valuable asset indeed. Tom had a reputation for honesty, never boasting of any feat of arms he could not perform.

'I grieve for Hal Plowman,' the sergeant said at last. 'A mighty man was thy father and a good one. His son would have found a place in our band, whate'er betide, for thou'rt a good fighter. Come thou to the armoury anon, for we must begin the hunt for those losels on the morrow, and need we every man we can use.'

So began Tom's short career as a soldier.

The Sheriff's men, fully armed and reinforced by some of the Duke's contingent, surrounded the forest near Gillingham the day after the next. Though they found the camp, there was not a trace of the outlaws themselves, except for one.

Frustrated, Tom took the sergeant to the spot where he had fought the

Boar. Sure enough, there he lay. Tom spat on the carcase and turned away. He wouldn't even help to bury the man.

Had the outlaws gotten wind of the soldiers' approach long before? The tracks out of the forest were old and bore all the signs of a panicked stampede, not a stealthy, ordered retreat. The local men of the town had gathered together in a tardy, half-hearted attempt to amend the situation, but none of them had ventured to enter the woods. Too many had done so in the past, never to return.

The sergeant made his report to the Sheriff, and thought little more of it, but it puzzled Tom somewhat. He suggested that a search be made, but the sergeant said there were too many other matters to attend to, and too few men to do it, let alone chasing elusive outlaws beyond the bounds of his writ.

A month passed, and Tom performed his duties faithfully. To ease the pain and emptiness in his heart, he drank and womanised as much as any other soldier.

His fellows developed considerable respect for him, not just for his fighting prowess, but also for his honesty and generosity. Although he had become grim and silent, he was always the first to buy drinks, and the first in to any conflict that was called for. He had a burning hatred for injustice and would swiftly avenge any hint of bullying among them or any oppression of the poor. But there seemed to be no progress in the pursuit of the outlaws, and he became impatient with the normal processes of justice.

At last, the emptiness inside him became unbearable, and his oath of vengeance came back to torment him. He decided to go his own road, much to the sergeant's disappointment. Tom was a promising warrior with leadership capabilities and could have risen rapidly in the ranks, but he would have none of it. He decided to work his own way around the south of England until he avenged himself on any of the outlaws he could find. Maybe then he could find peace.

First, however, he returned to his family's grave, and it was there that his life underwent the most amazing transformation.

Chapter 5: The Grim Reaper and the Lord of the Harvest

'For he that soweth in his flesh, of the flesh he shall reap corruption;
but he that soweth in the Spirit, of the Spirit he shall reap everlasting life.'

(Epistle to the Ephesians 6:8 Wycliffe-Purvey Translation.)

Standing over his family's grave, Tom took his knife from his belt and grimly slit the length of his hand until blood flowed.

'By my blood, and that of my father, mother and sister, I swear again mine oath of vengeance!' he declared defiantly to the surrounding trees. 'I will relent never, neither will I rest until the blood of my foes flows freely as did my family's! God and the Devil be my witness!'

Suddenly, as he stood upon the ashes of his past world, his earthly vision became cloudy and misty, and he was looking into the world of spirits. To his horror, he saw a black, shadowy chain had wrapped itself around his hands, feet and chest, drawing tighter.

Then, before his horrified gaze, a large and menacing figure seemed to arise out the earth, shadowy and shrouded in a cloak as black as the darkest night. Its face was partly hidden by the hood, but Tom could distinguish the bony jaw of a skull peeping out from under it. In its skeletal hand was a large and sharp scythe. It was the Grim Reaper!

The apparition pointed towards him with a bony finger and gave a ghostly, echoing cackle of glee. Immediately, other horrible apparitions arose out of the ground.

Frozen with terror, Tom could tell, without asking, that these were demons of Violence, Hatred and Pestilence (surrounded by demonic, flea-ridden rats). He discovered that the ghostly chain wrapped around him was attached to a loosened length of chain, and Hatred grasped the end of it. Somehow he knew the chain represented his oath, sealed with his blood.

The horrible apparitions leered at him for a moment, and the Grim Reaper spoke in glee with a harsh, rasping voice.

'Ha! Out of his own mouth is he ensnared. He reapeth what he soweth. Now we have him.'

Tom realised what he had done. In his folly, he had allowed bitterness to poison his soul and had fallen into the trap of his true enemies, the minions of Satan.

Then Violence came forward and was about to take a hold of him. Somehow, Tom knew he had a choice to make: to give in to the hatred that would possess him, living a destructive life of violence, or repent of his oath and relinquish his mission of vengeance.

His father's words, even those the Grim Reaper had uttered, came back to him. He fell on his knees in terror, crying for God's mercy.

Immediately, like a bolt of lightning from heaven, the shining figure of a huge heavenly warrior appeared, casting the demons to the ground.

The Grim Reaper slunk away, knowing his time was not yet, while the others fled in fear.

The light faded to reveal the great warrior more clearly. He wore the gear of a great Saxon Thane fully armed for battle, but his face was noble and kind. In his right hand he bore a two-edged sword.

Feeling like St Paul on the road to Damascus, Tom cried out, 'Oh messenger from heaven! I have sinned! What must I do to atone?'

In a voice that echoed with thunder, the shining messenger said, 'Fear not, Thomas Plowman. I am thy guardian and messenger. God hath chosen thee for a far greater destiny than a life of bloodshed. God hath permitted judgment to be executed upon Baldrick by thine hand, but vengeance belongeth to the Lord, and he will repay with far greater justice than thou canst do. Neither is it thine to atone for thy sins, for all thy works of righteousness are as filthy rags. There is a better way.

'Think not that doom hath come upon thee for thy past sins. God hath seen thine hunger and thy pain. He would fill up thine hunger with Himself, the Bread of Heaven, and would heal thy pain, for He is the Great Physician, and hath suffered greater than any man. Thus shalt thou find thy destiny, if thou wilt turn unto Him in repentance and seek His healing.'

Then the warrior himself fell to his knees and bowed to the ground, as

Tom became aware of a warming light behind him. It was as though rays of unconditional love were shining on him, beckoning him to turn around.

He did so and also fell on his face, trembling. For before him, he saw the Lamb of God, suffering on the cross.

The vision changed to a huge field of near-ripe wheat. In the midst of it was a great figure, His face glowing like the sun. It was the Lord of the Harvest Himself. He held out his nail-scarred hands to show the suffering He had been through to secure Tom's salvation. None of Tom's own pain could compare to it. Who was he to sit in judgment on his enemies and to presume to execute judgment upon them? Had not his mother told him what the Saviour had said before He died: 'Father, forgive them! For they know not what they do.'?

Tom wept tears of repentance.

'Now arise, Thomas. Thou art My Plowman, My Sower and Reaper. I have need of thee.'

The voice above him was as gentle as the breeze, yet more powerful than a thunderstorm.

In a daze, wondering why he was given the privilege of speaking face to face to the Lord of the Harvest, he timidly looked up and found that He had gone. In his place, a new messenger stood before him.

This messenger was clothed as a great Earl of the time of Harold. A glow and air of authority surrounded him, and in his hands he held a two-edged sword, a great shield and a sickle. He also spoke with a voice of rolling thunder.

'Thy chain is loosed! But not all.'

Tom looked down and saw that the chain had broken and was lying at his feet. There were still remnants of those chains on his wrists, but his deliverance was almost complete. Tom closed his eyes and breathed a prayer of thanks.

How could the Lord of the universe have need of him – a licentious sinner? What was the meaning of those gracious words?

Answering his unspoken questions, the messenger said, 'It is because He hath chosen thee as a chief labourer in the harvest that is to come to this land. Thou'rt called as a harvester of souls, a sower of the seed of the Word of God. But first thou must plough and sow into thine own life.'

The messenger brought forth the implements he bore.

'Behold! I bear the sword that thou shalt wield in great power to defend the defenceless and to strike down the enemy of men's souls. But thou must be exercised in the use thereof ere I give it thee.

'Behold! I bear a shield for thy protection. Thou shalt learn to lift the shield of faith to quench the fiery darts of the wicked one. It shall be thine anon. Bear it well.'

He held the shield out to Thomas, but when he received it, with a trembling hand, it seemed to melt into his being and disappear. Yet he felt a new sense of confidence, and that he could face anything that life, or the enemy, could throw at him.

The messenger continued.

'Behold! I bear the sickle – thine authority to go forth and preach the gospel, making disciples of many in this land. It shall be thine when thou'rt skilled to fight with the sword and the shield.

'Now arise, Thomas Plowman! Go thou north unto Oxenford. There thou shalt find thy chosen yokefellow by the name of William Shephard, a worthy man of God. He and others of God's servants shall instruct thee in the use of the sword and shield. Go forth! For God is with thee.'

And with that, the messenger was gone.

Shaking and wondering if it were all a dream, Tom stood looking around. Then he noticed it. The pile of ashes of his home was gone. There was nothing but green growth where once there was death.

He knew his family was safe in the arms of their redeemer. None would disturb their sweet memory. But he had learned his lesson now. He had an awesome call on his life to fulfil.

'...God aiding me!' he cried.

Shouldering the last of the worldly possessions he had in his sack, he set off north, on the long road to Oxford.

Tom's journey to Oxford seemed rather uneventful after the glorious visitation he had just experienced, but he was enjoying himself hugely.

He had never felt so free, now that the guilt and shame of his past life had been washed away, without the need to do penance or buy indulgences.

He had never felt so alive. He felt as though he was born anew, and an exciting new life had begun. A sense of purpose and destiny had taken hold of him.

He had never felt so loved, by a love so powerful that the One who loved him would shed His blood for him and ask for nothing in return for the gift of salvation.

The religion he was taught by Holy Church was pale and pathetic compared to this.

His old *joie-de-vivre* returned with a vengeance, and the smile that now lit his face came from a powerful fire deep in his heart.

As he travelled, Tom sang snatches of old songs that suited his elated mood, but often reverted to the Song of the Harvest, for he knew that the Harvest of Souls was his calling.

> 'Sing Hey for the sickle! Sing Ho for the scythe!
> For the heart of the reaper be merry and blithe.
> With joy shall we labour through rain or hot sun,
> Giving thanks to the Lord when the harvest be done.'

He had a fine, strong, lusty voice, and those who heard him would stop to listen. In taverns along the way, the local men applauded loudly and bought him ale in return for another song.

At other times in his journey, he would meditate deeply upon the things that had been said to him, both in the visitation and also by his parents over the years. He was largely recovering from the grief he felt for his family, gone forever, but an ache would sometimes surface in his heart. This made him feel more for the sufferings of the people he passed.

However, his buoyant spirit could never be submersed for long, and it was not long before he burst into song again. His meditations comforted and cheered him, meaning so much more than they ever had before. This was the second experience of the shield that the Messenger had given him.

His money lasted him for most of the journey, but such was the exalted state he was in, together with his new-found compassion, that he gave freely to those in need.

To supplement his dwindling resources, Tom hired himself out to farmers, and such was the volume of work he did that many asked him to stay.

Although he enjoyed the roving life, his heart was restless to see what awaited him at Oxford, and to meet this mysterious man, William Shephard, of whom the Messenger spoke.

At first, a little unwisely, he spoke about his visitation to fellow travellers or in taverns along the way. He was naturally gregarious and fell easily into conversation with strangers.

Many of the simple folk were awed at his experiences, and there was certainly a glow about him that could only come from meeting the Lord of life Himself. But some mocked and laughed. They had some cause to do so, for there was so much superstition around, and preposterous, conflicting tales were told, often fostered by the wandering friars. Tall tales sometimes generated an extra coin over and above the usual benefice that friars received. Many had long lost their credibility, for times had changed from when the friars first appeared as humble men, fired with zeal and true to their vows of poverty and a simple lifestyle.

Tom had a lot of easygoing tolerance, but if the mocker went too far, that gentry found himself head-down in the nearest horse-trough or miller's pond. Tom still had a few things to learn.

Finally, he crossed the Cherwell and found himself outside the Bull and Book tavern in Oxford. Entering, he discovered a much more congenial atmosphere than William had found a number of years before.

Much reconciliation had occurred since the riots at Merton College. Many students, mainly Wycliffites, had approached the townsfolk and addressed their grievances. Friendships had been made, and now the tavern was nearly full with townsmen drinking the health of the masters and students, and vice versa, much to the delight of the tavern-keeper whose business was thriving again.

One man stood up and called for a toast for 'Doctor Evangelicus, Champion of the poor.' Nearly everyone drank and applauded loudly.

Another, rather reprehensibly, toasted, 'Confusion to Courtenay!' which produced loud, ribald laughter. Tom learned later that Courtenay, Bishop of London, was a fierce opponent of Wycliffe and forbade him to preach in his churches.

One group of students, farmers and labourers, mellowed with good ale, hailed him genially, liking him on sight. They invited him to join them, and one bought him a drink.

The one who did this shook his hand warmly and said, 'I call myself Benjamin Abyngdon, master. A student of Merton College am I. It seemeth that thou'st journeyed long and sore, and a great journey's tale hangeth upon thy brow. Wherewithal can one be of service unto thee?'

'Thou'rt abundant kind to a stranger, Master Abyngdon,' responded Tom, touched and grateful. 'Thomas Plowman is my name, and I seek one William Shephard, a man of God. Dost thou ken of such an one?'

'Few that ken him not at Oxenford, Master Plowman. A busy man is Father William, but hath ever occasion to speak to any that hath need of his wise rede. I met him hither as a stranger in this very place, whence he rendered me kindness in return for the churlishness of myself and my companions. A more godlier man have I not found, and his fellowship do I value above all. Haply we will find him anon.'

So it was that the Shepherd and the Reaper finally reached their divinely-appointed rendezvous.

Standing before him, Tom saw a tall, bearded man, with a grave and kindly face, and latent laughter in his grey eyes.

A sense of destiny came upon him.

Chapter 6: Yokefellows

'And when they ministered to the Lord, and fasted,
The Holy Ghost said to them, Separate ye to me Saul and Barnabus
[part ye to me Saul and Barnabus],
into the work to which I have taken them.'

(Deeds of Apostles Chapter 13:2 Wycliffe-Purvey Translation/Revision.)

'Thou'rt a Dorsetshire man – even as I,' observed William, hearing the stranger's accent. 'Doubly welcome art thou, Master Thomas Plowman.'

He invited the two of them to dine at Hereford's quarters to hear his story. Such was the trust and esteem that his master had for him, William had earned the privilege of entertaining whomever he wished when Hereford was away.

Excitement grew in them all as first Tom, then William, shared their stories. Even without the naming of himself in Tom's visitation, William knew in his heart that they were destined to minister together in a powerful way.

Tom, with his budding intuition, could see that William was not only his chosen mentor, but a yokefellow in the Lord's work – a mighty work, such as had not been seen for centuries.

When asked of his immediate plans, Tom explained that he had nothing fixed beyond his meeting with William and his aspirations to become a preacher of the gospel. He was willing to sleep in the hay-barn of a local farmer he had worked for until he found something more comfortable.

'Holy Saints! In a hay-barn? God forbid!' protested Benjamin. 'Is there not a free bed in our dortoir at Merton, now Holloway hath departed? I shall speak with the Ward of Residence thither.' He cut short Tom's expression of thanks.

The next day, his friend brought him to Hereford's quarters again, where William awaited them. Abyngdon was in high fettle, very pleased with his find. This was the second stranger he had befriended who showed great promise.

'A right good fisher of men am I,' he boasted laughingly. 'Is he not an evangel sent of God, as Doctor Evangelicus hath so prayed for, Father William?'

'So I think, and so saith mine heart,' William agreed. 'It hath been in the heart of Doctor Hereford to begin classes for the training of these "poor preachers" that Doctor Evangelicus would raise up. Alas, we have not many students that art both graduate and willing to go forth among the poor folk. But need we a-many years of study for this task? Nay! Methinks that laymen will be needful, of especial them that be gifted and called for such a strange work.'

He looked speculatively at Tom and quoted a verse from Hereford's translation of the Book of Esther: 'Who knows but that thou art called into the Kingdom for such a time as this?'

'But withal respect to Master Plowman, sickerly he is not so goodly countenanced to look upon as were the fair Queen Esther!' objected Benjamin.

Tom laughed and riposted, 'Nay! Rather be I like to them that would have devoured the good prophet Daniel, or so 'tis said.'

William was too obsessed with Wycliffe's vision and their latest find to enter into the spirit of this. Smiling absently at the camaraderie of the other two men, he said, 'Doctor Hereford hath pledged monies and more for this vision, and Doctor Evangelicus himself also. They live frugally that they may give oft to the poor; hence do they gather wealth for the kingdom of God. But what of thine own wealth, Master Plowman? Wherewithal shalt thou sup and faire if thou wouldst join us?'

'Heed it not, Father, for labour I with mine hands for my needs,' Tom answered eagerly. 'Two farms hath I inherited and may be sold, if it be deemed needful to raise the wherewithal. But I be thy servant or disciple, yea, whatsoever thou would wish in all else, for so hath it been ordained, I trow.'

'Good man! Gladly would I disciple thee,' approved William, sensing once again the bond between them. 'Thou'rt lettered?'

'Father James of Gillingham hath so taught thy servant, and I read much when I may.' A mischievous grin emerged. 'But, alas, he hath not driven forth the demon of inquisitiveness that possesseth me a-times.'

'Ha!' commented Benjamin. 'I perceive that thou'rt a born scholar! Thou hast need to be so inquisitive, yea, and a little wood[12] also, *et abnormis sapiens.*'

As Tom looked mystified at this, Benjamin took on an air of superiority, in mimicry of the august Doctor Wadeford. 'To be interpreted: A Natural Philosopher, my son.'

'And I perceive that my friend shall instruct thee in thy Latin, God aid thee, e'er all is done,' observed William. 'Come thou to these quarters on the morrow, if thou wilt, and I shall observe thy cunning with the quill. Thou shalt copy some of Doctor Hereford's tracts with me. There be many a student that hath so repaid the Masters for their sponsorship, and thus have read the scriptures in the mother tongue. So shalt thou earn thy faire also.'

'Gladly will I do so, Father William,' said Tom gratefully, dizzy at the thought of reading the Holy Scriptures himself, in his own tongue. 'And I thank thee of thy kindness.'

'Yea! But 'ware the scourge of the dreaded *chorea scriptorum*[13], Master Plowman,' added the irrepressible Benjamin in a voice of grave admonition. ''Tis a grievous affliction that plagues us all in this task.'

Tom looked a little apprehensively toward William, as though he would be struck down by a demonic attack or horrible debilitating disease. William chuckled.

'Fear not the doomsome words of yon jobbardly Jeremiah, Master Plowman. He maketh merry with us all oft and anon, and 'twill be to his own undoing. But heed thou his warning that thine hand may have its Sabbath rest each day, that thy copying may not overburden it.'

Nicolas Hereford had been delighted to meet Tom when William explained his circumstances and his calling.

Like all of the leading Wycliffite teachers, Hereford sponsored some of the more promising, but indigent, students through their studies at Oxford. These were mainly young men whom he had met on his travels,

---

12   mad
13   Writer's cramp

while preaching in churches throughout Leicestershire and Gloucestershire. Fired with a call to preach the gospel, they would often approach him, or William Shephard, at the end of his addresses. Hence, many students automatically adhered to Wycliffe's movement at Oxford.

There were also a growing number of lay students, like Thomas Plowman, who had begun attending Hereford's special classes for lay preachers.

By contrast, Doctor William Wadeford and his followers only accepted the sons of gentlemen or wealthy merchants for enrolment in his courses; only those who could pay their own way. He sneered at the 'peasant-priests', as he called them, in Wycliffe's train, shaking his head disgustedly at how 'basely the clerical vocation hath descended'.

'How hath the mighty fallen!' he quoted derisively, referring to Wycliffe, his rival.

Thomas Plowman would never have been considered fit for one of Doctor Wadeford's classes, but with Hereford, it had been a different matter altogether. Based on his obvious intelligence, together with a recommendation from William, Hereford had willingly offered the young man a sponsorship.

'Mine exceeding and grateful thanks, good Doctor,' replied Tom with a kind of rustic dignity. 'Natheless, a proud son of the soil I be. I have vowed me that neither meat I shall take, nor bed shall I slumber in except that I have toiled for't. Forgive me if churlishness this may seem.'

'Thou'rt a man of honour, I deem, Master Plowman,' Hereford replied approvingly. 'Thy zeal doth commend itself to thy calling. But mark me well, there is a grave yoke that thou must also bear as an Oxenford cleric, and in especial one that be of Doctor Wycliffe's party.'

He went on to enumerate the study disciplines and responsibilities that would be expected of him.

'So this I would ask thee: Canst thou truly make provision for all thy need and yet attend unto all thine office?'

Tom opened his mouth to protest his capacity for an even greater load, but looked up at William, standing behind Hereford's chair, and caught the quizzical gleam in his eye. He bowed his head and smiled.

'Good Doctor, mine own father once saith unto me: Not even the strongest oxen can plough two furrows. I will accept thine offer with thanks.'

'So be it! Thou'st spoken as a true Wycliffite preacher, my son.'

'Amen!' agreed William, his smile broadening. 'An honest man is he. The labourer be worthy of his hire. And fear not, Master Thomas, for verily thou shalt labour for it indeed.'

When lectures were in recess, Tom joined William in going among the village folk, working and talking with them. This was as the breath of life to him. His sunny temperament, hard work and sparkling enthusiasm soon won over many hearts, and he became just as popular as William.

In the beginning, he observed and listened to William's style as he preached and prayed. Within a year, however, Tom's confidence had grown to the extent that his own voice rang out in the streets of local towns and villages.

William noticed that when Tom discovered some new revelation from the scriptures, he would share it fervently and skilfully with his street congregations, with powerful effect. Tom had a natural gift of words, a dramatic bent and a boldness that gave William a slight twinge of envy.

'Ah, well!' he said philosophically to Benjamin as they drank their ale at the Bull and Book. 'He is an evangel preacher, a reaper of souls. I am but a shepherd.'

'Aye, but one that feedeth those selfsame souls he reapeth, Father William,' said Benjamin firmly, with one of his occasional bursts of profundity. 'Ye are destined to labour together, both. Have I not seen it oft? What will it profit the soul if it be born, but to perish through want of feeding?'

''Tis soothly said, my sage, and I thank thee of thy kind rebuke!'

The only serious fault William could find in Tom was a certain impetuosity that characterized him, and sometimes got him into trouble. When injustice was being done, Tom could not stand by and watch without intervening. On one occasion, William witnessed two of the more unruly students, whom Tom had found harassing an elderly woman, having their heads banged together.

Tom also found it hard not to confront the hecklers and gainsayers in the street crowds that came to hear them. More than one student or cleric that was hostile to his message, and said so, found himself semi-baptized, face down, in the miller's pond or horse-trough nearby. It was not really a violent temper that prompted him to react in such a way. In Tom's youth at Gillingham, it was often considered the normal way of disposing of one's opponent to end a debate, whether verbal or physical. He sometimes did it before he realized what he had done.

William was usually able to smooth over the situation with diplomacy, and found it hard to castigate his erring disciple when he came to him later in genuine repentance.

One such incident occurred after one of Doctor Wadeford's followers was left with his feet sticking out of a thornbush, kicking wildly. Muffled noises could be heard emanating from within the bush. Although William was present at the time, it had all happened too quickly for him to prevent Tom's reaction.

Tom immediately realized the enormity of what he had done. Not only would he receive a raking down from his mentor, he knew a complaint was sure to be made to the masters – even Doctor Wycliffe himself. With a rueful lowering of his head, Tom turned to William, awaiting condemnation and an imposition of penance.

'*Eheu, Padre. Peccavi*,' he said soberly.

'So though sayest!' William snapped, rather annoyed. 'But "*Primum non nocere!*"[14] quoth I, thou jobbardly shakebuckler! Avoid him anon!'

But then exasperation slowly gave way to a smile on William's face as Tom hastily obeyed. Then an irrepressible chuckle arose from deep inside, which gave way to helpless laughter as Tom, doing his best to conceal his relief, apologised to the shaken victim. William walked away, shaking his head and still chuckling – a bubble of mirth that lasted well into the evening.

Tom largely grew out of such behaviour – once William convinced him that it did more harm than good.

'Hark ye, Thomas!' his mentor would say earnestly. 'Wilt thou impart wood justice? And wilt thou debate with the sword or strong arm of the flesh? If thou wouldst make enemies unto thyself, beware lest it be to thy gainbite[15]! Stint thou this witaldry! Mark thou the words of Holy Writ that

---

14 Above all, do no harm
15 Regret

sayeth: "Whatsoever ye mete shall be meted unto you." Wilt thou reap that which thou sowest?'

Tom was silenced, remembering the words of his father and mother.

'Well, be not discouraged, my son,' added William, relenting. 'Thou hast strange gifts for a strange task that is before thee, even more than I. Thou'st a great heart within thy breast, moreover. Thou'rt a shakebuckling rogue, Master Thomas Plowman, but I perceive we shall become boon comrades. And mark thou this: *Ab ove maiori discit arare minor.*'

Tom wrestled with the quotation for a moment, for his Latin was still only half learnt. Then it dawned on him. 'From the older ox the younger learns to plow,' he laughed. 'But what if the younger be a froward beast, Father Ox, and drag thee onward beyond thy measured ploddings?'

'Then shall I avoid me the yoke, and ride upon the plough to look upon thee as thou toilest alone, Master Plowman. And wield I the goad also.'

In spite of William's half-hearted attempts at disciplining him, the imp of mischief never really left Tom – even to the end of his days.

Chapter 7: The Lullards of Logic Lane

'So shine your light before men, that they see your good works,
and glorify your Father that is in heavens.'

(Gospel of Matthew 5:16 Wycliffe-Purvey Translation)

As with everything he put his hand to, Tom threw himself into university life.

He became close friends with Benjamin and also with William Thorpe, Master Smith's assistant. The three of them had the same zest for life that characterized most of Wycliffe's followers, emanating from the joy that welled up within them and their relationship with their God. They frequently asserted that they were God's children, forgiven and free, and in the words of the articulate Benjamin, 'full o' fanksgiving.'

The three of them had fine voices and sang together in the great Oxford Cathedral choir. They were called upon to sing a rendition of the *Baudette* at the dedication of the magnificent chapel of New College that Christmas.

Sometimes, when they were free from their studies, they marched down the street together singing in fine harmony, Thorpe's deep baritone undergirding the two tenors. The townsfolk used to wave a greeting, for the Wycliffite students brought a breath of fresh air to Oxford town.

'So shine your light before men,' quoted Wycliffe, as he preached from the chapel pulpit, 'that they see your good works, and glorify your Father that is in heavens.'

Inspired by this command, his students often went into the town and looked for ways they could spread some of God's light, and the three friends were no exception.

It was some time before the populace discovered who left the money inside Widow Hampton's door, or who fixed old John Hoby's chimney, or who carved the wonderful figurines for the little orphan girls at Christmas.

Finally, under the seal of secrecy, Widow Hampton shared the secret with old Mistress Joan, the town gossip.

'It were them lads o' Doctor Wycliffe's, it were,' she whispered to her old crony. 'But they were a-beggin' o' me not for to be a-tellin' naught nor no wight, God bless 'em. "Give glory unto the Good God alone, Ma'am!" quoth they. So tell thee not a soul, my dear.'

'O, nary a word, Widow dear,' promised the excited Mistress Joan, pleased, for once, to be spreading good news instead of the usual neighbourhood scandals.

As a consequence, any lingering resentment that the townsfolk had toward the university students, in general, quickly dissipated, and the memory of the Mob Quod Riots soon faded. The occasional angry words were expressed toward some of Wadeford's followers, but the people were largely becoming tolerant of their arrogance.

Admittedly there was still an element of riotousness among the students who lived in the poorer quarters, who had not joined the Wycliffite movement. Bad, even criminal, habits were hard to break. There had once been a time when lawless bands of students roamed the countryside, preying on whomsoever they could. Later, these same young men often took up posts as priests! But as long as the Wycliffite influence grew and remained, such criminal behaviour was largely curtailed.

Some of the eldest of these lads did their best to corrupt Tom, inviting him to their drunken routs and orgies. They were surprised to find that he was too busy enjoying life, and his call, and his love for his Saviour to be drawn away by such perilous pleasures. Besides, he had made a pact with his two close friends, as well as Father William, that they should be honest, open and accountable to each other regarding their 'daily walk'.

* * * * * *

One of Doctor Wadeford's young followers was Master Roger Dymok, a clever young clerk about to be elevated to the staff of the Archbishop of Canterbury himself. Dymok's invective against the Wycliffite party was well known. He was both envious and irritated by the young men who enjoyed the favour of the people and the Wycliffite Masters. He had never bothered to win friendships, since sincerity and loyalty were, in his view, both inconvenient and rustic. Yet he wondered why people flocked to hear men such as William Shephard, Thomas Plowman and William Thorpe speak on the streets, rather than his own scholarly and skilfully prepared harangues from the public forum.

One day, he stood upon the threshold of the cloister at New College as the three friends walked by singing.

Dymok, filled with pride over his imminent elevation, looked upon them with ill-concealed contempt.

'What?' he drawled, clearly enough for all the bystanders to hear. 'Sickerly but be this naught than the three Lullards of Logic Lane?'

He bowed in mock reverence.

'I bid thee good morrow, sirrahs. Dost thou serenade the ravens with thy lullaby? Witterly not the poor ears of the *Populori*? Ah, me! *Parva leves capiunt animas.*[16] But I forget me, do not I? Thou, Thomas Plowman, art of the *adscriptus glebae*[17], art thou not? Hence wouldst thou seek fellowship of the basest. I wot not wherefore that thy great Doctor Arch-Evangelicus doth open the hallowed portals of University College to such rabble. But 'tis all of a piece, and surely an ensample of such heretical bent.'

He gave a melancholy sigh as he stepped onto the pavement.

'O how have the mighty fallen!' he concluded, pleased with the poisoned barbs he had been longing to cast for many a day.

But his reflective and silken sarcasm gave way to a wail of dismay, as his feet slipped under him, and he came down on his buttocks with a resounding splat. Whether his nose was too far in the air to perceive the peril at his feet, or whether it was Tom's careless foot that partly tipped over a tub of rotting apples that sat near the entrance, or both, was unclear. His fall had been softened by the mushy and liquidly fruit, but the beautiful new cassock he had bought for his new post was ruined.

The audience that had gathered all roared with laughter. Luckily for them, Tom had somehow known it was coming and surreptitiously waved them all back, so none else had suffered the fate of the unfortunate Master Dymok.

Forgetting his customary poise and hauteur, Dymok struggled to his feet, slipping again and again.

---

16 Small things amuse small minds
17 Serf

'Hell and the Black Vomit seize ye, ye heretics!' he screamed at them. 'Ye shall be damned and shall fall…' but he slipped again and landed face first in the mush, his mouth full of rotting apple.

Benjamin Abingdon, once he had mastered his own mirth, came to Dymok's rescue. He grabbed a nearby bucket of grey-looking water and threw it over the unfortunate man and the cobblestones, making it easier for his feet to find traction. But the sufferer did not demonstrate any gratitude for this noble act, and spat forth at him both verbal venom and rotting apple flesh.

Dymok grabbed his dripping capuchon and glowered at the three grinning friends for a moment.

'Ye have not heard the last of this!' he fumed, then sloshed away, smelling of old ale and washing water, thoroughly humiliated.

As the three friends walked on, after apologising to the toothless old washer woman and refilling her bucket, Thorpe mused, 'The Lullards o' Logic Lane. That title liketh me well. Thinkest thou, Thomas, that we should wear it as our sobriquet as a minstrel troupe?'

'The toast of the Bull and Book shall we be, at the least!' laughed Tom. 'Let us go thence and sample of the new Oxenford beer we hear tell of, and share the geste of this day's adventure. Sing we some lullaby to put to slumber the drunkard.'

And so, strangely, the term Lullard, or Lollard, soon caught on among the townsfolk when referring to the Wycliffite students, but it was mostly given as a badge of honour rather than of scorn.

Master Dymok's complaint to Doctor Hereford notwithstanding, Tom continued to rise in William's esteem. He had made rapid progress in his studies and general training, and the rusticities of his former life had soon given way to a courtesy of manner worthy of the noblest lord of the realm. This was partly due to Tom's ability to adapt to his surroundings, his generous nature, and also the example set by most Wycliffites. Master Ashton proclaimed from the pulpit that true gentlemanliness was a Fruit of the Holy Ghost, quoting Chapter Five of Paul's Epistle to the Galatians.

Tom drank in all the teaching he received and began to grow rapidly in his faith and character. In spite of Tom's occasional mischief and impetuosity, William noticed that he showed wisdom beyond his years, and began taking him on more of his rounds of ministry, much to that young man's delight.

Tom soon dropped nearly all formality toward his mentor, for William put him at his ease and demonstrated a genuine concern for his welfare and growth. Tom was able to tell him all his hopes, fears and deepest pain, finding relief and healing through it all. He considered William the godliest and best man that he knew, without a trace of hypocrisy. Soon they had become like father and son.

Chapter 8: Miracle at Coventry

*'And it was almost the sixth hour, and darknesses were made
on all the earth into the ninth hour [till the ninth hour.] And
the sun was made dark, and the veil of the temple was rent
at two [and the veil of the temple was cut the middle].'*

(Gospel of Luke 23:44,45 Wycliffe-Purvey Translation/Revision.)

One of William's duties was to fill in as vicar for some of the local rectories
when the present incumbent was absent for any reason. This happened a
number of times after his ordination, partly because he had made a name
for absolute honesty and simplicity of lifestyle, and partly for his sermons
on a personal relationship with God.

Once, after he had spoken and ministered at a village church near
Coventry, the laity of that church petitioned his Lordship the Earl to offer
the vacant living to William, but somehow William knew he was called to
something different, although he did not yet know what it was.

The next time he visited Coventry, he took Tom with him. It was
Easter, and the villagers and townsfolk came together to witness and
enact the Easter Passion. They had seen various Miracle Plays before, but
William's preaching on the death and resurrection of Christ had inspired
them.

The only problem was, as the flustered verger informed them, they
didn't know the whole story. The last incumbents had instructed the
people on such things as the stories of the Saints and their martyrdoms, but
were a little vague on the necessary details of the real account of Christ's
life, ministry, death and resurrection. Thus, the organisers realised how
little they knew about these events, and were inclined to put in their own
inventions. This included, to Tom's barely disguised amusement, an all-in
brawl between the disciples and the temple guard who had come to take
Jesus away.

The uninformed players were shocked to discover that the disciples actually deserted Jesus, and that Peter (considered to be the first Bishop of Rome) actually denied Him out of fear of a young maid's opinion of him.

The verger was relieved that they had a learned man in their midst, just in time to organise the play.

The next problem was that none could be found to satisfactorily play the parts of neither the Saviour nor St Peter. Those who volunteered were howled down by their rivals as unworthy.

In the end, the verger himself was struck by a brilliant idea. Turning eagerly toward William and Thomas he said, 'Hither be our men! Father William be the Blessed Lord and Master Thomas be the good St Peter.'

All the players cheered, drowning out William's protests that he was not worthy of such an exalted role either. Tom laughed and urged him to play the part, since no one else would and he was universally approved. The show had to go on after all.

Tom revelled in his part, having a taste for drama and considerable talent for it – provided, he confided to William, he wasn't obliged to become a fat Bishop of Rome later.

Scandalised and delighted, William laughed and exclaimed, 'Blasphemy! A Holy Father! Thou? *Quod abominor!*[18]'

Once the pageant was ready to perform and the street stage set up in the main square, the crowds came gathering. It was a beautiful day, and everyone thought that nothing could possibly go wrong. The costumes had been elaborately made and every player seemed to look the part. The crowd hushed when the Christ and his disciples entered into the supposed Gethsemane Garden.

With great reverence, William played his part as the Christ suffering, and was so convincing that many of the ladies in the audience wiped their eyes.

There seemed to be a spirit of excellence that entered the players, for they threw themselves into their parts so much that the audience gasped at all the right times and hissed at Caiaphas the High Priest and Pontius Pilate as they pronounced the death sentences. They all cried out with dismay at the whipping and the *Via Dolorosa*[19] scene.

---

18   God forbid!
19   The Way of Suffering, the road Christ took to Calvary.

The crucifixion was where it became the most dramatic, and the most alarming, for either the weather (as the sceptics insisted) or Almighty God Himself took a hand.

The lashes and the wounds inflicted on the supposed Christ seemed so real that one sensitive woman in the audience fainted. Others wept, much the same as they must have at the real crucifixion. A few young loutish lads shouted along with the players who scorned the Christ. The older folk were shocked and turned on them indignantly.

But the words froze in everyone's mouth when William, as the crucified Christ, cried out, 'My God! My God! Wherefore hast thou forsaken me?'

Although there wasn't a cloud in the sky, a great and uncanny darkness crept rapidly and steadily over the summer sky, plunging the whole scene into an eerie twilight.

William was so intent on His role that he didn't notice the change that was happening. He cried out in a loud voice, 'Father, forgive them for they know not what they do!'

The lads who had previously mocked now looked at each other with white faces in the great darkness, then fell on their knees and hastily repented. Apart from that, there was stunned silence. Even Thomas took a while to recover.

Then William cried out even louder, 'Father! Into Thy hands I commit my spirit!' and bowed his head as if to die.

Immediately there was a distant rumbling in the direction of the great Coventry Cathedral, and the earth shook slightly.

The terrified simple folk still on their feet fell on their knees also.

The player who was the centurion lost his cue, or the words dried up in his mouth, as he looked around ashen-faced.

Tom had recovered quickly, even though it brought back memories of his own personal visitation. With great presence of mind, he walked behind the backdrop, came close to where the centurion would be and cried, 'Truly, this man was the Son of God!'

This helped the petrified players to pull themselves together. Most left the stage beating their breasts, even crossing themselves, but with more penitence than they had felt before when they had done so at mass.

The women and Joseph of Arimathea came to take the Christ's body down, and William opened his eyes briefly to see the real drama enfolding around him. It was then that he noticed the darkness and the fearful reverence on everyone's faces. He immediately looked up in the sky to see if there was an eclipse of the sun, but the moon was nowhere to be seen. He closed his eyes again in earnest prayer, wondering for a brief moment if the end of the world was near at last.

Recovering from his own amazement, he whispered to his frightened fellow players to take heart and continue the pageant, for God was playing His part as well. Taking heart in his confidence, they laid him in his tomb and gathered with the 'apostles', who were still shaking with unfeigned fright, and passed his message on to them.

The verger, as narrator, announced with a quavering voice that it was Resurrection morning, then froze again as he heard the rumbling as of a great stone being rolled away.

Immediately, the darkness that had swooped so suddenly over them, just as swiftly lifted. The sun shone overhead as though nothing had happened, and birds sang again in the rooftops around.

With relief, everyone began to breathe again and murmur among each other about the wonder they had experienced. But this was gradually drowned out and silenced by the most beautiful singing anyone present had ever heard.

The great wooden carving that had been painted to look like a stone was rolled away from the supposed tomb entrance, and the dark hole it was covering a moment before was filled with a light brighter than the sun. Rays of glory shone out upon the audience as the people gasped and cried out, this time in joy and wonder.

A figure was silhouetted against the light and came forth, reflecting the glory when he emerged from the tomb. Everyone fell down and worshipped.

The light and the music faded, revealing the very earthly and real William standing and looking around, a little bemused, at the worshippers.

'Pray, do it not good people!' he cried, distressed and shaken. 'God hath revealed His glory this day, that ye seldom will behold! But worship we the Risen Saviour in our hearts, not images nor a mortal sinner as I!'

But he was at a loss about what to do from there, shaken as he was by all the dramatic events.

Tom, however, knew in his heart that this was too good an opportunity to let slip. He leapt energetically on stage and stood with William.

'Verily! We be but mortal men as was Peter, whom I played in likeness. But God hath spoken unto us through this blessed pageant! A Miracle Play in more than name! Let us hearken unto the simple message of the gospel of the risen Lord. Them that come to the foot of the cross and receive His forgiveness shall also have the Glory of God shining through their lives, yea even as we beheld it in Father William. But mark ye! Father William himself would hasten to say that there be no need for priest nor confessor between us and God's Blessed Grace open unto us anon! For the curtain of the temple was rent in twain, and an abundant entrance into His presence was ope, even unto us all!'

Grateful for Tom's presence of mind and surprising insights, William pulled himself together and gave a firm 'Amen!'

He looked at Tom, and was about to expand on the theme of an open way to the Glory of God, when he was interrupted by a young boy's voice raised in alarm.

One of the bolder and more inquisitive of the altar boys had recovered quickly from the earth-shaking events, and raced off to investigate the rumblings they had heard from the cathedral. What he saw shocked him as much as the manifestations that had just passed. Not knowing that Tom was preaching to the intent audience, he cried out the news as soon as he was within earshot.

'Master Thomas! Father William! Come ye anon, I pray! 'Tis a terrible thing! The barrier o' the sanctuary! 'Tis fallen! 'Tis gone!'

Everyone snapped out of their riveted attention on William and Thomas's message, blessed themselves over this added wonder and raced off in the manner of sheep through a new gate to see for themselves. Even many of the wealthier folk, who had witnessed the drama from their upper windows, ran to see.

Tom and William followed, wondering what it meant.

They managed to make their way through the crowd enough to see that the elaborate, tall, but strong, lattice work that separated the sanctuary from the congregation had collapsed with a great thunderous noise. The dust was still clearing, and people gasped in dismay at the damage.

'It be the wrorth o' the good Lord!' cried one.

'Nay! Hit be devilish worrk, this!' cried another portly citizen. "Oo but the devil hisself would a-maken soch himpious mischief to hower blessed 'oly church, then?'

Quickly realising what had happened, Tom jumped up into the lower lectern and called everyone's attention. He still wore St Peter's clothes, and a mysterious ray of light seemed to shine down from above as he spoke, almost as a soft spotlight that shone from heaven to affirm what he had to say. Everyone fell silent.

'Neither be this God's nor Satan's wrath, good people! Mind ye not that the barrier fell as our Father William cried out the words of our dying Saviour?'

The people nodded dumbly, watching the glow around the commanding figure before them. William immediately understood Tom's strategy, and quietly climbed the main pulpit stair, as was his right.

Tom continued boldly and clearly, following the promptings of his heart.

'Wot ye not also the account of Holy Scripture? The Lord Our Saviour cried out those blessed words "It is finished!" and gave He up the ghost to His Father's keeping. Then behold! The veil of the temple be rent from top unto the base thereof, by the finger of God! Sacrifice, oblation and offering to appease the righteous wrath of a Holy God ceased! The way into fellowship with the Father was open unto us all, rich or poor, low estate or nobly born!

'Hath not the Lord God so shown us in likeness this day? Father William in like manner as the Living Lord did cry "It is finished!" and the memory hath stirred the power and grace of God to show that there be an open way, without barriers, into the very Holy Presence of God!'

Having come to the climax of the point he was making, he looked out toward the people, who were staring with open mouths and shining eyes. He was still feeling his way, and was not sure what to do or say next, so he looked around for his mentor.

'It is very sooth,' came a calm but clear voice from the pulpit. A similar glow and ray of light softly appeared around William as he took up the message from where Tom faltered. He went on to explain about the animal sacrifices of the Old Covenant and that the Lamb of God put an end to them all by His precious Blood. Not merely as a legal transaction, but as an expression of God's love, making a way for everyone to come into personal relationship and fellowship with the Father. No further works could ever win their way to God and to eternal life, according to the scriptures. In a dramatic way, God showed them that He wanted them to come to Him in their hearts, if they accepted Christ's sacrifice as being sufficient and called on Him to forgive their sins, without a priest intermediary, penance or further sacrifice.

This was radically new to the people of Coventry. Only the previous week, Friar Bentwood had thundered from the same pulpit their need for more penances, more tithes and the damning consequences of missing the confessional. Even then they would still have to pass through Purgatory before they had any hope of their heavenly rest.

It had been drummed into the simple, unlearned folk for so long that they would have been confused and suspicious of Tom and William's message of freedom in Christ had not God intervened with the mighty signs of that day.

'It be soothsaw! Yea! I believe!' cried one young woman, her heart responding, and she fell to her knees as she felt the love of God flowing in and washing her clean. Soon, most of the folk present were on their knees, weeping and opening their hearts to God's cleansing and loving presence.

To William and Thomas, it seemed this miracle was the greatest one of all that strange and wonderful day. William showed Thomas the practice of praying for and counselling each individual penitent until they had the reality of God's presence in their hearts.

Many of the older, more religious folk were wary of the whole business, although most could not deny the signs they had seen that day. The verger wondered what the bishop would say when he saw the barrier had gone.

The bishop did not know what to think, when he returned with the new incumbent. He had specifically asked for William Shephard to fill in, knowing him for a godly man, so how could he question the strange doings in his absence?

In the end, he played it safe and, for the sake of appearances, rebuilt the barrier, although not so high and exclusive this time, but he did not forbid William and Thomas from preaching in the immediate parish. He charged the verger not to say anything to the Archbishop should he visit.

'Tales of a naked woman riding through the town be ferly enow,' he said with a worried frown, 'let be tales of the Holy Christ crucified again in pageantry!' and he crossed himself.

However, the story of the Miracle of the Coventry Pageant was long talked of among the folk round about, and the largest Wycliffite disciple gathering yet was established there by William and Tom's labours.

More than ever, William was convinced of Tom's readiness to preach as an evangelist and as his yokefellow.

Chapter 9: The Council at Leicester

'And He said to them, There is much ripe corn, and few workmen.
Therefore, pray ye the Lord of the ripe corn, that
He send workmen into his ripe corn.'

(Gospel of Luke 10:2 Wycliffe-Purvey Translation.)

'And He gave some apostles, some prophets, others evangelists, others
shepherds and teachers,
to the full ending of saints, into the work of ministry,
into [the] edification of Christ's body.'

(Epistle to the Ephesians 4:11,12 Wycliffe-Purvey Translation/Revision.)

The vision of the Poor Preachers had been growing apace in Hereford and Wycliffe's hearts and minds, and a number of students and graduate students showed some promise. But could they cast these men forth as sheep among wolves? Without any means of support? Should they beg, like the friars?

'Nay!' asserted Wycliffe. 'The mendicants have a-wearied so many of the people of England with their simony and thrift while the poor suffer deprivation. But what sayest thou, Hereford, if there be preachers that hath known poverty, but with the fire of the Word in their hearts, and do toil with their hands for their daily faire? Would not the poor folk as lief hearken unto them than the mendicants?'

'Thou sayest sooth,' agreed Hereford, thinking of the growing cynicism toward the friar fraternities he had come across in his travels. 'An *Odium Theologicum*[20] doth prevail amongst the people. 'Twould be as refreshing rain were there penniless men that preached the Word of Life, but asked for naught in return.'

Wycliffe sighed and considered the vision for a moment.

---

20   Dislike of the Clergy

'Nonetheless, the task would be beyond the power of mortal man. To live and labour among the villagers, to face deprivation and hardship would be a mighty task alone. But gifted men they must be, called of God and instructed to divide the Word of Truth aright. Also, what if the lordings of the Church do lay hold of them? Many there are that care not, nor mind not, the affairs of their diocese, but they such as Courtenay and Mandeville would raise their hand against us, yea, even to do violence if they could. Will they withhold their wrath upon our poor preachers? I think not!'

He sat down, looking more tired and frail than Hereford had seen, brooding for a moment.

'The Gaunt hath turned his back at last, for he refuseth the changes for that I have petitioned,' he announced wearily. He slid an official-looking scroll that bore the royal seal across his desk. Hereford read it with growing dismay.

'What? Will he support the papal bull of transubstantiation? Methought he would break the power of the prelates and their arrogance! So quoth he oft and anon.'

'So quoth he,' echoed Wycliffe bitterly, dropping his quill into the inkstand with unwonted force. 'But statecraft is a fickle woman, my friend. A courtesan who will be bedfellow to whomsoever will give her the most. John of Gaunt and the Council of the Crown will soon give way to the young King Richard. If he will befriend us or no, I wot not. Latimer and sundry other shall speak on our behalf in parliament, but I fear me....'

He sighed again, but shook off his dejection. 'But God needeth not such men to perform his will!' he asserted, his customary mental vigour returning. 'Where the general faileth, the foot soldier shall conquer. Thou, Ashton, Swynderby, Parker, Smith, I and the others have laboured long, and we have seen some fruit in Leicestershire, Gloucester, Sussex. But what of the rest? What of the common folk of England? If God gave us but one sign, I would send out our men into the four corners of the land with the gospel, even anon! But is there but one man who would be ready to thus go?'

'Yea! There is even such an one. Nay, two at the least.' declared Hereford, brightening.

This caught Wycliffe's full attention. 'Whom, then?'

'Father William Shephard! Even anon he goeth amongst the peasant folk in our neighbour villages. They love him dearly and hence hath oped their hearts to the Word of God. He hath raised up many disciple gatherings amongst them.'

'God be praised! And who is the other?'

'His name is Thomas Plowman, son of a well-to-do Dorsetshire farmer slain by outlaws. But Master Thomas is called of the Lord to preach the gospel, I trow. He laboureth together with William Shephard in the harvest of souls also. An intelligent, gifted lad, right amiable, and hath a mighty thirst for learning. I have heard him proclaim the Word of Life with great passion and skill in our streets.'

He told his mentor of the Miracle of the Pageant of Coventry. Wycliffe listened in growing wonder, visibly brightening.

'A mighty sign indeed! Were not the Holy Apostles unlearned men in the eyes of the learned? Verily, gifted laymen with great hearts may avail where many a graduate faileth. But will Master Plowman abide all the years of study?'

Hereford explained about his innovative classes for lay preachers.

'An excellent scheme! Excellent indeed.' approved the Doctor. His lip curled and he added, 'But our beloved Wadeford, surely will he not approve?'

He gave his short barking laugh. Hereford chuckled appreciatively at the vision of Doctor Wadeford's reaction should he have the least suspicion of what they were contemplating.

The older man's sunken eyes gleamed as he sat by the window, watching a group of his more promising students walk by. The more he thought about the scheme, the more excited he became.

'Yea, by God! Raising up the poorest to minister unto the poorest. Speak if thou hast need of moneys, my friend. Nevertheless, I will not send them forth into dearth and danger without that the Lord command us. Come, my friend. Let us pray now and seek the mind of God in this matter.'

So the two men went down on their knees and prayed fervently that God, the Lord of the Harvest, would raise up labourers into the fields of human souls throughout the land.

In fact, prayer was rising up to Heaven from across the land.

The tragedies of the last several decades had shaken all of the foundations that many had trusted in for centuries. Now many were either falling into despair or falling on their knees in genuine repentant prayer, crying out for God's mercy.

Master William Smith called for all those that attended his prayer gathering to fast and pray that God would continue to pour out his Spirit on all flesh.

Pockets of people throughout the land, whose hearts hungered for more than the empty piety that traditional religion could offer, now cried out for Truth.

Even as far as Cornwall and the North West Cunningham District of Scotland, there were gatherings of celtic monks at the ancient cairns to pray for their erstwhile political enemies, defying the disapproval of their local abbotts.

Many hermit-monks of Wales came together in unprecedented unity. The cave of St David was full of weeping monks and nuns.

The mysterious Guardians of the Stones in Wiltshire assembled at Stone Henge, crying out to the living God.

The forgotten remnants of the communities of Iona, Tara and Lindisfarne knelt down every night among the ruins of their ancient power, and raised their hands and voices together for the sake of the land of England.

Members of the ancient and secret order of Culdees gathered together at Glastonbury Tor and petitioned heaven with tears, fearing for the dark chaos that was coming upon the land.

A few months later, in the midst of his translations, lectures and writings at Oxford, Doctor John Wycliffe dreamed a prophetic dream.

In the dream he was lifted up to view the whole of England, from sea to sea. But instead, all he saw was a dark night of despair below him, thick and heavy, with grieving people wailing around him.

He looked up to the heavens to beseech God's mercy upon the land, as he had for the last twelve months. Then he saw it appear – a morning star of hope.

The night below him became less dark and oppressive. He also noted that there were dim pockets of light here and there, often in unexpected places, where saints of God were gathering to pray.

Suddenly a mighty angel, shining and glorious, came down from the heavens above him and hovered over the town of Leicester at the very heart of England.

He was dressed as a glittering herald, as if sent from the King to summon his knights and nobles to a council of war. He bore a great silver trumpet. When he blew the trumpet, it echoed throughout the land, and Wycliffe recognised it as a divine summons.

Here and there, he saw pockets of fellow-believers, bathed in light, arise and follow the sound of the trumpet. They journeyed toward Leicester, the heart of England.

Returning to his own room, he packed hastily for the journey. Following the angel in the distance, he arrived at Leicester and found himself at the dwelling of his friend and colleague, Nicolas Hereford.

He looked upon the faces of those who were converging on the same house, but they were hooded and hidden from him. Hereford was expecting them all, however, and invited them to an upper room.

They sat at a great table, as in council, where the angel stood guard. The only ones Wycliffe recognised were William Shephard, Master Ashton and Master Smith, who were as mystified as he at the strange proceedings.

The strangers did not appear to be surprised.

Into their midst, a pure and shining white dove appeared and settled on the translated scriptures that Wycliffe had brought with him and laid upon the table.

Then a mighty rushing wind blew in. The book flew open and the pages took wing, blowing out of all the open windows and flying north, south, east and west throughout the land. They were fluttering and scattering everywhere, almost like a swarm of butterflies.

Looking out of the window, he saw raggedy people jumping up to catch them. Others shunned them and blew them away. Those who caught them and read them became transformed, and a light shone out from their hearts, like a mirror reflecting the sun. Those that shunned them seemed to have an aura of gloom and darkness wrapped around them.

Through the window, the dawn was approaching, but the morning star appeared to fade.

Wycliffe awoke to broad daylight streaming through his window.

He knew the dream was too vivid to be anything but a heavenly summons.

Trembling, he packed hurriedly, called his carriage and journeyed post-haste to Leicester.

Almost everything was arranged as in the dream. Hereford also had the same dream of summons, as did William Shephard, Master Ashton, Master Smith and the mysterious strangers. But the latter had received the summons a week or so earlier, and were walking down the road to Hereford's place at exactly the same time.

God's timing for their arrival was perfect.

Hereford's living was the parish of Saint Cleopas' church in the quieter streets of Leicester. His house was not large and imposing as many houses possessed by medieval Oxford Fellows, but met his needs comfortably. He followed Wycliffe's example of living fairly simply, with merely the basic comforts of a prominent professional of the day.

His house consisted of two storeys. Below, he had a comfortable parlour and hearth, with the kitchen and servants' quarters at the back. Up the broad stairs, with a beautifully carved balustrade, there was a large meeting room with a round table in the centre. His study was adjacent to this, with walls crammed full of books. The meeting room had windows with views out over the roofs and streets, looking north, south and west, having pleasant views of the river and the countryside.

When they had been made comfortable, the strangers each introduced themselves.

They were all clergy or members of different and remote orders that only Wycliffe and Hereford were familiar with, but all with a common bond – a fervent love for God and His people.

They had their roots in the ancient Celtic Culdee or Ceile Dei movement that had not fully yielded to the Roman traditions, but continued many of their own, mostly in secret.

The strangers each had been praying and fasting that God would open the way to preach the gospel to the far corners of the land, and they knew God had answered their prayer in the heavenly summons. The Spirit of God had also given some of them a particular message, which they each shared with the Oxford men.

As host, Doctor Hereford felt he should be the convener of these strange proceedings, overawed and nervous though he was. After they had gathered around the great table, he provided refreshments and, glancing at his mentor, invited the strangers to speak as they felt moved by the Spirit of God.

The first to speak was a middle-aged man with dark hair and a slightly rugged countenance. He was wearing a simple habit with a fine woven Celtic cross on one of the hems. He spoke with the cultured voice of a learned man, with the slightest suggestion of an Irish accent.

He had introduced himself as Father Dermid Maconnaughie. He was a scholarly man of the Order of St Columba, official keeper of the archives of Tara, where many ancient documents and traditions of the ancient Celts were kept. He had corresponded occasionally with Doctor Wycliffe, so both he and Wycliffe were delighted to have finally met, for they had so much in common of professional interest.

Father Maconnaughie had travelled from Antrim to pray and seek God's direction amongst the ruins of the monastery on the Isle of Iona. It was there he heard the supernatural summons weeks earlier.

'This day,' he announced solemnly, standing before them, 'I break the tradition of silence sworn to by disciples of the *Ceile Dei*. As God Himself hath summoned us and commands us to speak, so all human vows of silence are made void.' He looked toward the other strangers, and they all nodded their heads in agreement.

He went on to explain that he followed the ancient *Ceile Dei* traditions, adopted by St Patrick and the ancient Celtic saints. Also, he kept alive the ancient druidic centres of learning, centred at Tara. These were the equivalent of universities, but greater than any others of their day. Many had come from near and far in ancient times to learn their lore from their large accumulation of wisdom and knowledge.

The druids had fallen into disrepute when some turned to pagan gods, and so the official church looked askance upon them. Most of the holy druids had become priests and been absorbed into Holy Church by Patrick himself, but they still kept most of their own traditions under an oath of silence, holding to the scriptures as the ultimate authority in the Earth, and rejecting many of the Roman traditions that were gradually introduced, and also the authority claimed by the Bishop of Rome.

'And the *Ceile Dei* shall never die!' he said defiantly, and others murmured a fervent 'Amen!'

'As long as there be a true church militant,' he went on, 'whatsoever banner ye march under, the *Ceile Dei* will labour and fight to advance the Kingdom of God. This be my calling!'

Maconnaughie studied the scriptures, native history and all other ancient documents he could find. He also collected and sifted folktales and legends from the last of the wandering bards of Ireland, Scotland and Wales, looking for any grain of truth in them before their lore was lost.

His mission to the Council of Leicester, as it became commonly called amongst them, was to represent the church militant of the past.

As a historian, he had traced the roots of British Christianity from Joseph of Arimathea, through St David, the Irish missionaries to Cornwall, and onward to the present day.

He also translated portions of scripture into his mother tongue to share the gospel with those who would listen and had begun to question many of Rome's traditions. However, he admired many of the godly men who clung to the Roman communion.

He spoke of the division within the Culdee church when the leading bishops had met with Augustine and the Roman legates at the Synod of Whitby. Many of the more remote clergy of the Culdee tradition felt they had been sold out to the Romans, and only superficially made their submission to Rome.

'Doom came upon the Culdees, for as Laodicea had they become in those days,' he said with a sigh. 'They contended but for Holy Days, rather than for the souls of men.'

He went on to speak of the cycle of struggles that the true church militant in Britain had been through.

'Whene'er the hour was at its darkest, as it be at the present, God always caused the church militant's light to shine the brightest. Mine heart telleth me that dawn is at hand.'

He smiled at the two translators.

'In every generation, there were them that translated the holy scriptures into their mother tongue, but few have translated the whole as ye have, gentlemen, save King Alfred the Great.' He bowed to William, a Dorsetshire man. 'But few hath passed them on to rich and poor alike. Satanas, the enemy of men's souls, hath sought to destroy such a work if he but could. In the past, communities have risen, served their God and fallen into the shadows. Many portions of scripture have been translated and lost. Single men and women have declared the Word and some have died for it. That is passed. But if the whole body of Christ be joined as one? What a mighty manifestation of God's glory 'twould be!'

He looked at the Oxford men with a challenge in his eye.

''Tis a soothsaw that they who hearken not unto the lessons of history, doomed are they to repeat them. Will ye rise up and follow in the steps of them that have gone before, and fulfil the will of God for this generation? The great cloud of witnesses, the saints of old, are gathering to see the glory of God revealed among ye, gentlemen. The hour is struck!'

With that, he sat down.

The Englishmen exchanged glances in wonder. So much had been confirmed by what this godly man had said, and they were so encouraged. They felt a sensation of being swept up onto the crest of a huge spiritual wave, whose groundswell had been building for centuries. At the same time, they also felt the security of travelling down a well-trodden path, in the footsteps of powerful men and women of God.

The next to address them was a tall, red-headed and red-bearded Scot with an air of authority, as one who had addressed kings. His habit was as simple as Father Maconnaughie's, with the same Celtic cross on the hem.

He was Charles McGregor, the Abbott of St. Andrew's monastery of Aberbrothock. He was known by name only to Wycliffe, for he was a man who travelled widely and sometimes ran diplomatic missions for the Scottish king during times of tension between England and Scotland. He was highly renowned internationally for his wisdom, godliness and scholarship.

Though fiercely a Scot, he had not a trace of accent, having studied for a time at the new university of Cambridge.

Secretly, however, he was also a member of the Culdee tradition.

'Gentlemen,' he said in his deep, cultured voice, 'I speak for the church militant of this present hour.'

He revealed that while he travelled widely on his international missions, he secretly kept in touch with what he called 'glowing embers' – lettered men who earnestly studied the scriptures, translated portions into their mother tongue and copied them.

He had spoken to a number of recusant Franciscans, as had Wycliffe, during his state missions to the continent.

He had been led into the remote mountains of Southern France to speak to the surviving Waldensian enclaves, encouraging them.

He had conferred with the great Jan Huss, the Bohemian reformer who had been inspired by Wycliffe's writings. The Abbott and his associates acted as a courier for many copied portions of scripture and reformist tracts where persecution from Holy Church became severe. He had the gift of gathering information throughout Europe.

There were pockets of believers, he had discovered, also in England where the light of God still flamed. Through many miraculous circumstances, God had shown him where they were, and he kept in contact with them whenever he could, forming a network.

This was dangerous work, but God had protected him time and again.

All the Oxford men had heard of some of these movements, but none, not even Wycliffe himself, had known of them all. Hearing of these, they began to feel a sense of God at work in their generation also. He was calling on them to ride on the rising wave of His glory, soon to be revealed.

'Doctor Evangelicus,' McGregor said, 'My message from the Almighty be the same as God said to Elijah in the desert, that He hath many "hidden prophets who hath not bowed their knee to Baal." Fear not, for thou'rt not alone in this battle. Thy fame hath gone forth to many lands, and they pray to the heavens for thee, that thy courage faileth not. But the time hath come that these glowing embers in this land must join to show the flammentation of God.

'But who shall take the fire unto them? Send thou forth preachers into the villages and towns of England. Let them be humble and holy men that bear the fire of God unfeigned in their hearts, and the Word of Life – in the mother tongue – in their hands.

'Anon it is the season to challenge openly the corruption of the false shepherds that devour the flock of God, even like to wolves in sheep's raiment. Anon it is the season to send forth labourers into the harvest to preach the gospel.'

He paused, sensing the rising wave in the hearts of all who heard him.

'Thy brethren in Scotland stand with thee. We be not at war, for in Christ there be no Scot nor English, serf nor nobleman, male nor female.' He bowed toward another stranger, a lady who had heard the summons. 'If we can aid ye in thy task, whatsoever ye need, then speak ye the word.'

Then he indicated a young man who sat at his side.

'I ask also that my companion here may be taught in the ways of lay preaching, that we may spread this fire in our homeland also.'

Then he bowed and sat down.

Chapter 10: Vision and Commission

'Preach the Word, be thou busy suitably without rest,
reprove thou, beseech thou, blame thou in all patience and doctrine.
[Preach the word, be thou busy to opportune and inopportune,
reprove, beseech, blame in all patience and doctrine.]'

(Second Epistle to Timothy 4:2 Wycliffe-Purvey Translation/Revision.)

Next, the lady, whom the Scottish abbot had indicated, arose. She also had an aura of authority about her, as well as the poise and grace of a queen, but without arrogance.

Nearly the entire Oxford contingent had heard of the Lady Eselde of Tregowan, Prioress of the Nunnery of St Mary Magdalene at Tintagel in Cornwall. Upon her introduction, Master William Smith had exclaimed, "Tis the Lady Mother herself!' and bowed reverently before her.

'Then thou'st heard but the good report of me and not the ill, Master Smith?' responded the lady with a twinkle in her calm grey eyes.

She was highly regarded for the considerable work she and her ladies had done among the poor, and for their single-minded devotion to prayer and good works. Tales had spread of the miraculous happening in response to their prayers.

A godly Cornish woman of noble birth, and greater nobility of heart, she was also a member of the secret order of the Culdee.

Her deceased husband was Sir John Tregowan, a renowned Cornish nobleman who, it was said, traced his lineage back to Sir Gawain, a knight of the Round Table of King Arthur. Her own lineage, the House of Trelawney, was said to go back to Sir Galahad, the most noble of all. But after her husband's death in France, she forsook her worldly title and privileges and entered Holy Church.

Being a woman of considerable force of character, it was not long before she rose to become Prioress at St Mary's. She was unique among her peers, rejecting the profligacy as practiced by many of her fellow prioresses, she wore a simple habit and concentrated on reaching the poor, sick and suffering.

On one of her regular pilgrimages to Glastonbury, she met some of the Culdees gathered at Glastonbury Tor. Such was their impact upon her that, from then on, her abbey carried on many of the pre-Roman practices of the Culdee movement, and she had the same beautifully designed cross sewn into her habit.

Being so well known, not all of her practices and beliefs could be kept secret, and there were some whisperings about unorthodoxy at St Mary's. However, the common folk adored and revered her, calling her the 'Lady Mother', and some even asserting that she 'be a Holy Saint of God'.

At times she had a farseeing look and somewhat of a reputation of a prophetess, even though this was not recognised by Holy Church, which was a little suspicious of her unorthodoxy. None had challenged her, however, partly because of the air of authority she bore like a royal robe, and partly because of the hawk-like look she gave that seemed to penetrate one's very soul. Even the Bishop of Truro could not look her in the eye, and normally looked the other way if anything unusual occurred, which it frequently did at St Mary's. As long as the authority of Holy Church was not directly challenged, the prelates could afford to be tolerant – for the moment.

The prioress and her ladies had prayed and fasted for reform within the church and for revival of the simplicity of the early apostolic faith throughout Britain. She was fully aware of the growing discontent and despair among the common folk.

Now, standing in Hereford's upper room, she spoke with a low, resonating voice, but with a fraction less than her usual poise. She had not been involved in events of this magnitude as yet.

'Good gentlemen and brethren in Christ, glad am I that the brethren of the Culdee have spoken, for now am I emboldened to speak of strange things indeed. Spake they of things past and things present; I shall declare unto thee of things to come.'

She gathered her cloak around her and fixed Wycliffe with her characteristic faraway look.

'I and my sisters have been much in prayer and fasting for this hour, that the church militant may arise. Two sennights gone, we were so in prayer. Then my worldly vision faded and the Lord sent unto me a great ghostly vision of dark portents and strange doings.'

In the vision she had seen a great lion, lying on a hill of gold, silver and great luxuries, and guarded by half-grown lions and wolves, also sleeping. On a separate hill, of similar wealth, lay a woman in rich raiment, guarded by fat shepherds, all fast asleep.

Out of the surrounding towns and villages came many thin and starving farm animals, driven by desperation rather than evil. They would have slain the lion and the woman and devoured all the luxuries.

Then a tall, thin shepherd appeared with a flock of lean but sturdy-looking sheep. He called on the woman to awake and feed the animals with the luxuries that surrounded her, since that was her designated duty.

Disdainfully, she threw a few crumbs out to them and called on the lion to chase them all away and leave her in peace. But the lion was becoming weary of her demands and refused her.

Then the shepherd, in righteous wrath, berated her and begged the lion to remove her luxuries and feed the animals. The lion was reluctant to disturb the status quo, but neither did he refuse him, conferring with his entourage to see if he had the might to overthrow the woman and take her treasure.

Meanwhile, a white dove descended on the shepherd's shoulder and spoke with him. Then the shepherd produced a great loaf of bread, broke it into pieces and bade his sheep eat it, and also go and feed the animals with it.

When the sheep ate of the bread he provided, they grew larger, and some changed into shepherds similar to the first. Then they went out among the starving animals and fed them also. The bread kept multiplying, similar to the biblical feeding of the five thousand, and many of the animals gratefully accepted and followed the shepherd.

Observing this, the woman and her entourage screamed with jealous rage, declaring that the animals should be following her, not the shepherd. She claimed the bread was poisoned.

The lion restrained her from attacking the shepherd for the moment. He seemed pleased that her authority was being challenged, having an eye to her riches himself.

Some of the animals, however, were not content with the wholesome bread distributed by the sheep. They fancied the delicacies the woman could provide, and so joined her part.

Others were impatient with the sheep's distribution, or had not seen the shepherd's bread and challenged the guardians of the king's feast, even slaying some of the fat shepherds to raid their food.

The woman falsely accused the shepherd of inciting the rebel animals, and this finally convinced the lion to release his restraint on her, even lending some of his guardian beasts for her use. She then ordered the guardian beasts to slay the shepherd and his sheep and destroy the bread. The wolves began to obey and slew or chased off a few of the good sheep and the lean shepherds.

A few of the young lions reluctantly obeyed, but a number arose in righteous wrath and, with the shepherd's followers, tried to protect the shepherds and the sheep.

Then, as battle was joined, a cloud of dust arose and the vision faded.

As the prioress came to the end of her narrative, she covered her face and wept, knowing the conflict and bloodshed that was coming. Wycliffe and his followers were awed and deeply moved. Eyes were wiped. There was little doubt of the main meaning of the vision.

She dried her eyes and stood tall again, awaiting their response.

'For two days I held my peace, for I knew not the signification thereof,' she said quietly. She indicated her companion seated quietly nearby – a sharp-featured sister with dark and fiery eyes.

'Then Sister Iofa, one of my maiden-warriors of prayer, beheld the selfsame vision. Shaken with fear, she declared to me the exact likeness of all I have declared unto thee this night, though she wot not that I had seen it also. We prayed that God would make the meaning plain unto us, and in answer, I received the Dream of Summoning, as have ye all. Then did I begin to understand, and what the brethren of the Culdee have uttered this night hath made it plainer.'

She produced a small roll of parchment and laid it on the table.

'I have put quill to parchment that I forget it not. Use ye it according to your wisdom, brethren.'

A profound but eloquent silence filled the room for a full minute.

Characteristically, it was Wycliffe that broke the silence. His scholarly mind had to make sure he had all the facts right – not that he, nor anyone present, doubted the truth of the message.

'Lady Prioress, wilt thou interpret for us the meaning of this vision? Dark sayings and strange doings indeed! The lion, I trow, is England's crown? The woman, Holy Church?'

'Yea, fair to look upon once she was, Doctor Evangelicus, but she hath become haggard and fat from indulgence, greed and even gross sin. The famine-smitten creatures are the common folk, some of which shall turn to the sword and bloodshed.'

A spasm of grief passed briefly over her face, and Wycliffe nodded in understanding.

'Lady, this also we have foreseen. The seeds, alas, have also been sown amongst us at Oxenford. But what of the shepherd in thy vision?'

'It is the only man and his followers that hath had the courage to cry out like unto the voice in the wilderness, that the nation and Holy Church should turn again in repentance for their manifold sins.'

She brought the faraway look into focus again upon her hosts, and bowed toward them.

'That shepherd and his yoke-fellows are seated before me, I deem.'

The Oxford men digested this, finding both encouragement and a challenge in the commendation she bestowed.

'I deem the young lions and the wolves to speak of the lords of the realm and their might,' she continued, 'but their hearts will either be noble and courageous enow to embrace the truth, or cruel, cowardly and full of greed.'

'God save us!' muttered Hereford, thinking of a few noblemen in both categories.

'And the good sheep, Lady Mother?' asked William Shephard, knowing the answer in his heart.

She smiled at him. 'Humble messengers are they, Father William. Courageous, obedient, pure and compassionate men, with the heart of the Great Shepherd within. They will go forth and feed the poor folk with the Bread of Life. Yea, even to the four corners of this land.'

William's heart flamed within him. His own vision and calling became clearer.

The prioress suddenly seemed to be transformed before them, as though the Warrior Queen of old, Boadicea herself, briefly stood before them.

'Doctor Evangelicus! Gentlemen! The time hath come! The trumpet hath been sounded to prepare for battle. In this conflict that draweth nigh, I and my web of praying warriors will fight for thee. For, as Father Dermid hath said, the battle hath ever been won on our knees ere the army marcheth off unto war.'

The warrior-queen image faded. She bowed her head as though she were a tired mother who, having delivered her children to their new masters, was in need of rest. She sat down.

'So be it, Lady Prioress,' responded Wycliffe. 'And we thank thee.'

Finally, Father Euan ap Owain, an itinerant Welsh priest of the Order of St Dafyd, arose and addressed the assembled group.

He was a member of the Ceile Dei, a branch of the British Culdee brotherhood. He was a close friend of Father Dermid, and also Abbot Charles' contact in Wales.

Owain was renowned throughout Wales, Scotland and Ireland as a mighty singer and inspiring preacher. He was sought after in the courts of princes and churches alike, and could have become a minstrel-bard for one of the Welsh lords, and been given a position of great honour and privilege. But after his own personal encounter with the Living God, wealth and fame became as nothing to him. His joy and calling, he discovered, was to encourage and inspire the pockets of Cymry believers scattered throughout Wales, and proclaim the Word of God in song, in the *Cymraeg* tongue.

Although he passionately desired Welsh freedom and independence from English domination, he had learned, under Father Dermid's wise council, to recognise that the ties of the family of the Kingdom of God were stronger by far than those of country, blood and kin. A hard lesson for a true Welshman, but hence he was able to minister even to some of the English settlers, and at times mediate between them and hostile Cymry villagers, preventing much bloodshed.

He was not so welcome in England, partly through the cultural and political tensions with the Welsh, and partly because of the arrogance of many English noblemen and prelates of Holy Church toward the Welsh. It was noted also that he did not promote the traditions of Rome, and the hierarchy were suspicious of him.

His father had been the last of a great order of ancient bards, claiming descendency from the greatest of all the Celtic bards, Taliesin.

Father Owain's English was not yet very good, even though he understood most of what was said, so he spoke mostly through a young interpreter – a Welsh-born brother from the monastery of St Peter and St Paul in Shrewsbury.

He spoke of the pockets of believers and hermit monks that occasionally assembled to translate portions of scripture into their mother tongue and to discuss them and pray. Sometimes he would put some of these scriptures to music and sing them.

Prophetically gifted, he was so inspired by all that had been said at the council that he took up his harp to sing an ancient Welsh hymn. It was one known to the others of Culdee tradition, who took up the song with great fervour and power.

The atmosphere of the room became electric and thick with the manifest presence of God as they sang, and the awed Englishmen listened and drank of His presence

Then a spirit of prophecy came upon the Welshman, like he had never experienced before. Supernaturally, Owain cried out in clear, cultured Middle English.

'Behold! Lift up thine eyes, for the season of harvest hath come in this land. Also a time of sowing is at hand for a later and greater harvest.'

Although he had not read them, he quoted from Wycliffe's translation of the scriptures.

'"The fields are white unto harvest! Pray ye the Lord of the Harvest that He would send forth labourers."

'The Lord of the Harvest, He shall pay thy wages. Look not unto man for thy supply, although men shall pour their wealth into thy labours at times.

'The Lord of the Harvest, He knoweth well the seasons – let Him guide thee unto the ripest fields. Hearken unto thine heart, not unto what thy senses would counsel thee.

'The Lord of the Harvest, He shall give thee the strength and skill to fulfil thy task.

'The Lord of the Harvest, He shall watch over thee and rescue thee from the snare, the storm and the sword.

'And though thou goest forth with tears and toil, bearing the precious seed of the Word, thou shalt doubtless come again with rejoicing, bringing thy sheaves with thee. Then shall the Lord of the Harvest say unto thee, "Well done, thou good and faithful servant!"'

Such was the power of God upon him at that moment that Owain spoke fluent English from that day forth. Delighted with his new gift, he offered his services to Wycliffe and his followers, then sat down and played the hymn again softly on his harp as everyone quietly worshipped and revelled in God's presence.

When the music faded, Doctor Wycliffe arose and spoke in a subdued but clear voice. 'Lady Prioress. Brethren of the Culdee. Strange things and dark have come to us tonight, yet there be much that hath been made clear. I have no need that I should open to ye all that which God hath sown in my heart and in my friends and comrades, for already have ye beheld and heard it. Indeed God hath confirmed and watered that seed through the messages ye have come so far to deliver.

'How can we show our gratitude? With all that lieth in my province, our faculty is open unto ye all, and I pray ye shall accept our hospitality for as long as ye will. Indeed, we would humbly pray that ye abide awhile and impart unto us your rede and wisdom. In thy turn, use of whatsoever we have of our lore and our writworks that ye will for your purposes.'

He went on to explain the main details of his and Hereford's vision of the poor preachers, of which even their other comrades had not heard. The Culdee exchanged glances as they saw how the separate parts of the picture were falling into place.

With William's aid, Wycliffe stood shakily to his feet and in a voice full of exaltation announced, 'The time is come! God hath spoken! Tarry we no longer! With God's good aid, we shall send forth the labourers into the Harvest!'

'Amen!' they all cried as one.

The Spirit of Prophecy seemed to descend upon the great theologian. He raised his trembling hands and looked toward the heavens.

'Almighty and ever-living God, Lord of the Harvest and great Shepherd of the flock of God, we worship Thee. Forgive the sins of this people and have mercy upon us. Who are we, but sinners, that Thou wouldst deign to entrust Thy precious Word unto us? In our frailty, send unto us Thy might and power that we may impart Thy Word unto the furthest corners of this land, yea, even beyond.

'Raise up godly men from among us and fill them with zeal, wisdom, valour and hardihood to go among the people. May Thy message touch rich and poor alike, to bring healing and cleansing to this land. May thy servants take the written Word in the mother tongue and dispense it to the hungry of heart, even as Thy Blessed Holy Son did divide the bread to the manifold thousands. May these evangels bear the sickle to the ripened harvest and the staff of a shepherd for Thine elect sheep. Let Thy Kingdom come and Thy Will be done on Earth as it is in heaven, to the praise and glory of Our King, the Lord Jesu Christ we pray this.'

'Amen!' they all cried as one.

Father Owain began the Celtic hymn once again and everyone stood to their feet. Such was the power of God among them, even the Oxford contingent found their tongue and joined in, even though they did not understand all that they were singing.

Finally, the weight of God's Presence seemed to lift. It was as though they all awoke from a beautiful dream to a new day of great promise and hope. The first rays of dawn were beginning to dim the light of the candles in the room. Hereford stirred, recalling his duty as host.

"Twill be a night ever burned within my memory. Come gentlemen all, beds we shall find for you all in mine humble abode if you will. Ladies, shelter for you we shall seek at my Lord of Leicester's castle, if it please you. Her ladyship hath taken our part and would delight to extend unto you her hospitality.

'Rest we all shall need for further councils we must take for this glorious emprise that we are called unto this new day....'

Chapter 11: Preparation and Departure

'A priest should live holily, in prayer, in desires and thought, in godly conversation and honest teaching, having God's commandments and His Gospel ever on his lips. And let his deeds be so righteous that no man may be able with cause to find fault with them, and so open his acts that he may be a true book to all sinful and wicked men to serve God. For the ensample of a good life stirreth men more than true preaching with only the naked word.'

(John Wycliffe, writing on the 'ideal minister of the gospel'.)

Master Wycliffe again pressed the Culdee visitors to stay for a while, offering them accommodation at Oxford and Lutterworth, his parish living. All but the Abbot from Aberbrothock accepted the invitation.

The abbot was a busy man, with matters of state as well as those of God's Kingdom to attend to, but he hoped to maintain correspondence and visit again when he could.

He was delighted, however, when Wycliffe presented him with copies of the English scriptures and some of his writings to copy and distribute to other English-speaking peoples.

The following morning, the abbot rode off with his cortège, but his young compatriot stayed behind to attend the class for lay preachers, as had been requested.

The young Scot's English was barely intelligible, but what he lacked in English, he more then made up for in enthusiasm. He haled from Kilmarnock in the Cunningham District in the West of Scotland, and was keen to return equipped to preach the gospel. Although there was a general distrust of Scots, the more tolerant scholars, such as Thomas Plowman and William Thorpe, took him under their wing and made him feel welcome.

He insisted that he sleep with the windows kept wide open – even in winter. Being a hardy highland man, he made light of hardships and cold weather.

'Och, noo! Gi' me a gude bed o' Heeland heather, ho' porridge i' the morn and God's freesh airr!' he would boldly declare, much to Thomas' delight. 'I dinna want na mair tae keep oot the cauld.'

During their time with the remaining Culdees, Wycliffe and Hereford discussed the logistics involved in the commissioning of the itinerant evangelists.

To their excitement, they all discovered there were already a large number of both graduates and laymen-adherents who wished to be commissioned. They were willing to go wherever God would lead them – sacrificing everything.

Chief among these were Father William Shephard and Thomas Plowman.

God had called many to be at the right place at the right time, each one with their own remarkable story.

Renewed in health and vigour, now that he knew what to do, Wycliffe organised some final preparation to augment the lay preacher's training. They had been trained in evangelistic theology and basic strategy, and had been in prayer and fasting to find the specific will of God for each one.

Although the lay-preacher's course had been a small class to cater for such gifted young men as Thomas Plowman, there was also considerable interest from the graduates and under-graduates training for priesthood among the Wycliffite students, and they attended when they could.

Wycliffe looked proudly upon the group of bright-eyed young laymen and the more seasoned warrior-priests as they stood to attention before him, like an army of keen recruits.

'Behold, Gentlemen!' he announced to his closest following with his characteristic bark of laughter. 'We have before us the Order of Poor Preachers.'

Wycliffe, Hereford, Waystract and Smith threw themselves into this period of preparation and, when classes were in recess, gathered all the most promising of their students together and invited them to Wycliffe's own church at Lutterworth.

He had begged the Culdee visitors that they could help in the final preparations, and so they stayed with him at Lutterworth for an extra few days.

One morning, after prayer and fasting, they all met in Wycliffe's church, sitting near the sanctuary, together with the candidates for the first evangelistic thrust.

After a time of worship, Father Owain called Tom forward. Speaking prophetically, he said, 'Behold, a labourer for the coming harvest! Much hast thou sown, now anon is the season of reaping, for thyself and for many. Receive now the sickle from the Lord of the Harvest.'

He looked intensely at the young man, who was trembling with excitement as the power of God coursed through him.

'I sense in thee a gift of prophecy, my son. Hearken to the still small voice within thine heart, not unto the clamour and the storms around thee, and thy gift shall blossom and bring forth much fruit for the Kingdom of God! Sing thou the praises of God, for it shall sustain thee in thy labours and shall bless many.'

Under the direction of the Holy Spirit, the prioress then arose and called William forward.

'A shepherd art thou by name, and a great shepherd's heart bearest thou. Go forth, O shepherd, and gather the lost sheep, that they may hear the Word of God and that they may find pasture. Take thou the Bread of Life with thee, for there is a famine for it in this land. Thou shalt walk ancient pathways, yea, even in the steps of saints of old and gather many that are afar off. In places unlooked for shalt thou find God's people, and thou shalt unlock the Holy Scriptures unto them, and rightly divide the Word of Truth. Go forth!'

She looked on the tall, lean man and felt something of a kindred spirit. Smiling at him, she added, 'I know thee not but by the name of Father William Shephard, and that only at the council at Leicester. Yet thou'rt one that mine heart tells me I could trust with my very life. If it be the will of the Almighty to send thee south and west unto the corner of this land, even Cornwall, then come thou to the Priory of St Mary Magdalene's at Tintagel. Thou and thy companion may overwinter, if ye will, for there is rest and refreshment in good measure there.'

William smiled back gratefully.

'If it be the path that the Great Shepherd would send us, then gladly would we come to thee, Lady Mother, and I thank thee.'

William Thorpe was also one over whom Father Owain prophesied.

'O faithful servant of God, thou hast bowed thy neck to the yoke and plodded with measured step without stinting, neither hast thou murmured at thine hardships through which thou'st toiled. Now the Lord of the Harvest calleth thee to reap of that which thou'st sown, and great shall be thy joy.

'Yea, strange doors and great shall be oped unto thee at times, for lords of the realm and of the church shall enquire of thy message. Indeed some of the great shall call thee to account in strife and wrath, but fear not! Stand strong and speak My Word boldly as did the prophets of old before kings. I shall stand with thee and shall deliver thee from the hand of the evil one.'

Thorpe took a deep breath and closed his eyes.

The Welsh prophet-bard then turned to Abyngdon, who was chuckling with delight on his more serious-minded friend's behalf.

'O thou man of laughter and song, go forth and spread thy joy abroad to them that do sorrow. Thy yoke-fellow at thy side shall speak more of the weightier matters of the kingdom, but thou shalt lighten the hearts of his hearers, even in the face of thine own hardships.'

Abyngdon stood open-mouthed and wide-eyed for so long, even Thorpe had to laugh.

Father Owain gave another general exhortation to them all, revelling in his new-found English tongue.

'Brethren, if God send thee, then shall He confirm thy calling and His Word with signs following. Hast thou not read in the Holy Gospels that the Lord Jesus Himself went forth, not but to proclaim the gospel only, but to do good? He healed the sick, He raised the dead, He cast out devils. Yet also He embraced and forbade not the little lambs to come unto Him. He did eat and drink with the publicans and sinners. Will ye walk in His steps to heal the pain and shed forth the love of God? So shalt thou win the hearts of the people for the Kingdom, and many shall flock to hearken unto thy message.'

William Shephard, Tom and his friends smiled at each other, for that concept of ministry was becoming clearer from their own experimentation. However, they also felt rather inadequate.

'Wherewithal shall we work thy miracles, Lord God?' muttered Master Harold Ravenswood, a keen but anxious young intern. 'We be not Holy Apostles as of old. Neither have I the boldness thereof so to proclaim Thy Word even as they. God aid us!'

'Fear not!' exhorted Father Owen, fixing his eyes briefly in Ravenwood's direction, as though he had heard him. 'Be ye strong in the Lord, and in the power of *His* might! Look not to thine own strength nor holiness. For this battle is not thine, it is the Lord's!'

Harold lifted his head and closed his eyes in a silent prayer of thankfulness.

More prophetic words were spoken to others individually at the gathering, then when all was done, Wycliffe himself arose and addressed them with all the austerity the solemn occasion demanded.

'Gentlemen and brethren. We must decide this day whom we shall send forth for the first wave of our Evangelical thrust. There hath been naught the like of this commissioning for an hundred years, since the first mendicant friars were sent forth. This be no simple task, for this shall be your devoir:

'That thou shalt go among the poor as poor preachers, without money, nor possessions, but even as the Lord's disciples went forth with naught but God's provision.

'Thou shalt not beg, but shalt work with thine hands for thy living, unless that the Lord stirreth the hearts of the people to give willingly and without request.

'Thou shalt go forth as two companions, even as the apostles of old, to strengthen and encourage the other. For we cannot succour thee from afar.

'Thou shalt journey from village to village and from town to town until the Holy Ghost doth guide thee else.

'Thou shalt preach only the pure Word of God, for we proclaim the gospel to reach the souls of men and women.

'Thy message is one of grace and truth, that men and women may know the forgiveness and presence of God Almighty in their hearts, *without* the need for dead works of piety.

'Proclaim thou the efficacious power of the Blood of Christ alone.

'Rebel not against Holy Church and the lords of the realm, for that is not thy mission.'

At that moment, Swynderby's fiery intern, John Ball, looked up, glowering, for the fire in his bones burned to rectify the glaring social injustices around him, but he said nothing as yet.

'Thou shalt rebuke all evil practice that thou behold wherever thou goest, nonetheless. And more, it behoveth thee to live a life worthy of thy calling, in all veritable piety and simplicity. For if thy light shineth not brighter than the friars nor corrupt clergy, who shall hearken unto thy message?

'Thou shalt at times face enmity and strife. Think not that thou shalt escape the hatred of Satanas, the enemy of the souls of men. He shall do his utmost to prevent the propagation of the truth, but Almighty God is with thee. The state hath shielded us hitherto, but lean thou rather upon the Rock of Ages for thy security, for the arm of flesh is vain and will fail thee.

'Thou shalt spread forth the light and love of Thy God whithersoever thou goest, to work the works of the Lord, even as the good prophet, Father Owen spake by the Holy Ghost. Go ye as far as the Holy Ghost would lead thee and no further. Turn neither to the right nor the left, but walk the strait way to that which God hath called thee.'

He paused, looking on the faces of his hearers. Many appeared daunted at the difficulties put before them, but some eyes shone with anticipation, relishing the challenge. Most notable was young Thomas Plowman, Hereford's protégé and William Shephard's disciple. Yes, he would surely be a candidate, and Wycliffe took heart at this.

'I ask, brethren all, that none but the willing among ye shall signify if ye hear the call of God in all this. There is no shame if thou hearest not such a call, for I have not hid the perils and hardships of such a vocation, and but for the grace and a veritable call of God, ye will fail. Peradventure thou'rt destined for the second or third wave of preachers, for some are ready, and many yet are not.

'But if such is thy calling, to be our vanguard, to bear the honour of the first in the field – then arise! Stand forth anon and we will speak further on this thy call.'

Immediately twelve men sprang to their feet.

Father William Shephard.

Master Thomas Plowman, as a lay-preacher.

Master Benjamin Abyngdon – soon to be ordained.

Master William Thorpe – soon to be ordained.

Father Richard Brandon.

Father John Ball.

Master Harold Ravenswood, also as a lay-preacher.

Father John Haswell.

Master Lawrence Parsons – also soon to be ordained

Father Simon Cole.

Master Peter Hallworthy – lay preacher.

Father Edward Smithdon.

That evening, these men gathered in the priest house of the church for further briefing. It was noted that most had had prophetic utterances spoken over them by the Culdees.

Hereford eyed John Ball with some misgiving. *Well, if God has truly called him,* he told himself, *He surely will soon tame his wildness and bitterness against the aristocracy,* or so he hoped.

Meanwhile, Wycliffe asked the brave band of volunteers to pray and seek guidance regarding who they should team with, and whither they should be sent.

William Shephard and Thomas Plowman had already ministered together too long to be separated, although they would have loved their friend Abyngdon to have made a third. He had already been out preaching in the streets of Oxford, Coventry and the back streets of London, his hometown, together with the bold, young William Thorpe.

The others were not so easy to team, as none could relate well to John Ball. Although they respected his courage and endurance through the sufferings he had experienced, they thought him too much the angry man to be able to labour with him easily. His obsessive hatred for the rich prelates and the aristocracy seemed to override all else when he preached. He was all for radical social reform, by violence if need be. He was impatient of any counsel to modify his stand and tread more gently.

This apparent rejection by his peers aroused his ire.

'By the splendour of God!' he exploded. 'Are ye all so malten-hearted that ye dare not proclaim the truth boldly? Are ye men? Dost thou cower beneath the heel of the fat ones that oppress us? Then so be it!'

He stalked toward the doorway, turned his stormy eyes upon them and raised his fist.

'If none come with me, then go I alone to mine own people in Kent! There be stirrings among them to throw off the yoke and be free men once more. Thus shall I speak forth as a free man and will not be silenced by womanly milksop rede! I have been whipped and bound in chains for this cause, and dreadless shall be again until we see all Englishmen as free men!'

He stormed out, and was never seen in Oxford again.

This left an uncomfortable gap in their midst, but there was also a sense of relief.

Hereford sighed. 'I feared that such would be. Oft have I reasoned with him to regard the fruit of gentleness and speak words of graciousness, but he would have none. He is bent to his own scathe and, I fear, ours also. God save him, and soften his heart!'

'A great loss,' agreed Wycliffe grimly. 'None could daunt him, and he could have been a mighty weapon in God's hand. But he is fey and redeless in his bitterness. His hurlings may bring shame upon us, but we must not let disquiet to make us waver from our course.'

He staggered a little with weariness, and his friends jumped up, concern on their faces.

'Take thou the helm if thou wilt, Hereford,' he muttered, 'for I am weary.'

They helped the frail old warrior to his bed to rest a while.

In his absence, Nicolas Hereford and senior Master Richard Waystract, with their boundless energy, organised the rest. It was agreed that the two older priests, Simon Cole and Edward Smithdon, take Peter Hallworthy, a young and eager layman, as a third in their mission.

The next day, as they were discussing some of the lesser details of the missions, the Prioress of St Mary's walked in with a triumphant smile on her face. She was bearing a russet coloured friar's robe, together with a sturdy ash-plant staff.

"Twas the only tailor in Lutterworth who had such cloth, Doctor Hereford.'

'Bless thee, Lady Mother, but thou needeth not to run a handmaid's errand,' protested Hereford laughingly. 'Brethren, behold! The livery of thine office, as we agreed. Doth it accord to thy vision, Father William?'

'The robe of the Great Shepherd?' responded William, coming out of his own meditations on the prophetic messages from the previous day. 'Likeness in the colour, indeed! There were also the blood-stains of his blessed wounds, but methinks 'twould be irreverent to stain our garments in likeness. What thinkest thou, Lady Mother?'

In response, she opened up the robe to show a dark red lining.

'Shalt be cleansed of this if thou so counsel it,' she said, looking enquiringly at both William and Hereford.

'Nay!' smiled William. 'I am content, if so thou art, Doctor Nicolas. To keep the robe and the blood colour before mine eyes haply will mind me of our mission. What say ye, my comrades all?'

The other evangelists were satisfied with the concept, and Tom volunteered to try it on over his layman's clothes. His shoulders were too large, so the robe did not close around his chest properly, much to Benjamin Abyngdon's amusement.

'The tailor had cloth enow for but twelve robes,' said the prioress in a housewifely manner. 'Eleven robes we need, thus make we a larger one for thee, Brother Thomas. 'Tis done. Rude cloth but it beareth toil and travel well. I counsel ye all that thou wear thy lay-garments under these when there is need to keep ye warm, and take also spare clothing so that ye may wash the toil and assoilment from the past day's clothing.'

She smiled deprecatingly. 'But I become a mellsome old woman. I cry ye pardon.'

Hereford laughed. 'Not for naught call we thee "the Lady Mother", Madame, and we thank thee. Wherewithal didst thou pay the tailor monies of this, I ask of thee? Hast thou laid forth of thine own stipend? God forbid! The cost we must repay.'

She smiled triumphantly again.

'Nay, good Doctor. A new sponsor and mighty have we,' she said mysteriously.

They all waited expectantly as she savoured the mystery.

'Her Royal Highness, the Queen Mother!'

There were gasps from all but Doctor Hereford.

'Ah! Blessed lady! She spoke in Doctor Evangelicus' favour when he would be tried for heresy. Ever our champion hath she been.'

'A true Princess of Wales and Queen is she then, a daughter of the King of Kings,' commented Father Euan ap Owain.

Next, Hereford held up the staff.

'Behold, Brethren, the sceptre of thine office, even as Moses and the prophets bore. 'Twill also aid thee in the weariness of thy roilings[21].'

''Twill also aid thee to scratch the fleas on thy back, Father William,' whispered Tom disrespectfully to his fellow-evangelist.

William choked and whispered back, 'Or mayhap as a rod for thine own, young scapegrace.'

Tom chuckled quietly. He had long discovered William's dry sense of humour, and had thoroughly enjoyed their preaching tours of the local villages together, especially the miraculous visit to Coventry. This mission was simply doing the same, but on a much larger scale. He couldn't wait to start.

Leather footwear was provided, but most quietly decided to stow them in their packs for the coldest weather. They had found that going barefoot among the poor folk built a greater rapport with them. On more than one occasion William and Thomas had given their footwear away to the most desperate.

'Desperate indeed were they,' observed Tom, 'that they would bear the odour therof.'

'Thine be the odour!' replied William caustically. 'Mine be washed and clean.'

'Soothly said, O Father William of the holy foot. But mine labour more sorely.'

'Verily! But if they run not swiftly, my staff shall be as a rod for thy back, my lad,' laughed William.

Finally, Hereford pulled forth a beautiful hand-drawn map of England, a rare treasure in those days.

'Brethren, we are commanded to send forth the gospel north, south, east and west. Have ye all settled in thine hearts whither ye be sent?'

21 Wanderings

Each mission had prayed earnestly for direction, and they had decided it in this wise:

Father Simon Cole, Master Peter Hallworthy and Father Edward Smithdon would travel north to Lincolnshire. Peter Hallworthy knew it well.

Father John Haswell was a Norfolkshire man, so he and Master Lawrence Parsons would journey east.

Father Richard Brandon and Master Harold Ravenswood would journey to the Suffolk region.

Benjamin Abyngdon and William Thorpe had elected to journey southeast to Essex and Kent.

Father William Shephard had felt drawn toward Cornwall ever since the prioress had given him the invitation to St Mary's. This would mean they must travel the furthest before overwintering on the way. Yet more than that consideration drew him westward. He had a strange sense of destiny both in Glastonbury in Somerset, and at St Mary's itself in Cornwall.

As for Tom, he would follow anywhere William wanted to go, as long as the harvest of souls was plentiful and ready.

The prioress was delighted to hear of their decision.

'I will not hold thee to thy word, Father William,' she assured him, 'for but by the grace of God do we make our plans. But I must away regardless and return to my folk at St Mary's, for I have tarried overlong in the glory of this thy commissioning. I will speak to my friends in the way, that they look to thy needs should they find thee near. God speed thy mission, brethren all, and the prayers of all our folk go with thee.'

William and Thomas could not speak, so they bowed in deep respect to express their gratitude. The prioress understood.

Would they make it all the way to Cornwall? Only God knew.

The next day, the prioress and her companion left as swiftly as they had come. She was a woman of boundless energy, and was often on the road, guarded by her grizzled and faithful Cornish henchman, Jory, and his men.

So it was, very early on the first day of May, at Wycliffe's church at Lutterworth, the leaders and the remaining Culdees gathered around the evangelists and prayed with them, wishing them Godspeed.

Wycliffe and Hereford presented them with as many copies of the portions of scripture in English that they could spare, or were complete. Hand copying was a long and tedious labour, had it not also been a means of memorizing God's Word.

Goodbyes, benedictions and bear hugs were exchanged amongst all the comrades, together with some light banter, in the typical English manner on such important occasions.

'*Salve, clerici vagantes*[22]!' said the lively young Benjamin to Tom as he wrung his hand. 'Alas that thou dost forsake the minstrel troupe – the Lullards of Logic Lane.'

'Nay! *Altiora peto* – I seek higher things, O fellow priest-errant,' responded Tom, revealing his progress in the Latin tongue. 'Thou hast the august William Thorpe to keep thy wayward foot upon the straight way, and I have the good Saint William to guard my waywardness.'

Wycliffe stood before them all and quoted the final words of the Great Commission of Christ from his and Purvey's translation, followed by his benediction.

'The Grace of the Lord Jesus Christ, the love of God and the fellowship of the Holy Ghost be with ye!

'Brethren! Go ye forth!'

They all responded with a fervent 'Amen!' and then quietly departed into the thin morning mist, parting at the crossroads that went north, south and east, each mission to their own destiny – to shake the nation of England.

---

22   Farewell, wandering scolars.

Part 2:

The Missions Go forth

Chapter 1: Beyond the Horizon

'The highest service to which man may attain on earth is to preach the law of God. This duty falls peculiarly to priests, in order that they may produce children of God, the end for which God had wedded the Church. For this cause Jesus Christ left other works and occupied himself mostly in preaching...'

(John Wycliffe on Preaching, modernised version.)

'Whither away we, Father William?' Tom demanded with a laugh as they marched rapidly down the road south of Lutterworth. 'Should any fellow-wayfarer we meet inquire what be our goal, what say we? "Withsoever the Lord leadeth us," quoth I, "Then 'Tis folly!" quoth they.'

Father William Shephard, ordained clergyman and Master Thomas Plowman, lay-preacher, were on a journey to a destination they knew not where, barefoot, with no idea of their next meal or resting place.

'But soothly quoth thou, and soothly quoth they,' answered William seriously, although the corner of his mouth crinkled a little. 'Such is the road we tread. Folly doth it seem, but the wisdom of God is foolish to them that mind but the world and its wisdom. But if God calleth us and leadeth us, His will shall be done – and in His manner. Was it not a mighty lesson we learned? That we beheld the power and grace of God, as did we in Coventry? That lesson is worthy of every toil or tear we suffer.'

'Yea, by my fay!' agreed Tom, his heart stirring at the memory, 'But wherewithal know we whether we tarry or go forth as God listeth? Shall He send us dreams and visions at every turn? Can we bring salvation to all? We are but two small drops in an ocean of need.'

'Art thou overwhelmed, O' Thomas the Strong? It is well. So also am I, but so it must be. God will manifest His strength when we our weakness confess. We fail, else. But I bear thee witness, that when thou didst but submit thyself unto Him, He put it in thine heart what thou shouldst do. Let it be our guide. The still, small voice of God the Holy Ghost faileth us

115

not, where the clamour of our thoughts may do so. Hath He not called us to this road? Therefore, shall He not guide our steps?'

'Soothly said also,' nodded Tom, but added ruefully: 'But are we not but flesh and blood? If our sinful hearts beguile and betray us, what then?'

'Thou showest humility and wisdom beyond thy years, my son. But be sure the good Lord shall order our steps, correct or chasten us should we err. Mind ye also: *Casis tutissima virtus.*'

The corner of his mouth crinkled and he glanced sidelong to see how Tom's Latin was progressing.

Tom's brow furrowed momentarily in mental effort, then he gave a crow of triumph.

'"Virtue be the safest helmet." A sooth-saw indeed. Kind-wit the ancient Romans possessed in some measure then. Though they knew not what scourge they would lay upon the backs of poor clerics as we, that must needs be schooled in their tongue, God wot.'

'Art a scholar, my son, so instructed in the scholar's tongue thou must be.'

'Wherefore not mine own mother's tongue?' countered Thomas, mildly rebellious. 'What ails it, then? Do we not read the sacred scriptures and preach in God's English?'

'Sooth, but little hath been so written save the great works of Doctor Evangelicus and his masters.'

And so the discussions continued over the many miles southward down the main highway.

They turned aside briefly to call on some disciples from a previous visit. This was the little hamlet of Cotesbach, on the border of Leicestershire.

''Tis Father William and Master Thomas,' cried the village children who danced out to meet them. The next moment, dozens of children were crowding around them, begging William to tell them another story, or Tom to play another game with them.

As soon as the nature of their journey was known amongst the villagers, and that they were travelling on foot, they were almost inundated with offers of hospitality. They would not hear of them working to earn their bread.

The two men stayed briefly to strengthen and encourage those disciples, then moved on. Hence, they were able to journey into Warwickshire on the next day. The disciples all came to see them off, offering them wayfaring food and ale.

The local church was the centre of village life. If the majority of the people who attended, great or small, concurred with the Wycliffe's message; then Wycliffite disciple gatherings would soon be found throughout that county.

Across the border, it was a different matter.

Coventry and its surrounds was the only area that felt John Wycliffe's influence in Warwickshire. The bishop of Coventry had a profound respect for William Shephard, hence he had asked him to fill in until a new incumbent for a little parish had been found.

When the Miracle of the Coventry Pageant (as the locals referred to it) occurred, it totally overset the bishop's comfort. He knew that Courtenay, Archbishop of London, strongly opposed John Wycliffe and his influence, but he was dismayed and astounded to learn that William was of Wycliffe's persuasion.

The simple-minded verger, full of excitement, had naively informed Canon Abel of Neville about both the miracle and the message. The Canon, being a champion of the status quo and a confidant of Archbishop Courtenay, was furious. He ordered the quaking verger to repair the fallen woodwork and rode immediately off to the bishop's residence to inform him of a dangerous heretic that had bewitched and deceived the people of Coventry – an evil, renegade priest by the name of William Shephard.

'Nay!' protested the bishop, visibly shaken. 'But ... but ... is he not too godly and scholarly a man to be an heretic?'

The canon gave him a full account of the so-called miracle, but from his own perspective of course. The miracle took on the aspects of an elaborate and sinister deception, with a touch of black magic to ensnare the unlearned populous of Coventry. He respectfully but sternly warned that he was due to visit Courtenay the following day.

'The Reverend Father shall hear of this outrage!' he said stiffly, in cold wrath.

The bishop was a weak man, and knew that Courtenay had enough influence over Canterbury to remove him, so he hastened to reassure the fiery canon that stern measures would be taken.

Publicly, he forbade William from preaching in any more of the churches in his diocese.

Privately, however, he drew William aside and tried to explain his predicament.

'I cry thee pardon, Father William,' he said, fidgeting and dithering. His eyes shifted and fell under the steady gaze of the tall man's grey eyes. 'I know thee for a godly man, but ... er ... well ... the Reverend Father, the Archbishop of London, as thou knowest ... well ... surely thou'ds look upon mine unhappy besteadance in this with understanding. My diocese would be lost to me and...'

'Fear not, and be at rest, Very Reverend Lord.' William calmly reassured him, taking the situation in his stride. 'If it is forbidden that I preach in thy pulpits, so be it. But grant me leave, I pray, that I may privily shepherd them that have need within thy diocese.'

Relieved, the bishop assured him of his full approval, unaware that amongst those that "had need" in Coventry, there was a strong and growing disciple -group of Wycliffites.

However, in Warwickshire, the southern mission encountered the iron rule of Ralph Morton, bishop of Worcester and cousin to the Earl of Warwick (with whom he quarrelled regularly.) A very different man to the bishop of Coventry, the Very Reverend Bishop Morton was autocratic and querulous, and took a hard line against John Wycliffe and his men.

'Neither that evil man of sin, nor his pernicious Lollard masters shall place one heretical foot within my diocese!' he roared to his trembling clergy.

His diocese included much of Warwickshire as well, so William walked on perilous ground if he tried to preach in any of his towns, let alone the churches.

What neither of the bishops realised was that a powerful movement was beginning in the rural villages. If the churches were closed to the evangelists, many a cottage, farmhouse or hovel was not.

The bishops, like most of the church hierarchy at that time, largely ignored the peasant folk. Hence there was little interference to the work of Wycliffe's evangelists among the peasant folk – at that time at least.

William and Tom were, therefore, about to embark on one of the most incredible, perilous and miraculous journeys that anyone could have ever experienced.

They were now in unfamiliar territory and had no idea what lay in store, whether good or bad. It bothered them little, for they fully believed that God would guide and protect them. And if not?

'Yea! Then we suffer for the Lord's good name!' cried Thomas Plowman joyfully.

Tom had found his true vocation. He felt on top of the world, and let the world know it. He lifted his voice and sang some of the many miles away.

Sometimes he sang the "Song of the Wayfarer," clear and strong:

> *'Whither the feast, the song and the lyre?*
> *Whither the hearth and whither the fire?*
> *Whither the slumber that night doth send?*
> *They abide for us all at our journey's end.*
>
> *'Then onward. And whithersoe'er we go,*
> *Tarry we neither for rain nor snow.*
> *Over the hills or through vale so green,*
> *Undaunted our feet from morn unto e'en.'*

William could not sing, or so he said, but he took out a tin whistle he made himself back in his shepherding days, and played along, that is, when he had the breath for it, for Tom set a rapid pace.

Sometimes they discussed passages of scripture, or discussed and sometimes argued over some points of doctrine. William had the advantage in this mostly, since his knowledge of scripture and his insights were far superior. Occasionally, however, Tom's keen intellect pointed out something that William hadn't noticed. So the miles passed swiftly for them to the next village.

* * * * * * *

Father Richard Brandon and his disciple Master Harold Ravenswood also had a number of miles to cover, for there were a few deserted villages in the Suffolk region, looking forlorn and empty. Most of them had been swallowed up as larger pasture-holdings, reflecting the trend towards sheep and cattle grazing in the midland regions.

'Whither the villein folk, Father Richard?' Harold wondered, inspecting the crumbling longhouses and cots as they rested briefly at one deserted village. 'Surely 'tis not the Black Death that hath done this? These are but, mayhap, one twelvemonth bereft of habitation. Was not the last scourge of the plague in thy youth?'

'Yea. Yet 'twas more than but the plague, dreadless,' opined Father Richard grimly. He had also lost his mother and his siblings to the plague in his youth. The memory was only slowly fading.

'Methinks the Black Death began an exodus a-many a twelvemonth gone, but the lure of the town-life hath turned the trickle into a flood. If a serf may dwell in a town for a year and a day, a free man shall he be – so saith the law. There be good livings to be earned in the towns, for there is need for labour a-plenty. Mark ye not Oxenford and Coventry that they have grown manifold in numbers o'er the short years thou hast been with us? Chapmen[23] and guildsmen grow apace in the towns anon, so also the labourers. Yea, and so also the kennel-hoves[24] in which they dwell, alas!'

They sat down by a small stream and opened their limited provisions to fortify themselves for the road ahead. Harold pondered Father Richard's words.

'The power of the landlord passeth with the passing of the manor-bound serfs, unless this Statute of Labour be enforced.' argued the young man knowledgably. 'But who shall regard such a law? Can the gentry enchain the wandering labourer for ever? Tis folly! And the people are very roth.'

'Verily. 'Tis fuel for John Ball's witless rebellion forsooth,' sighed Richard, a recognised Jeremiah in his day. 'Methinks rivers of blood will flow if this madness be stayed not.'

---

23 Merchants
24 Slum

'Yea, 'Tis grievous.' agreed Harold blithely, munching on some wayfarer's bread and fresh cheese. 'Surely the judgment of God is upon the nation, yea upon the Church also, for many a monk did perish in the Black Plague…. and suffer Hell's torment for their sloth, likerousness , covertise and idolatory. And so perish all that heed not the Gospel of Christ!'

An expression of satisfaction spread over his face, and he added:

'So fair a cheese I have not tasted!'

He happened to look up at his older companion at that moment. The expression on Father Richard's face seemed to turn the cheese to wormwood in Harold's mouth.

The older man considered him for a moment, and the younger man trembled a little.

'Have I spoken amiss, Father…?' he faltered. 'Surely…Is it not sooth…?

'Thou'rt full young and heedless still' said Father Richard in tones of quiet displeasure, 'therefore shall I stay my full wroth. Zeal and wit hast thou in abundance, but thou speakest as one that wanteth in heart and compassion. Wist thou not that God alone is judge of all men? It is not for us so to judge, even of our gainsayers. Know also that God looketh upon the heart – of the brethren and sisters of the cloister also. Not all are given over unto the Sins Seven, as 'tis commonly said. Mind thou also that Christ came not into the world to condemn it, but that many through Him might be saved! Hast thou not been amongst us long enow to learn of this?'

It was rare that gentle Father Richard spoke such words of stern rebuke to him.

Harold hung his head. The cheese fell from his hand into the dust. Seeing this, Father Richard heaved himself to his feet and put a hand on his shoulder, speaking in a warmer tone.

'Come, come, my lad! Be of good cheer! Much is there for us all to apprehend. I have seen pain and grief – thus greater do I feel the great heart of the good Lord Jesu, that it breaketh and grieveth for all men. But neither do we forsake the fear of God, and thou speakest sooth indeed of His just wrath. Mind thou this also: A true preacher of Christ's gospel speaketh from the heart as also from the head. Yet I ween that a good preacher of His Word thou shalt be, dreadless. Be not cast down – I would not have chosen thee as my wayfellow else.'

121

He reached down and retrieved the morsel of cheese, rinsed it in the stream and put it back in young Harold's hand with a smile, as though he was symbolically restoring the young man's calling and authority.

'Teach thou me then, father,' pleaded the young man earnestly, lifting his head and crushing the cheese into crumbs in his intensity, 'that I may preach from the heart like unto thee!'

'Life itself and the path that God hath laid before thy feet shall be thy mentor, my son. But I shall do what little I may. Lo, alas! We behold such a lesson before us even anon. Stern lessons these, and many have learned of them too late.'

They both surveyed the depressing scene around them for a moment.

After a short depressed silence, Harold straightened his back, gulped the remaining crumbs of the cheese down and threw his breadcrumbs to the sparrows.

'So be it, if it must be. But such is not our road, and ours be a brighter destiny. Let us seek the land of the living that they may hear the gospel and find life more abundant, mayhap, than their fathers.'

'Amen! Spoken in the manner of an hearty preacher of the gospel! Onward, then.'

* * * * * *

Young Father William Thorpe felt a little unsettled.

He had, of course, experienced the initial enthusiasm and euphoria as all the missions went out from the great Doctor's presence, the words of his blessing ringing in their ears. He never doubted that this was God's calling for him, and had been prepared all of his life for this very season. But now the enormity of their task was dawning upon him.

He was more serious-minded and practical than his fellow priest, Benjamin of Abyngdon, who was only one year his junior. The latter sang as lustily as he ever did as a member of the famed "Lollards of Logic Lane," an unofficial trio of what he referred to as "God's Minstrels". But for once, he won no response from his companion, even one of their favourite airs.

'*Quo vadis*, brother William?' he rallied cheerfully. 'Dost thou dream that art not given unto dreaming? Wherefore this glumpousness of countenance and dark thought? Brother Sun rideth the heavens with joy and the fowls of the air would laud unto God His praises … but thou wilt not?'

'I do but meditate upon the way before us, thou wastrel!' retorted Thorpe, glancing up with a flash of a smile. 'Saint Francis thou art not, and thou reck little of the morrow. But soothly I say this: Had we not the seer-saying of the good Lady Mother and the command of Doctor Evangelicus himself, then would I say that this mission is but roiling madness!'

'But these signs we have indeed! What dost thou fear?'

Thorpe considered before he gave his answer.

'We are called to bid the folk of England to throw off the yoke of Rome and all its might. 'Gainst us in numbers uncounted are many friars and more mighty foes of the true gospel of Christ. We see not our path clearly before us with its snares and pitfalls. No warm hearthside living is this, that many a priest new ordained would covet. We take not provisions for the way save copied portions of Holy Writ. Yea! *In veritas*, these things will God provide if He calls us to walk such a road. Natheless, I am one that would see my path clear and plain, and with steps well-ordered. Much to learn still have I of faith in God's providence, brother Benjamin.'

'And learn these things thou wilt, *condiscipulus*.[25] Therefore what dost thou truly fear?'

William stopped in his tracks and soberly faced his friend.

'Nay, to hide mine heart and mind from thee I cannot. I will speak then of my greatest fear: that I would fail of the task before me. In my youth my sire feared likewise, and 'tis a yoke wherewith he hath ever since burdened me. O that I were a sanguine soul as thou and our brother Thomas Plowman, and had the wisdom and authority of Father William Shephard!'

Seeing how vulnerable he was, Benjamin stepped up and grasped his friend urgently by the arms.

'Hearken unto me, my brother. I am more like to fail than thou. Have I not seen thy labours and thy goings in times past? Thine is an heart of a warrior, of a watchman full faithful. Thine eyes are as the lynx and thy mind as one of the wisest in all England. Do I not therefore look to thee as elder brother and first in this mission? Disputations and offense there shall be twixt us, times and a-times, but thy disciple am I from henceforth.

25 Classmate

Where thou goest, I will follow. Such is my faith in thy judgment and kind-wit. God is with thee! Thou shalt not fail! If we fall short as a'times we shall, then God Almighty will raise us up and fill up that which we lack.'

They looked each other in the eye for a moment as the bond between them strengthened. They were comrades-in-arms, fellow labourers in a friendship that would last through the most difficult of times.

'Cast off therefore this demon from thy neck! Thou shalt not fail!' reiterated Benjamin vehemently.

A sad smile dawned on William's countenance.

'Is this wisdom or folly, or but goodly fellowship only? *Alter ego est amicus*[26]. Well, if thou shalt be fool enough to follow where my stumbling great feet leadeth thee, then so be it. But soothly did the Lady speak, when she called thee to be my fellow-labourer. Such is my need. Let us call upon God to strengthen us for the road before us.'

Their custom in the past in times of spiritual need was to kneel before a chair in one of Master Smith's spare chambers and cry out to God with hands raised. Not having immediate access to the old prayer-warrior's rooms, nor his fatherly presence, they settled for a private glade in the forest, away from the road, with squirrels and a badger to watch over them. Kneeling on a low bank, the levy of a small but noisy stream, they lifted their hands and poured out their hearts to God Almighty. William was not ashamed to even shed a few tears as he felt the tension and fear wash away from his soul.

At last they washed their faces in the clear water and stood to their feet, refreshed and encouraged. William blew his nose noisily.

'Let us onward then!' he recommended, in a more decisive tone than he had just previously spoken. 'Nightfall cometh a-pace and we must seek shelter and toil-fare for the morrow.'

'And the path beyond?' inquired Benjamin, brushing the mud off his russet robe. 'Wist thou whither it leadeth us beyond our sight anon?'

'My thought is that it leadeth unto Kent, mayhap even Canterbury itself. What sayest thou?'

Benjamin stooped again to fill their water-skins, then bowed in mock humility before his senior.

'I shall follow thy lead, my liege, as God guideth thee.'

---

26 "A friend is another self."

William laughed.

'O wise fool! Come then, brother Lollard. The burden of the journey we shall make lighter as we sing for the edification of the squirrel and badger and whatsoever else would dare to hear. Let us sing the "*Te Deum*" that we rendered afortime in Logic Lane. Alas, that Master Thomas is not in our midst!'

Benjamin lifted a waterskin in a toast.

'Wassail, cry I! Wassail to Master Thomas Plowman, mighty singer and preacher full gifted! May he ever be a-prospered in his way!' and he launched into the opening bars of their favourite Latin psalm, this time with William's deeper voice in harmony.

Chapter 2: Rugby Aroused

The Spirit of the Lord is on me, for which thing He anointed me;
He sent me to preach to the poor men, to heal contrite men in heart,
and to preach remission to prisoners and sight to blind men,
and to deliver broken men into remission;'

(Gospel of Luke 4:18 Wycliffe-Purvey Translation.)

The celebrated third member of the minstrel trio, meanwhile, was journeying south. There was no question in Master Thomas Plowman's mind about who should lead the southern mission, as that leader was Father William Shephard.

They reached the outskirts of the town of Rugby one midafternoon. There they came across an old farmer, a tenant of the Earl of Stafford, harvesting his strip. The way his back was bent and his frequent pauses and grimaces seemed to indicate that he was either injured, sick, worn-out or maybe all three.

The old man stopped when he saw them coming down the road, and looked at them in interest. Few travellers came in twos these days, with the roads becoming more dangerous because of the increase of lawlessness.

When he saw their habits, however, he drew a world-weary sigh, turned away and continued on with his painful toil. He had little to offer supposedly hungry begging friars. They were usually much fatter than he anyway, and he had no stomach for their empty piety. He had seen more than enough in his lifetime.

Even without conferring with one another, the two evangelists knew what to do.

'Good morrow, good father!' cried Tom cheerily, 'Wilt thou accept aid from two travellers in exchange for a bed and a meal? If thou canst spare neither, why, let us ease thy burden natheless. Am I not also a son of the soil as thou?' and he swept off his outer robe to reveal his sleeveless working smock, broad shoulders and muscular arms.

126

The old man blinked and gaped at him, for he knew a good worker when he saw one.

'But be ye not brothers that beg?' he asked incredulously. 'Never hearen I aught of friars that toil for their fare. Neither hearen I o' them that would toil for naught. There be many and a-many that will a-toil not a whit in yon monkeries.'

'Neither monks nor begging friars are we.' said William, removing his own clerical robe. 'Give us shelter only and we are content.'

The farmer hesitated, but he knew that he could use all the help he could get, for his back was painful and the last of his barley was in need of harvesting before it spoiled, so he gratefully accepted. He warned that he had almost nothing to offer them, but would feed them as best he could.

Touched by the old man's generosity, Tom offered to finish the field for him, while William helped the man to his house to rest.

In response to the farmer's curious questions, William explained something of their mission along the way. The old man was impressed. Once again he regretted that he has very little to offer the two evangelists to eat, although they were very welcome to sleep the night. His sons had gone off to war in France and had not returned. He was very poor, for rent and the new poll tax had been heavy. His back was worn out and arthritic and his old cow was sick, so there was no milk. He said all this, not in a complaining spirit, but merely stating facts to explain why he could not feed them well.

William was well aware of the plight of the many struggling farmers in those days, and it grieved him.

'Fear not, father. We have come to bless thee, not to devour thy last crumb. The Lord provideth for His children, and regardeth the plight of the poor.'

As they stepped over the threshold of the rough wooden longhouse, the typical and familiar smell of smoke and drying herbs greeted them. Rough and barely serviceable furniture, a beaten earthen floor covered in rushes and a black-stained and well-used cauldron on a smoky fire all gave mute witness to the old farmer's straightened circumstances. The larder door stood half open and its contents were woefully bare.

William felt a stirring in his spirit. Somehow he knew that the farmer's circumstances were about to change – and sooner than expected. Echoing the words of Jesus' disciples over a thousand years before, he spoke: 'Peace and thrift be unto this house!'

It was the custom of some orders of friars to bless a hosting house they entered in such a way, but there was such a ring of prophetic authority in William's words, the old man blinked and eyed him in wonder.

Then William prayed a blessing of health and abundance on the old man and his house with such sincerity and feeling that the farmer was deeply touched.

'Amen! And my deepest thanks, Father William,' he said, raising his bowed head and fixing his faded blue eyes on the kindly man. 'Thy prayer be like them o' the good Saint Francis hisself, I trow. May the good God send the answer surelye and anon, and bless thee also.'

He wiped his brow with his battered old hat and sat down painfully.

'I be called Old Ned, I be. And folks hereabouts wist Old Ned for a man o' his word, yea, and a giver. If I have naught but a loaf as remaineth in my breadpot, o' which dreadless I have, then shall ye good brothers have it, that I swear, and God will repay me.'

Ned went straight to his breadpot to show that he meant what he said. But when he lifted the lid, he staggered back with a startled oath, then crossed himself.

'Whence came this?' he whispered. 'It be a miracle! A holy miracle!'

William got up and looked. The first thing that he noticed was the delicious fragrance of fresh, recently baked bread. The breadpot was completely full of it.

'Bless my beard!' he muttered to himself. 'Did not Father Owain prophesy of signs following?'

The realisation of the miracle had only just struck them, when they heard the sounds of slightly distressed bellowing from the cow byre up the end of the longhouse.

'Auld Daisy be none too weal o' late.' explained old Ned, coming back to sad reality again. They both listened again, a little puzzled. 'But naught hath she to sing of like unto this.' he added.

'I have toiled a little among milch cows ere I were in ministry, Master Ned,' stated William, casting aside his russet robe and rolling up the sleeves of his working clothes, 'But by my beard, the song she singeth is too robust to be that of an ailing lady. She calleth for her daily milktake more like, methinks. Suffer me, that I may so do, and earn of thy toothsome miracle bread. At the least shall I look to her udders, that they be hale.'

'Her milktake? But how can this be?' wailed old Ned as William grabbed a clean bucket and disappeared through the door, 'She maketh not milk this last sennight or more!'

He followed William out to where old Daisy was waiting and stamping impatiently.

She looked a little askance at a stranger approaching her, but soon recognised the touch and kind words of a master cow-handler. Sure enough, her udders were full to bursting, much to old Ned's astonishment and delight, and not cracked and scaly as he saw them that morning.

'Wonder o' wonders! Another holy miracle this be!' he cried.

The old man watched William's skill and quick hands with approval. However, they had no sooner returned to the parlour carrying the brimming bucket, when Old Daisy summoned their assistance once more. Even William was astonished to see her udders were full again.

The old man cackled gleefully. Grabbing another bucket, he gave it to William to milk her a second time. 'This be another day o' wonders, by my faith. Make I some cheese for the winter, be sure.'

He regarded William with deep respect as he laboured, his head pressed against Daisy's flank. How many holy men would be found in this position and work miracles as well?

'Be thou an Holy Saint, Father William?' he asked, awestruck.

William, chuckling, began to deprecate any pretence to sainthood in the traditional sense, but a knock on the door interrupted him. Old Ned went to the door in the house while William continued with the immediate need to relieve Daisy of the life-giving liquid.

There was a good community spirit in the immediate neighbourhood, and they all loved old Ned. He was well known for his honesty and generosity. The old lady next door had prepared an evening meal out of her own rather limited bounty, knowing Ned's present need, and had brought it at that moment.

'Well, that be right good-hearted o' thee, Widdey Bessie,' said the old man, touched by her generosity, 'but will ye not as lief come and feast o' my bounty then?'

He chuckled secretively, and beckoned the mystified dame to come over to the breadpot. She almost dropped the dish she held when she saw the abundance before her.

'Master Baker never bake naught o' this!' she gasped. 'It be better nor like o' Mistress Mary's! Whence came..?'

Old Ned cut her exclamations short, bidding her grab a loaf and sit down while he told her animatedly of the amazing events, and the "holy miracle man" that came to his gate.

This was too good for the local gossip to keep to herself. A simple and devout country dame, she didn't doubt a word of it, so she immediately left Ned to eat his meal while she spread the news.

William came in shortly after with the second bucket brimming with rich creamy milk such as Ned hadn't tasted for years. The bread seemed to melt in their mouths and was still a little warm. Soon more of the locals dropped in and were invited to a feast they hadn't experienced for a long time, yet the bread bin didn't seem to become depleted at all.

'Be not this the holy miracle o' the Good Lord Christ Hisself – the feedin' o' the fifty thousand?' cried one bright young lad, crossing himself. 'Be it not loik as Father John be a-tellen a' Lord's Day last?'

William gently corrected the minor numerical inaccuracy, but recognised it as a cue. He had a very attentive audience, so he commenced to talk about the Lord Jesus as the Bread of Life.

They all paused in their feasting and listened spellbound as he emphasised the need to feed upon Christ in the spiritual sense. He boldly contradicted the tradition of the transubstantiated bread of the Roman Eucharist, but urged them rather to seek and find a personal relationship with the Bread of Life to strengthen them daily. He spoke clearly and in a manner they all understood. The miracles before his hearers were so real, how could they dream of questioning the doctrine of such a "holy saint"?

These were revolutionary concepts, especially for the older ones to take, steeped in their traditions and relying on a priest to intercede for them. A few tentative questions were raised but were easily and convincingly answered. There was such a sense of conviction and wonder amongst them all, many of the listeners had left their bread unfinished. It was nearly dusk when William decided that they were ready for the next step.

Most of the younger ones present did not hesitate to respond to his invitation. They could not help but note the stark contrast between the wholesomeness of the message William presented and what now seemed like the emaciated superstitious fairy tales, the hypocrisy, and in some cases, the immorality of many local monks and friars.

'Besoid, think ye our holy fat abbot o' St Simeon's be a-worken a holy miracle-feast for us loik o' this?' said one boldly. This was applauded with laughter and caustic comments on the abbot's life and morals.

Tom came in quietly, happily wiping the sweat from his brow and dusting the barley straw from his clothes. Seeing him, Old Ned whispered loudly to the other older folk: 'That be Master Thomas as were a-harvesten o' my barley – aye – and would do it for naught if need be.'

Such a gesture so impressed his older friends, they were inclined to think that the message of these two men must be true, no matter what 'the fat brethren o' St Simeon's would be a-sayin' contrey.'

Soon almost the whole local neighbourhood at that end of the town had come to faith in Christ, and made the nucleus of a strong disciple gathering. They reluctantly dispersed before midnight.

The two evangelists helped old Ned get out his best spare bedding, gave heartfelt thanks during their evening sacrifice and retired, deeply contented and encouraged by the day's work.

If any further proof of their calling was needed, this day's events certainly supplied it.

Early one morning, they had barely finished morning prayers, when they heard old Ned cry out in the cow byre. The two men came running to investigate.

What had happened was that old Ned had risen shortly after the two guests had, still wondering if the events of the last few days had been a dream. But the bread was still there, as fresh as ever, and still one full bucket of fresh milk, despite the previous two day's feasting. He was also aware of a joy in his heart and a sense of freedom he hadn't experienced before. The air seemed to tingle with it.

He began humming to himself as he was preparing breakfast for them when he heard Daisy's now familiar summons. Shaking his head in wonder, he went down to milk her, forgetting that his back could not bend in that position the day before. He had half-filled his bucket before he realized what he was doing.

'By all the Holy Angels! Be I hale o' my back then? Aye, and the leg too!' he shouted in his amazement. He jumped up to test it and bend it. Sure enough, there was no pain, whichever he bent and stretched.

The men ran up to find him running around his croft cackling to himself and stopping to pull out those stubborn weeds that he had been obliged to ignore before.

Naturally, the news of this spread fast, even beyond the disciples' circle of acquaintances. Soon there was even more talk of "Holy Saints that be come down o' heaven." People came running to see for themselves and ask questions.

Seeing them gather at his gate, old Ned suggested to the two evangelists that they go into the town square to preach to as many of the folk as possible.

William characteristically remembered Daisy, who was complaining about their neglect, and suggested Tom take old Ned with him to show the folk the miracle of his healing. He himself would attend to Daisy, and would join them later.

He winked and nodded at Tom to indicate that he had full confidence in him to handle the situation.

Old Ned demurred at first, saying 'It be not meet for Saint William to be a-milken a cow.' But crowds were gathering to hear. So at William's insistence, he and Tom led them all to the square.

Tom, gratified that William showed confidence in him, found the town crier's stand in the middle of the square and mounted it boldly.

In the manner of the town crier, Tom made himself heard above the crowd.

'Hear ye! Hear ye, good folk of Rugby! Great miracles we have seen these last few days a-gone! Behold good farmer Ned! For has he not been made whole by the hand of God?' and he summoned old Ned to come up and demonstrate his new-found health and to explain to the awed crowd what God had done.

Tom then followed on from where Ned left off, proclaiming the message that Christ came to heal their wounded souls as well as their bodies. He brought greetings from Doctor Wycliffe and declared his message of salvation without confessions, penances, good works or striving in one's own righteousness.

John Wycliffe's name and his championing of the poor had spread rapidly throughout the land. Although the older traditionalists murmured a little about 'heresy 'gainst Holy Church,' the younger ones cheered at the mention of Wycliffe's name. This gave Tom even more encouragement, and he challenged them to follow the way of the Holy Scriptures, even where it disagreed with their tradition. He thundered out John Wycliffe's denunciation of the abuse of power of the prelates and their social injustice, but the sins of the common people also received a stern tongue-lashing. Many in the crowd turned pale and trembled.

William had joined him by that time, pleased that Tom had found his feet so quickly. In fact, William had become convinced that Tom was much more the evangelist than he himself was.

His entrance could not go unmarked. When his tall figure was seen on the outskirts of the crowd, there were enough folk that recognised him and whispers of 'Behold! It be the good Saint William hisself!' and 'He be a-worken holy miracles, witterly.'

So he joined Tom on the stand, resigned to his unwilling canonised status. Maybe they could use it to Kingdom advantage. Therefore he did not need Tom's introduction, for everyone gave him their full attention. An eerie hush fell upon the town square. "Saint William" was about to speak.

When William looked out over the sea of awed faces, they seemed to be like sheep without a shepherd. So, in his own clear but quiet voice, he summed up what Tom had said, explained their need for a personal relationship with the Saviour and invited them all to pray a prayer of repentance and faith in the blood of Christ to cleanse them from sin. He prayed with such earnestness and compassion, and the sense of the Presence of God was so real, that some folk (notably some men first), began to weep.

Suddenly, one beggar on the edge of the crowd cried out 'I see! Mine eyes – they be opened again!' and waved high the dirty rag that had covered his eyes. 'No more a-beggen' I be! Glory be to Gawd a'moity!'

He was so delighted with his sight, he went from person to person, peering into their faces and embracing them, or gazing at the colours around him with almost idiotic and child-like delight. Pandemonium broke out at this. Many fell to their knees to repent of their sins, crying out to God for mercy.

Tom, swept along in the tide of the river of God's power, went out amongst them to pray and minister as William had shown him at Coventry. William ministered from the other end of the crowd.

A few misguided folk begged 'Saint William' to heal their coughs and sore toes. Acutely embarrassed, he explained that he was no saint in that sense, and that God alone was the healer. He urged them to seek their own healing, for he did not feel any healing power upon him at that time.

Some went away disappointed that no more spectacular miracles were forthcoming, but those whom God had truly touched stayed on to enjoy the presence of God.

Old Ned's neighbours remarked with great satisfaction to the erstwhile doubters, 'Said I not so? He be Saint William as worketh holy miracles.'

Many more were added to the disciples that day – at least half the town. The day was half spent by the time the two men returned to Old Ned's farm, tired and more than a little dazed at the wonders they had seen.

Old Ned was still in seventh heaven and said little.

'Hast done well, Saint William,' commented Tom mischievously.

William smiled wearily 'Silence, impious wastrel! But by my beard, thou'st also done very well, my son. Yea, abundant well.'

Tom coloured a little, pleased.

William looked hard at his companion's lion-like profile.

'Furthermore, methinks thou'rt called to be the [27]vaward of this army, my lad. Thou'rt an evangelist-born, I deem. Mine is but a shepherd's calling, and so shall I gather and tend them. But to strike the first blow calleth for the boldest and most froward in our midst. What sayest thou, soldier? Art willing?'

The eager expression of excitement on the face that was turned to him was all he needed to know.

Chuckling, they sat down to a midday meal that Widow Bessie had prepared for the three of them. They toasted her health and God's blessing with a tankard of Daisy's creamiest and set to.

---

27   vanguard

The next day, William went out to help Daisy produce more milk, and then Old Ned led her out to happily graze on the barley stubble.

William was soon commandeered by eager disciples and other townsfolk who asked him many questions. Some merely wanted a touch or a blessing from the good "Saint William", so he was kept busy for quite a while, disabusing their minds of their misapprehension. A few of the more intelligent tradesmen and merchants were interested in the subject of hagiology, so he gave a simplified discourse on true biblical canonization, based on a theory put forward by the Wycliffite master, Master Ashwardby, at Oxford.

Meanwhile, Tom helped old Ned to gather, bind and store the last of the harvested barley, then turned his attention to some young lads playing on the common over the road.

They were playing a rough-and-tumble game they had invented – or so they claimed.

Tom thought at first that it must be a game of Folk Footbale which he used to play in his youth, from which few came away unscathed. But then he realised it was not so.

The game reminded Tom of another childhood game he used to play called "Keeper o' the Bale," where a small bag stuffed with hay was thrown among members of one team until stolen by the other team who gave chase. They could not afford the bouncing pigskin balls that the wealthy manor children had, but the poorer youths were wizards at improvisation.

Furthermore, the local lads had added a more physical aspect to it: The possessor of the bag had to race to a pair of sticks at his end of the field and touch down under or kick the bag over a crossbar which was tied halfway up the sticks. The other team had to tackle him to the ground to stop him, and if he dropped it, they possessed themselves of the bag and raced for the corresponding sticks at the other end. The game had become very popular, even though no one throughout the town could agree on a name for it.

Tom was intrigued.

Seeing Tom there, leaning on the dry stone wall and watching, they recognised him and invited him to join in. He proved a handy player, although he was a little too chivalrous for some of the larger, rougher lads. Tom also insisted on making some fair rules, which gave the smaller ones a chance. This impressed many of the weaker lads, for even the biggest among them had nothing but profound respect for Tom, especially his brawny arms and huge shoulders. In the end, Tom became a kind of adjudicator who enforced the rules. He drew boundaries with pieces of twine and lined each team up in an orderly fashion. Such was the justice and fairness of his decisions, smaller players discovered skills and talents they had never dreamed of before. Brawn alone no longer counted unless it was skilfully and fairly mixed with good tactics.

These innovations were so well-received (by the majority at least) that it was almost unanimously decided that Tom would hold his new office in future games forever. Tom, a little dismayed at this, hastily demurred and recommended that another wise and respected adult be given the office.

Old Farmer Ned and William watched and cheered them all on. Soon a small crowd of adults gathered as well. Some of the men became so inspired by the game, they began to discuss tactics and rules.

'Wherefore do these lads alone be a-playen this?' said one. 'A fine thing this be.'

'Aye!' said another. 'This be men's work, this be!'

And soon, a game for men only was planned. They then turned their attention on Tom.

Simply because of Tom's sense of fair play, a few more youths came to believe his message and later joined the disciple gatherings.

Inspiration came suddenly upon Tom. So at the end of the game, he gathered them all together and spoke to them in the adults' hearing.

'Lads all, wot you not that the Good God calleth you all unto the game of Eternal Life? Will ye take his part and be yoke-teamed with the Good Lord Jesu as your captain? But mark how that when ye worked as true yoke-fellows and abided by the laws o' the game, then ye conquered.'

And so he continued, expanding on what William later laughingly called, "The Parable of the Prodigal Sons of Rugby."

Both adults and boys were struck by this illustration, and many inquired further. More disciples were added. William was impressed.

'"Twas well done, O Thomas the evangel.' he said as they retired that night.

William spoke every night to the disciples, giving them scripture portions and asking for scribes to make copies. He exhorted them to grow in God and meet regularly to pray and read scripture portions.

When the morning soon dawned, however, they knew it was time to depart.

For one thing, the local priest did not like the rumours he was hearing, especially about these miracle-working friars. Like old Ned, he had had a surfeit of friars, some of whom worked bogus miracles for gain. Word came to the two evangelists that the priest was demanding their instant removal.

Ned begged them to stay, offering to hide them in his loft, but Tom was keen to move on for the sake of unreached people in other towns and villages. William reluctantly agreed, but insisted that they meet once more with the disciples before they left.

All the disciples were a bit teary, but understood that the gospel must be taken to other counties and towns. They offered gifts of food to help them along to their next destination. This was often a feature of their whole mission, which helped the evangelists to cover many miles.

Before they left, Widow Bessie gave them the name of her cousin in Warwick town. Her name was Mistress Mary Langland, a middle-aged widow who was considered by many to be a modern day Dorcas, known for her charitable works and hospitality to strangers. Her brother had become a scribe in London and was becoming an author of note. He occasionally sent or brought her moneys to support her works of charity.

'Langland?' muttered William to himself. ''Tis a name that stirreth a memory, but whomsoever he be, I wot not.'

Armed with the widow's information, the two evangelists waved to their friends and set off.

Chapter 3: Peace to This House

And when ye go into an house, greet ye it, and say
Peace to this house.
And if that house be worthy, your peace shall come on it;
But if that house be not worthy, your peace shall turn again to you.

(Christ's instructions to his disciples.
Gospel of Matthew 10:12,13 Wycliffe – Purvey Translation.)

The wild roses were in full bloom in the woods north of Warwick, but Mistress Mary Langland had no time to enjoy them. She was at her wits' end.

There had been a terrible windy spring storm the night before, which had blown away the loose thatching on the northeastern corner of her cottage. This had been followed by heavy rain that morning, which had drenched the floor of her own bedroom, as well as the bed coverings. She had become drenched while attempting to cover the gap with whatever straw she could find – only to see it falling or blowing off again.

Most of the men of the neighbourhood were in their fields and could not help her until nightfall.

Her dwelling was at the windiest end of Warwick town.

'Oh! Would that his lordship had but spared the trees nigh o' the new assart!' she wailed as another load of straw blew off the roof with yet another gust of wind.

No sooner had she said this, than she heard an ominous squawking. Looking out the window, she saw half a dozen hens running out into the road from their enclosure. She threw her hands up in dismay and groaned, for she realised the door of the henhouse had also blown off again.

She had spent so much time keeping her guesthouses in good order, she had neglected her own.

She gave chase, thinking how foolish she must look as she ran hither and thither, trying to round them up. Exhausted, she had almost shepherded most of them into her croft shed, when who should appear out of the shed, but her faithful Barnabus, wagging his tail and looking for a little sport.

One bark made the nervous fowls run under Mary's feet. Of course, this was a clear invitation to Barnabus to give chase – or so he thought. Soon they had scattered to the four corners of the croft, many running out onto the road again.

Deaf to his mistress' exasperated commands, the delinquent hound ran in all directions, barking encouragement to the frightened fowls, inviting them to share in the fun.

Mary staggered out into the road, and collapsed onto a low rock wall, sighing.

'Oh, Lord God! Aid thou me and spare me mine hens o' the foxes.'

Bedlam raged around her. More straw blew off the roof.

She covered her head with her hands.

Suddenly, she looked up at the sound of approaching footsteps and groaned again. Visitors were coming. Normally, she enjoyed having strangers seeking haven from a long journey, even if they were begging friars as these appeared to be. But with her household in turmoil and Barnabus barking hysterically at them, she wouldn't have been surprised if the travellers nervously passed by.

But the two men stopped. Though friars they seemed to be at first glance, as she studied them closely, they had neither the pale, disapproving mien of the ascetics, nor the more common well-fed look of the conventional friars. They were both well-proportioned, strong-looking men with a certain *joie de vivre* rarely seen in any clergy. She did not recognise the order their habit proclaimed.

In spite of this, past experience with friars taught her to expect them to pass strictures on the disorder of her household and pass on, or ignore her plight and demand free hospitality for the night as their right and privilege. She waited with a sense of helpless resignation, hoping they wouldn't waste too much of her time, so she could continue her hopeless pursuit.

The younger stranger, however, the most powerful-looking of the two, cheerfully introduced himself as Thomas Plowman, a lay preacher.

'Ho! Mistress, thou'rt caught in a veritable tempest!' he observed, loudly and jovially. 'Surely we are sent from Above to rescue them that have strayed from the paths of righteousness.'

Off he went in pursuit of the furthest wandering fowls.

The other man, calling himself Father William, had the kindest face she had ever seen. He helped the harassed spinster to her feet. Together, they joined the pursuit with the young man, who was making joyous hunting calls and laughing as he weaved here and there after the wayward fowls. He reminded Mary of her brother, when he was a lad.

But they made little progress, and the combined din of the recalcitrant canine and the rioting birds became almost deafening.

Father William knew it was no use, and that soon many chickens would be lost to predators in the woods. Not knowing what else to do, he prayed.

Into his mind came the prophetic dream that Brother Joseph, his first mentor, had told him of the staff of authority. He also remembered the passage of scripture where the disciples of Jesus entered a household on their mission to proclaim the coming of the Kingdom. He had read it in the vulgate, so without bothering to translate and pronounce the conventional household blessing, nor stopping to think how foolish it must seem, he raised his staff and cried '[28]*Pax huic domui!*'

To everyone's astonishment, including William's, everything instantly calmed down.

Faithful Barnabus immediately stopped barking and returned submissively to his mistress, panting contentedly, his tongue hanging out. The hens halted their headlong panic, and even began drifting back towards the house, picking at grubs and seeds as they came. Between the three of them, the humans were able to gently herd the now docile birds back to their coop, and Tom immediately jammed the broken door in its place to be mended later.

Even with the wonder of the homely miracle still fresh in his mind, William nearly burst out laughing when he saw Tom's face.

'Bless my beard!' William remarked, ''Tis a useful piece of weaponry this.'

''Tis a powerful incantation thou'st invoked, Father Wizard,' commented Tom, looking at William with renewed respect. 'Or be this but the power of "the good Saint William" then? What was't?'

The grateful lady, who came up beaming all over her homely face, interrupted them.

---

28 'Peace be with this house!'

'Thanks be to God! Good brethren, if ever guests be welcome to Langland house, thou'rt the most. Be that a holy miracle I beheld, or be mine aging eyes awry?'

Tom turned to her, surprised.

'Be thou Mistress Mary Langland, then? Thy good cousin Widow Bessie sendeth thee greeting and commended us to thine hospitality if thou wilt. Mine holy companion be naught else but Saint W... Ow!'

William had rapped Tom on the ankle with his staff before his friend had the chance to mischievously mistitle him. Some decorum had to be maintained before the lady, after all.

'Thy pardon I beg, Father,' continued Tom, in a deceptively penitent manner, tempering his introduction. 'Madame, this be Father William Shepherd, a godly man.'

'And this young man is Master Thomas Plowman, a lay preacher and a truly worthy man, madam.' added William, with a stern eye on Tom's grinning countenance. 'Natheless, he is still but apprenticed.'

Having hopefully put Tom in his place, he went on.

'Sent from Oxenford are we, by Doctor John Wycliffe, to proclaim the gospel of the Holy Scriptures to all, throughout the land. Soothly we seek shelter and fare, but we beg not, and will labour for our bread.'

'Ye beg not, brethren? A strange thing is this also of all ferly wonders I have beheld this day,' declared the lady. 'But ye have earned anon more than what would be needful, good sirs, if I asked it of thee for gold or silver. But come ye in o' the chill wind.'

It was then that Tom noticed the large gaps in the roofing.

'Tempests be common and hands be few to amend the wounds thereof, Master Plowman.' said the lady fatalistically, when Tom drew their attention to it.

'Our hands be few,' answered Tom, 'but we will essay if thou'st the thatching straw, Mistress.'

'Oh, if ye but would!' cried the grateful lady, and before she knew it, both men had shed their outer habit (which was strangely dry despite the morning's rain) and were gathering the straw they saw which had blown or was heaped in a corner of the shed.

She cooked them a delicious soup, selecting the best ingredients she could find in the house, while the men set to work.

By the time they sat down at table, they had not only repaired the roof so it would last a few years, but they had also fixed the chicken coop door with a strong latch.

Overcome by their goodness, Mary said 'Gentlemen, for soothly ye seem, ye shall ever find an open door and fare abundant and free, if ye pass this way again.'

She laid soup and her best bread and cheese before them.

William gave thanks and prayed a blessing upon the house. He prayed with such sincerity and conviction, Mistress Mary felt as though the answers had already come.

As they all ate, she confided to them of a dream she had a few years ago.

She loved God. It had become an obsession to know Him more, but her traditions had taught her that none but priests and the holiest of holy saints could approach Him, such was the sinfulness of mankind. In spite of this, her desire to draw near to Him grew in intensity. Every night, she prayed that He would reveal His love to her. She had more than once considered entering one of the local abbeys, but she was not impressed by the conduct of many sisters and monks she had seen, and she also felt she should support her younger brother, who had gone to Oxford to study.

One night, she had a vivid dream. She saw two angels who came knocking at her door, asking for hospitality. They looked like ordinary men, but their faces were not clear in her mind. When they had eaten, they produced a book from their waybag. It looked like rough stained leather binding on the outside, but when they opened it in front of her, the pages shone with a heavenly light. She somehow knew that she would find in it what her heart had been yearning for all of her life.

At that point, Tom immediately reached for their waybag, but William quietly put out his hand to stop him and slightly shook his head. Mistress Langland continued, unaware of this.

Golden words shone out to her from the pages in her dream, but all she could see were three words:

'God so loved.' They were in English.

Then the book was opened again, this time to the story of the Apostle Peter raising Dorcas to life again. The words shone like gold. Then they seemed to lift off the page and float into her heart.

At that very moment, much to her disappointment, she awoke.

Nonetheless, the memory of the dream stayed with her and occasionally reoccurred. She concluded that she was called to serve God and serve people in the area of hospitality and good works for the poor.

With part of the legacy her father, a well-to-do craftsman, had left her, she and her brother William built Langland House, the guesthouse nearby. She welcomed strangers and travellers of all walks of life, even the poorest of the poor who could not pay. She spent the rest of her days mending and making clothes for the more desperately poor among the locals.

William Langland had discovered in himself a gift for writing. He had studied at Oxford, and was now in London. Although times had been lean for a while, he was also making a reasonable living with his writings, and brought her money on his occasional visits.

'William Langland,' echoed Father William thoughtfully, as he turned a questioning eye to Thomas, who wrinkled his brow in an effort of memory, and shook his head.

'Have ye seen or heard tell of him at Oxenford, brethren?' she asked hopefully.

'Not of a certainty, mistress. But pray, continue thy tale.'

She still hoped one day, of course, that the angels would drop by as she had seen in her dream.

William, warmed by her generosity of spirit as much as by her soup, raised a finger to gain her full attention, then reached for his waybag.

'Mistress Mary, no angels are we, but mortal men (although this thy brose hath the savour of heaven on't.) Natheless, we would show thee a book that hath revealed unto us the selfsame soothsaw as that which thy heart hath yearned for, though it be bound in stained leather, and gloweth not to earthly eyes.'

But he was mistaken.

He retrieved his precious bound copy of the translated scriptures, then opened it at random. Mary gasped ecstatically. It was not the story of Dorcas, but the pages fell open to the words of John, chapter 3. Verses 16 and 17 glowed with the same heavenly golden light that she remembered in her dream:

'But God loved so the world, that He gave His one begotten Son, that each

man that believeth in him perish not, but have everlasting life. For God sent not His Son into the world, that He judge not the world, but that the world be saved by Him.[29]

'But how can this be?' she cried. 'Ever have I struggled to find His love, but failed. Fastings and prayers and penances have I offered. Never failed I o' confessional and mass. Saint Julian have I ever faithfully served and prayed unto. Many a charitable deed do I. But still my heart findeth not peace, but rather guilteousness o' my sins. Wherewithal can I but believe, yea, without good works, to find His favour?'

So it was that William showed her, via the scriptures, the way of salvation through faith in the all-sufficient blood of Christ. He explained how true good works flowed naturally from a redeemed and grateful heart. This totally went counter to everything that Father Richard (the rector of All Saints Church in Warwick) had told her over the years.

She could not deny the evidence of her eyes, evidence enhanced by a heavenly confirmation, and these were the most godly men she had encountered. Her heart was bursting as revelation came to her of the relationship with God that she had longed for all her life.

'More than ever shall I serve my good Lord!' she declared rapturously, tears of joy filling her eyes. She embraced both men. 'I serve Him as a free and grateful handmaid. A bond-thrall unto guilt and fear shall I be no more!'

They invited her to join in their evening sacrifice before they retired to the guesthouse.

As the two men settled down in their beds, they discussed the wonders they had experienced that day. God was indeed confirming their mission with signs following. It seemed, observed William, that their path was already laid out for them. All they had to do was follow it and wait for God to show them the next move.

Mulling over this, a thought occurred to Tom.

'William Langland, her brother. Was he not of Master Ashton's lads, thy messfellow at University College?'

'Beard o' Moses!' exclaimed William sitting up. 'The selfsame William

---

29 Original Wycliffe/Purvey translation

Langland it must be. Had forgot him. Gifted of the poets tongue and of quill is he.'

'Witterly! His sister would be a-proud to hear him. He hath writ mighty works, methinks. Whither went he when he departed Oxenford?'

'To London. as a clerk and copier did he live, but "The Creed of Piers Plowman" should gain him a better living, dreadless. A bold work, and anon many there be that read it. Many more shall, I deem.'

'Yea, unless Courtenay and Arundel read it first.'

'Courtenay and Arundel? A scrivener-clerk despised would he be to their exalted besteadance[30]! They would heed him little. But many a good plowman and artisan, if he be lettered, shall heed him indeed!'

As William began to doze off, another thought occurred to Tom as he meditated over Mistress Langland's dream.

'Fellow angel!' he called softly. 'Whither thy wings?'

'Oh, fly thou unto the habitations of sleep, thou redeless yellowbeak!'

---

30 position

Chapter 4: Warwick's Wounds

'And when they had given to them many wounds, they sent them
into prison, and commanded to the keeper, that they should keep
them diligently. And when he had taken such a precept, he put them
into the inner prison, and restrained the feet of them in a tree. And
at midnight Paul and Silas worshipped, and praised God; and they
that were in keeping heard them. And suddenly a great earth moving
was made, so that the foundements of the prison were moved. And at
once all the doors were opened, and the bonds of all were loosed.'

(Deeds of Apostles 16:23-26 Wycliffe/Purvey Translation)

The next morning, after prayers, Mistress Mary made breakfast for them with fresh eggs that the prodigal hens had just laid, and fresh milk just delivered by a farmer friend.

She was delighted to hear that they knew her literary brother. Being barely literate herself, letters from him were welcomed but a little pointless, and he could only occasionally visit her. To her added delight, William offered to read them to her.

Tom made some further repairs to her cottage with Barnabus in attendance. He had a predilection for Tom's company rather than his fellow-labourer, much to William's chagrin. William took pride in being prime favourite with all animals.

'Hast stern Father William done scathe unto thy sensibilities, Master Barnabus?' said Tom sympathetically, holding him up by his front paws. 'It is well with thee that thou knowest the fear of the Lord.'

The amiable animal wagged his tail and returned cheerful but monosyllabic answers.

Tom was referring, of course, to the word of command William spoke the day before. Barnabus had held him in awe ever since.

'Sely creatures are ye, both.' observed William in passing, carrying firewood and fresh water. He was helping Mary clean up both dwellings, bedding and so forth, in spite of Mary's protests that 'it be not meet work for holy men.'

At William's request, Mary had spoken to the peasant farmer, a personal friend, who had delivered her milk that morning. He was pleased to receive help in the form of manual labour in return for meal and bed, especially anyone recommended by Mary.

They met the man an hour later. He was redheaded, ruddy-faced and weather-beaten but an honest-looking man of William's age, and they liked each other on sight.

Giving them a hearty handshake, he spoke in a peculiar growling voice, a legacy of his military days in France. A swordstroke would have cut his throat if his chain mail vest not intervened.

'So ye're Mistress Mary's miracle men, be ye? That's as may be, but ye been abundant kind unto Mistress Mary, I trow, and that be true holiness i' my mind, by the saints. Simon Hawkes be my name, good brethren, and I be a-needen o' holy miracles messell, though I be a-cheered enow with four-so-much good hands to aid me.'

'Be our hands, feet and shoulders at thy service, good Master Simon.' replied Tom cheerfully, shaking hands almost as large as his.

The preliminary courtesies concluded, Simon showed the two men around his fields where he was ploughing for the wheat sowings.

'But mine old Samson be hip-halt, alas!' he said with a deeper growl than usual 'and I be obleeged to a-borrow o' John Mulwood's mare 'til Samson be hale again. But that be a sennight gone and him with a touch o' the [31]accesse, poor old soul.'

William asked to see old Samson's leg, since he had treated farm horses before. Immediately he saw what the problem was – an infection on the fetlock, still festering due to unskilled treatment. He removed the rough makeshift cloth that covered it, cleaned the sore, and made up a special herbal poultice. Applying this seemed to have some soothing effect on the wound immediately, much to the relief of both the horse and his master. Both recognised the hand of a master and both gave him added respect accordingly. The horse would be better in another few days.

---

31   fever

'Sickerly, thou workest holy miracles as Mary hath said, Father William.' commented the farmer appreciatively.

William shook his head. "Tis naught but the common miracle of herbs of medicine, Master Simon.'

Tom worked the plough steadily and efficiently while the farmer and William did some much needed repairs on the longhouse.

The grateful farmer fed them well and asked them about their mission. What they told him made him blink in wonder.

'By the saints! Thy message be one that all men should take heed of, honest or no!'

He was especially interested when they mentioned John Wycliffe's name.

He looked up with a grin and demanded, 'Be he the one as a-pullen Archy-Bishop Courtenay's noäse?'

Then he slapped his side and roared with laughter.

If he had been disposed to help them before, he was now a fervent partisan. He offered to gather as many friends as he could in the town square the next day so the two evangelists could deliver their message to as many as possible. He knew the inquisitive nature of the Warwick townsfolk well. A cheering crowd would inevitably attract a bigger crowd. It was also market day, so many folk were sure to be there.

Everything was going to plan until his wor'ship the mayor of Warwick happened to be riding through the square with an armed following in train.

He was a very ambitious man, bent on gaining as much favour from persons of great consequence that he possibly could. He had just returned from a journey up northwest to see the Bishop of Worcester. He had also somehow manipulated an acceptance from his lordship, the Earl of Warwick, to dine with him that night. Consequently, he was in an exalted frame of mind, feeling that he had gained new heights.

Bishop Moreton of Worcester was still simmering and spitting venom over the bold remarks by certain Oxford Dons. Above all, he was stung by Doctor John Wycliffe's diatribes in his polemic tracts circulating throughout many ecclesiastical and academic circles, challenging the authority of prelates and clergy whose morality was called into question. Already angered by events in Coventry a few years ago, he was so infuriated by Wycliffe's stern (and in the bishop's case, rather accurate) accusations, he unwisely stormed into the courtroom of his cousin, the Earl of Warwick, demanding that he use his influence to silence, if not remove the renegade John Wycliffe. Far from being sympathetic, the earl, deep in John of Gaunt's confidence, just laughed in the bishop's face. This, of course did nothing to heal the longstanding enmity between the cousins, or the bishop's temper. Even his peers seemed unconcerned, even lethargic about Wycliffe's complaints, with the exception, of course, of Courtenay, Archbishop of London and the Bishop of Lincoln. They, at least, were aware that if this dissention spread, with the support of the Crown, it may lead to some uncomfortable reforms amongst the higher clergy. There had already been calls in parliament for more accountability of the clergy. But most of the prelates thought that nothing would come of it, and laughed it off.

'Well,' cried Bishop Moreton, 'If the great heed not the wynd, then the lesser shall be a-winnowed!'

He summoned all those that had any influence at all, whom he knew were under his influence, and poured out his frustrations on them, (except his humiliation before the Earl, of course) urging them to at least remove any support from Wycliffe and his following. He even stooped to share his complaint with previously ignored and disdained persons such as the ambitious Alderman Gerard Pugsley, Mayor of Warwick.

Gratified at such condescension, he listened to the bishop's tirade with obsequious shocked dismay.

"That malapert Jack-eater, John Wycliffe..." the bishop fumed, had dared to question the authority of Holy Church, and had even questioned some of her traditions on the grounds of Holy Writ. Although he did not unburden all his heart, he said enough to make his guest take note.

Pugsley was neither a scholar nor an astute politician, although he dreamed of joining the elite members of the House of Commons one day. He had become a successful master merchant, but he no longer paid enough attention to the simmering factions and underlying power struggles of high state, and cared little for ecclesiastical matters unless it advanced his own interests. He immediately recognised an opportunity to do so.

'As a true son of Holy Church,' he vowed to the bishop with great fervour, 'mightily shall I resist any heresy-make within an hundred leagues of Warwick.'

The bishop bowed his head in gracious thanks and gave him a thin, artificial smile. A proud and arrogant man, he still had no stomach for sycophants, least of all ambitious lowborn merchants. But many of the truly influential personages of the land, including his hated cousin, would love to get their hands on the massive wealth within Holy Church's coffers, and hence were often taking Wycliffe's part. Winning support from those who recognised his authority was a necessary evil to defeat the undesirable popularity of the Wycliffites, however, so he concealed his contempt.

In happy ignorance of this, Alderman Pugsley rode into his little kingdom with a glowing sense of triumph, dreaming of the social heights he was almost assured of. His pleasant reverie was interrupted by a clear voice raised above the hubbub of a crowd gathered around Warwick central square.

He reined in and listened. Even his bored entourage of men-at-arms looked up and listened. They were a little surprised, for there had not been any friars preaching in the streets for several months. The existing limiter[32]-friars had settled comfortably into fat livings, or were well catered for in any case. Others were too busy trying to weasel money out of the wealthier members of society, or dallying with pretty village maidens to return to street preaching. The citizens of Warwick, although irritated by their ceaseless demands for money, and mildly disapproving of their moral aberrations, generally tolerated them for their papal authority to absolve all their frequent sins.

Occasionally, the richer classes could obtain indulgences for feast days for an exorbitant sum, much of which stayed in the pardoner's pocket. But the bishop had paused in his cathedral-building of late, which meant no indulgences had been forthcoming.

Alderman Pugsley was not overly fond of performing his penances. He had gotten in arrears with his last diet imposed by his confessor. He patted his bloated belly rather ruefully. He had previously negotiated with his confessor to go on pilgrimage instead, but his spiritual guide had been

---

32   Friars limited to begging in a defined region

a little too avaricious of late, and would not budge on his demand for extra tithes in exchange for absolution, nor on the penitential gastronomical restrictions.

His reflections were again interrupted, and his attention caught by a name spoken by the vigorous young preacher in the square. A hum of excitement went through the crowd, followed by a hush which indicated that the speaker had their full attention.

'Yea! Doctor John Wycliffe himself!' cried the powerfully built preacher, so unlike any of the portly friars the Aldermen knew. 'He would have thee read the Holy Scriptures in thine own tongue, and see the simple truth for thyself, not the fables and saint's tales that ye have heard oft and lome. He hath sent us to declare the simple truth of salvation without intermediation of nor priest nor friar nor bishop...'

That was quite enough for Alderman Pugsley. It was heresy-make! This was the opportunity he needed to gain favour from the bishop, and hopefully from the Earl also.

Here is a God-given opportunity, he told himself, to show the world (all that really counted, at least) that he would be doing his duty and ridding society of troublemakers and heretics. Had he not so sworn to My Lord Bishop? It was also a good opportunity to show the citizens that he was one who ruled with a strong hand.

Roused to righteous wrath, he spurred toward the crowd, shouting 'Make way, there, make way! 'Tis I, the mayor of Warwick! Way there!'

He forced his way toward the front of the parting crowd, his men-at-arms close behind. The citizens muttered at his approach, for he was not too popular among the common folk of late.

The mayor glared up at Tom, standing on the town crier's dais with arms folded.

'What be thy meaning, thou young malapert! Dost thou fleer at my lord bishop – nay! – at Holy Church herself?'

A tall, bearded man in similar habit stood next to the young preacher and responded in a deeper, cultured voice.

'Nay, your worship! We give respect where it is due. But we assert and declare that Holy Scripture taketh higher authority than any man, even though he bear the office of the Bishop of Rome or, indeed, Worcester.'

The crowd murmured agreement, generally thinking this was a

reasonable statement, since Tom had previously reminded them that the scriptures were written by the Holy Apostles and Prophets. Holy Church itself claimed its authority on the basis of scripture, after all.

But his worship the mayor had no time for theological accuracy or truth. Political expediency was his religion.

'Heresy! Heresy! 'Tis shendful!' he blustered forth, turning red in the face at this seeming impudence. 'Do ye dare challenge God's authority upon the Earth? Repent ye and recant anon, lest the avenging hand of righteousness falleth heavily upon ye! Wilt thou be put in the stocks? Or worse?'

Many in the crowd looked surprised at such heavy-handedness. Others, having taken his wor'ship's measure, drew the right conclusions.

'Ah! Dreadless the old bretheling be done a-favel[33] o' Bishop Moreton hisself.' commented Simon Hawkes caustically to his neighbour.

'Aye!' replied the other scornfully 'And with ten o' his alaunts[34] at his beck, he do fancy hisself right barful.[35] Orgulous dotard!'

Tom spread his arms and met the fulminating look in the mayor's fat face with his cheery smile.

'But wherefore be we punied for but preaching God's truth, your wor'ship?' he protested mildly.

'Ha, then!' cried the mayor, bristling. 'Dost thou recant not? By the beard o' St Edmond, thou *shalt* be a-punied then, obdurate young jack-eater! If my warnings thou heedest not, then mayhap the iron fist of justice will!'

He spun around to face the weary sergeant at his side.

'Seize them!' he roared, 'And place them in the stocks!'

The sergeant was looking forward to his dinner, so he decided to get it over and done with as quickly as possible. But the younger preacher looked rather powerfully-built, and might make good account of himself, his habit notwithstanding.

He caught the eye of six of his men and with a gesture, indicated they approach the dais from both sides. The men thought arresting holy men was pretty poor sport, but were too well trained to hesitate.

---

33 flattery
34 Fierce hunting dogs, also a derogatory name for men-at-arms
35 dangerous, ominous

Trapped by a wall at his back, and four men approaching each side of him, Tom had instinctively stiffened, ready to fight for freedom.

William laid his hand on Tom's shoulder and in a tone of quiet authority, murmured 'Nay, Thomas. No hurlings here. We bear adversity like men, and men of God. He will fight for us in His time.'

Tom relaxed, albeit reluctantly. He managed to smile upon his captors as they marched him and William over to the far end of the square, pushing through the muttering crowd.

'Master Alderman!' bellowed Simon Hawkes furiously, his ruddy face even redder. 'This be not justice!'

He would have said more, but William intervened.

'Peace, Master Simon, but we thank thee,' he said firmly, turning his head. 'To make garboil would be a sleeveless cause. God's will shall be done, even in this. Prithee, seek thou Mistress Mary, that ye make intercession for us.'

The two men had their necks and wrists firmly placed in the large wooden stocks, side by side, and sealed with a monstrous iron padlock.

The soldiers were not rough, partly because they had some respect for these unusual supposed felons, one of whom seemed very much more like a saint than a sinner. But "horders be horders," as one of them apologetically explained to William.

The mayor was a little disappointed that there wasn't a struggle. It would have emphasized the righteousness of his actions if the two heretics had tried to run or fight. As it was, the crowd's sympathies were now with the miscreants. But the mayor was no longer sensitive to popular opinion unless it worked to his advantage, so he laughed and sent a final warning to the captors.

'If this thy heresy shall abide beyond four-and-twenty hours, we shall hie thee to the bishop to abide his doom. Think well on this.'

He rode off to his quarters, very pleased with the performance of his duty so far. He would have something of which to boast to My Lord the Earl that evening.

If the interest of the crowd had been tickled by these unusual and radical preachers before, it was fairly caught now. These men were prepared to face the humiliation of the stocks and maybe even imprisonment for what they believed in. Although some were cautious about upsetting the status quo, there was enough cynicism toward the fatter members of the clergy and their love of money and power to make the stance of the two preachers from Oxford rather refreshing.

Most of the original crowd remained, their normal market-day business forgotten. Questions were asked and William calmly answered them as though he were comfortably seated in Doctor Hereford's study, rather than locked in an uncomfortable and vulnerable position. His answers, his manner and his attitude impressed many of those present.

Tom also commented occasionally, and even laughed at his own predicament, giving thanks to God for the privilege of suffering for Christ and the truth. Many of the citizens present began to draw parallels with the stories they had heard of the Apostle Paul's sufferings.

However, there is always an empty-headed and loutish element in any society. The mayor, on the way to his quarters, saw a few of these lads lounging about, and told them there was some good sport to be had at the stocks.

Although these lads had no good opinion of the mayor himself, they were bored enough to try a little bear-baiting, as they called it. They gathered all the rotten produce they could from the kennels by the market-place and hurried to the town square.

They were disappointed to see a crowd still gathered closely around the men in the stocks, an unusual occurrence which hindered their aim. But this did not deter them.

One of them tried lobbing a moist missile over the crowd's heads, and it landed 'Splat!' right in the centre of the crowd, splattering rotting fruit flesh in all directions. This had the desired effect of scattering the crowd, who had no wish to share the fate of the condemned men. This cleared the way for some unimpeded target practice for the youths, and soon the missiles were coming thick and fast.

William resigned himself to this humiliation, knowing it was all part of the risks of his calling, but Tom fumed inwardly, longing to get his hands on them, and rub their faces in the muck they were throwing.

A few pieces hit their faces, which occasioned much delight and ribaldry from the lads. The other citizens watched in silence, neither supporting the pastime, nor committing themselves to a cause they still knew too little about to get their hands dirty.

There were some however, who *were* so committed.

Simon Hawkes and his best friend and neighbour, John Mulwood had not been idle all this time. Simon had hurried off to see Mary as William had asked him, and he and John also had a word with a few of their closer friends out in the fields. They knew that the inevitable consequences would soon be under way, so they wasted no time.

Mary hastened around to her friends, mainly the wives of the farmers that Simon rounded up, and soon they were on their knees for the holy men she had told them about that morning.

Armed with pitchforks and old coats, Simon and his friends ran back to the town square before the youths had warmed to their task.

'Ho! The young wolfheads!' growled Simon. 'Well, we shall storm this affray full soldierly.'

He and his men gathered in a line at the end of the square. They grasped their pitchforks, and removed their old garments, holding them like shields in a manner that reminded one old soldier among them of a famous attack at the Battle of Poitiers. He was a former sergeant of the Earl's foot soldiers, so he took command.

'Form ye rank, then!' he ordered. 'Lower y'r spears! Raise shields! ...... Charge!'

With yells and war cries, the farmers charged.

History, however, did not repeat itself in this case. Seeing a line of deadly pitchforks advancing rapidly toward them, the youths did not even consider making a courageous stand as did the foot-soldiers of France. Crying out in dismay, they fled, throwing some of their ammunition wildly in the direction of the grim-looking farmers. Those that hit their mark were turned aside by the makeshift shields.

One of the leading youths slipped and fell, covering himself and one other with the half-decomposed missiles he had dropped. Two others fell over him in their haste and landed face first in the quagmire the first had created. They only just escaped the advancing prongs. But one did not get away.

The spectators were thoroughly entertained by this spectacle. They laughed, clapped, jumped and cheered.

'*Sa, sa, cy avaunt!*' cried one gentleman-hunter among them, gleefully waving his cap as if he was at chase.

Some of the other old soldiers among them, stirred by the memory of their past glories in France, shouted 'Saint George for Merrie England!'

Once the show was over, the victors congratulated and toasted, and the affair had been well discussed and laughed over by the populace, most of them began to go about their business. Some stayed, however, interested to see the response of the two men condemned to a night in the stocks. One kindly dame retrieved some water from the town pump, meaning to clean up the mess on the two condemned men's faces and garments.

Mistress Mary, meanwhile, left the farmers' wives in fervent prayer and hurried to the square to witness the last of the death-or-glory charge and the ensuing rout. Although she enjoyed seeing the enemy's retreat, she had other business, so she hurried to the stocks, muttering indignantly under her breath about 'redeless, malten-hearted gigelots that labour not a full day's honest toil, the nithings!'

She had brought clean cloths, some rough soap and a clay pot full of clean pump-water, so she set to work on William and Tom, tenderly washing the last of the defilement from their faces and what she could of their garments.

She took the water offered by the other kindly dame, and rinsed them off as best she could. She held cups of ale to their lips and gave them pieces of bread and cheese. She decided against giving them the pieces of fruit, considering the circumstances.

Tom was almost helpless with laughter over the stirring and somewhat farcical battle, and so forgave the young fools. He realised that he must have looked a little ridiculous himself. Was he not a young fool himself once?

Turning his head as far as he could (his bull-like neck was very tight in the opening) he noticed that William had taken it all without a blink, although he chuckled a little over the battle scene.

'Dost fit the mold of saint better than I, Father William.' said Tom.

William had no chance to reply, for at that moment Simon and the old retired sergeant came marching up to them, almost dragging a whimpering young lad between them. Tom recognized him at once as one of the youths who had recently indulged in target practice at his expense.

The old sergeant commanded the prisoner to halt, then held up his pitchfork in a military salute.

'One prisoner o' war have we a-taken, m'lord, capting SIRRAH!' he barked, thinking for a moment he was reporting to his commander on the battlefield.

Simon, even more ruddy of face than usual, gave a short laugh. He shoved the young offender forward roughly, growling 'Yea, Martin Gateshead, thou shendful young suckfist! Thou shalt abide the doom of the men thou defilest, by the Beard o' St George, thou shalt!'

The young man trembled before the men in the stocks.

'Grant me ruth[36], good brethren friars,' he stammered out. 'My gokey play-fellows did compel me.'

'Jack-stew!' scoffed farmer John behind him. 'Thou didst hurl as hardily and laugh as loud as t'others o' that shendful frape. What shall we do with thee for thy penance, eh? Face down in the kennels?'

Both Simon and Tom were of a similar opinion and opened their mouths to suggest some embellishments to John's suggestion.

'Nay, Master,' came a quiet but firm voice from the other side of the stocks. 'Much do we owe thee and thy comrades-in-arms for our deliverance. But neither shall I pronounce such a doom on one who hath indeed been led astray.'

William looked steadily at the young man, who turned towards him, trembling with hope.

'This then shall be thy doom, Master Gateshead. The bread of idleness shalt thou eat no more. Thou shalt eschew the company of them that corrupted thee. Rather shalt thou give aid to the worthy folk that hath need, whether for wergild[37] or for naught. Mistress Mary shall give thee good rede in this, if she will, but God and the Holy Angels be my witness if thou dost backslide. Then, woe betide thee!'

'Sickerly shall I counsel him, good Father William.' said Mary, impressed by the forbearance and the wisdom of William's judgment.

36   mercy, pity
37   reward, payment

'Young Master Gateshead hath lost his mother as a child, and gladly shall I succour his young redeless soul.'

All the other witnesses who had remained were equally impressed, and more astonished discussion ensued. They had expected vengeance of the severest kind to be meted out, and this mercy spoke more to them of the kind of gospel that the two evangelists declared than all the preaching in the world from the pulpit.

'Well, by the saints, thou'rt a ruthful man, Father William,' remarked Simon, rubbing his chin, a little ashamed. 'Methought that a severe penance was meet, but I assieve o' thy kind-wit[38] withal.'

He looked sternly but not unkindly at the young man, overcome with relief at his emancipation.

'Mistress Mary be in the right on't, Master Martin Gateshead, and much o' thy tomfoolery be due o' poor ensamplement. Thy father drank hisself a' grave's death. But mark me, then. If thou'lt look to goodly folk anon and be a-leered o' them and fear the good Lord … well … I can give thee labour with pay a' my farm then.'

'Mighty handsome o' thee, Master Hawkes,' said the grateful young man. 'A-farming be what I be a-wishful of for to do. Thanken thee o' thy kindness, Father William. I repent me o' my wood witaldry. God send I be worthy o' thy trust!'

He went off to the pump with Master Hawkes, to wash off his own defilement.

His last statement sparked off a few questions from the assembled audience. They had rarely seen a display of such mercy before. So they asked William's views regarding sin, guilt, penances and redemption. This was an open door too good to miss for Tom and William, and for the moment they forgot that they were bound in stocks for a night and a day, awaiting a hostile bishop's wrath.

The day was fading as the last of the crowd drifted away, but more than a dozen new adherents stayed. Beside Mary and Simon, young Martin and most of Simon's neighbours who had joined in the Battle of Warwick Square, as Tom called it, stayed to guard any other possible attacks on the

---

38   common sense

evangelists. They chatted well into the evening, and Mary fed the captives well, although it was a little messy.

Finally, William persuaded them to leave, for they had their own affairs to attend to, and he wanted them to avoid attracting the unwelcome attention of the authorities. Once or twice, a soldier had been seen crossing the square. He had glanced curiously in their direction, noting the crowd but not interfering.

Tom and William were finally left alone in the dark. Their wrists and their necks chafed at their bondage, and their feet grew weary from constant standing. William wondered aloud if the bishop was aware of their exploits at Coventry.

Then a thought occurred to Tom.

'Father William,' he said conversationally, as though at a meal-table, 'did not the Apostles Paul and Silas pray and sing praises in like bestadance?[39] Did not the good Lord send forth a fearsome earthquake to deliver them? Wherefor do we not pray and sing praises unto God for our deliverance also?'

He spoke as one putting an interesting theory forward, but not treating it seriously. To his surprise, instead of pouring scorn over his suggestion, William thought about it awhile, finding the idea rather appealing.

'Ferly though it seem, I fleer not, Thomas,' he said deliberately.

'Nay!' he laughed as Tom tried to turn his head in astonishment toward him. 'I say not that God shaketh the earth for us anon, for unwilling is He to bring terror on the townsfolk. But my heart tells me that we are called onward, and neither lock nor stock nor bar shall stop us if we be about the King of King's business. There is some sooth in thy janglery.[40] Yea! Let us sing and give thanks even as did the Holy Apostles, whether God deliver us or no.'

Tom laughed at this, thinking what fools they must appear, but thought – why not? What had they to lose? God had commanded them to give thanks in everything – and to rejoice when they were persecuted for Christ's sake. So he began to sing some of their favourite Oxford hymns. William joined in as best he could, and soon they found joy and confidence building within their hearts. They felt strength coming back

---

39   circumstances
40   jesting

to their weary feet, and Tom felt the urge to dance for very joy. They sang louder.

Suddenly, without warning, the huge padlock sprung open and the upper half of the apparatus flew up and open. The two men, being released so suddenly from their bonds, fell over backwards with a startled cry.

Lying on the cobbles, they looked at each other for a moment, then began to laugh uproariously.

Tom sprang up and investigated the locks, wondering if there had been some weakness, but they were sound, well-oiled and solid.

'Come, Thomas.' commanded William, still chuckling. 'We have been given an open door unto freedom. Let us go through without delay. We must return unto Mistress Mary's guesthouse and see what the morrow bringeth.'

'Oh! But that I could look upon his wor'ship's countenance on the morrow when he seeth this,' gasped Tom, between gusts of laughter.

They were also surprised to find their packs and scripts at the foot of the stocks, untampered with. William could have sworn that the soldiers had confiscated them.

Mistress Mary was still in fervent prayer for the two men when Barnabus pricked up his ears, sprung up and raced to the door, barking hysterically. This was followed immediately by a knock at the door.

Suspicious of anyone knocking at the door that late at night, she ran to fetch her brother's club from the corner and returned to the door. But then she discovered that Barnabus had changed his tune, wagging his tail and making cheerful woofings – as to friends.

Nonetheless, she opened the door cautiously, club at the ready, and nearly fainted at what she saw.

Tom laughed, and picked up Barnabus, giving him a friendly shake as the hound tried to lick his face. William helped the flabbergasted dame to a chair.

'But ... but ... Alderman Pugsley would relent never!' she protested. She was rendered almost speechless when William quickly explained the situation.

After she had recovered, stopped blessing herself and shaking her head in wonder, she got up and set about making some supper for them in a businesslike manner. She stopped only to anoint their chafed necks and wrists. The fragrance of pig's lard hung about them for days.

They were about to go and wash their stained habits, but Mary would not have it.

'Get ye to bed, blessed brethren, and I shall be thy lavender[41] this night. Thy stained habits leave ye outside o' thy door. What with all thy faithful labours and sorrows, and to be used despiteously so, then a-working o' holy miracles withal, mighty a-wearied ye must be, dreadless. Ah! Blessings upon ye both, good saints, and goodnight.'

Almost dropping with weariness, the two men kissed her gratefully on the cheek then collapsed on their own beds in the guesthouse. They felt they had already held their "midnight mass" at the stocks.

---

41   Washer woman

Chapter 5: Freedom from Bondage

'Therefore if the Son [shall] make you free, verily ye shall be free.'

(Gospel of John 8:36 Wycliffe/Purvey Translation/Revisions)

That same evening, his worship the mayor was still floating on his cloud of supposed grandeur when his lordship the Earl of Warwick arrived.

Everything of the best had been purchased. Alderman Pugsley had laid out a pretty penny to impress his noble guest.

The Earl of Warwick was a powerful man with large estates and considerable influence with the crown. He was known to be a personal friend and confidante of the Duke of Lancaster, John of Gaunt. A grim-faced, dark-haired aristocrat with a proud bearing, he was not a man to be trifled with. Like most of the austere family Beauchamps, he did not suffer fools gladly.

His lordship arrived arrayed in splendour, although in fact he was certainly not in his best attire, and only brought half his customary retinue. Neither did he assume his best social manner. He regarded his host as a mere common alderman after all. Aldermen, especially men of Pugsley's stamp, were barely tolerated for their occasional usefulness.

His lordship had matters of high state on his mind, together with his quarrels with the bishop of Warwick, his cousin. On top of this was the total rebuilding of his family's pride – Warwick castle. This was a mammoth and complex task, for he was adding huge outer walls and towers. Consequently, he was a little out of temper.

He would have cancelled his engagement if he could, but it was part of his breeding to keep faith with his vassals and others within his influence. Having a rigid sense of duty, he considered it beneath him to be capricious – although there were certainly times when he lapsed.

He greeted his host's bowing and scraping with a curt nod and swept past him into the dining hall.

After the customary trivialities, civilities and courtesies of the occasion had been exchanged (mainly by the host), the mayor began to speak on the matters close to his heart.

Pouring out his best wine in person, he began his carefully rehearsed speech, couched in copious amounts of flattery and simpering that his guest found rather irritating.

Like his cousin, the bishop, his lordship had nothing but contempt for sycophants. But there his similarity in tastes with his cousin ended, and thus did his host display his glaring ignorance and make his biggest blunder.

Alderman Pugsley assumed that all members of the noble house of Warwick were of like mind in upholding the status quo, and held each other in the highest esteem.

'My lord,' said he ingratiatingly 'Be thou greatly assured that thy servant be exceeding zealous to maintain law and peace within thy lordship's realm.'

He raised his own goblet in a toast.

'May the shire of Warwick for aye be weal and the greatest in the land, and redound unto thy glory, my lord.'

His lordship felt a sense of boredom creeping over him, but he bowed his head graciously and lifted his own goblet to his lips without comment.

In happy ignorance of this, his host continued.

'And so great is my zeal, my lord, that straightway have I executed my devoir[42] upon the prayer of thy noble cousin, the bishop.'

The earl immediately put his cup down and looked sharply at his host, his attention caught.

'Say on,' he said in a deep voice, like the calm before a storm.

The mayor was now firmly convinced he was playing his guest like a fish on a line.

'Knowest thou then, my lord, that yester e'en thy venerable and holy cousin did alert thy servant unto the accursed heretical sect of that man of sin, John Wycliffe' he confided, savouring the moment. 'This very day did I happen upon two of his followers – in guise like to our holy friars, markest thou – a-preaching of their damnable heresy in this our town square.'

---

42   duty

163

He became a little discomposed at the look of intense and grim interest on his formidable guest's face, and hastened to reassure him.

'But indeed, I arrested them straightway and placed them in the stocks to await thy noble cousin's pleasure ….'

His voice trailed away as he saw the thunderous look grow on the earl's face.

His lordship sprang up, his eyes blazing, spilling his wine.

'Arrested? The stocks? My cousin's pleasure?' he roared. 'Holy Virgin, thou whining dog of a bretheling! Art thou so redeless as to crawl to that gigelot, Morton, with thy glosery?[43] Him that dare nameth me cousin?'

It seemed to the Mayor that the earth was crumbling beneath his feet.

Pale of face, he stammered 'Pardon... pardon, my lord! Methought….'

'Think then no longer, thou snivelling lurdan,' snapped the earl, 'if thy redeless pate can do such.'

He threw his chair aside, stood over his shrinking host and gripped his collar with his left hand to draw him nearer. His dark eyes glared into the fear-filled lacklustre eyes before him, and he held his index finger in his face. He spoke deliberately, softly but no less menacingly than his outburst.

'Thou shalt go without, yea, even anon and immediate, and release these men. Thou shalt treat them with great worshipfulness. From thine own purse shalt also pay them recompense, *en foison*,[44] for the scathing thou hast done unto them. Dost thou presume to do sheriff's work? And mark me well, Master Mayor. If I hear of such usage of Wycliffe's men at thine hands again, thou shalt be naught but mawtrews.[45] Indeed, in the selfsame stocks shall I lock thee and another shall be mayor in thy place. Dost thou mark me?'

His victim opened and shut his mouth a few times, then nodded. His throat was too dry for any utterance other than squeaks and gulps.

Having completely annihilated the man into a quivering wreck, his lordship threw him back into his chair and felt better for it. He stepped back.

'Then go! I shall await thy return.'

---

43 flattery
44 in abundance
45 pounded meat

The mayor rapidly gathered the shattered pieces of his dignity together, staggered to his feet and ambled off as fast as he could go to the soldier's mess in person. He didn't dare send a servant. He also felt he needed some fresh air and a liquid restorative when his errand was complete.

The men in the mess were broaching their second keg of beer when he burst in, demanding to know where the sergeant was.

An embarrassed silence was broken by his second in command. 'He ... er ... hath gone without, your wor'ship,' he stammered, his voice slightly slurred.

'Wenching, dreadless!' fumed the mayor. 'Thou, man! Hast thou the key to the stocks? Take thou some men and fetch me those prisoners hither. Anon and straightway!'

The flummoxed soldier turned to obey and the mayor called after him

'And mark thou this! Treat them with all honour and courtesy. They shall have all meat and drink to their full desire and to my charge.'

The astonished men muttered among themselves when he left.

'Would that the chincherous[46] old fripperer ope his hutch for us in like manner,' grumbled an old soldier 'Wherefore be he forestraught o'er the prisoners?'

His fellow shrugged his shoulder, being too drunk to think profoundly, belched loudly and poured himself another beer.

The soldiers charged with the errand took a lamp and staggered into the dark. The fresh night air cleared their heads somewhat, so they made haste to the square.

They stopped dead and goggled at the spectacle of the apparatus tidily locked and clean, but empty.

No prisoners were in sight.

The corporal wondered if the beer had deceived his eyesight. He rubbed his eyes.

Trembling, he plucked the mayor's sleeve as that worthy sat, humiliated and silent under the contemptuous but amused stare of his formidable guest. The soldier whispered into his employer's impatient ear.

---

46 tightfisted

This added complication to a disastrous night startled the mayor into unguarded speech.

'What? Gone? Mother of heaven! Wherewithal can they be free?'

'Ho! So the birds have 'scaped the fowler indeed?' came that dreaded mocking voice nearby. 'A sorry warden art thou, Master Mayor. Thou wouldst apprehend innocent men, condemned without trial, then through gross lachesse,[47] they flee?'

The mayor did not know what to say. How many more disasters could happen that night? One more came.

'All shall be amended, my lord, I swear thee,' he protested desperately. 'I shall find of them and recompense of mine own purse.'

'Do so!' came the stern reply. 'His Royal Highness John of Gaunt, hath cast his mantle of protection over that godly man, John Wycliffe. That arrogant papelard the Archbishop and his frape of shapsters would have his head, else. Speak evil of him on thy peril. Mark thou also this, jack-fool: Thou shalt lout and make losengery[48] unto my fat cousin no more, for in two sennights, thou shalt give account – yea, *full* account – of thine office.'

The mayor groaned at this final blow, for there were a few little matters of business he was not too anxious for the earl to look into – nor anyone else in authority. Perhaps he could still win back some favour if he carried out his instructions to the letter, and showed himself a reformed character.

A few desperate transactions with a few corrupt brothers at St Matthew's priory may be necessary before all the books were opened for the earl to see, but it would cost him a pretty penny.

With these gloomy thoughts, he bowed deeply before the terrifying nobleman before him, vowing eternal compliance. The earl left the hall immediately, gathered his following, and proceeded on the journey back to his manor in high good humour. He rarely had the chance to enjoy such sport lately.

The mayor stood watching him go, the ruins of his dreams lying figuratively all around him. He finally retired in a shattered condition to his chambers to spend a sleepless night, planning a rather bleak future.

---

47   negligence
48   'lout' – bow, 'losengery' - flattery

The next morning, he rode into the square with a few soldiers and the sergeant, who was recovering from the consequences of the previous evening's activities.

They had to push through the curious crowd that had gathered around the empty stocks, trying to fathom how the two men had escaped.

Some crossed themselves and muttered, 'Witchcraft!'

Another cried out: 'Nay! It were not witchcraft. Holy Saints they be. Have we not sinned? Like to the good St Paul in prison, dreadless. Come they back in holy wroth to bring doom on our heads.'

'There be earthquakes, and prisoners a-'scapen, then,' prophesied another knowledgeable citizen with a voice of doom, although his facts were a little inaccurate. 'Shut up thine house! Lock up thy daughters!'

'Jack-stew!' bellowed the irritated sergeant, suffering both from a bad headache and from a tongue-lashing by his employer. 'The locks be but a-broken, dreadless. Give way there!'

He and the Mayor closely inspected the huge locks for damage. Finding none, they were mightily mystified. The mayor looked suspiciously at the sergeant.

'Hast thou but two keys? Can aught other ope the lock?'

'Naught else, I swear it your wor'ship!' asserted the harassed officer.

At that very moment, Tom, William, Mary and Simon were passing through the square on the far side. Tom and William's faces had become too well known for them to pass unnoticed. Soon the cry went up from those nearest them.

'The holy men! The Wycliffe preachers! The workers o' ferly wonders, by the faith!'

Many crowded around them, asking how they got out and whether they were Holy Saints or Evil Warlocks, as they crossed themselves.

Of course, this was too good an opportunity for Tom to pass up. He leapt up to the town crier's podium again and held up his hands for silence.

Spurning any charge of witchcraft or undue sanctity, he told them all frankly what happened. He waited a while as all the excitement and buzzing of 'Aye! It were soothly a miracle!' died down. He had their attention now.

Beginning with the obvious theme of freedom from bondage, this time he preached the gospel without interruption. Their persecutors, even though they were present, were silenced and in a chastened, bemused frame of mind.

'Satan would have ye all bound in the stocks of dead works, penances and empty piety,' Tom declared, barely restraining his laughter at the awed expressions on the faces of his listeners. 'But Christ hath come to set the prisoner free! Yea! Free to find salvation through His grace alone. Free to love the Father and pray to Him *without* intermediary – save Christ. Free to taste the joys of heaven. But what, then, be the key? Wilt thou place thine affections on God the Father and Christ His Blessed Son? Or wilt thou cling rather to vain religion and empty piety? That is thy choice. That is the key.'

Then William took up the theme and quoted from Wycliffe's translation.

'Thus said the good Lord Jesu to the Jews that believed in him: "If ye dwell in My word, verily ye shall be my disciples; and ye shall know the truth, and the truth shall make you free."'

The people were amazed to hear the Holy Scriptures spoken so freely in their own tongue, and many felt the power of it gripping them.

William went on to urge them to follow the scriptures rather than the traditions of men, even if these came from supposed spiritual authorities.

Despite some murmurings from those who were still steeped in tradition, many more believed because of the miracle of their release from the stocks – and the release they themselves were experiencing in the power-filled preaching.

At least thirty more committed themselves to new faith in Christ, joining the swelling number of disciples. Others were seriously thinking about it.

The two evangelists were kept busy as a new gathering of disciples was established. Mary Langland offered her guesthouse as a meeting place.

When he had the first opportunity, the mayor approached them and humbly apologised, hat in hand, more with a view to prevent legal reprisal and to appease the earl than from any change of heart. He was very pragmatic about his spiritual state.

He felt himself caught between the hammer of the earl's wrath and the anvil of the bishop's inevitable wrath. The two evangelists had become a major embarrassment, but he could not stop them now.

'The very reverent Bishop Morton loveth not thy master, Doctor Wycliffe,' he urged persuasively, 'hence thy weal be imperilled should he find you in this place. I beg of you, sirrahs, delay not thy departure.'

He offered them a 'parting gift of goodwill' as reparation for their mistreatment at his hands. He pulled out a large cloth purse that jingled. Midst the "Oo's" and "Aah's" of the crowd, he placed it in Tom's hands and would not listen to his demur.

Tom and William had already planned to continue their journey in the next few days, so they graciously accepted the mayor's apology and promised to leave soon.

The mayor was relieved and left, not knowing what to make of them.

Tom shook the rather heavy bag handed to them and discovered that it was full of golden coins. He whistled softly. But after exchanging nods with William in tacit agreement, he gave the bag to Mary.

'Mistress Mary, we ken of naught that would use this as sagely nor as honestly as thou and Master Simon. Wilt thou share it as thou reckon 'twould be meet among them that have need?'

Mary held the bag with a look of dazed wonder, her eyes filling with tears. Her selfless prayers for many poor folk were being answered. This was a happy day for her in another way as well.

'Keep thy tears for our wedding day, Mary my dear,' said Simon in a rallying tone, pushing through the applauding group of disciples.

'Ah, 'Tis fortunate for thee we be handfasted[49] this morn, Simon Hawkes" riposted the lady, wiping her eyes happily and taking his hand. 'Else the good folk be a-thinken o' thee as had covertise withal, and would wed but a bag of gold. But anon have I a man at hand at last! If the roof faileth or the fowls do avoid their pen once more, I shall be at rest.'

'Then peace hath come to thine house at the last,' laughed William, embracing her and wringing the hand of the groom-to-be.

Tom and William spent the last days answering questions of the interested, and strengthening the new local disciples. Their numbers grew rapidly

---

49   betrothed

One of their new disciples was one of the earl's huntsmen and astringers, who could read and write. He was delighted to comply with William's request to assist Mary to read scripture portions regularly at the disciples' reading circle. He also gleefully regaled them with the tale of Alderman Pugsley's discomfiture, although it had been a little embellished in the manner of servants' gossip. It did not take long for the story to spread among the populace.

Needless to say, the evangelists and their disciples were greatly encouraged by the spectacular evidence of God's divine intervention, and Tom never ceased to shake his head in wonder at it. The former sergeant, now demoted for dereliction of duty, often visited the stocks to try to fathom the mystery, even to his dying day.

Waving farewell to the saddened but grateful disciples, the wayfaring preachers travelled further south.

Tom sang lustily:

> 'Nor lock, nor bar, nor whip, nor goad
> Keepeth the wayfarer from his road.
> For naught on earth a power there be
> To keep him from his destiny.'

Chapter 6: Out of the Mouths of Babes

*'Truly I say to you, whoever shall not take the Kingdom
of God as a child, he shall not enter into it.'*

(Gospel of Luke 18:17 Wycliffe/Purvey Translation)

Not all of the missionaries' stops were as eventful as at Warwick, but for Father Richard Brandon, journeying east with Master Harold Ravenswood, their stay in the village of Quainton was one of the highest points of their entire mission.

Just as their colleagues on other missions, Father Richard and Harold soon developed a daily rhythm that served them well wherever they went.

They prayed together early each morning, seeking direction from the Holy Spirit, wisdom and strength for the day.

There had been, however, a few mornings when Harold awoke to find Father Richard already on his knees, agonising in prayer, looking as though he had hardly slept.

Concerned, his disciple once asked him what the problem was.

'My mind is under siege, Harold lad,' he said wearily. 'I wake to a deluge of thoughts of mine unworthiness. Mine own sinful follies of youth returneth in terrible gainbite.[50] Thoughts of fear, yea, even impurity. A-times I meditate a-till my mind churneth unto a garboil. But it then it passeth.'

He covered his head in frustration.

'Pray thou for me, my son.'

Although he had not experienced such attacks, Harold prayed with him as best he could. He appreciated the humility of the man in admitting his weakness, but it shook him a little to see this broad-shouldered man, whom he had come to regard as a solid rock, so vulnerable.

---

50 remorse, guilt

Earnest prayer and study of the scriptures brought temporary relief, but for how long?

Nonetheless, weak or strong, their mission called them onwards, so they prayed for direction, as was their custom.

Normally they felt drawn toward the villages eastward of their position.

If God had not already opened opportunities for them, they would approach the first freehold farms they could find and offer to give the farmer a few hours' labour in return for a meal and a place to rest, even if it were only a bed of hay in the cow byre.

The surprised farmers agreed to such generous terms almost without fail, since skilled labour was rather scarce or too expensive. This often led to interesting discussions where the evangelists could share their message in a way the villagers and labourers could understand. What many farmers and workers ignored or dozed through at Mass, they gave a willing ear to out in the field – especially if the preachers wielded a sickle as willingly and ably as Harold and Father Richard did while they preached. Both had been farmer's sons before they heard God's call, although Harold had also been a wainwright's apprentice for a season.

One farmer told him of the need for a wainwright in Quainton. This inspired Harold to suggest that they try the village directly. Who knows? Maybe they would find an apothecary, herbalist or physician that could give Richard some relief from his insomnia. Father Richard, looking heavy-eyed, nodded his head in tired acquiescence.

And so they arrived at the village of Quainton.

It was normally a quiet and picturesque village, but on this occasion it was buzzing with excitement. The villagers and many from neighbouring Waddeston were gathering at the big cross to watch the last touches being put on their new church.

'Our own church it be, thanks be to God and the blessed St Mary!' cried an ecstatic young matron proudly, hugging her youngest child.

'Yea and verily,' said the reeve, standing on the uppermost step, nodding his satisfaction. 'The Lord's Day nigh, we be a-trampen weary feet to worship at Cuddington and Aylesbury church no more.'

The newcomers, wearing russet habits were very soon noticed. The peasant folk, in their simple goodwill, welcomed them as holy men.

'Ye come in a good hour, brethren! Come ye and rejoice with us!' called the reeve above a chorus of welcoming voices. 'Give them a tankard o' thy good ale, Master Taverner.'

The villagers gladly gave them work as they requested, and rewarded them with the warmest hospitality and a ready ear for their message. They listened in wonder at the Word of God spoken in their own tongue. Even at the first invitation, a good number stayed to hear more, and not a few committed their lives in response to the Spirit's call.

The reeve, although he was rather cautious about '..this ferly foreign preachin'..', was impressed by the missionaries' honesty, fervour and simple lifestyle.

'But more godly men do ye seem than many a freer that do abide among us, Father Richard,' he admitted.

Although no one in the village had even basic literacy, the new disciples faithfully and earnestly memorised the English scripture portions that the missionaries patiently rehearsed for them.

'Worthy folk, these,' observed Harold appreciatively, 'The backbone of England. The salt of the earth.'

'Witterly,' affirmed Father Richard, collapsing wearily on his bed of hay. 'There be hope for this land if there be many such.'

* * * * * *

Meanwhile, the southern mission under Father William Shephard and lay preacher Thomas Plowman continued to prosper, although local superstitions were a little inclined to impede the message occasionally.

One farmer's wife ran into her neighbour's place, big with news.

'Martha, my dear!' she panted excitedly, 'I beheld me a holy vision o' heaven! It were the good Saint Francis hisself, it were. He be a-sitten in the swine's sty with our sickened piglet on his knee, a-tenden it. And he a-holden speech with my Walter – as vowed he never again would hearken to the liesings o' them false friars. And mark ye this: my Wat be a-hearken full earnest, aye, with tears a-pouren down his chaps. 'Tis soothsaw, I tell thee!'

'A holy miracle it be then!' said Martha, round-eyed with amazement. 'What sayeth he him – the good St Francis?'

'He were a-tellen a tale – e'en a Parallabull – as did the good Lord Jesu Himself.'

They both piously crossed themselves.

'What manner o' tale be this …. Parallabull ?' enquired her neighbour, a little awed at her friend's theological superiority.

'It were a tale of a wastrel son as did spend o' his father's liven, but found his gainbite in the swine's wallowings – or such ... I stayed not for the rest, lest the good saint did frown upon my boldiness. But to beholden my wild Wat a-weepen afore Saint Francis hisself! ... Aye! An holy vision it be dreadless!'

Village folk and townsfolk alike found the two men a refreshing change from the motley of friars, pardoners and palmers who came begging and even demanding meals or money from them – hinting at Divine Wrath if they refused.

But these new ministers of the gospel were also learning valuable lessons themselves as they were busy imparting truth. Among other things, they learned that God has a wonderful sense of humour.

They were washing in the cold, clean waters of the river Stour. William was vigorously drying his hair. Suddenly, he put the cloth down and sat in troubled thought. In spite of all their victories, he felt like a failure. He was unaware of his good friend Richard Brandon's similar struggles.

'..And the Blood of Jesus cleanseth us from all sin,' he quoted aloud, as though trying to convince himself. 'Wherefore then do my sins come back to torment me, Thomas? Must we seek forgiveness again and yet again for what is passed, to find our heart's release? Whither the good 'Saint William' now?'

'I wist of thine heart's cry, Father William, but too well,' replied Tom with unaccustomed gravity. 'Time was when I regarded not the depth of my failings, trusting to the priest's assoilment, but that is vain as we know well. We reap whatsoever we sow, for God is not mocked. After such a sacrifice at Holy Cross, why do we still fail and fall? Is our mission but in vain? Are we not indeed unworthy of this calling?'

But his solemnity could not last. He jumped to his feet.

'But fie upon these dark thoughts! Sinners we be, but also redeemed by His grace. If we our message believe not, then how can we proclaim it?'

William threw the cloth aside and got wearily to his feet.

'That is sooth, O my young sage. 'Tis spoken with a lion's mouth also. Well … if true saints or holy angels there be naught so to do, then fallen man must proclaim God's truth. God save us and aid us.'

It was not the first time these fits came upon him. Sometimes this burden of guilt would cast a pall on their mission, but their sense of duty never wavered. There was a task to do, whatever their own inner struggles may be.

They walked on toward Shipton on Stour. Their path was unexpected crossed by a tall, blond-haired, ugly but cheerful-looking freehold farmer in his thirties, walking over to his fields from his house.

He bade them a friendly, 'Good morrow, good brethren. Friar-brethren do ye seem, yet ye have the likeness o' real men. Whither are ye bound?'

They explained their mission and offered to give him a hand in exchange for a meal and a bed.

Surprised and delighted, he gratefully accepted. He looked at their habit curiously, but shook hands and introduced himself as Farmer Oswald. He would have freely shown them hospitality in any case, even without their offer to lend a hand – such was his bigheartedness. However, he was hurrying to complete his first harvest before the dreaded Spring-rot spoilt it, so he was grateful for any help, especially if it was virtually free.

His two youngest children came out to watch as the three men and his oldest son laboured quickly and efficiently through the morning.

William also went off to attend to some problems with the farmer's livestock.

'Mighty welcome ye be any-days, good brethren,' declared farmer Oswald, clapping them both on the back when the last bale was stored high and dry.

'Aye!' affirmed his taciturn son, plodding along behind them. He was as large as his father but not as outgoing. Shy at first, he had thawed considerably under the strangers' benign influence and was not a little in awe of their strength and skill.

'Yea, even so sayeth my lad, as is wont to be a-sayen naught,' laughed his father. 'The barley harvest be done and the ewes be a-lambing right well, to thy thanks a-plenty. Ye have earned ye your meat, yea, manifold and more. Come ye in for bread and cheese and meat. My good dame be the finest and fairest cheese-maker this side o' the shire.'

Inside his farmhouse, his worthy dame, a comely and kindly woman, fed them well. Her lord's boast had not been an empty one, for her cheese was the best the two men had tasted, and they said so. The good woman kindly promised to pack some away when they were to journey on, since it kept well.

As the men sat back, sipping their mead, the youngest daughter of the household came and stood before Tom, looking up admiringly and inquiringly at him with large, liquid blue eyes. Although she had her mother's good looks, she also had her father's outgoing nature.

'Pwithee, Mathter Thomath,' she lisped with all the forthrightness of an innocent seven-year-old, 'wherefore doth Fwiar Jonath beggeth and pweacheth, but thou and good Father Thaint William do both work and pweach?'

Tom's sunny smile broadened into merriment and he looked toward William to see how he liked his title.

'Thy fame goeth before thee, Father "Thaint" William,' he commented softly.

Their hosts roared with laughter. William forced a smiled that went awry.

The lady of the house, unaware of the battles that occasionally raged in William's soul, explained with a smile how little Elsbeth had said that William resembled her idea of Saint Francis. He looked so kind and had made her pet lamb better.

Tom lifted the young lady onto his lap. 'Little Lady Elsbeth,' he said in a grave, avuncular manner, 'Good Friar Jonas be an holy man, surely, or so hope we.'

The farmer snorted in derision. Tom ignored it and continued.

'But neither he nor we, nor even Father William be as holy as the good Saint Paul the Apostle. Did not he labour full well as a maker of tents and preach also? Was not even the good Lord Jesus Himself but a carpenter and wandering preacher? We but pursue their holy ensamples, sinners though we be.'

The girl thought about it for a while, then flung her arms as far as she could around his neck, much to his surprise.

'Thou be-etht no Thinner, Mathter Thomath, thickerly,' she objected with a giggle.

Tom was absolutely delighted. He was obliged to exercise powerful self-restraint lest the little lady be offended at the bubble of merriment which threatened to burst out of him. Her father was not so restrained, but she ignored his unseemly mirth, hopped off Tom's knee and approached William shyly.

She fixed her large serious eyes upon his smiling grey ones.

'Father Thaint William. Dotht thou not heal people like ath thou didtht heal my Bethie?'

Her mother, torn between her own mirth and disapproval of her lord's, explained to Tom that "Bethie" or Bessie was the name of Elspeth's pet lamb.

The reluctant saint put his hand on the engaging child's shoulder.

'God alone doth heal, my little one, this time with the blessed herbs of His creating. Yea, and if thou wilt also eat of the good herb thy dear mother put before thee at meat, thou also shalt be as blithesome and quicksome as thy little Bessie. But Master Thomas speaketh wisdom, my child. We are not Saints, but sinners saved by the Grace of God.'

She continued to stare at him as she digested his words.

'Then, if it be by the Gwaithe of God that thou'rt thaved, thou'rt no more a Thinner, Father Thaint William,' she argued.

The childlike wisdom of that eternal truth, coming from a seven-year-old's lips, struck William like a bolt of silent lightning. He sat there stunned. It was God speaking, through a little girl's lips.

Why could he not simply accept God's grace even as did the child who stood before him?

'Bless my beard! Is that not the armour I need?' he thought. 'Have I been so sand-blind, priest and preacher of the gospel though I be? 'Tis such a simple truth, even a sely child may comprehend.'

Thomas was also struck by her statement of faith and turned a glowing face toward William.

'Out of the mouth of babes and sucklings hast thou ordained strength,' he quoted.

The little girl gave William a big hug and then ran out to play with her twin brother.

Tom and his hosts could finally give vent to their pent-up laughter. But to William, the moment was too precious to laugh at.

Ever after, William had a special welcome for children.

When they had eaten, farmer Oswald arose.

'Come ye and meet our good neighbours, if ye will. Ye have won me spare hours to play with, so mayhap the Harwells or the Trents be glad o' more hands. It be a rare treat for us all that holy men be a-worken right hearty o' their hands for us, by my fay. And as hearty and robust be thy message, by the Saints. Aye, and too good for but one old jobbard's ears to be a-hearing. What say ye?'

Happy to gain a wider audience for their message, the two preachers agreed, and the three sallied forth down the road to the next longhouse, with Tom and Oswald still chuckling over the little girl's profound wisdom.

It wasn't long before three families had both heard and received the message of God's grace and salvation. They formed the nucleus of a new disciple gathering. One young woman, the oldest daughter of the Trent family, was sufficiently literate to read regularly the portions of scripture that William could spare. She had taught herself to read determinedly, in spite of the local parson's disapproval. In his view, women were house-keepers, not scholars. In the end her perseverance caused him to relent. It wasn't often that a charming young person came to him for tutoring.

She sought out Tom whenever she could while they stayed, and discussed many portions of scripture. She marvelled at his knowledge and quick wit. When she learned that he was a lay-preacher and not subject to a celibate vow, her visits became more frequent.

When the evangelists announced that it was time for them to leave, she was deeply disappointed. She confessed her feelings for him to her mother that night, holding back her tears bravely. Her mother, a wise woman, conceded that he could be good husband material, but his calling was paramount at present.

'But only God knoweth, my child, the path before him and thee. If it is written above, he shall return. If not, there be a-many and a-many worthy swains that would seek thine hand.'

This did not particularly comfort the girl, but she conceded the possible truth in it all.

Tom, however, was too taken up with his call to be distracted by a pretty girl. She was a sweet child, as he had said when William made casual enquiries about her frequent visits. It was Tom's opinion that she would make a good wife for a fortunate young man, but she would never be seriously interested in a penniless preacher. William was rather relieved.

At the end of each day, the two men had what William called, the "evening sacrifice" where they gave thanks for the day's successes, debriefed and prayed for God's blessing on those they had touched.

Tom sometimes called it 'Vespers' or even 'Midnight Mass' if it was rather late.

On the day that little Elspeth had taught him such a powerful truth, William prayed with even greater fervour than usual.

'Blessed God and Heavenly Father, how we thank Thee for Thy glorious grace. Thy blessing bestow upon the little one that showeth us the path of faith to receive thy "gwaithe". Who are we to eschew such a blessed gift in despite of Thy holy command?'

This revelation gave him the strength he needed whenever the enemy tried to attack his mind again. In the end, the tormenting thoughts stopped coming altogether.

* * * * * *

It was night in Quainton village.

Father Richard Brandon could not sleep.

The more fervently he preached and read the scriptures to the people,

the louder the mocking voices of condemnation echoed in his head. In the
end, he asked Harold to finish the work that day.

'Thou'rt a wise minister of the gospel and showeth great skill, my son. I
shall hie me to my bed, for I am a-wearied more than my wont. Methinks
it be weariness of heart.'

His disciple nervously took on this responsibility, glancing anxiously
at his mentor's drooping frame as he went into the night.

But after tossing and turning in frustration upon his bed of straw,
Father Richard felt that the night air would be more beneficial.

He found himself walking, almost as though being drawn toward the
new church. He liked the smell of freshly hewn and chiselled stone, and
he was curious to see how it looked on the inside. It might take his mind
off his troubles.

In the light of the moon, he noticed that the door had not yet been
issued with a lock. He had little regard for the local taboo that prohibited
villagers from entering an undedicated church, so he pulled open the
freshly-stained door and walked in undaunted.

In the dim light, he noticed that benches had been installed, so he
knelt in a dark corner and bowed his head in prayer.

'God, have mercy upon me, a sinner,' he whispered.

There was a very light footstep at the doorway.

He stopped and listened. Was that the door opening? There was no
wind.

He could hear the unmistakable soft padding of a child's gait, and
then a small shadow approached the railing before the sanctuary and knelt
down. Father Richard was sure he had seen him before.

Of course! He was the little boy that had sat in on the disciple
gatherings, hanging on every word that the missionaries had said. The
child had not been told that it was sacrilege to be in an un-consecrated
church, let alone wandering off from home at night alone. He didn't see
Father Richard kneeling in the dark.

Then he prayed, softly but clearly, a prayer that Father Richard never
forgot.

'Faver, Lord God, good Lord Jesu, I fank Thee. Fank Thee that Faver
Richard and Masser Harold have come. Fank Thee for a Holy Bible we can
know full well. Fank Thee that it saif that good Lord Jesu did die ....'

For a moment, his young voice was suspended with tears. He sniffed loudly,…. for all my sins, and I be forgiven, and I go to heaven. Fank Thee that Faver and Movver love Thee and love each ovver anon, and do strive and shout no more. Thou makest me so happy. I want to be a preacher when I be a-growed, and make all men to love Thee also, just like as do good Faver Richard and Masser Harold.'

He blew his nose, got up and skipped out of the church, humming the tune of a hymn that Harold had taught them.

To Father Richard, it seemed as though all heaven stopped to listen to the child's prayer. The faith-filled words seemed to echo throughout the church: '….good Lord Jesu did die …. for all my sins, and I be forgiven, and I go to heaven.'

A voice in Richard's heart spoke: 'Unless ye believe ….as a little child …. for such is the kingdom of heaven.'

Richard wept with repentance at his lack of childlike faith, and suddenly felt the cloud of guilt lifting and blowing away in a sudden gust of joy. He jumped up and ran out of the church and into the woods near the common, where he could safely vent the laughter that was bubbling up from within him.

When he returned to the house where he was staying, he found Harold, looking worried, walking around outside with a smoking torch, looking for him. Father Richard came up laughing and embraced him in the biggest bear-hug Harold had experienced. He gasped for breath. Father Richard was no weakling.

Instead of the burdened and tormented soul he last saw, Harold found him standing tall, strong and confident.

' "For such is the kingdom of heaven." Remember it well, my son,' he said joyfully, and laughed when he saw his disciple blink at him, mystified.

'Shall expound it thee a' morning's light, my son. Soundly shall I sleep this night.'

Chapter 7: Rich Man, Poor Man

"Lythe and listin, gentilmen,
That be of frebore blode;
I shall you tel of a gode yeman,
His name was Robyn Hode."

-A Gest of Robyn Hode

(An early printed Robin Hood ballad – author unknown)

'Behold, brethren!' announced Father Simon Cole in his usual dramatic style, throwing his arms wide and turning slow circles as they passed under the ancient branches, 'We are come to Sherwood Forest at last. Ever have I desired to walk in its glades, to feel the phantom of the great Locksley himself therein. Swift and true were his shafts, and seldom did they fail of their mark!'

'Verily, and so it is Sherwood,' said Father Edward Smithdon, carefully checking their bearings with the hand-drawn map he carried everywhere. 'That fat rascal taverner spoke in very sooth, though I doubted his word.'

Edward was equally fascinated by the Robin Hood legends, but more from an academic and historical perspective than from the sense of romance of his more fanciful friend. They stared in wonder at the great mass of ancient Oaks, Elms, Beeches and many others that once formed the green mansions of the most famous outlaw of all time.

But Sherwood's fair robes of green were changing hue with the coming of Autumn. Gusty winds swirled orange, red, gold and brown leaves around their bare feet as they trudged along the old road that transversed the ancient wood. Some of the russet leaves indeed almost matched the colour of their habits and cloaks.

The trees swayed and bowed and creaked, waving their branches majestically as they joined in the merry song and dance with the exuberant winds and chattering leaves. It almost sounded like the laughter of a merry band of elvish children, dancing through the glades, running rings around the strangers and leaping from branch to branch, as though celebrating harvest time.

The younger man with them, although interested and proud of the local the legends (being locally born), was not quite as enthusiastic as his elders. He was raised near the border of Nottinghamshire. Local folk often take local famous landmarks for granted. He was keen to move on to the next village, for Master Peter loved people. But being the apprentice, so to speak, he had only limited say as to their agenda.

'Peter, my lad,' said the ever curious Father Edward, 'thou'rt Lincolnshire-born, art thou not? What sayeth the Lincolnshire village folk of the great Locksley? Was he truly the knight in Lincoln-green armour that is said of him, or doth legend but lie?'

Peter thought for a moment, scratching his nose.

'Some folk there be that do swear by the tale as God's gospel, but others – indeed, at harvest's end yestere'en, Master Adamson o' the Blue Boar declareth that there be many Locksleys. "And scoundrels all be they!" quoth he, "for in the days o' my great grandsire they would come a-drinken all o' his ale and pay not a farthing."'

The good mimicry of the fat taverner's voice and manner made Simon and Edward laugh.

'Ha!' scoffed Edward the sceptic, giving Simon a mildly derisive eye. ''Tis as I deemed, brother. Even an old wives' tale to enthral the simple.'

'Not so!' asserted Simon the believer, staunchly. 'False and scurrilous heroes, these braggarts, but Robin Hood lived! And liveth doth he still within the hearts of them that seek to right the wrongs of this iniquitous age. Do not we so do? Perchance there be men in these very woods that hath the spirit of the Hood within them.'

'And sayeth the good folk that there be outlaws dwelling in these woods still?' Edward asked Peter, looking warily at the trees they passed.

'Nay, 'Tis safe indeed, Father, else would I have spoken,' answered Peter. 'For the King sent his men to aid the sheriff to rake the woods clean of lawless men. Many fled southward. With the ebbing o' the Black Plague, labourers were in great need, so many there were that returned to honest toil once more, 'Tis said. Naught hath been seen or heard of outlaws these days. Natheless, poachers still roam the woods oft and anon, seeking the king's deer and other game.'

This rather prosaic explanation of the state of affairs in Sherwood was rather disappointing to Simon Cole, the orator of the three companions. Although he was thirty-eight summers, well educated and hardened in limb, he still viewed life as a romantic adventure.

'Alas! Gone are the days of great chivalry and noble deeds. O, that men would arise once more and assail injustice, bringing hope unto the hopeless, cheer unto the cheerless, as friends of the friendless...'

Edward shook his head at him in friendly mockery.

'Wilt thou hearken unto the ravings of Father John Ball then, my friend?'

'God forbid! Yet did even he have a noble vision ere he fell into a gall of bitterness.'

Peter turned eagerly toward him.

'Ah but, Father Simon, doth not Doctor Evangelicus take up this thy call to champion them that be oppressed? Are we not sent forth to bring hope, to befriend the friendless? There be some that speak of the ghost of Locksley himself that roameth these very woods, wreaking vengeance upon the unjust and the oppressor.'

'Ha! Soothly said, my son. The spirit of Robin of Locksley is upon us still; yet we steal not, nor rob. Rather do we save from the hand of the great fiend whatsoever he would kill, steal and destroy...'

'Say also that we defeat his lies with the Truth of the Word of God,' Edward interjected tartly. 'Have done with these ferly fables, Simon. We fight with weapons that are not carnal. Therefore, did not Robin Hood – if indeed he be truly one man – did not he do ill that he fought evil by the arm of the flesh?'

He was a lawyer turned theologian. Truth and plain facts were his passion.

'Nay!' objected Simon, 'God shall call us a-times to smite the ungodly with the edge o' the sword, even as King David of old smote the Philistines.'

'No longer do we live in such perilous days, Simon. War hath ceased in France. God send this peace shall last! War is an evil beast that devoureth good men, our precious victuals and the wealth of the land. Strife enow is there 'mongst our own people – even within Holy Church.'

'And what of the poor common folk?' interjected Peter, the young shepherd. 'Will not they suffer and starve whilst we debate matters of law and right? Locksley, though thief he was, did but aid the poor. His day is passed. Who anon shall champion their cause in his stead?'

Edward, the lawyer-theologian thought about this for a while. He felt equally as strongly about injustice after all.

'But to defy the powers that be? Nay! Saint Paul himself forbade it, my son. Doctor Evangelicus himself declareth their plight where'r he goeth and hath won greater following than the Hood, I deem. God hearkeneth to the cry of the needy. Methinks our missions shall be of greater good than rebellion and the taking up of arms ever shall.'

Simon only partially agreed with Edward's wisdom, and the debate continued for the next few miles.

After that, the three fell silent as they turned onto the larger road that came up from Southwell. The wailing and whistling of the wind drowned out the steady crunch and swish of their shoeless feet wading through the drifts of restless leaves.

That was why the poacher was taken completely unaware when they came upon him around a sharp bend in the road. As they approached, he was furtively and rapidly stuffing a dead forest pheasant into a dirty cloth bag. His blond hair and beard were dishevelled and he was obviously not well-fed. He bore all the appearance of having been driven by desperation to a vocation he was not at all comfortable with.

Peter raised his finger to his lips and arched a questioning eyebrow to his seniors. The others exchanged looks and nodded, tacitly agreeing that they would not interfere. The poacher typified the many desperate men who had hungry families, and went looking for illicit means when law-abiding means fell short of filling their stomachs. Even Edward, a strong advocate for integrity and adherence to the law, could reluctantly sympathize – in his previous calling he had not always been guiltless himself.

The poacher had his back to them as they passed quietly. With the sounds of nature vociferously drowning most others, he would never have known of their presence, had a twig not snapped loudly under the toughened sole of Simon's bare foot. The man spun around with a startled cry and bolted with his booty. In his haste, he did not see a protruding tree root. His foot caught and he fell heavily with a groan of pain and anguish. Dazed, he tried to rise again, but swore when he tried to stand on his right foot, and collapsed in a pile of leaves. (If the good Saint Aidan heard what the unfortunate man said then, he may have been rather indignant – if real saints had that kind of dignity.)

Hagiology, however, was not on Peter's mind as he ran forward to assist the fallen sinner.

'O master, what folly is this? We be no foemen that thou shouldst so flee thus heedless.'

Without awaiting permission, he whipped off the old worn-out boot from the man's injured foot, as another saint's name was loudly and irreverently invoked in response to the surge of pain that followed. It was hastily muffled as the man realised that he was in the presence of holy men. He took off his rather shapeless cap and buried his face in it with a moan of despair and pain.

'*Not* one of Robin's merry men, methinks,' Edward remarked dryly and came up to tend the ankle with some herbal remedies he carried in his scrip. He pulled a face at the unnatural shape of the anklebone.

'Fear not, my son,' said Simon reassuringly, sitting on a small bank nearby. 'We are come not to condemn, but to bring hope unto the hopeless, and help unto the helpless as my comrade-brethren would say.'

'Nay, brethren … fathers,' groaned the man in his broad Norfolkshire brogue, 'there be no hope nor help for me. I be accursed o' heaven for my sinnin' I be, thankin' ye fo' y'r kindlyness. Tell ye not his Lor'ship, I beg o' ye, or I be a-losen o' my right maw – and halt-foot into the bargain.'

He winced at Edwards gentle but firm ministrations.

'God ha' mercy! My only sin be a-carin' over-much for my Mary and the little ones all, that they famish not. Winter's wastening be on our heels, and naught to stave off our want save a fistful o' corn ungrounded. My fellows all, that have naught o' kith to mind, they did bolt fo' the woods, and be a-findin' open-handed masters that pay just wages. Ah, but his chincherous lordship (Lord Southwell he be) do he make remembrance that I keep my post then? No. Rather doth he ply the whip to work the work o' them that be gone and pay me not near my worth. He setteth his fat pigeons to devour mine own corn, my livelihood – and woe be to the poor wretch that bid them begone!'

He winced again, wiped his nose with his sleeve, then chuckled reminiscently.

'But there be pigeon-brose in the pot a-time and anon, and his lor'ship none the wiser.'

Realising how imprudent this boast was, he studied his new clerical acquaintances warily.

There was something different about them.

Peter was trying to hide a smile, while the older men looked sympathetic rather than disapproving. Edwards hands were noticeably tough and calloused, as he deftly bound and splinted the ankle,. The poacher scratched his head, disturbing a few fleas.

'Be ye friars then, brethren? Thine arms, thine hands be as they that wield a sickle full mighty, be sure. Ne'er seen I the colour o' thy cloth aforetime.'

Peter grinned at him as he knelt to aid Edward in his work.

'Verily, not a few have so spoken, master. But doth not the name of John Wycliffe be of significance unto thee?'

The fleas' nest suffered another earthquake. The name did sound familiar.

'Wycliffe? As clear as St Ninian's well be that name,' muttered the poacher 'Clear but not clear enow. Mayhap there be some tale a' the village on him. Be he the head o' thy brotherhood?'

In answer, Simon immediately launched into a glowing tribute to the great man. This naturally led onto the message of their mission, which he delivered with great vigour and passion, striding back and forth and stopping to sit by the fascinated man as he explained a relevant point.

Simon had studied hard under Master Ashton's tutorage, but his fervour, honesty and love for the Author of the message was what impressed his audience the most. Even Edward and Peter never tired of hearing him preach, and they paused in their administrations and listened.

Simon was reaching the climax of the story of his own spiritual odyssey when the sound of a horse's whinny in the distance interrupted them. The wind had died down a little, and the unmistakeable thud-thud of many approaching horses could be heard, together with voices raised in argument.

Natural instinct immediately overrode spirituality.

'His Lor'ship! Sheriff's men!' the poacher whispered, and staggered rapidly out of sight.

Not a moment too soon. Eight riders came around the corner at a leisurely pace.

The leading rider was richly dressed, richly mounted and richly endowed with flesh. He did not appear to be enjoying his riches, however, judging by the peevish expression that seemed natural to him.

His companion, although better proportioned, wore a plain but obviously well-made knight's habit. His air and demeanour were sufficient to proclaim an officer with authority, even without the device on his sword and shield. He also wore the expression of a man nearly at the end of his patience.

Six stolid-looking men-at-arms followed on plain troopers' horses, two bearing the Southwell livery. The other four, as Peter immediately recognised, wore the insignia of Nottinghamshire.

'My Lord,' the Sheriff was saying in a weary voice, 'to pursue thy vassals unto the far corners of the land is *not* within my writ.'

'And what then of the Statute of Labourers, my Lord Sheriff?' came the peevish reply. 'Do we make our laws but to flout them? How shall we work our lands, else? Many and a-many of my plowmen have forsaken their posts and fled, curse them, and now it doth appear that my best labourer Rolph hath taken to poaching, if he hath not fled unlawfully also.'

The sheriff was striving to keep his temper in check.

'Thy good neighbours, my lord, have used their vassals with greater wisdom than them that did pass such a law. Good wages do they pay. The Statute, my lord, is a law most ill-conceived that...'

At that moment, he noticed the travellers on foot. Peter had hidden the telltale boot under his garments just in time. Edward was putting away his herbal concoctions, while Simon leaned on his staff, looking intently at the fat nobleman in growing disapproval. Lord Southwell raised his eyebrows in mild surprise.

'Holà, good brethren!' he said with some semblance of courtesy, reigning in and staring hard at them. 'Travelling friars from the south art thou? Hast thou seen a rag-dagged scoundrel, Rolph Howard by name, in thy journeyings? Or hast heard rumour of his goings? An ill-favoured rascal, white of hair and white of beard. I misdoubt me that he hath a-stolen of the king's game and forsaken his plough. Hence I have called upon the good sheriff to aid in my pursuit.'

'And hath wasted four-and-twenty hours in this sleeveless hunt,' muttered the disgruntled sheriff. His men began to murmur agreement but thought better of it.

The three travellers were extremely reluctant to betray the poor man, but their commitment to speak truth, part of their code of conduct, presented them with a dilemma.

Simon solved their dilemma as his zeal for justice and mercy rose in him, burning fiercely. He stood in his lordship's path, his dark eyes smouldering like hot coals, his fine voice carrying over the rising howl of the wind.

'Nay, my lord, no scoundrels have we seen. Rather have we beheld hungry men that strive to feed their wives, their little ones, yet fair wages are withheld by their vavasours wrongfully. The Statute of Labourers? What of the law of justice and mercy? Doth God not behold it from heaven when the poor are oppressed? My lord sheriff is in the right on it. The labourer is worthy of his hire – so saith holy scripture.'

The sheriff's eyes gleamed with amusement but his lordship became furious. No friars or even bishops had ever presumed to challenge him like this before. He dismounted so he could confront this audacious cleric at his own level. He would have done better to stay mounted, for Simon's imposing height and mien put the nobleman at a disadvantage. Nonetheless, Simon's stinging rebuke made him sufficiently angry to disregard it.

'Who art thou, Brother Priest, to preach thy preaching at thy betters? Wist thou not to whom thou speakest? If the labour laboureth not, shall I pay him his hire? I ken not what manner of order thou art, but be sure I shall put complaint to the head of thine order for thine audacity.'

It reminded Peter of a spoilt, fat little spaniel barking and snarling at a large sheepdog.

'The head of our order, my lord, is of like mind,' interjected Edward, coming forward to stand with Simon. 'Hast thou not heard Doctor John Wycliffe berate such injustice as this?'

Gripping his staff pugnaciously, Peter also stepped forward to stand with his companions.

My Lord Sheriff, meanwhile, was one that did recognise Wycliffe's name, and favourably. He was a decent man, in stark contrast to his famous (or rather infamous), predecessor. He was a proud man of good birth, but had a strong sense of duty and a passion for justice also, in his own way.

'Ah! Doctor John Wycliffe? Now there is one I call a worthy Englishman. Are ye his men then? O that there were more men his like that would stand 'gainst the fat Papelardy that doth plague Holy Church. Many and a-many be the times when priestly-garbed felony we take in the net of the Law, but "Clergy! Clergy are we!" cry they and wave their robes insolently. And do they meet justice for their crimes when haled before the Archdeacon? Or before the Abbott? Nay! But for a dozen "Paternosters" and some monies in the bishop's coffers, they are free!'

He glared at Lord Southwell as he vented his frustration.

'It is my devoir, or so it doth seem, to seek poor half-famished men that must die or be maimed for petty thievery – good men that turn to evil in their despair. The king's justice this may be, but God's justice it is not.'

Loud applause greeted this soliloquy from the three brethren.

'We laud thy noble sentiments, my lord sheriff,' declared Simon loudly. 'Such is the message we proclaim: God's justice.'

'...And the Word of Truth,' added Edward.

'...And God's Mercy and Grace,' supplied Peter.

The sheriff laughed.

'If this be a new order of clergymen, worthy men that proclaim a worthy message, then ye are welcome to our shire brethren all.'

Lord Southwell was not satisfied with the way events were progressing. He had no interest in either theology or jurisprudence except where it suited him.

'But what of my lands, my lord sheriff?' he complained loudly. 'Shall I be bereft of labourers in the peak of harvest? What of the law of the land? Dost thou condone thievery and abandonment, contrary to the Statute? Wherefore art thou appointed then to thy post if thou perform not thy devoir?'

That was the last straw. The sheriff, fuming, turned his horse northward.

'Go, then, my lord, and seek to perform this, thy precious statute without mine aid!' he growled over his shoulder. 'If thou wilt not get wisdom as hath thy neighbours, then wield thou thine own sickle when all thy men forsake thee, or die. Two days have we pursued and have found naught of thy fugitive. I hie me to the castle anon. Other tasks, more fruitful, now call me. Good morrow!'

He began to ride off and his henchmen, grinning, followed suit. Then, as an afterthought, he paused and called back to the three missionaries.

'Brethren, if ye come to Nottingham, thou'rt welcome to my board at the castle if ye will. Fare ye well and God speed thy mission!' He rode off.

The brethren bowed and waved their thanks. It was heartening to see some evidence that Wycliffe's influence had already taken effect among the aristocracy.

The local aristocrat, however, far from heartened, was now in a foul mood. Swearing, he struggled, with some difficulty, back into his saddle and scowled at his own men who were trying hard not to grin..

'So this losel sheriff hath proved himself unworthy of his post!' he snorted defiantly. 'Then shall I seek this miscreant with mine own strong arm. A mark shall be added to thy pay, whosoever shall first take him.'

Totally ignoring the three missionaries, he rode off in a southerly direction. But this was where Peter made a mistake.

So relieved that he had gone, Peter threw the worn boot he had been hiding into the bushes. But one of his lordship's men, trailing the others, was sharp-eyed.

The sound of the horses' hooves were soon drowned in the wind's song and dance, and soon there was a rustling sound nearby as Rolf emerged from hiding.

'God ha' mercy! There be mighty trouble if I hie me not home, and right speedily,' he said in haste. 'My thanks be for thine aid, brethren, but fare ye well. May God speed thy labours.'

The three men replied in kind, but looked concerned.

'Shalt be a burdensome journey with an halt foot, my son,' said Edward.

'Aye, but so be it, Father Edward. Thine healing hath assuayed the worst, natheless. Blessings upon thy kindness. I need use o' both feet anon.'

He looked around for his boot, and Peter recollected where he had thrown it. Rolf put it on with some difficulty.

He was about to retrieve his plunder when suddenly a man-at-arms sprang from behind a tree and brought him down.

At the same time, Lord Southwell walked around the bend with a triumphant smirk on his fat face. His other attendant, looking aggrieved that he had missed out on the extra pay, was leading all three horses.

It had been a cleverly planned ambush.

Rolf, head bowed and unresisting, was brought before his gloating employer.

'How now, thou miscreant Rolf Howard! So didst thou deem to have escaped the net and forsake thy rightful place? Or dost thou rather pursue the king's game?'

'Nay, my lord!' protested Rolf, lifting his head. 'I but seek the last o' the berries and herbage o' these woods to feed my little ones.'

'Ha! So thou sayest. What then of this?'

Lord Southwell indicated Rolf's old sack that his soldier carried, now opened to reveal the dead bird.

Rolf groaned.

'My lord, ha' mercy, by the love of God!' he cried, in complete despair. 'Wilt thou take off mine hand, then? Slay me, and my wife and children then, for we all die else!'

'Have pity, for the love of Christ!' echoed Peter, distressed.

But his lordship seemed to revel in wielding the rod of authority, even in the teeth of clerical disapproval.

'An ensample shall he be to all that dare defy me,' he decreed grandly. 'His hand shall be spared, for there is much harvest yet to do. But fifteen lashes shall he suffer in the sight of all the insolent villeins at Southwell village.'

Rolf groaned again and fell on his knees as all three preachers protested loud and long.

'Silence!' shouted the unrepentant peer, leaning against the trunk of huge elm, arms crossed arrogantly. 'Keep thy preaching for the unwashed masses. Ye shall all learn that the house of Malet shall not be mocked. Hear ye the motto of my house: "I hold and hold well." My vassals will bow unto my will, or flout me at their peril.'

Edward refused to be silenced.

'But wilt thou flay the poor wretch, wasted as he be? I wist somewhat of medicine, my lord, and can tell that he cannot take fifteen lashes and not suffer great scathe, mayhap even death.'

'Eight lashes, then,' temporised his lordship. 'Neither more nor less. That is my last word.'

Shocked that his lordship would stubbornly adhere to such a brutal policy, the preachers did not know what else to do. Peter bowed his head in prayer.

But someone else did know what to do. The wind dropped abruptly.

Into the eerie stillness came the whirring sound of an arrow flying – stopping abruptly with a woodpecker's knock. A gasping cry of fear issued from the nobleman's mouth, causing everyone to turn in his direction. An arrow had all but pierced and pinned his right ear to the elm tree behind him.

His lordship froze, his already protuberant eyes positively bulging with fear. Everyone gasped, but not before a second shaft almost pierced his left ear. His mouth moved noiselessly. Everyone waited with baited breath for a third bolt from nowhere to find its fatal mark. Nothing happened and no one spoke for a full minute.

Such was the seeming accuracy of both shots, one of the soldiers whispered, 'Sickerly, Locksley's ghost it be.'

Simon, recovering from his own stupefaction, took advantage of the situation.

'Behold! True justice hath revealed her hand!'

Addressing the terrified and vulnerable nobleman, he read him a very telling homily for the next two minutes, on "To the merciful, God Himself is merciful" and ended by pressing the need for kinder treatment of his vassals – otherwise the next arrow may find his heart.

'Behold, the spirit of justice abideth still in the heart of these woods. Flout it at *thy* peril, my lord.'

Peter approached the petrified nobleman, taking care that he did not block the aim of the hidden marksman.

'My lord, wilt thou release this man and render him just wages?'

His lordship tentatively nodded his head.

'I r-release him. Doubled – nay – three-so-much shall his wages be.'

The soldiers, fearing that they may be the next target, stepped quickly away from the suddenly radiant Rolf. He limped to the edge of the road clearing in the direction that the arrow feathers pointed. He peered into the trees, removed his hood and boldly addressed his hidden deliverer.

'Many thanks be to thee as of old, thou blest ghost o' Master Robin. May thy spirit ever abide in honour in Sherwood and justice for the poor.'

There was no answer from either human or ghost, unless it was a brief roaring and creaking in the treetops, heralding the return of the gusty winds. It died down again.

Rolf turned toward his overlord and spoke with rustic dignity.

'My lord, hearken unto me. If thy word be good and thou be a-payen unto me three-so-much as thou a-swear me, then three-so-much shall I serve thee. This I swear a-fore God, a-fore the saints and...' he pulled off his threadbare hood again respectfully, '... a-fore the ghost o' Robin 'ood.'

The shaken nobleman stepped away from his bizarre imprisonment, glanced fearfully at the trees opposite, then in Rolf's direction with reluctant respect.

'So be it then.' he said curtly, once he had found his own dignity again. 'Even so do I swear. A man of my word am I.'

Without another word, he mounted his horse, gave a valedictory nod at the three clerics and spurred southward. Obviously, he was anxious to get away from the hidden and ghostly menace, but he held his head high, trying to look as though he had not been humiliated in front of his own men and three common clerics.

Peter looked in awe at the feathered shafts still stuck fast in the trees. Edward was studying them closely and shaking his head.

'Will his lordship hold to his word in sooth, think thou?'

'Surely,' said Simon the orator. 'The next shaft shall be his death should he betray his oath.'

'Simon! Simon!' Edward shook his head at him again. 'Wherefore givest thou heed to such Jack-mullock. There be not ghosts but living men that inhabit these woods once again. Cunning with the bow and with the spirit of Locksley within their hearts, I grant thee, but mortal men, dreadless. Mark well the shafts. Plain is their device, but phantom arrows they be not.'

He turned and addressed the trees in a clear voice.

'Greetings, O marksman of Sherwood! Come forth, if thou wilt, that we may have speech with thee.'

But while he spoke, as if in mockery, the trees began to sway, sigh and creak again as the gusty winds and leaves resumed their complicated dance. No other human-like answer came to Edward's challenge.

'Behold!' laughed Simon in mock triumph 'Thou'rt answered, thou unbeliever. But peradventure the good Lord hath sent his holy angel to right this wrong. Did not the psalmist say that "…. if the wicked turn not, the Lord shall whet His sword and He hath bent his bow …."?'

This explanation appealed to Peter, who eagerly turned to see Edward's reaction. Even Edward could not fully deny the possibility, although he had no recollection of any similar angelic or even divine intervention with the use of arrows in scripture.

The more simple-minded Rolf had no doubts whatever.

'Nay, brethren! Master Robin's ghost it be, and so shall I be a-swearen of it unto my dying puff, by the saints.'

He turned his weary limping feet toward home, but paused and looked back at the three missionaries.

'Thanks be to God 'o thy kindnesses, brethren, that thou didst take my part in the face o' his lordship's wroth and scorn. It be not ever forgot, and Doctor Wycliffe's name be ever blest, so it be. No more a-poachen will I, but mayhap his lordship be a-usen us all gentily henceforth, so there be no need.'

He sighed and turned away. It occurred to Peter, feeling compassion stir for the man, that he would be going home empty-handed to a hungry family. He ran after him, fumbling in his script for the remains of his wayside bread.

'But stay, Master Rolf, take of this for thine eventide meal, meagre though it be. Thy children have the greater want than I.'

He produced, to his own surprise, a whole round loaf instead of the half he thought he had remaining.

His colleagues, prompted by Peter's generous gesture, produced respectively and in like manner: a whole cheese and a full skin of ale. There was enough for Rolf's family and to spare.

Edward, surprised but ever sceptical, shrugged his shoulders and opined that their host at the Blue Boar had stacked their scripts generously and secretly for all their hard work. Peter laughed at this.

'Nay! Half a loaf did we eat from my script at noontide, Father, and no more and no less.'

'The cheese in like manner,' added Simon, triumphantly. Edward said nothing, but wondered why the ale had somehow replenished itself. He had drunk heartily after their morning's hard journeying. Whatever the case, whether it was a miracle or not, he knew the value of giving. He handed the full skin over to the poor man, avoiding Simon's eye.

Overwhelmed, Rolf could hardly speak. He stood looking down at God's provision in his trembling hands, shaking his head in disbelief. Finally, he crossed himself and looked up at them.

'Will ye not turn thy steps southward to my haven, holy brethren? If this goodness be thy message, then ever thy disciple shall I be. Come I beg o' ye, that ye have shelter o'er thy heads this night, humble though it be. On the morrow, I bring my kinsfolk, nay, all the village to hear o' the holy Word o' God.'

* * * * * *

A few hundred miles south and west, Father William and Thomas were making steady progress, but their scripts were much lighter. Their supply of English scripture portions was running low. They had been rather generous in distributing them, for many of the disciples prized these even above their next meal. Folk that could read begged for more copies, and spares for their friends.

Finally, William was forced to restrict his copies only for designated readers of each disciple gathering, or faithful scribes who were committed to making copies for other readers.

William and Tom decided to take the east road from Chipping Norton toward Oxford to replenish their supply if they could. Ever since the Council of Leicester, copying of English translations had intensified, so there would be a goodly supply in any of the Wycliffite Masters' offices.

'Would that we had great seals with these scripture portions set therein,' suggested the innovative Thomas, as they trudged further south.

'Yea, even great machines that would stamp them on mighty tablets of wax. Or mayhap manifold copies of parchment or paper, covered of wax on which the seals be stamped with multitudes of their message. Then, farewell *chorea scriptorum!* What thinkest thou?'

'Naught but the rich could pay for such,' William objected mildly, but the vision did secretly appeal to him, which prompted him to add: 'But mayhap 'Tis possible. Nay! Quill and paper never shall die.'

They argued the matter all the way to the village of Long Compton, where they stopped for lunch, hungrily consuming the last of that excellent cheese.

An afternoon's work at a farm gave them a bed of hay and a small morsel of food from a farmer with a sour expression on his face.

Tom was rather indignant at first, especially after a hard half-day's work. He had worked up a hearty appetite, and when a tiny meal of horse-bread was served them, he muttered something about "mumpish and chincherous old morpets..."

A look from William, half stern, half understanding silenced him.

Then William gave such heartfelt and sincere thanks to God for their meal and bedding, the farmer felt ashamed. He mumbled something about his straitened larder, but got up and put a half-eaten pigeon in his big cauldron on the fire, stirring in a few herbs to make a broth. William wondered where the man got his pigeon from, since most were the property of a local landlord. But he said nothing. Poaching was quite common in those days, and he had done something of it in the past.

While the pigeon was cooking, the farmer, who called himself Harold, apologised for his seeming miserliness. He explained that most folk in Long Compton were sullen and discontented with their lot, with the heavy rents, extra taxes and hard times. They blamed the government, the local landlords, the local priory brothers, even the parish priest.

'Some there be that even a-cursen of...' and he lowered his voice and crossed himself '...good Saint Martin hisself.'

He was only mildly interested in the message of the gospel, thinking more about his poverty than the state of his soul. His response was that the locals had too much to think about just getting by without arguing over theological questions.

'If such mumpishness prevaileth in this place,' confided William sadly during their evening sacrifice, 'then little hope have they to hearken unto our message. We must away at dawn, methinks.'

They made good progress to Chipping Norton, from whence they would turn southeast to Oxford the next day.

As they approached the town, William noticed with his shepherd-trained eyes, how healthy and thick the wool was on the sheep. The hillsides looked so green and lush, covered with sheep. There were also fascinating limestone rocky outcrops everywhere, enough to build whole towns and cathedrals.

This was the gateway to the famous Cotswolds of England, and they could see for miles from the hills on which the town was built. The view of the Stour Valley was so enthralling, it reminded Tom of a verse from the Song of the Wayfarer:

> *Master Hawk! In thy soarings, look down to behold*
> *The vale and the river; the blue, green, the gold.*
> *And I, the wayfarer, shall join in thy flight*
> *On the wings of my song from the morn unto night.*

They obtained work at a nearby manor of a wealthy land-owner.

The bailiff, once he recovered from the shock of friars asking for work instead of alms, heard that William had been a shepherd. He watched William shearing some of the thick quality fleeces from a few sheep nearby and was impressed by his speed, skill and gentleness. Being short of such skilled shearers, and being rather late in the season for shearing, he offered very good wages if he would stay indefinitely. William shook his head.

'Alas, Master Bailiff, rather is my calling unto the flock of God. Natheless, we shall abide with thine until our new flock is gathered and fed.'

The bailiff did not quite understand, but shrugged his shoulders, grateful that he intended to stay for the moment. He took them to his nearest flock and set them to work.

Tom watched William's quick hands with a pang of envy, but soon became quite skilled for a beginner, under William's patient instruction.

The bailiff, whom his workers called Master Bernard, gave the shearers beds for the night at the servants' quarters at the manor and paid them well. He was still hoping William would stay awhile, so he invited William in for a tankard of his best beer. He discovered how knowledgeable William was of the wool-trade, so they exchanged notes. William in turn learned about the growing trade in that area, and the international demand for such high quality wool.

It was not long before the bailiff became intrigued about William and Tom's present vocation. He thought it strange that such skilled and hard-working men were not making their fortune, instead of wandering around the countryside as penniless preachers, and said so.

'Nay, Master Bernard,' answered William with a confident smile. 'Ne'er have I felt so rich. These be not sleeveless roilings.[51] Rather, we are about the business of the King of Kings. Great are our wages of joy and peace as we walk in obeisance unto Him. For the blessing of God maketh rich and addeth no sorrow to it.'

'Would that I had such a blessing!' confessed Master Bernard enviously. 'But though I be not penniless as thou art, yet oft and anon do I feel wretched and poor within mine heart.'

William saw this as an opportunity to explain the way of salvation to him, according to the scriptures. Unfortunately, the bailiff still valued his well-paid and prestigious position too much, and was not ready to pay the price of defying the *status quo* as yet. If he defied the traditions of Holy Church, and his noble employer or the bishop found out, anything could happen.

He treated the two men with deep respect nonetheless.

Tom, meanwhile, was having a drink with the other shearers, and was soon telling them of their mission. A few stayed to listen, fascinated by the concept of working preachers, especially men highly skilled in agriculture. Most, however, were more interested in making as much as they could in this comparatively well-paid job, and moving on when the shearing was done.

Comparing notes at evening prayers, Tom and William decided to see if they had better success in the town next day. They slept on comparatively

---

51   roving about

comfortable beds that night, but William could now sleep like a baby even if it were but hard ground, for little Elspeth of Shipton's words of wisdom echoed through his dreams:

'If it be by the gwaithe of God, and thou'rt thaved ... no more a thinner art thou.'

Chapter 8: Pardon for the Pardoner

'By this fraud have I won me, year by year,
A hundred marks, since I've been pardoner.
I stand up like a scholar in pulpit,
And when the uneducated people all do sit,
I preach, as you have heard me say before,
And tell a hundred false jokes, less or more.'

(from "The Pardoner's Prologue",
'Canterbury Tales' by Geoffrey Chaucer.)

Faversham was a thriving seaport town in Kent, growing richer every year from the burgeoning wool export trade, not to mention the constant flow of pilgrims to Canterbury. But wealthy towns often attracted trade of a different sort, as young Father William Thorpe commented grimly to his companion, as a flock of Barnacle Geese flew over a heavily laden ship leaving for Ghent.

'Dost thou speak of the smuggling trade, brother William?' yawned young Father Benjamin Abyngdon, stretching tired muscles. 'Mayhap the Roiling Ram hath good French wine from Ghent hid deep in its cellars that could quench a weary labourer's thirst.'

'Nay, thou wine-bibber,' returned his friend, relaxing his customary grave expression a little, 'I speak of a darker trade in that which men would put their very souls in great peril.'

His more light-hearted yokefellow grimaced, becoming decidedly less light-hearted.

'The pardoner's trade? Yea. It is a wine full seductious that turneth even good men unto beasts under its evil spell. Hast heard tell of such trade in these lands, brother?'

'In the orchards of my lord Faversham this very morn did I hear of it. The chief husbandman, who laboured at my side in the gathering of the fruits, did grutch in bitterness of the matter. I had hoped to speak the Word of God unto him and of God's grace, but he showed a face of wrath, a little. "Art thou yet another holy man that would corrupt good men that they forsake their ploughs and pruning hooks?" quoth he. Then he crossed himself and turned him about in shame and asked my pardon that he spake so freely. My pardon I granted him freely, for it seemeth that he spake from just grievance, but enquired the reason for his saying, "Thou'rt not then a pardoner, Father?" quoth he in surprise, "But for this I should have reckoned me, for thou art not fat bellied and doth labour full well as any honest man. I cry thee pardon of my folly, but I spake from the fullness of mine anger without giving thought to it." Then spake he of many and many a good farmer, labourer and shepherd that had fallen into evil ways of revelry, gluttony and licentiousesse. They forsake their spouse, their families, flout the avenging arm o' the law and a-times would even lose their life and soul, so hell-bent were they. And wherefore? "Grace o' the Holy Father o' Rome!" cry they and wave of their pardons under the nose of his lordship's steward.'

A passing middle-aged fisherman with an inquisitive nose and only one good eye overheard the young priest's grimly-spoken anecdote and paused to join in the conversation.

'Ah, brother freer, thou be a-speaken o' poor Simon the Soak, do ye not? God rest his soul.'

He crossed himself, sat down on a wooden crab-trap nearby and fixed his good eye on William. The other was covered by a rough cloth that passed as a patch. This did not stop the good eye from gleaming expressively with news to tell.

'Him and his good brother Adam did fine fishermen make, did they'm. Many and a-many were the good gest and tale that Simon he would be a-tellen o'er a good flagon at yon Roiling Ram, be sure. But likerous o' the bad brew were he and Adam, give ye they them half chance. And Master Pardoner o' Canterbury did given they them that evil chance. Cozened he many a hardlye-worked-for mark from Simon and from Adam's purse for to sell them pardons and indulgences, aye, and narey a few. Soon it be low-tide o' moneys and high-tide in bad brew for the poor lads, folliards though they be....'

'....Aye! Caught by his lor'ship's men, were Simon, when they be a-reeven in his lor'ship's cellars.' volunteered a big fish-trader, one of many dockside folk who stopped to listen. 'No pardon o' Rome left to cover them then. Lost, his right hand be by my lord sheriff's command, a'though young Adam ran free a'fore they took o' him. Simon be gone to God … or mayhap the Devil, God rest him. Evil brew were in his blood, and his arm be a-rotted a' gangrene's rot for the wound o' his lost cammet, poor jobbard that he were.'

The gathered assembly shook their heads in sorrow and murmured regretfully as the two young priests exchanged horrified glances.

'What of Adam, his brother?' asked William.

'We wist not whither he went, brother,' answered a rather withered-looking housewife in her forties. 'Mayhap he a-joineth the cursed corsairs. Some there be as a-sayen he leapt to his death from Longman's Ridge in his desperence,' and indicated the direction with her basket of fish. 'He once be a-sayen as his pardons be more a curse than a blessedness. And this be the tale o' many a good man and nary a few womenfolk with gold for to cast away.'

There were more head-shakings and signs of the cross from the muttering crowd.

The fisherman brought his bright single eye back toward the young priests.

'And so then, brethren, be ye a-coomen hither a-sellen o' pardons and indulgences?'

'Pardons and indulgences!' fumed Benjamin with uncharacteristic heat. 'Veritable tools of the Devil, are they, wrapped in pious altar cloth to deceive sely folk. Baited hooks to drag the credulous unto damnation, while the fat prelates stuff their coffers and St Peter's shrine is shrouded with gold. Little wonder is it that Doctor Evangelicus raiseth a storm on the matter.'

'And what better place for the pardoner to ply his trade than the pilgrim road to Thomas a'Beckett's tomb,' added William Thorpe, looking around him, 'where sely pilgrims seek assoilment for their sins….'

'…Or seek for praise in the eyes of their fellows,' added Benjamin.

The assembly were a little shocked to hear these bold young preachers speaking out so freely against the establishment.

'But, brethren,' asked the housewife tentatively, 'be it accepted a'fore the good God and His holy angels if it be that the Holy Father give o' his blessen?'

'His blessing?' echoed William, irritated. 'Doth a good tree bear fruit corrupted, judge ye? Nay! Know ye all that Doctor Wycliffe, the mightiest theologian in the land, and many of his mind also do heartily condemn such doings – even though they be done in the name of the Reverend Father or the Bishop of Rome himself.'

His audience reacted a little nervously at this forthrightness, but one powerfully-built and cheerfully belligerent labourer spoke up. He had the manner of a leader of men – or rather, a pack-leader.

'Doctor Wycliffe, say ye? Ah, brethren, then ye be o' like-mindedness wi' Father John Ball, ye be. He be south away yonder, a-shaken his staff at the fat landlords and bloaten bishops who thrive full well a-whilst good common folk do starven. God 'ild him, say I! A mighty man o' God be Father John Ball! If united we be, then can we throw off this damned yoke and be free!'

His voice rose as he spoke, ready to take over proceedings.

'Aye and amen!' roared a group of shabby and dirty labourers behind him almost in unison. They appeared to be the man's followers, even a kind of bodyguard.

A few locals glanced nervously at the big rebel orator and felt it was time to leave, while others growled their agreement. William and Benjamin exchanged glances again, a little anxiously this time. The name of the fiery rebel-priest was not unknown to them. Doctor Wycliffe warned them there would be trouble wherever John Ball went, and they had witnessed this during his sojourn at Oxford.

'We have no part in Father John Ball's rantings,' answered Benjamin heatedly. 'He will seek to fight evil with evil, and would have us all to take up the sword in dissention. They that do so will but die by the sword. We speak of the evils within holy church alone, and that all may turn from their sin and seek God as Father through faith alone.'

The big labourer spat and swore, cheerfully grinning still.

'Ho then! If ye fight not like all true men o' Kent, then we have no part with ye, O milken-priests. Father John be my man. Come lads, seek we the valiant and strong for our cause. We find naught o' that hither.'

He stalked off noisily with his following. The fisherman, glancing over his shoulder at them, shook his head and laughed shortly.

'That be Wat Tyler, brethren,' he informed them. Lowering his voice with a touch of rustic prophecy, he added: 'Born to hang, he be, and many o' his train with him, more be the pity on't.'

'God forbid!' uttered William in dismay.

The crowd was dispersing, but the fisherman stayed and chatted, feeling a certain affinity with the two missionaries. He called himself One-Eye Jacob.

'Ah well and well, Father William and Father Benjamin, men indeed do ye be in my sight, though my sight be less than it were, for ye speak boldly o' matters that many dare not, whate'er Tyler be a-sayen. Jacob o' the One-Eye do rarely mistaken his man. Comen ye unto the Ram, that we slake our thirsts o'er a tankard or three. Preachen be thirsty work, surelye?'

Glad to have made at least one friend, they assented, although the three tankards he proposed were in doubt, as William explained, due to their vow of temperance.

They walked down the street toward the tavern, watching the comings and goings of this thriving and growing portside market, when they noticed a colourful group of travellers that had just arrived through the southern gates. They were typical of a company of varied rank returning from a pilgrimage to Canterbury. It was customary to travel together where possible, since travelling alone was becoming more dangerous due to the increasing lawlessness in the land.

Some of the travellers, being high-born, accepted the hospitality of Lord Faversham, the local overlord. The travellers of lesser consequence had to seek shelter in the village.

William and Benjamin adhered to Doctor Wycliffe's policy of poverty, so they had given most of their wages to the almoner at St Genevieve's. Benjamin, however, insisted on retaining a little to sample the local beer, which was of high repute, and a sustaining meal. William saw no harm in it, although the Wycliffites discouraged regular visits, and banned drunkenness altogether. He noted that two of the pilgrims, Franciscan friars, entered the Roiling Ram tavern before them.

Within the tavern, they passed the two friars, seated together at a table. The friars regarded them with a mixture of curiosity and suspicion, obviously wondering who this new order was, noting their russet-coloured habits. Curiosity got the better of them and they approached the two evangelists, asking if they may join them at their table. They seated themselves without waiting for a reply, completely ignoring the presence of the fisherman. The latter took it patiently, being used to snubs from most of the clergy, and watched with interest to see how his new clergy friends would react to the Franciscans' arrogance.

These introduced themselves as Friars Charles and Stephen, returning from pilgrimage to the shrine of St Thomas A'Becket at Canterbury. They took it for granted that this conferred a certain distinction in the stranger's eyes.

In the eyes of the strangers, however, they appeared as two overfed, arrogant clerics who were there to sniff out their business.

Benjamin's hackles rose a little, but William was willing to give them the benefit of the doubt. The order of Saint Francis had noble beginnings after all, even though he strongly disagreed with their theology and many practices. Besides, it was best to handle any potential conflict carefully.

Friar Charles took a pull at his beer and wiped the foam from his greying beard with his sleeve, all the while staring at the strangers. 'And who art thou, brothers?' he finally demanded. 'Be thou Franciscans? Palmers? Pardoners? Thine habits proclaim an order beyond my ken. Speak ye!'

William put his hand in Benjamin's shoulder to check the hasty words that rose to his lips.

'Neither and none, good brothers,' he answered cordially. 'No order are we, save that we give obeisance unto the order of Our Lord Christ Jesu, Who commandeth us to preach the gospel and gather the lost sheep. Like to thy worthy selves, we are *clerici vagantes*.[52] Natheless, we are not mendicant and will toil for our meat.'

His answer appeared to both impress and annoy the friars, for they could see just by the look of the strong, work-hardened strangers that it was no idle boast. They were now at a disadvantage by this evidence of humility and simple faith. The fact that these men appeared to be bursting with health, yet were as lean as greyhounds in comparison to most friars, was evident to all. They did not show the signs of the lucrative sponsorships and benefices that was many a friar's portion in those days.

---

52 Wandering scholars

Friar Charles was forced to defend his position as a begging friar and was annoyed at the necessity.

'Hold we to an oath of humility as prescribed of our order. Thus do we remain lowly men of God, not proud men that labour.'

This defence seemed so lame, even in his own ears, he sank into furious silence.

'Who are ye then?' demanded Friar Stephen sternly, still trying his best to assert some kind of superiority, 'if ye be not recusant Franciscans? Do ye preach? The accursed heretical *Spirituales* speak as ye do. Wot ye not that De Montfort and Mitterand were burnt at the stake not three years gone? Beware lest ye follow the same path unto perdition.'

He ended on a patronising note, and took another pull at his beer.

Benjamin and William remembered the bitter division between the two main branches of the Franciscan order. The dominant and comfortable *Conventuales* were the only branch of the two that were endorsed by the pope, and some of the leaders of the ascetic *Spirituales* were cruelly made examples of. Some were still secretly of their persuasion, so they had heard.

Before William had the chance to answer them, a loud laugh was heard halfway across the room.

'Ha! There be two holy men more anon, by the face!'

Friar Charles knew the voice. He bowed his head onto the table and groaned as if in pain.

'O Mother of God! For my sins!'

'Behold, Father Benjamin, it be Master Pardoner as we wot of,' the fisherman whispered to Benjamin.

Friar Stephen glared over his shoulder at a fat and boisterous figure who was descending upon them. He turned and looked back at William and Benjamin, his face eloquent with annoyance and distain.

'Well, brethren. His presence endured we perforce all the long leagues from Canterbury. Like unto purgatory it was, God save us! Liefer would we your fellowship seek than that of this malapert, cautelous bretheling!'

The unwanted guest heard the last comment quite clearly, but rather than being offended, gave another of his loud and hearty laughs and slapped the hostile friar on his back.

'What! Friar Stephen!' he cried in the noisy, boisterous manner habitual to him. 'Thou mumpish, wey-faced old jobbard! Hast thou not stint of thine envy, that I have the blessed Holy Father's benefice of holy indulgences and thou hast naught?'

His victim coughed and spluttered as hastily swallowed beer almost choked him, and his tankard spilled half of his contents on his habit.

Benjamin and William looked the newcomer over with both amusement and mild aversion.

Although the man spoke with the refined accents of a learned priest, he was characterised by a brash, insensitive manner and a devil-may-care attitude that showed little respect even to great dignitaries. His habit proclaimed a special envoy of the Papal legates, a pardoner who sold indulgences to raise money for crusades, papal wars or lavish building projects.

Benjamin also found himself surveyed by a bold pair of bloodshot and cynical eyes, set in a bulging face as subtle as a fox with a wide, toothy grin and dirty brown stubble on his chin. Signs of overindulgence and dissipation were all over him.

'Ho there and well met, my noble brothers!' he belched out genially, grabbing their hands and shaking them vigorously. 'Aloysius Morton, am I. Third cousin o' the Bishop o' Worcester himself.'

He grabbed a stool from the nearby table and sat so close to them, they could smell his unwholesome and wheezy breath.

'Methinks I see the signs o' true holy demeanour upon you, for there be not an ounce o' lard upon thy bellies. Dispense I to ye holy pardons in vain, sickerly? Ye'll have naught? Well, fear not! Have I not wares that be the covetise o' many a palmer, by the living Moses! Treasures for truly holy men, these be.'

He reached into his script and whipped out two sealed wooden boxes, ornately carved. He leaned over to his audience with an air of conspiracy mixed with awe and held forth the relics.

'In here be two splinters o' the left kneebone o' the holy faithful hound o' good Saint Francis himself.' he uttered, lowering his voice impressively. 'The bones o' that holy hound be blessed of great virtue, brothers. Let it be sit in thy tankard or brose for two-and-twenty breaths, and thou'st a sure curative o' thy ventosity.[53] Aye! And many and many another accesse[54] also.'

---

53   Colic
54   sickness

He sat back with a smile, putting on a more businesslike, yet persuasive manner. 'Beg of thy sponsor but two marks apiece, good brethren. Aye, soothly quoth I – but *two marks!* and the miracle be thine own. What say you?'

'Beshrew thine importable liesings,[55] scoundrel!' growled Friar Charles, hostility and disdain flickering in his little eyes. 'Hast thou not essayed such fetchings[56] upon thy pilgrim-companions? Aroint thee, say I, and fetch us some peace!'

'Ho! Dost thou doubt me indeed, thou rump-fed papelard?' retorted the pardoner with another loud laugh, and pounded the table. 'May the blessed Saint Francis that ye serve strike me if I shew ye not the truth withal o' my words.'

He jumped to his feet and grabbed his opponent's tankard, drawing it toward himself.

'I give thee wager, Master Friars!' he cried aloud in challenge. 'Will not these holy relics show thee their virtue, even anon? All the golden rings that adorn thine hands 'gainst mine own purse o' gold.'

In a dramatic gesture, he swept out his bulging purse and threw it on the table. The strings were not tightened, and a few shining gold coins scattered out over the table. The friars' eyes glistened as they saw them. He was, in effect, offering them odds, for there seemed to be at least fifty marks in the purse, whereas their rings were worth only about five. The fisherman whistled in awe.

His boisterous and noisy challenge soon attracted the attention of many other drinkers in the room, and they crowded around to see what was happening. Master Morton was delighted, for this gave him a greater audience to sell his wares.

Holding up one of the relics so all could see, he announced to the whole tavern with his powerful voice in the manner of a market street-crier.

'Behold, good townsfolk, the power of good Saint Francis himself. Were not his holiness and grace be imparted unto his beloved creatures? His own hound did take his healing virtue unto many whom he sent, when the blessed saint did lay his hand upon him. Witterly, it be so! Can

55 lies
56 crafty schemes

these worthy Franciscan Friars deny the virtue o' their own patron? Yet they do so!'

Benjamin and William had to admire the showmanship of the man, setting aside the unfortunate coarseness of his manner, and the propagation of such fables and superstitions that were prevailing in the land.

Benjamin became conscious of the still, small voice of God as this performance was going on. He became alert, wondering what God was about to do.

Master Morton was revelling in his particular limelight, and he held everyone's attention as he pressed his point home.

'So the worthy friars doubt the power of their own patron? So be it! He himself shall rebuke their little faith.'

He went on to expound on the supposed wonderful properties of the virtue within his precious relics before him. Then he looked boldly upon his opponents, and repeated his challenge.

'So? Well, holy brethren? Think you not that I can show the power of thy holy saint? Is it a wager?'

'Would the blessed Saint Francis hearken unto a redeless rushbuckler as thou?' cried Friar Stephen scornfully 'Think you we be all awhape for all thy bobance? I take thy wager!'

He ripped off all his golden rings, and slammed them confidently on the table next to the bag of gold.

'And I also,' said his fellow, following suit. 'Wilt thou invoke our Holy Saint? Do so if thou hast the gall. Peradventure this will school thee to shamefastness hereafter, by my fey!'

A look of deep satisfaction crossed Master Morton's face as he eyed the rings. 'So be it! The blessed Saint himself shall decide between us who beareth the folly.'

He held up the tankard before him, raised his hand and closed his eyes in a dramatic show of piety.

'O holy, sublime and blessed Saint Francis, hear thou my prayer!'

Such was the deep reverence in his voice, that most of those present bared their heads and closed their eyes in holy awe. It was well known that Saint Francis loved his animals, and many tales had been spun regarding the blessings and grace he had bestowed, especially his holy hound. Who would dare to make a mockery of such a prestigious Saint as the blessed

Francis himself, after all? Even the friars, now not so confident, bowed and prayed fervently on their own account. Surely, their own blessed patron saint would not fail them.

There were two in the room, however, whose eyes were definitely not closed, and they prayed, but not to Saint Francis.

'Reveal thy power, O blessed Francis!' the saint's supposed devotee cried, as if calling down fire from heaven. 'If my words be sooth, then let thy blessing well up within this common beverance that be before thy servant, as I cast the holy bonesplint of thine holy hound within, on whom thy blessing abideth. Anon, even-Christians all! Behold ye the miracle!'

He paused as they all opened their eyes, and looked expectantly at the tankard before him.

'Behold! The virtue of the Holy Hound of Saint Francis!' he declared, holding one of the small relics in the palm of his slightly dusty hand, then threw it into the tankard and stepped back.

To gasps of astonishment, the beverage began to bubble, then it foamed and overflowed all over the table before the dismayed faces of the friars.

'An holy miracle o' good Saint Francis hisself!' said the fisherman and crossed himself. Benjamin and William were whispering to each other.

With a loud laugh of triumph, Master Morton gathered up all the riches from the table before the beer reached it.

The two friars, furious, totally humiliated and confused, made to leave as inconspicuously as possible.

'What say ye, even-Christians!' their tormentor challenged, addressing his audience 'Wilt thou not keep fey[57] where these foolish friars did doubt? There be more of the splinters of the holy hound o' the good saint for thy benefice if ye have patience. They be but two marks apiece, a bargain indeed for relics of mighty virtue. Thine own eyes beheld it.' On and on he went as one wealthy merchant approached him with golden coins in his hands, while others crowded around him, pledging to pay him once they could beg, borrow or steal the means. Chuckling, he pulled forth parchment from his scrip, and called noisily to the ale-draper for quill and ink. Business appeared to flourish that night.

'Hold!'

57 Faith

A clear voice rose over the hubbub, surprising everyone to silence. All eyes turned to Benjamin.

'A mighty miracle it seemed, Master Morton,' said Benjamin clearly, looking at the showman with an amused smile, 'Yet cannot such a sign be contrived?'

Murmurs began amongst the gathering at this and they looked toward Master Morton for his defence. The friars stopped short at the door and spun around.

'God's life! Thou wouldst question the power of Saint Francis?' blustered Morton, turning a little pale. 'Malapert young jack-eater! For shame! And thou in holy friar's raiment.'

Benjamin, still quite affable, came up close to the man.

'Saint Francis in heaven may smile upon my janglery, Master Morton, but nor he nor the God Whom he serveth will smile upon thy cautelous liesings, and steal honest men's gold.'

Before the accused could bellow out his refutation, Benjamin swooped. Not for nothing had he laboured in many a field. With his strong left arm, he held the startled pardoner's arms pinioned to his side, while he reached around and pulled a little satchel of dust from the man's script.

This he held high, standing on a chair so all could see, and the stunned showman could not reach. Morton's mouth had suddenly gone dry, and he was uncharacteristically silent and trembling. Another murmur arose from the crowd who looked accusingly at him.

'Sirrahs-all!' said Benjamin clearly, 'Know now that as our pious chapman here did pray so holily, I and my comrade, who are but simple preachers of the gospel, and regardeth not false piety, we beheld a cunning sleight of hand, as our holy pardoner dipped his holy relic in this satchel. Behold!'

He pushed his own tankard before them and sprinkled some dust from the satchel into it. Almost immediately, the liquid bubbled, even spurted over the sides – more vigorously than the earlier demonstration.

'Mighty virtue there be in this holy powder, master tregatour,[58]' taunted Benjamin in cheerful derision, as the fountain subsided. 'Wherefore didst thou as lief not merchandise it as those vain relics?'

The room exploded in outrage, led by the two friars, who charged back

---

58   Illusionist, magician

through the crowd crying 'Blasphemy! Lewd sacrilege! May Saint Francis strike thee dead, if we do not!'

The unforunate trickster fell to his knees and covered his head as men beat him. The merchant demanded his money back, while the friars wrested their rings back off him.

'Mercy! I cry ye gramercy, good sirrahs!' he wept 'I will amend! But spare me my life!'

This seemed a little doubtful as the enraged men, led by the friars, began to execute mob justice upon him in supposed righteous indignation.

'Hold! In God's name, stint this fraperous murdering!'

Even Benjamin jumped, never having heard his friend's voice thunder like this. Such was an authority and sternness in William's voice, that all the crowd were struck to sullen silence even in the midst of their outrage.

'Even-Christians-all!' cried William, looking very much like Saint Francis must have looked when he discovered a mob of youths tormenting a small pig. 'For shame! Dost thou sit in the place of God, Who alone is the righteous judge? Verily, this man hath greatly sinned and must pay recompense of his fetchings. Yet there is more to this. Mark ye!'

The crowd turned with reluctant respectfully to hear William, forgetting the battered and bleeding wretch at their feet for the moment. The indefinable dignity of this holy young man addressing them had caught their full attention. The two strangers had discovered the fraud, after all. Even the dazed and broken pardoner listened, half in hope.

William launched into the account, as recorded in the gospels, of the woman caught in adultery. The Pharisees had hoped to trap Jesus into either doing some uncharacteristically judgmental act, or contravene what they claimed was the Law of Moses and insist the girl should live.

Jesus did neither.

'Let him who is without sin, cast the first stone!'

The words of the Lord Himself seemed to hang in the air, and William waited as the men looked at each other sheepishly. The point had been taken.

With some grumbling and murmuring, the local men finished their drinks and gradually, a few at a time, went home, but not before removing what they considered was their own (with interest) from the bag of gold on the table.

In the space of ten minutes, the only men left in the room were William and Benjamin, the two friars, one battered and weeping pardoner on the floor, the fisherman (deeply impressed) and a bemused and anxious ale-draper.

William called on the draper for hot water and bandages as he pulled out a small bottle of ointment from his scrip. He and Benjamin set to work on the broken sinner.

The two friars were still angry at being so fooled, but their conscience also smote them at William's words. They stood and glared at the three others for a moment.

'But will ye not give him in arrestment unto the sheriff?' demanded friar Charles at last.

William paused, pulled over the bag of gold from the table, and threw it to the friar in exasperation.

'Lo, thou hast the weregild of thy wager, brothers. Take it then!' he snapped. 'I council ye that ye 'ware the wrath of the Reverend Father of Canterbury who sent this man. He hath betrayed trust, sickerly, but is answerable to him that sent him, not to us nor to the sheriff. Let Canterbury judge him. But what of grace? He is penitent. Wilt thou throw the first stone then?'

He looked sternly at the friars for a moment, who were apparently hesitating between pride and shame.

'Think you that Saint Francis himself would have so done this?' William pursued. 'Nay! Jesu Christ Himself came but to bring sinners unto repentance. Justice must be mixed with mercy.'

The friars stood for a moment, struggling with their pride. Whispering between themselves, Stephen expressed his admiration for the wisdom, quick wit and humility displayed by the two strangers. He even admitted the possibility that he let his avarice and his self-righteousness rule him. Charles merely pshawed and disclaimed.

Disregarding his companion's attitude, Stephen addressed the two preachers in a milder voice than he had used toward them previously.

'Brothers, who are you? Who sendeth you?'

Benjamin got to his feet, shook out his robes and simply said 'Doctor John Wycliffe.'

That was enough for Charles. 'Ha! That tempestuous heretic! 'Tis he that bringeth the wrath of ....'

'Charles! Hold thy peace!' interrupted his colleague, irritatedly. 'Mind thou not Friar John Walter's words on the matter? He stood with Wycliffe as his advocate before the Archbishop of London.'

Friar Stephen shut his mouth with a snap and swallowed. His colleague turned to the strangers before him.

'Brethren, I understand aright anon, for this friar John was our own mentor, a godly man. He spoke highly of thy master, though we believed him not therebefore, for so were we instructed of my order. But what I have seen this day hath assuaded me that Friar John spake sooth. If ye be his disciples, then a godly man indeed is Doctor Wycliffe, though our superiors would say other.'

Friar Charles opened his mouth in protest, but seeing William on his knees, treating the wounded sinner, he shut it again, fuming a little.

William looked up and smiled amiably.

'Friar John Walter is indeed known to me, good brother. Doctor Wycliffe will never forget the four valiant Franciscans that took his part when he and the Gaunt came before the Archbishop. Our master hath spoken strongly of the corruption in Holy Church, but there be many that still strive to serve Our Lord as best they may. Gramercy, good brothers.'

The two friars bowed and walked slowly away. One, at least, seemed chastened somewhat in spirit, yet strangely uplifted and encouraged by William's gracious parting words. He had much rethinking to do.

The sufferer on the floor groaned as he tried to sit up. Gone was the swaggering self-confidence he had twenty minutes earlier. He was shattered in spirit worse than in body.

'Brethren!' he croaked, for there was some damage done to his throat. 'I wot not wherewithal to thank ye. Ye are my judges and my saviours, both... I ... I be humbled o' your graciousesse, and repent me o' my wickedness.'

He grasped William's wrist urgently.

'Make I my confession for absolution before thee, Father William? What must I do to be safe o' Saint Francis' wroth?'

Benjamin and One-eye Jacob were a little sceptical at first, after witnessing the old conjurer's amazing and talented performance in assumed piety. They both agreed that these could be crocodile tears, hoping he may escape retribution.

'Take ye all my gold, brethren,' insisted the penitent desperately. He produced a small bunch of keys and held it out to Benjamin. 'Behold: the keys o' my casket and my chamber. Take thou every whit. Give to them that I have so grievous wronged. Manifold, if need be. Many a time have I cursed this demon o' greed and lost sleep on't, but it would ever return to bind me to my woe. Now the bond is broke, and I need it not. A conscience cleansed be riches enow, though I starve in a kennel. Take it all, brethren, I beseech ye.'

By this time, even the world-weary fisherman and ale-draper were moved.

'Never be'eld I the loik, Maester Jacob!' the draper commented in wonder as he set about the task of cleaning up blood and spilt ale. Jacob was for once unable to comment, so he just nodded and gave the draper a hand.

The incident reminded Benjamin of something he had read in his devotions that morning, but could not quite remember. He said as much to William, but his companion had other things to think about.

Ignoring his whimpering protestations of his unworthiness of their aid, they supported and half carried the broken and bleeding man to his own quarters to further tend him.

But this incident was only the beginning of stirring events that were about to occur in Faversham.

Chapter 9: True Treasure

'...But gather to you treasures in heaven [but treasure to you treasures in heaven], where neither rust nor moth destroyeth, and where thieves delve not out, nor steal. For where thy treasure is, there also thine heart is.'

(Gospel of Matthew 6:20,21 Wycliffe/Purvey Translation/Revisions)

Acting on the advice of the knowledgeable One-Eyed Jacob, who was familiar with the mood of the local populace, and knew the busiest time and place in the town, bold young Father Benjamin Abyngdon mounted the town-criers podium in the town square.

Business was in full swing, but the locals never seemed to grow weary of another diversion, even if it was just another preacher. Friars would occasionally mount the podium and hold forth either with an entertaining story of the exploits of their patron saints, or harangue them for their shortcomings – especially when the speakers themselves were running low on financial resources. Nonetheless, people always stopped to listen, partly from habit and partly from curiosity. Wagers were sometimes made between the irreverent, over what the topic of the sermon would be. This was the information Jacob supplied the two evangelists before melting into the crowd.

A crowd soon gathered around the podium when Benjamin stood up to speak. It gathered in size as they noticed the unfamiliar clerical robes he wore. These were russet coloured, a little frayed but clean and without any of the usual adornments or rosaries the populace were used to seeing on begging friars. Strangers, obviously, and may have something new to say.

Next to Benjamin stood Father William Thorpe, not only wearing the same clerical robes, but also an intangible aura of authority which made him look older than his years. It was just as well, for next to him stood a trembling Brother Aloysius Morton, former pardoner designate of the Archbishop of Canterbury, former palmer and once a vendor of holy relics. It was almost as though he was straining at an invisible leash, getting ready to take flight. One or two men in the crowd recognised him, and pointed in wrathful astonishment, thinking he had already done so.

William had talked to him all evening at his temporary quarters, patiently bringing him to an understanding of the plan of redemption as presented in the scriptures. The man's broken state was both a help and a hindrance to this process.

'But… but, good father…' he pleaded conscientiously, '… can I not do penance? Wherewithal then can I cast off this great burden of guiltiousness? I would chastise my back until it bleedeth… all I possess I would give to Holy Church…to thine order… to the almoner …oh… if I could but find peace… so saith Father Harold of Feaversham…'

William's patience became very slightly frayed. He had heard that plea time and time again. It had become so entrenched in the minds of the populace, and many an unscrupulous clergyman had grown fat on it.

'Nay! Penance is verily a deceit from hell!'

He closed his eyes in silent and frustrated prayer, biting back hasty words in his exasperation which, he knew, would not help. Then it came to him that he once had the same struggles. He continued in a gentler vein.

'Have I not also felt the pain of such bondage? My friend, thou sufferest needlessly, and it will do naught but despite unto the grace of God. So saith the holy scriptures, though even thine archbishop would say other… peace thou shalt find if thou'st made thy peace with Almighty God, and laid all thy sin by faith at the foot of the cross of Christ by faith. "Good father" thou callest me? I am but a sinner as thou and as all men, so saith the blessed Saint Paul. But the blood of Christ – and that alone – availeth for my redemption as it doth for thine.'

But years of tradition and a huge weight of guilt made it almost impossible for the man to comprehend that God's forgiveness could come so easily. William closed his eyes again and prayed for inspiration.

An image flashed into his mind of a moment in his own youth. His intrepid nature and inquiring mind had led him into mischief at times. His father, a big-hearted, god-fearing man, had not shielded him from the consequences, but had always loved him in spite of his occasional annoying behaviour.

Inspiration! William told him of his brief vision, comparing God as a loving Father against the commonly held view of God as an angry judge.

'What was it that thou sayedst at Matins on Lord's Day last? *"Pater Nostra...."* What is its meaning?'

It made an instant impact. He could see hope dawning in Aloysius's face.

'Our Father...Who art in heaven...' he whispered. 'Now do I see it.....
It is a mighty wonder.' Then his face fell. 'Yet have I taken of much filthy lucre. It weigheth heavily upon mine heart. It is a wall that prevaileth strong between I and the Father in Heaven...'

Another word of wisdom was dropped into William's heart. He stood up and shook out his robes.

'Then we shall cast down that wall,' he said vigorously. 'All penance is vain, but if thou hast not the peace of God in thine heart still, mayhap there is need for retribution.'

'Retribution? W-what is this? Is it the wrath of God on my sin?' Aloysius trembled.

'Nay! That is not God's way. Say rather repayment to them that thou'st wronged ... and....'

It suddenly occurred to William that this situation could be turned into a powerful opportunity to present the gospel to the people of Faversham.

Thus, it was that the next morning, Brother Aloysius Morton limped along to the town central place of meeting, the young preachers who had saved his life at his side. He stood, almost covered in bruises, nursing a black eye, a broken nose, his left leg in a makeshift splint, with his head down, wondering if he would survive the day. Behind him, in a wooden wheelbarrow, Jacob bore a large wooden chest.

And the townsfolk were ready and waiting. The word had got around that these young preachers with the unfamiliar message had exposed a terrible fraud by a fat pardoner, who had taken advantage of their piety. Anger had been growing among many of the poorer folk, a fire skilfully fed and fanned by Wat Tyler, the rebel leader. Politics were largely forgotten, however, when the two preachers mounted the podium. The tale of the exposure of the cheat had spread rapidly, and now most of the audience knew who had done it. A great cheer went up.

219

Benjamin was a fine orator, one of the famed Oxford Master John Ashton's most promising pupils. He raised his arms high to silence the crowd.

'Behold and mark ye well, even-Christians all! A miracle of God's grace stands before you in this man at my side. For until the time of yestereve he, by many cautelous fetchings, did take money wrongfully from some of you. He did make merchandise of false holy relics and deceived honest, believing folk of their labour's fare.'

This caused a sensation among the crowd. 'Aye, that be the lieserer we beheld within the tavern, beshrew him!' cried one big man in the crowd, shaking his fist at him. He would have said more, but Jacob the fisherman, mingling with the crowd, whispered something to him. The man blinked and gaped in astonishment.

One well-dressed dame stepped forward agressively.

'Is't Brother Aloysius? Sayest thou that my precious talisman be but jack-mullock?' she demanded indignantly. She pulled out a small object hanging around her neck, ripped it off the string and threw it at him. It missed his misshapen nose by only inches. 'Repay me those marks anon, miscreant!'

The accused shifted his bruised feet and kept his head lowered.

But Benjamin held up his arms, and the mutterings and shouts subsided.

''Tis the young preacher as did esspose that rogue Morton's fetchery,' whispered many of the men to their spouses. More local folk arrived as word spread about the happenings in the square.

'.... But all that which he hath done is past, anon!' Benjamin's strong young voice silenced the last of the mutterings. 'Such is his hearty repentance, he will repay you all that he hath wronged. Yea, again I shall say it: he hath purposed to repay you – and more. God hath worked on his heart and he hath determined to restore where he may. Even this day – even anon.'

He gestured to the injured dame who had demanded repayment.

'Good lady, wilt thou not come forward to receive thine own again? This be no more falsehood. Come forth, I pray thee.'

Amidst more incredulous mutterings and wonderment from the crowd, the woman pushed her way to the podium, hardly believing her good fortune. She blinked as she stood before the man who had betrayed her trust only the day before. He reached around and gathered a good handful of golden coins from the wooden chest, something he had kept hidden for years, and held it out to her with a beseeching look.

'Forgive me, good lady. Accept thou thy wealth again, yea, repaid four-so-much.[59]'

Even William was surprised by this generosity. A man would have changed indeed, if he gives away more than he has to. This also had a familiar ring to Benjamin, who quickly whispered to William while the people wondered and blessed themselves over this gesture. William immediately fetched his precious leather-bound manuscript and found the place that Benjamin wanted.

A few others came forward, and were paid the same, the poorer they were the greater were they reimbursed. There were one or two that came forward that Master Morton could not remember having made any transactions with. William raised his clear blue eyes and looked gravely and steadily into those of the would-be claimants. That indefinable aura of authority that hung about him had its effect. One of them retreated hastily back into the crowd. The other looked away, but being ragged and obviously poor, he sighed as his uncomfortable conscience deprived him of a helpful mark or two.

Master Morton, however, was not going to be a spoilsport. He was beginning to feel an acceptance and a joy he had never felt in his life.

'Await, good sir. Take o' these to succour thy little ones, as a gift of God Who forgave such a lewd blackguard as I.'

He slipped a generous amount of coin into the astonished peasant's hand, cutting his thanks short.

Then he saw a little ragged girl standing nearby,, looking hopeful and slipped another handful of coins into her little hands, as much as she could hold, and was rewarded with a rapturous, 'Bwessings be unto thee, goob Bwuvver,' and a kiss on the cheek. She ran and poured the coins into the hands of her approaching mother, a pleasant but harassed-looking woman in ragged clothes. The worthy woman turned and blew a kiss to her benefactor.

Tears were appearing in more eyes than Master Morton's.

---

59   fourfold, times four

The mood of the crowd changed dramatically after this, the chest was rapidly running empty, and Benjamin felt it was his moment again.

'Hearken unto me, good folk! This is God's doing. 'Tis a triumph of His great grace. For this cause hath my companion and I been sent, to proclaim the Holy Word of God in thine ears yet in thine own tongue. Hearken ye unto the Holy Scriptures. It is the Word of God that Doctor Wycliffe of Oxford would have ye all to hear.'

As always, there were some that had heard of Wycliffe's brave stance for the downtrodden. They cheered and informed the crowd that '... these be Wycliffe's men – champions o' the common folk of England.'

Meanwhile Benjamin, ignoring these accolades, turned to the manuscript and read out the story of Zacchaeas from the Gospel of Luke. The cheating little tax-collector who had climbed a tree to see Jesus walk by, had been invited to meet with Jesus. When he emerged with the Saviour, he announced to the crowd that he would give half his goods to the poor, and ...' Benjamin paused and glanced at Master Morton's smiling face and continued more deliberately:

'.... Quoth he and mark ye well: "..and if I have any thing defrauded any man, I yield four-so-much."'

Master Morton chuckled through happy tears. The Holy Scriptures even foretold his own story.

Benjamin, with dramatic emphasis, came to the climax of his reading:

'Jesus saith unto him, "This day is salvation come to this house..."'

He closed the manuscript. Everyone present broke into thunderous applause and cheering. With that pronouncement by the Saviour, Aloysius Morton felt the chains of his avarice and guilt falling off him. He was coming into a full experience of God's love, not only as a spiritual son of Abraham as Zacchaeus was by flesh and blood, but as an adopted son of the Father God. He wept.

Hearing the scriptures spoken openly and boldly in English was yet another refreshing novelty to the townsfolk, so used to being excluded from the mysteries of Holy Writ.

As the emotion of the moment began to ebb, William Thorpe then took the podium to relieve Benjamin, who stopped to cool his dry throat with a tankard of ale, bought to him by the ever-helpful Jacob.

'People, beloved of God, hearken unto me!'

William did not have the same oratory flair as his colleague, but his fine, grave baritone had a carrying quality. This, together with his air of authority and deep sincerity had an immediate and profound impression on his listeners. If this was not enough, he had won considerable respect from many of the men in the crowd who had seen him labour with his hands, and many had witnessed his bold and compassionate stance at the tavern the evening before.

'Wot ye not that these same scriptures do show us the way to find the same salvation as this worthy man hath found? And mark ye this: there is no intermediary, nor confessor, nor pardoner, nor even any good works that can stand in the place of God's abundant grace.'

He brought out one scripture after another as he presented the message of forgiveness through faith, and a cancelling of the debt in God's books because of Christ's death on the cross.

Then he boldly condemned the sale of indulgences, and his cultured voice rose with his righteous anger.

'It is Simony! Did not the blessed Apostle Peter himself condemn the same Simon who dared to buy the gift of God with money? Nay. Hold not the grace of God in such contempt.'

Aloysius bowed his head in shame.

'Neither shall ye do despite to God's grace through penances,' the deep voice thundered in the silent square. 'What? Shall ye earn God's free gift like wages? An insult to the precious blood of Christ is this, and will but shut the gates of heaven if ye trust in good deeds for thy salvation. For all our good deeds are as filthy rags, sayeth the Holy Word of God...'

He came to his terrible climax.

'And the wages of sin is *death*!'

The word "death" seemed to echo around the square. The people trembled.

After a moment of fearful silence, William appeared to relent.

'...But the gift of God is eternal life. Yea, He giveth greater grace. Have I not received of it, a sinner also?'

There seemed to be a collective sigh from many in the crowd. William indicated his protégé with a sweeping gesture.

'Do we not behold it this day in our brother Aloysius before you all?

His good deeds ye have witnessed this day are but the fruits of repentance. Such is the power of God's grace. Do we sit in judgment on this man, who now hath God's forgiveness? Who indeed among us can cast the first stone? So will not I! So will not our Blessed Saviour.'

Aloysius brightened and stepped forward, showing a glimpse of his former boldness, although his voice was a little husky with emotion.

'Amen, say I and thanks be to God. Let it be known among ye all that from henceforth I sell indulgences and relics no more. I renounce it in Christ's holy name, though mayhap I bring the displeasure o' the Reverent Father upon mine head. So be it. My greatest treasure be now the love and forgiveness of mine own Heavenly Father.' He paused to master the lump in his throat. 'But I shall seek rather to work with mine own hands in honest toil, God aiding me.'

Cheers and murmurs of approval greeted this speech as he stepped back to where Benjamin awaited, smiling proudly.

This encouraged William to think that that many in their impromptu congregation were ready for the greatest decision of their life. He called on those who would hear and receive more of their message to gather round. With many mutterings and head shakings, some of the crowd dispersed to go about their business, but an encouraging number emerged and gravitated toward the podium. William came down so he could converse with them more personally, and to answer many questions. Not a few of the littlest local urchins sat at his feet to listen.

Meanwhile, Jacob approached Benjamin, bursting with excitement. He was leading, almost dragging a big, weather-beaten man forward. The man had a bushy white beard and the same rolling gait as Jacob – not to mention the distinctive odour of fish that characterized an experienced fisherman. Benjamin noted that he had the dazed and slightly bemused expression.

'Hail ho and be'old, Father Benjamin,' Jacob announced, with the gloating expression of one who had caught the biggest fish ever seen. 'I a-bringeth thee none else than the grand master o' the Fisher's Guild o' Feversham – even Master John Pike hisself.'

Benjamin looked at the man with interest, recognising him as the same who had shaken his fist at the former pardoner a little earlier. Brother Aloysius became a little apprehensive seeing such a large man bearing down on them, but was reassured when he stopped and brought his huge, calloused hand up to touch his forelock and bowing in respect to Benjamin. A deep but respectful voice came from within the white bushiness that covered most of his face.

'Hail and ho, Father. Mighty be the grace o' God – even on the stubborn heart of a fisher as I be.'

He turned his head to Aloysius and his voice almost became a growl. 'Had I not seen thine open-handedness, brother, I be one as would ha' truly cast thee overboard, bound o' mine own rig-ropes, be sure.'

Aloysius knew that he would have made enemies, possibly for the rest of his life. He nodded dumbly.

'But for God's grace, say I,' continued the deep voice. 'For the child thou didst bless wi' thy gold be my sister's youngest daughter. For this I thank thee.'

Jacob nodded his head and cackled in corroboration. Aloysius gaped with surprise, then glowed with jubilation.

Big John bowed his head and hesitated before speaking again. 'Nor do I be as one a-casting o' stones upon thee, for I be one that hath used others despiteously, God forgive me.'

He crossed himself as his audience looked up at him in astonishment. Even the canny Jacob was taken by surprise by this confession. A tear ran down big John's cheek and was lost in his snowy whiskers. He sniffed and wiped it with a dirty sleeve.

'It were the time when the herring were abundant a' the spring haul last. Mine old nets they be a-worn thin and tore grievous. The guildsmen, my fellows had paid o' their rightful guild-duty, but o' mine own – I had no wherewithal to buy or make new nets, for all my means be gone to feed my little ones and my widowed sister and her child also. God forgive me, but I bought me new nets o' the guildsmen's monies, and ha' not repaid. Oft and anon have I a-purposed to repay, for my nets are accursed for my sins, and the sea yieldeth little herring o' late, though I prayed full earnest to Saint Peter to bless them. For 'tis rieving and treachery when all be said. Wilt thou not assoil me o' my sin, father Benjamin?'

Benjamin was still explaining to the confused and guilt-laden fisherman that absolution need only be done through God alone, when Aloysius, who had slipped away unnoticed, returned bearing a bulging purse.

225

'Take this I pray thee, Master John Pike, for the guildsmen's duties. Was I not a fisherman in my youth ere greed and ambition possessed me? Happy days and sely were they indeed. Alas that I left that worthy calling. If aught remain, feed thine own.'

The big man stared at him in wonder. A huge grin parted the white bushiness momentarily. He took the purse in his left hand, but held out his calloused right hand in a gesture of friendship. But it was also a symbolic act of the transaction taking place in his soul.

"Tis God's gift, be sure, and I humbled be and will take it with thanks, fisher brother, for thus call 1 thee fro' henceforth. If thou canst toil and catch for thine own fare, thou'rt right welcome to sail at my side then, if thou wilt. God send that together our repentance bring greater blessing to our nets, and then shall I pay o' my debt. Twice, nay, thrice have I seen the goodness o' God in thee. If the grace o' God be as free as this, then I give mine all to the Giver of all – this do I swear for as long as I puff.'

Aloysius took the offered hand gratefully. It was the beginnings of a fine friendship and a better business partnership than he had ever experienced, though he knew it would take months before he would acclimatize to his old trade. All he could say was 'Sweeter shall my repose be this night.'

Benjamin was moved to applaud loudly.

'A rich man art thou indeed, fisher brother Aloysius, though all thy riches thou givest away. For great is thy reward in heaven.'

Yet even during the deepest of heart-searchings, a master-fisherman will still be aware of the elements. He lifted his head to look at the heavens and sniffed the air.

'Yon clouds that be a-comen in be great with rain.' He looked around as William approached, still counselling new disciples and speaking to many lingering enquirers.

'Hail ho, Father. As one that findeth grace o' the good God, I would serve thy cause if I may. Come ye all to the Fisherman's Guild hall, that ye be not a-soaken and catch ye'r death.'

Chapter 10: Fighting at Faversham

Therefore Simon Peter had a sword, and drew it out [Therefore
Simon Peter having a sword, drew it out], and smote the
servant of the bishop, and cut off his right ear. .....
Therefore Jesus said to Peter, Put thou thy sword into thy
sheath [Send thou the sword into the sheath]; wilt thou not,
that I drink the cup, that my Father gave to me?

[Gospel of John 18:10,11 – Wycliffe/Purvey translation.]

The Fisherman's Guild Hall became the new disciples' regular meeting place at Faversham.

Many of the locals, especially those who had witnessed the recent dramatic events, approached the Wycliffite preachers to enquire about this exciting new movement. Benjamin and William were both kept busy for the rest of the week. John and Jacob especially brought many of their colleagues along.

Aloysius resigned from his lucrative post as pardoner, even forsaking his Franciscan orders.

'Brother Aloysius no more am I!' he announced with a laugh, casting his clerical gown aside with a flourish. He had regained his dramatic flair. 'Henceforth call ye me fisher brother Francis, a fisher of men, an humble servant of God.'

He draped a fishing net over his shoulders like a clerical robe, picked up a fishing hook and bore it like a crozier through the fisherman's guildhall in the manner of a lordly bishop.

The guildsmen laughed and cheered, thoroughly entertained.

'Brother Fisher Francis?' chuckled Jacob, in an aside to big John. 'It liketh me well. Anon the guild be a-blessed of its own jester belike. But be his arms as mighty wi' nets as be his speech, thinkest thou?'

'Well, let be a'til a twelvemonth, say I, and he will be a-hauling as strong as any,' answered John tolerantly. 'An apprentice full willing he be, and the good God hath blessed our haul o' late. I be content. Fisher's cunning be in his fingers, and so his boast be good, but his arms be oversoft for want o' use. But by the Rood...!' he rumbled with deep-chested laughter, '....A mighty crier he be at market. He a-selleth our fish better nor like to his days a-sellin' his Pope's pardons.'

Father William Thorpe, furthermore, asked Aloysius (or Francis, rather) to be principal reader of scriptures for the Faversham disciples, leaving the Wycliffite preachers free to preach and to pastor their flocks elsewhere. He was delighted, and Benjamin gave him one of the last of their dwindling stock of translations. Francis used his oratory skills in this new office to such purpose, that even the children of the disciples loved to sit at his feet and listen attentively as he read.

In spite of the blisters on his hands, the smell of fish on his garments and the gathering wrath of his former friary, he was revelling in his newfound sense of significance, his friendships and inner joy.

Word of these amazing events spread even to Canterbury. The young preachers found themselves in regular demand at the podium in the town square at Faversham, as the numbers in their street congregations swelled from folk even from the furthest parts of Kent. The Guild Hall was beginning to overflow with new disciples. William Thorpe began to entertain hopes of spreading the word even in the hallowed streets and halls of Canterbury itself.

But wherever the Kingdom of God advances, the kingdom of darkness will always attempt to destroy, or at least mar it.

It was ten days since the confrontation with the pardoner in the Roiling Ram.

William and Benjamin were leaving the Guild Hall after their morning prayer with the disciples. They were walking through the square, debating whether they should journey further south to Canterbury or start their return journey, when Benjamin stopped and lifted his head to listen.

It was a strident, angry and vaguely familiar voice with a vaguely familiar message coming from the very same podium they stood on the previous day.

'.... For this tyranny of men that ruleth o'er men was not so ordained at the very beginning.

> *When Adam delved and Eve span*
> *Who was then the gentleman?'*

There was a roar of agreement from his audience at every intake of breath by the speaker. To William's experienced ear, this crowd's response seemed rather well-rehearsed, lacking the spontaneity of his own street congregations over the past week. Nonetheless, the disciplined cheers seemed to enhearten the orator, who took in audible, hissing breaths as he harangued the moving and shifting populace.

'Are we not one in the sight of Almighty God? He is no respecter of persons, though they call themselves a lord of the realm or holy bishop. Arise therefore, brethren! We have mightier strength than they, for we are many. They are but few, yet they would keep all of earth's treasures unto themselves. And be not deceived by the holy demeanour and liesings of these fat princes of Holy Church. What? Have ye not heard of the Devil's fetchery that was exposed afore ye all by us, who are sent by John Wycliffe? That deceiving Brother Aloysius hath confessed it, but pray, who sent him to bewitch ye all? 'Twas none but that arch-demon himself, who calleth of himself the Reverend Father Archbishop of Canterbury. How long will ye bear his burdensome tithes and collections......?'

Benjamin stood on the edge of a nearby well to get a better view of the speaker, and gasped. William, however, knew who it was without looking.

'John Ball! Ever hath he been a thorn in Doctor Wycliffe's side.'

They hurried over to join the crowd.

John Ball! The bitter young priest at Oxford who burned with fierce, unrelenting, uncontrolled anger at the injustice of the whole social order. But rather than change the hearts of people by the grace of God, his was a gospel of violence. He had alienated his colleagues, and once again the authorities were after him. He left Oxford in frustration, shaking his fist in Wycliffe's face, vowing to raise the men of Kent in rebellion and revolution. Now it seemed that he was carrying out his threat.

His strategy was clear. He had become aware of the Wycliffites' hard won favour of the people and was clearly trying to use it to advance his own cause.

Wat Tyler stood at his side, but his characteristic grin was fading a little, watching with frustration the lack of response from the locals. His own band of followers did their best, cheering whenever John Ball paused for breath, but only a small handful of the younger local labourers seemed to be inspired.

In fact the revolutionaries were even met with some hostility.

'Liesings!' yelled someone from the crowd. 'Thou speakest not sooth! Doctor Wycliffe, God aid him, be a-preachen peace and godliness, nor would he move us to hate and violent deeds....'

William recognised the heckler as Dick Brand, an ardent, hotheaded disciple from the Fisherman's Guild. He would speak to the more overzealous of their disciples at the next meeting, but there was no time to think about what he would say just at that moment.

Wat Tyler took note of the counter-dissenting voice, caught the eyes of a few of his largest henchmen, then jerked his head in young Dick's direction. These gentry converged on their target, but not without opposition. The Fishermen's Guild were a close-knit brotherhood, and would not stand by seeing one of their own victimised. Tyler's men were immediately turned on. This sparked outrage from Tyler and the rest of his followers. Some apprentices from the Carpenter's and Baker's Guilds who were at least sympathetic to the Wycliffites, joined in. Soon an all-in brawl seemed to be under way, and the yells of mob war drowned out even John Ball's angry voice. Women and children screamed and ran for cover. Chaos reigned supreme.

'O for the strength of Sampson,' prayed Benjamin aloud, dodging blows and falling bodies as they pressed through the milling crowd to the podium, 'or even the strength of Thomas Plowman.'

'O for the wisdom of Solomon.' puffed William at his side, 'Or even the wisdom of Father William Shephard.'

Before they reached their destination, thou found the wild-eyed John Ball, robes and all, roaring out curses on all Wycliffites and swinging punches at any man who came near him whom he did not recognise.

The quick-witted Benjamin dodged one of these wildly flying fists, grabbed his arms from behind in an arresting motion and pulling him back toward the foot of the podium. Being a tradesman's son and supporting himself with the work of his own hands in the course of his ministry, Benjamin's strength was superior to that of John Ball.

'Fool priest!' he hissed in John Ball's ear. 'Breakbuckler and want-wit! Think thou that souls can be saved from hell by such usage? Stint thy snarling, thou gokey wolf's head!'

John Ball struggled to free himself in vain, but laughed.

'What? Gentle Father Benjamin of Abyngdon is it?' he hissed defiantly. 'Save thou then thy timid souls, if thou canst so do. To free these souls from their hellish captivity of all fat lordings is my mission, God aiding me. Release me! Stay me at thy peril.'

Meanwhile, Father William Thorpe had finally pushed his way to the podium. With John Ball not in the position to contest the stage, William raised his hands to gain attention. His clear baritone voice seemed to pierce the cacophony of yells and curses all around him.

'Cease! Cease this gross witaldry! In the Name of Christ Jesu!'

The disciples recognised his voice at once and calmed down, causing their antagonists to pause in surprise and look toward the podium. The authority in his voice and the Name he invoked had an immediate effect.

Now that William had their attention, he hesitated. He realised that a theological treatise on rioting was useless here. He tried to appeal to their common sense.

'What is the meaning of this madness? Think ye that such rioting will not reach the ears of the powers that be?'

But this was like throwing down the gauntlet to John Ball. He cast aside Benjamin's slackened restraint and strode forward, puffing and fuming like an angry bull about to charge.

'The powers that be? A fig for the powers that be! Fool and blind that thou art, that thou canst not see. Doth it say not in thy precious Wycliffe's translation: "The Kingdom of God suffereth violence... and the violent take it by force?" Mark me well, o ye of womanly counsels that hath arms of iron: we shall raise an army of true men that shall shake the very foundations of the Devil's strongholds in this land....'

Another roar of agreement from his followers answered this, but this was immediately followed by an uneasy silence.

It was the unmistakable sound of marching feet and trotting of horses' hooves approaching, as though in answer to William's summons.

It was the Sheriff of Kent's men. Thirty foot soldiers and ten mounted troopers followed a fully armed and proud-looking knight – obviously an officer of high rank, bearing the arms and insignia of the county. Riding safely behind this formidable show of arms was an equally proud-looking cleric on a showy white horse.

Although the soldiers were outnumbered by Wat Tyler's men, they were armed to the teeth – and with crossbows at the ready. They looked prepared to take on a crowd thrice their number.

Benjamin laughed, 'Behold, the powers that be!'

Wat Tyler spat, cursed, then barked out an order. He was too good a tactician to risk his men at this stage. There was also no doubt that his men were very well disciplined, lightly armed though they were. They drew rank together with surprising speed, lining up behind the podium. The rest of the populace scattered, except for several men of the Fishermen's Guild, bruised and bleeding from their valiant stand. They were still prepared to fight Tyler's men – even the sheriff's men, should they prove to be a threat to the young preachers.

The commander of the troop halted and raised a richly embroidered gauntlet languidly. The armed men, also highly disciplined and well trained, halted as one man. The two armies faced each other silently for a moment. Benjamin, although relieved that the situation had been diffused for the moment, had a mild sense of foreboding. He looked nervously across at his colleague, standing calmly on the podium. One-eyed Jacob, his single eye blackened from the fight, limped up to Benjamin and whispered in his ear.

'That be the Sheriff's deputy-sheriff, Sir Ralph o' Mortemain, a puissant officer he be. Full pursuin' o' the rebels in Canterbury were he, but wherewithal he wist o' Wat's men in Feaversham I cannot tell.'

He glanced at the clerical gentleman who was making his leisurely way around to the front line of the armed men.

'Ah, then! Mayhap that be our informer. The ven'able Archdeacon Thomas o' Dunaway. A mumpish, barful, mellsome man with a nose for trouble, be sure.'

Having updated Benjamin with this intelligence, Jacob shuffled back to his post, standing with the guildsmen.

The commander, in strong contrast to all others present, was very elegantly dressed in military fashion. Bare-headed, hardly a hair was out of place, and his armour was so well polished it reflected the sun like a mirror. He leisurely walked his highbred horse back and forth in front of the podium, looking over the ragged army with evident disdain. He finally fixed his hooded gaze upon William as the one man apparently in charge of the situation.

'Who art thou that bringeth rancour unto the King's peace?' His tone, although languid, would have suited the late King Edward himself. 'Did mine ears deceive me? The rumours of riot and tumult could be heard, yea, from beyond the river. Answer me! Are ye the rebels whom I seek?'

Wat Tyler and John Ball, in spite of their boasted readiness to take on the might of the state, decided that discretion was the better part of valour in this case, and stayed out of sight.

'Nay, my lord, for we honour and serve the king.' answered William calmly, convinced he had nothing to fear from enforcers of the law. 'Men of peace are we, my colleague and I. Preachers of God's peace and grace we are. It is sooth that our flock have been overly zealous in defence of their own 'gainst ...'

William hesitated, not liking the role of talebearer, even against the troublesome John Ball. His forbearance was wasted, however, for at that moment, the Archdeacon rode up and took centre-stage of the unfolding drama. Portly, as most high-ranked churchmen were, he had a somewhat porcine, inquisitive nose and a dour and overbearing manner. He pointed an accusative finger at the two preachers.

'Ha! Splendour of God! Yea, false priests are ye, for thy cursed russet habits betray you. Are ye not Lollards, both? Disciples of that eternally damned John Wycliffe? As is that rebel-priest John Ball? This heresy shall be routed out, by God it shall! Hath not his lordship the bishop of Lincoln so given warning unto my master?'

Before William or Benjamin had a chance to defend themselves, the clergyman swung his horse around to face the deputy-sheriff's men.

'Seize them! They shall answer to my master, the Reverend Father himself.'

This act of arrogant presumption irritated Sir Ralph. The clergyman had never been a welcome addition to this expedition, but had to be tolerated for his rank's sake.

'O venerable and holy archdeacon,' drawled the captain, his voice and manner dripping with contempt and sarcasm, 'great is thy zeal for thy master *en assuivant* of these Lollers, or whatsoever thou wouldst name them. Natheless, to command my men is not within thy writ. 'Tis sheriff's business that calleth me hither. Questions of heresy or apostasy are not mine to consider, unless my lord sheriff willeth it so. Seek thee thine own men-at-arms if thou wilt apprehend these men, but 'ware lest thou usurp the authority of the sheriff of Kent.'

The archdeacon's face turned a deep red in his fury at this perceived insolence. He puffed and panted to regain his self-control.

'Mine is the authority of Holy Church! And do I stand in thy place, Sir Ralph, to mind thee of thy devoir to sheriff and king?'

He waved his hand at the two silent figures standing on the podium.

'With the advent of these turbulent priests, riot and tumult there hath been. My master's pardoner hath turned apostate and hath forsaken his post and his vows and these miscreants are the cause thereof. Do I inform my master, or indeed thine, that thou shalt do *naught*?'

In spite of his extreme reluctance at having his hand forced by a mere clergyman he heartily disliked, Sir Ralph had to concede the point. He sighed heavily.

'Art full hasty, O venerable Thomas, but so be it. Apprehended they shall be for questioning. Sergeant, take thou them, but with all due courtesy if they come willingly...'

Threatening growls of protest came from the fisher guildsmen, preparing to do battle in defence of their spiritual leaders. Firebrand Dick strode forward to give his candid opinion of the venerable archdeacon, only to be grabbed by the shoulder by Benjamin's strong hand. The men-at-arms who had stepped forward to make the arrest stopped at these threatening signs and their sergeant barked his orders. Being well-trained and disciplined, they levelled their crossbows as one man at the crowd.

'Peace, brethren!' intervened William with a stern voice, turning around. 'Be ye patient. Ours is a just cause, so no fear of the Law have we.' Turning back to the arresting sergeant, he spoke courteously.

'We come willingly, sir. Lay down thine arms, I pray.'

Having their own brand of discipline, he and Benjamin stepped forward but stopped as a new voice came from behind them.

'Hold, Father William. Hold, my lord deputy-sheriff, I pray!'

Everyone turned in surprise to see none other than the former pardoner himself running and panting, forcing his way though Wat's men up to the podium with the big fisherman by his side. Although he looked much healthier in colour than he did a week past, and had lost a little weight, he was still unmistakably the same cheerfully impudent and flamboyant showman that he ever was – but with a difference. His cheerfulness seemed to come from within, not from any self-confidence. He seemed to take charge immediately.

'Hail, Sir Ralph, and well met, my venerable Lord Thomas of Dunaway. 'Tis a merry meeting this day, is't not?'

The archdeacon, after a brief moment's unrecognition, pounced metaphorically upon him.

'Rood of Christ! 'Tis the apostate himself. Aloysius! Hast thou no shame that thou wouldst stand before thy betters in brazen insolence? No more shall I call thee brother, ill-mannered, brazen, ungrateful renegade, for thou'st fallen greatly from grace. Thou shalt answer before my master and thine for thy treachery and thine heresy. Whither thine habit?'

The former pardoner just laughed impudently and indicated his ragged and stained fishing garb.

'It is before thee, venerable lord. Nay, call me brother Aloysius no more. Fisher brother Francis am I from henceforth.'

Cheers came from his fellow guildsmen. Big John, who had just come from a late haul was being updated on the current state of affairs by Jacob. His heavy face became rather grave.

'Wilt thou so detain me, o' venerable Thomas, my lord?' Francis raised his hands in a fatalistic gesture. 'So be it. Willingly shall I be apprehended and stand with these worthy men before the sheriff. Yea, he shall have a full and faithful account of all my doings, forsooth.'

Then he leaned toward the fuming clergyman and gave him a broad wink as if to a fellow conspirator.

'For peradventure I have much to tell him that he would fane be wist of, sayeth thou not so, o my venerable lord Thomas?'

The venerable Thomas of Dunaway suddenly lost his composure. His rather protuberant eyes almost burst from their sockets. He turned pale, gulped and glared back at the chuckling scapegrace before him.

'Surely thou wouldst not dare,...' he whispered. Then he looked about him in doubt and embarrassment, as a few of the fishermen cackled with delighted anticipation, sensing a new scandal.

'Ho! But pray what is this, my lord?' came Sir Ralph's drawling voice, obviously relishing his unwanted guest's discomfiture. 'Hath an holy man truly done despite unto the King's law?'

Furious that he had betrayed himself, the archbishop tried to make a recovery.

'Nay and never, Sir Ralph!' he cried in accents of outraged innocence. 'Rather is it a matter of grave and grievous import that concerneth none but the reverend father and myself, and ...' he said, drawing himself up in his full dignity, perceiving a powerful defensive argument, '...and mark ye all, this matter beareth the seal of the confessional, and cannot be spoken of! Do not dare to do violence to such holy affairs ..... or ye shall abide the wrath of God!'

He glared around challengingly at all his hearers in an attempt to cow them. A few of the older and simpler folk present whispered, 'The wrath of God!' and made the sign of the cross.

'Ah, soothly said, my venerable lord. Ware we all the wrath of God indeed. Greatly do I fear it, yea even above the wrath of the Reverend Father of Canterbury. But surely it is also a grievous sin to conceal sin, is it not? And as I also am privy to these "holy affairs," surely I must speak of them should my good lord sheriff so demand it of me ... else would I abide the wrath of God.'

He made the sign of the cross also and turned a mock pious face toward the archdeacon who now looked rather nonplussed.

'O, the cunning fox!' whispered Benjamin in high glee. 'I would wager he hath perilous intelligence on many a high churchman. Were I not an holy priest, greatly would I fane hear of this holy, or unholy affair.'

'But thou art an holy priest ordained of God,' retorted William softly in mild rebuke, hiding a smile. 'Therefore hold thy peace and be content with blessed ignorance.'

But not for nothing had Thomas of Dunaway risen in the ranks to oversee the ecclesiastical matters of the diocese of Kent. Recovering his dignity, he turned his fidgeting horse toward the Canterbury gate and looked over his shoulder disdainfully at his graceless tormenter.

'Very well and so be it, thou talebearer and ingrate renegade. If thou wilt break faith and speak of matters that are not of thine order, then thou shalt bear the doom of everlasting hellfire. It shall not be said that the venerable Thomas of Dunaway did expose an humble penitent to public shame, therefore I withdraw my demand for thine apprehension and those of yonder heretics, and thou holdest a knife at my throat. Thou shalt buy thy freedom with silence for a space. But ware ye the vengeance of Holy Church upon them that flout her.'

He spurred past Sir Ralph saying loftily, 'I take my leave, good Sir Ralph. But this I say unto thee: Ware thou also of these turbulent Lollards, for ever there shall be strife whithersoever they goeth.'

With that parting shot, he rode off in the direction from which he came, looking as though he had won a great victory.

The fishermen and Wat's men alike, now in temporary alliance, muttered their approval of his departure.

'Aye, get ye hence, thou porcous-bellied polax,' growled out the young firebrand. He would have expanded on this theme had not big John put his arm around his shoulder warningly.

'Wilt thou a-fright the fish still, Dick lad?' he muttered in his ear. 'There be still work to do ere we a-haul in this net anon.'

The perilous situation had not yet passed, even with the departure of Dunaway. All attention, still with a little apprehension, was now on the deputy-sheriff and his men.

Sir Ralph had mellowed a little with the defeat and departure of the eminent clergyman.

'A wearisome jealous jade is Mistress Duty, alas...!' he complained, polishing the jewels on his left gauntlet and holding them up to inspect them in the dimming light, '....that I must bring the king's justice upon them that also bring me merry relief in all this burdensome business.'

He sighed, shook his head and lifted his languid eyelids to look upon the former pardoner, calmly awaiting his pleasure.

'Well and well then, Brother Aloysius... but stay ... Fisher Francis is't not? I would fane have had thee apprehended in the king's name to hear of what manner this terrible sin would be. Natheless, I have anon no foundation for such an arrest, for his venerableness hath so denied it. Holy Church will suffer none to bring judgment upon her own. If the nets of a fisherman giveth thee greater joy than an holy pardoner's hoards, then go in peace and prosper if thou'rt able. Natheless, these lollard priests are another matter.'

The tension among the fishermen had relaxed momentarily with the release of brother Francis, but a sense of foreboding came over them when Sir Ralph began, with indolent austerity, to address the two preachers.

'Father ... William Thorpe is't not? Heretic or no, I care not for such matters. But the matter that cometh within my writ is that these troubles and strife 'gainst the king's peace hath its root in thee, thy brother priest and that curst rebel gutter-priest John Ball.'

He did not notice the hasty movement from behind the podium by the same rebel gutter-priest. It was quickly suppressed, so he continued unchecked.

'Ye are all of John Wycliffe's party, so 'tis said. If the venerable Thomas speaketh sooth, strife shall ever follow thee and of this we have been witness this day. Whether wittingly caused or no, this vulgar furore my lord sheriff will not countenance. Look not to Holy Church to extend her mantle over you, for ye have offended her grievously, I deem. I say not that ye are fully rebellious as thy fellow, John Ball, else I would apprehend you indeed. Honest but overly zealful men do ye seem, so I withhold mine hand. But banished from Feaversham, yea from Kent, ye must be. I have spoken.'

Both he and William raised their hands to check the resulting storm of protest. Dick Brand was like a mad dog straining at the leash of big John's restraining arm. Even some of Wat's men expressed some sympathy and respect for the brave young preachers. Benjamin shook his head in frustration. He would have spoken some hasty words himself, but decided against it. The sounds of discontent died down.

'If that for us is thy doom, my lord,' replied William steadily, his deep and crisp tones in contrast to Sir Ralph's languorous superciliousness, 'then we shall endure it, unjust though it may seem to us. But mayhap our work is ended in Kent, and God will have us to return from whence we came.'

'Then the oracle of God am I,' returned the deputy-sheriff ironically. Then he relented a little.

'A full two days shall I give you both ere ye depart, Father William. But break faith, or trouble ye the king's peace again, then beware the sheriff's wrath. I shall abide at his lordship's castle against thy departure. Fare ye well.'

Sir Ralph bowed his head and turned his horse, signalling his men to about face.

As they marched away, a few soldiers, in the manner of town criers, were sent to the podium to announce a curfew imposed for the rest of the day.

'A bounty be upon the heads o' the rebels John Ball and Wat Tyler,' they cried sonorously. 'Whomsoever will bring tidings o' these, whom be named wolf's heads, and should they be a-taken, to him shall be given five marks a-piece ... Hear ye... Hear ye!'

A sheet of parchment bearing the same message was nailed to the market signpost.

Wat Tyler, observing this, cursed, laughed and spat. His fierce grin did not seem to abate. He seemed to revel in his notoriety.

'Ho then! The hunt is up, and the wolf must seek his lair for a season. Come, Father John.'

But John Ball had not quite finished his business. He was pleading vigorously with the two preachers.

'Behold now how such false justice hath been meted out unto you by yon tyrants. Do you not now wonder at the wrath of the common folk? Such is their usage unto us all whilst they feast as we suffer famine. Come ye with us and fight with us, I beg of you, Father William, Father Benjamin, for many good men follow you, and ye betrayed us not to our adversaries. Strike hands with us, and together cast we down that same tyranny that hath wrongfully banished you.'

This was too much for Benjamin's self-restraint. He jumped from the podium and stood nose to nose with the the rebel priest, his fists clenched, his own eyes flaming wrathfully.

'And shall we strike hands with thee?' he growled through his teeth, 'Liefer would I strike maw with the wild wolves, for I would trust them more. Thou wouldst broil good men in thy violent deeds. Innocent blood is shed. Thou wouldst beat upon our men for they assent not to thy madness. Ye cower behind our robes at the advent of the sheriff's men. Thou namest the good Doctor Wycliffe as thy patron, thus damning him in the eyes of the law. And for this we are banished wrongfully. Get ye gone, thou make-bait priest, ere I forget that I am a man of peace!'

Before the two angry priests got at each other's throats, both William and Wat Tyler stepped in.

'A-done do, John, thou fool!' hissed Tyler, holding him back, uneasily aware of the unwelcome attention this new incident would attract. 'Wilt thou betray us? This be no place to raise our army. Cowards and women-hearts rule in Faversham, more's the pity. We must away to Canterbury ere we be discovered or betrayed.'

'Ye name us cowards?' Benjamin stormed, as William restrained him with a hand on his shoulder. William turned and addressed John Ball and Tyler with his customary composure.

'Vain is it Father John, Master Tyler, to seek our aid in thy cause, for as far as the ends of the earth are our minds in this matter. Though my brother priest would fight in his hot wrath, yet seek we but the souls of men as doth our Holy Lord Christ. The path of the violent shall win naught but death for many. Mark the words of Our Lord Christ Himself: "He that liveth by the sword shall die by the sword."'

But Tyler and John Ball were too hell-bent on destruction and hatred to listen.

'Craven counsel!' cried John Ball as Tyler virtually dragged him away. 'If I die for my cause, so be it. We shall wade in blood ere the end.... But ye ... ye shall ever be slaves!'

His voice trailed away into the distance.

'Willing slaves of the Good Lord Christ are we' Benjamin shouted at the receding figure, 'not thralls of the great fiend as are ye!'

'Have done, my friend' William's calm voice admonished him. 'Slaves of Our Lord are we indeed, and he commandeth us to show wisdom and restraint.'

Benjamin was still fuming too much to heed him.

'O that I had but choked the life from such a losel. *Bonis nocet quisqus malis perpercit.*[60]

60 Whoever spares the bad injures the good (Publius Syrus)

'*Compesce mentem,*[61] my friend.' William said patiently, 'Cool thy wrath. Nay, greater scathe wouldst thou have done. But come! For much we have to do ere we depart.'

Having set all in order as best they could in the time given them, the two banished evangelists crossed the mighty Thames into Essex two days later.

Benjamin could see that William was taking his banishment badly. The memory of the parting with the grieving disciples weighed heavily upon him. His grave face was set in stern lines and his head was down as they trudged north and westwards.

Benjamin's own buoyant spirits now asserted themselves.

'Be of good cheer, brother. We have not failed. We have begun a fire in Kent that neither the sheriff, nor John Ball, nor Satanus himself can quench. And by the Living God, good fisher brother Francis shall fan the flames full merrily, I trow!'

William smiled a little.

'Mayhap thou'rt in the right, but ....' his smile faded, 'I fear me that Tyler and John Ball shall also ignite wildfire, and peradventure much shall be burned, and grievously. Such was the foreboding of Doctor Evangelicus ere our commissioning.'

'So say not I!' objected Benjamin, the eternal optimist. 'Their rebellion will fail as the Jacobean hordes of France fell also.'

'So do I hope. Natheless, hasten we unto Oxenford to bear report to our masters. The disciples on our journey we must meet but briefly.'

'A mighty tale of deeds do we report indeed! Shall our exploits rival those of William Shephard and Thomas Plowman, think you?'

William laughed. 'I think not, for full gifted and greater of heart are they, both. How fare they, I wonder, whithersoever they fare?'

---

61   Control your temper

Chapter 11: Go Ye forth ….!

*'Therefore go ye, and teach all folks, baptizing them in the Name
of the Father, and of the Son, and of the Holy Ghost; Teaching
them to keep all things, whatever things I have commanded to you;
and lo! I am with you in all days, into the end of the world.'*

(Gospel of Matthew 28:19, 20 - Wycliffe/Purvey Translation)

The next day was showery and gusty as the two men passed through the crumbling northern gates of Oxford, gates that were no longer deemed as necessary for the town's protection as they were in more politically unstable times. But warfare of a different kind was raging within and without the decaying walls of Oxford town.

Nothing seemed to have changed outwardly. The great towers and steeples stood as strong and impassive as before, impervious to the changeable weather. Scholars, friars and townsfolk with their livestock went about their business as they always had done for centuries. But William became aware of a slight tension in the air. Where was the vendor's cry? Why could he not hear the laughter of children, who would normally be playing in the streets? Instead of the customary loud and cheerful exchange of opinions one would hear in a market town, people spoke to each other in subdued voices.

William also noted that they had not yet seen any other cleric wearing the russet coloured habit, which proclaimed adherence to John Wycliffe's movement, especially the masters and ordained priests. When people passed the two travellers, they stopped and stared, then whispered to each other.

Once a passing group of student-clerics looked up at the two missionaries and said "God save John Wycliffe!" in low but fervent tones, then hurried on. Tom waved genially to a whispering group of housewives who were staring rather furtively at them. One waved back, but immediately they all glanced up and down the road and hurried into their respective houses like frightened rabbits in their burrows.

'Wherefore these whisperings?' Tom wondered aloud. 'Are we wolfsheads that folk look upon us so?'

William, sad but not particularly concerned, shrugged his shoulders fatalistically.

'Of late much simmering brose of enmity hath there been twixt Doctor Evangelicus and them that oppose him. We wear the garb of his henchmen, so are marked men also. Alas! A-times 'twill erupt into garboil and strife upon the clerks and townsfolk of Oxenford. Such are the times in which we live, Thomas.'

They drew near to the Angel tavern, its sign creaking on its hinges each time a gust of wind took it, beckoning invitingly. Tom, who was both thirsty and hungry for information, glanced suggestively at William, who hesitated. He glanced down the street, eager to press on to their destination, but not wanting to disappoint Tom. The beer at the Angel was of high repute after all. A gust of wind blew the hood off his head and a brief shower of rain smote his face. That decided the matter. He pushed open the well-worn oaken door, saying 'We will await the weather within. But mark: One drink only will I suffer....'

The words died on his lips as they shut the door. He had spoken above the wind, expecting to be drowned out by the noises within the tavern. But he may as well have been singing loudly at a funeral in a quiet chapel, so incongruous it sounded. Sad and morose faces turned to him in surprise, exchanged meaningful glances with each other, then turned away again. One student-cleric caught Tom's eye, shaking his head and putting his finger to his lips in a kind of warning. It only served to sharpen his curiosity.

The tension in the air was even stronger than ever. It reminded William of the first time he walked into the Bull and Book down the other end of town ten years earlier, dressed in labourer's rags and smelling of sheep.

The normal mixture of labourers, apprentices, clerics, tradesmen and students sat at various tables, mostly with their peers. One would usually expect to experience the customary hum and buzz of congeniality punctuated by the occasional cheerful and loudly proposed toast or drink-fired song. Instead, most of the drinkers sat silent, glum or glowering, giving reluctant attention to a group of friars and churchmen of various orders and ranks, seated around a large table on a central and elevated platform.

These venerable gentry seemed to have taken over proceedings. They were all wearing an expression of benign self-satisfaction as they sipped their wine. One particularly large cleric, his manner as imposing as the proportions of his stomach, was standing on a low stool as a makeshift pulpit, and holding forth dramatically. His raiment and ornately carved staff proclaimed him as a churchman of rank.

Tom and William had apparently missed the beginning of an important proclamation.

'.... And thither he shall stand before the Reverend Father himself,' the speaker announced with obvious relish, 'and before an holy convocation of legates shall he stand to answer for his damnable heresies and his insolence. If he returneth unto Oxenford, yea, *if* he so do, it shall be as a penitent truly disgraced and humbled, a black sheep that returneth unto the fold.'

A firm "Amen!" in chorus came from the central table, although the effect was slightly spoilt by a hiccough from the most enabriated amongst them.

'Mother church suffereth not such dark disobeyance, and the Almighty shall avenge it by the strong arm of His Holy Legates. Take heed from this, therefore. Fear and learn! As for those pernicious poor priests he hath sent forth....'

The orator glanced in the direction of the newcomers who interrupted his homily with their entry at that moment. Staring at them as they came into the light of the great torches, annoyance turned to scorn on his countenance as he saw the colour of their slightly ragged raiment.

'Hola! Speak we of demons and, lo! They come as if summoned. Two poor Lollard preachers have we amongst us! God save us! Are ye not of these beggarly men that be too haughty to beg?'

His belly wobbled vigorously, a little out of rhythm to his sneering titter. The stool he stood upon creaked in protest.

Focus now shifted on to William and Thomas, for the most part sympathetically. The general expectation was that they would suffer a complete verbal annihilation.

'Prithee, sirrahs,' continued the mocking, suave voice, 'do ye preach the gospel unto the swine? Do ye kneel in the grime to bless their children? Is the hayloft thy pulpit? Surely ye must wash ere ye enter the sacred portals of Oxenford.'

Loud, even drunken laughter came from the central table. Stony silence came from the rest of the room. The objects of his scorn stood impassively with arms folded, although Tom's jaw hardened somewhat, the latent laughter clouded over a little.

'We behold before us two lewd foot-soldiers of a ragged army of rebels and brigands. And they bereft of their great general, alas! And what is this command and commission by which they are sent? Is it not "Go ye forth… unto perdition"?

So delighted by his own wit, he almost doubled over with laughter, as far as his stomach would allow.

This was too much for the stool, already struggling under the immense weight it had to bear. One of its legs gave way and the noble churchman stumbled and fell headlong into the dust on the lower floor.

A roar of gleeful surprise went up from many of the drinkers, hastily checked. Tom approached him, ignoring a restraining hand from William. He shook his head and sighed with exaggerated concern as he bent to help him up.

'Alack, my venerable lord! Great is thy fall… greatly hast thou become despoiled, yea, grievous soiled. This we must amend! Did I not espy an horse's trough without this place? Waters of great healing virtue are found therein, so 'tis said.'

Before he or his colleagues knew what was happening, the fat fallen churchman, already whimpering with pain and shock, found himself plucked from the floor and carried like a squealing pig on large and very strong shoulders out through the gathered throng. There were gasps and guffaws as Tom and his wailing, struggling burden disappeared out through the door out of sight.

The sound of protests, pleas and rather unclerical-like curses that came in through the door were abruptly smothered by the sound of an unmistakable splash, followed by a series of very watery whimperings, curses, threats and spluttering, fading into the distance.

'Excommunicate shalt thou be for this, thou lewd Lollard heretic!' shouted one of the church officers as Tom returned, drying his hands on his habit. However, sizing up the powerful frame of their colleague's assailant, and the genial challenging posture he took up before them, none of the others made a move to avenge the humiliation of their esteemed spokesman.

Moreover, the mood had changed throughout the tavern. Tom's impudence had broken the sense of awe the churchmen had managed to impose upon the assembled company.

A student jumped up at his table at the other end of the room and raised his tankard in a toast to Tom.

'Lo, is this not Samson that returneth triumphant from the slaughter of the Philistines?'

His fellows broke into laughter, exploded to their feet and raised their drinks crying 'Hail, Samson, scourge of the Philistines!' and 'God save Doctor Evangelicus!'

Another vociferously argued that he was rather a David who had smitten him a fat Goliath, which provoked another wave of laughter. It was like a refreshing wind passing through or a ripple effect as nearly every table shook to the thunder of men rising to drink the toast. It was open rebellion, although some of the older men shook their heads and one muttered something about 'a-poked of the wild boar's rump' and that evil consequences would arise from this extreme act of defiance.

The remaining un-slaughtered Philistines rose as one man (with the exception of the most drunken cleric among them, who had to be dragged to his feet by his neighbour) and departed in a haughty and dignified manner, not deigning to comment nor even look at the young Samson who had committed such an outrage upon their august colleague. Samson bowed mockingly as they passed, restraining a strong impulse to speed their departure with a right foot to their posteriors.

He turned and bowed again, acknowledging the thunderous acclaim of both students and townsfolk throughout the tavern. He would have accepted a tankard of good beer from a grinning apprentice nearby, had he not found Father William standing austerely before him.

'Hail Samson indeed. But know anon that thou'rt a marked man.' His stern tones were tempered a little by the sympathetic twinkle in his eye. 'Thou'st sown to the wind, 'ware now the whirlwind! In greater force will the Philistines return in vengeance for thy folly, so we must away, and that straightway. Come! Let us make haste to Master Smith's abode. There perchance shall we find an haven for this storm of thy creating for the nonce.'

Tom looked longingly at the proffered beer as he obediently followed William out the door, hesitated, then grabbed the tankard for a quick pull and ran out the door before he incurred further rebuke.

Hastily wiping the foam off his face, he caught up with William, walking rapidly in the direction of University College.

'Thy pardon I beg, father. 'Twas witaldry, this I confess. But his insolence! Wouldst thou have me not answer the challenge to that ass's brayings? What manner of man is this pompous bag 'o bobbance?'

'A bag of high consequence is this, thy braying ass, my son,' answered William calmly, without turning his head or slackening his pace. 'Twas the Bishop of Lincoln's man: the venerable archdeacon Thomas Wynham, and none other.'

This revelation caused even Tom to blanch a little.

'Merciful heavens! I am a marked man indeed! Liefer would I have baptized the Pope himself. Wherefore didst thou not bid me refrain? Hadst thou but spoken a word...'

William shrugged his shoulders and gave a short laugh.

'Tempted was I to smite him down with my staff.'

He walked on, smiling at Tom's reaction to such an admission, but William's amusement soon gave way to slight anxiety.

'"Bereft of their general...." quoth he?' he muttered to himself.

Finally the travellers turned into Logic Lane and could see Ockham House, an elegant but solidly built Masters' residence at University College. Coincidentally, they discovered Master Smith taking the air just outside the gates, and hailed him.

He had just emerged from the wrought-iron gate, and was looking keenly around as though he was expecting them. When he saw them approaching, he almost ran to meet them, ringing their hands fervently.

'In a good hour! Is it not God's season, forsooth? I felt it within mine heart that your countenances I would look upon this day. Come ye into my chambers, my friends.'

He ushered them up ornately carved stone stairs, down echoing passages and up wide marble stairs to his quarters.

They chatted about recent events along the way. The master was hugely entertained by Tom's exploit at the tavern, but agreed that it might have led to trouble if Tom had been recognised and apprehended.

'Abide this night in this place, my son. If the enemy press thee closely, we shall conceal thy person within an hay wain for thy journey onward.'

Tom laughed but then realised that the master was not joking.

When asked about Doctor Wycliffe, the master was able to partially relieve William's mind, for the Doctor had been summoned to Lambeth to face a convocation of Bishops. Although Master Smith looked a little concerned, he brushed it aside with a dismissive gesture.

'Feints and sleeveless threats to affright us all, these. Have ye heard hearsay that the Doctor and his following will suffer loss? Do the townsfolk hide in fear of men-at-arms that come to seize us all? Liesings! Phantoms are these, sent by our foes to affright us, that we may bow and lout unto the fattened popish lordings, hold our peace and stay our protestations of the evils within the church. Hold we our peace? Ha!'

He led them down the final corridor and paused before his great oaken doors, defiance fading as he looked upon his guests.

'Natheless, this summons to Lambeth bodeth ill. Yea, ill doth the good Doctor bear it, and is fully irate. Ever he will give blow for blow upon his gainsayers, alas! He is one that will ever beard the lion!'

Then the sober expression lifted as he opened the door.

But will the bishops at Lambeth defy the Gaunt and others among the great that take our part? I think not. The doctor's task is not yet accomplished, and will not be stayed by fatted churchmen. A conflagration hath been lit that neither Lambeth nor the very pontiff himself can quench. And ye, good brethren, are chief among them that shall bear the flame.'

William and Tom exchanged glances of wonder as they followed him inside.

His rooms were unpretentious but comfortable, located in the most remote and quietest part of the building. He had dispensed with most of the ornaments that one would often see in a great man's residence, notably an absence of images of the Madonna and Child – not even a crucifix on the wall. Instead, his study walls were filled with shelves of leather-bound books and scrolls. William had sat with Master Smith many times during the years of study, and always felt at home, and yet still with a sense of awe. There were times in that room when he felt the presence of God so strongly, he had fallen on his face. It was almost as overwhelming as his first encounter with the Great Shepherd. He looked over to a seat in the remotest part of the room, and noted the two worn patches in the carpet in front of it, where the Master had knelt in prayer, and the moist stains on the seat where many intercessory tears had been shed.

For the moment, Master Smith's attention was on his guests, and he motioned them to some comfortable chairs by his table, littered with paper, inkhorns and quills. He seemed to be pregnant with news and suppressed excitement.

'Have ye broken your fast? Ye have? Sit ye down, for verily this is God's time and occasion.'

He rang the service bell, and a demure housemaid answered, bowing silently at his request for tankards of his best ale. Shutting the door, he sat down at his desk opposite them. His normally dreamy brown eyes seemed very much alive and alert.

'This very morn have I been a-praying for ye both, for burdened has mine heart been for ye of late. Hereford hath come and gone, for he is called to Cheshire to preach on the morrow. But he hath informed me, to my joy, of the sending forth of the Poor Preachers. O that I could have been present at the commissioning! But there is much a'do here of late. In especial have I called our intercessors together. So are we all on our knees here at Logic lane for ye all. All is well? Tell me, how fared ye?'

They told him briefly what had happened so far, and he listened in rapt attention, shaking his head in wonder over the examples of God's intervention. The housemaid brought in the ale, smiling especially at Tom before she left, but he was too engrossed in the stirring events unfolding to notice.

Master Smith pondered over his ale for a moment, stroking his beard. Suddenly he looked up and fixed his eyes on at them intently, aglow with the fire of prophecy. The two men sensed the presence of the Spirit of God, as they often did when Master Smith was in this mood, and waited expectantly.

'Brethren!' the Master began, with a voice throbbing with authority and power, 'In my devotions, God granted me a vision on thy behalf, and I wist not the wherewithal that I should impart it, for it was of great import but I knew not whither God had led you that I may tell it you. But God hath brought it to pass. Now ye are with us, ye shall hear it:

'I beheld thee both in my mind's eye, walking swiftly with winged feet both South and Westward. Ye both became as firebrands, burning with great zeal, and setting hearts on fire as ye journeyed, and journeyed far. Then it seemed that I was lifted up and saw beyond your steps that a path was laid out for you, lined with dried piles of tinder-wood. Through many counties this path passed, even to Somerset, Devon and even unto Cornwall. These piles and fires are gatherings of disciples, I deem, that hath been prepared to hear the Word of Life that would set them a-flame. As ye spread the fire and tend it, these flames shall be spread outward to other piles that await their time.

'But mark this, servants of God, turn not to the right not to the left. Satanas would essay to lead you from your true path. Tarry not overlong in each place ye are sent until ye find your journey's end. If ye so tarry and your gait would falter, the enemy may quench the fire and despoil them that await your coming, if ye stay not true to your calling. The whispered voice of the Holy Ghost in your hearts will guide you, whether ye must tarry or go on in each place that He will send you. Strange and dark things shall ye see. Signs and ferly wonders shall follow you as ye believe. He will give wings to your feet, words in your mouths, strength to your arms and his holy angels to guard you whithersoever God leadeth you. For He himself shall journey with you and will labour at your side. Go ye forth, and fear naught!'

His voice seemed to resonate around the room and through their whole being. They all sat for a moment, overwhelmed by the awesome presence of God.

Finally, William quietly broke the silence.

'This timely message hath greatly enboldened us, Master Smith. Surely it hath confirmed much that hath begun to take root in our hearts.'

'Amen!' agreed Tom, moved to prophetic utterance himself, and speaking with wisdom beyond his years. 'A task beyond the measure of our strength is this mission. Many tests shall we meet upon the way. Battles shall we fight that cannot be won by the arm of flesh. Thus, all the more need we His power and wisdom, but God hath spoken and the task shall be done. Thanks be to God and thy faithfulness, good Master.'

'Well, well. Thou'st been my best students, and greatly shall ye be missed at Oxenford,' said the old prayer-warrior. 'The blessed Holy Ghost alone is now thy Master, not I, nor none other. Mine heart telleth me that ye shall learn more in this journey than have ever I, nor any of the masters of Oxenford. Our prayers go with you. Ye shall sit at meat with me once more ere nightetale, and shall sleep on down and under cover this time, though ye sleep on earth and hay hereafter. But is their naught else we can supply you?'

'Yea, and verily, Master Smith,' said William, indicating the mass of papers on the table with a smile. 'For this purpose do we invade thy sanctuary – that we may harvest a-many of the good Doctor's copies of Holy Scripture and of them as much that our way bags can hold.'

Their bags were indeed bulging yet strangely light when the two missionaries set forth again the next day, now with renewed energy and confidence. Nevertheless, they hid their customary habits as a precautionary measure in case Tom was discovered and arrested.

They proceeded south through Kennington to Abingdon. These towns had heard much preaching from the Wycliffites, and William's face was also not unknown among the townsfolk and villages. Small disciple groups had sprung up wherever Wycliffe's influence had been felt. They needed as much encouragement, teaching and copies of English scripture portions as the two men could spare.

William decided it was better if copies were only given to those who were willing and able to make more copies or lead a reading circle of the followers. He found it difficult, however, to refuse some of the unlettered child-like folk who wanted to merely touch the Holy Word, hoping that some virtue would be imparted. Forestalling Tom's stern homily on idolatrous practices, William gently explained that, "...The letter killeth, but the Spirit giveth life."

They visited Benjamin's family at Abingdon and gave them tidings of their eldest son and his own mission to Essex and Kent with William

Thorpe, only to find that they had already dropped in briefly from their journey southeast. They had missed him only by two days, so the mother said.

Benjamin's father was the town's wheelwright, as highly regarded by his neighbours for his generosity and hospitality as for his family's antiquity. The Abyngdon generations went right back to the foundations of the town in King Alfred's day when it first received its charter.

'But come thou in, Father William. And thou also Master Thomas.' boomed Master Jonas Abingdon, beaming all over his honest and homely face. 'Ye shall sup with us, find repose and break your fast with us also.'

He held up his hand to pre-empt any protestations and insisted.

'Ye shall not say me Nay, for my sely young cub Ben holdeth ye both in high regard and speaketh much of ye. So then shall we.'

Tom could see from whence his young friend inherited his overflowing friendliness.

As they dined with the family, every member, even little Rosalind and restless young Edmund hung on every word their guests said. The father and mother also asked many questions about their son. Tom recounted, with considerable embellishments, many of the pranks that he and Benjamin had got up to, and though they had heard about them before, they all laughed heartily.

'Didst thou truly cast o' that fat friar into the miller's pond, Master Plowman?' asked young Edmund eagerly, recalling one of his big brother's anecdotes that Tom had avoided mentioning.

The family laughed uproariously and begged Tom to recount the incident. Tom turned a rueful, laughing countenance toward his mentor. He picked up the boy and sat down with him on his lap.

'Alas! Thou'st betrayed me unto my master, O Master Edmund. Behold, I tremble before Father William's just wrath, and must suffer stern rebuke and mayhap chastisement – even grievous sore penance.'

'But will it change thy ways, O thou young scapegrace?' retorted William.

'But, Father William, Ben sayeth there be no penicences no more!' objected little Rosalind, shocked.

'Verily thou sayest sooth, my child. We do but jape and jest on such dead works that papist friars and priests would yoke us with. But confession

I will make that temptation lay heavily upon me to do likewise unto the same fat friar. A vain and pompous morpet was he, though I lack good Christian charity in so saying. As penance (*not* penicence) Master Thomas, thou shalt humble thyself, stay thine own boasting and praise the exploits of thy fellow Lollard instead, for the edification of his good kinsfolk.'

Bowing meekly, Tom launched enthusiastically into a humorous eulogy of Benjamin's deeds, both virtuous and otherwise. He spoke of many of the good deeds his friend had done together with himself and William Thorpe in Oxford town. They were mostly Benjamin's ideas. He also spoke of the exploits of the "Lollards of Logic Lane," the name that Benjamin had laughingly given the impromptu trio he had formed with Tom and William Thorpe.

'Prithee, Mama,' inquired little Rosalind, watching Tom from the safety of her mother's lap with shy child-like hero-worship, 'What be "Lollards"?'

No one seemed to have a definite answer – not even William. It was meant to be a derogatory term, possibly derived from a group of long-forgotten heretics in Holland. Tom, thinking of his would-be minstrel comrades, claimed that it had arisen from the frequent song that burst from the lips of Wycliffe's followers. Finally, it was left to Madame Abingdon to give what Rosalind considered was the most satisfactory answer.

'Rosie liefest, Lollards be good, wise and fully brave preacher men sent by Doctor Wycliffe to show all folk the way to our good Saviour Lord Jesu. Thy brother be one o' them, be sure.'

William, ruffling the little girl's hair, began to speak of Benjamin's natural gift for winning friends and how he had turned it to good account in their evangelistic efforts. He praised the young man's energetic and passionate style of preaching, reflecting his convictions and zeal.

The father's bosom swelled with pride. Nonetheless, he had a word of warning for the missionaries as they retired that night.

''Ware the black friars, brethren! Bitter enemies of Doctor Wycliffe are the Dominican brethren. They have vowed to do great scathe unto the Christian Brethren and will stop at naught to withstand you if they wist of thy presence in this place. They prowl the streets like to wolves, and woe unto them that they find who wear the russet. Garboil and violence will they do if need be.'

'Ha! Will they so do?' Tom was defiant. 'Let them come. They shall find themselves duly baptised in yon miller's pond should they essay it.'

William sighed and shook his head at him, but refrained from rebuke. Instead, he related to Jonas the recent events at Oxford and the farce at Lambeth. Jonas guffawed at the tale.

'God's breath!' he gasped, wiping his eyes, 'What want-wits be those holy bishops, forsooth! Would that thou wert sent to Lambeth also, Master Tom, that they be baptized in yon miller's-pond with thy friars.'

'Dreadless they then will find wisdom,' responded Tom, rather doubtfully.

Fortunately, Tom's boast was not yet put to the test, and the two preachers were able to carry on their work unmolested.

A small but strong following had already been established and was growing rapidly in spite of the threat of the Black Friars, and the disciples were meeting regularly in the Abyngdons' home. Soon, Tom and William felt the call to move on, knowing the flock was in good hands.

'Go forth, good brethren, and haste ye back!' boomed Jonas' voice above the farewells of the disciples, gathered to see them off from his doorway. 'Our prayers go with ye.'

They obtained work, meal and lodgings at the village of Steventon. Over the following weeks, they did the same at Milton Hill and Chilton, where they spoke to the farming communities with varying results. Not everyone was willing to abandon the supposed security of their religious traditions, but there was hardly ever a village or town they preached in that yielded no soul responses from the folks at all. Nonetheless, it bothered Tom whenever the response was poor. He could never understand why some would walk away even when he preached his heart out at them.

'How is this, that ye do despite unto the grace of God? With mine own eyes I beheld Him!' he pleaded as a few older, hard-faced folk crossed themselves and turned away.

Crossing the Chiltern Hills the next day, they paused on a high pass that overlooked the delightful Berkshire countryside and rested on a large rock by a forest of fine Birch. They ate a few morsels of bread and cheese provided for them by a grateful Chiltern widow.

Tom leaned on a low branch and looked down into the valley below. It was a clear day, the morning mist had long gone. He noticed a farmer in the distance hard at work, sowing a freshly ploughed field. He would occasionally stop when he heard a flock of birds gathering where he had sown. Not wanting to break his stride, he called out in his frustration to a small urchin climbing a tree nearby, and whose task was evidently to keep the birds away from the freshly sown seed. The boy jumped down ran among the birds to scatter them, then reprehensibly returned to his tree.

As Tom watched, instead of amusement, he felt a pang of grief. Recollections of his past life came back to him, of when he was as young and adventurous as that small child, and the vexation he caused his patient father at times. He had never had a chance to say farewell and thank you to that estimable big man who had shaped his character in his earlier life.

Brushing crumbs off his habit, William walked over to see what Tom was staring at with such an unusually sad expression on his face. Looking down at the homely scene below, he soon understood Tom's mood but kept a sympathetic silence.

Tom, however, was not naturally given to gloomy introspection, so it was not long before he shook off his dolour and wiped his eyes with his sleeves.

Looking up, he saw a skylark performing some spectacular aerial acrobatics and others nearby that filled the air with song.

'Behold the fowls of the air yonder, Father William,' he commented cheerfully, 'that they abide not forever in their nests, but will fly free. So may my life be henceforth, God aiding me.'

William's lip pursed thoughtfully. He had often wondered about Tom's ultimate future.

'Yet peradventure, thou shalt establish thine own nest in years to come, yea, with chicklings that flout and grieve thee also? Or wilt thou rather fly free for aye, wearing the robes of a priest ordained?'

'None and neither, Father,' Tom laughed. 'I am doomed to "flee the fair fowler's tender snare, be she ever so fine and fair" – so the bard singeth. And I am full content to be but Thomas the Plowman, lay preacher of the Christian Brethren.'

The next day, they went to mass at St Mary's outside the delightful village of Wendover, wading knee-deep through meadows of grass, poppy and cornflower that welcomed the summer in a riotous display of frivolity.

They passed a couple of old watermills, dutifully resting on the Lord's Day. Out of curiosity and a fascination for things mechanical, Tom reached over the edge of the mill-run and pushed one of the great wheels a little to hear it squeak and groan. Instead, there was a great squawking and some herons erupted from within the wheel, taking exception to having their Sunday repose disturbed. Tom was so startled he slipped and nearly fell into the water, had not William been nearby, and quick-witted. He grabbed Tom from behind by his hood.

'Saints be blessed! My thanks, Father William,' laughed Tom, 'else I would have entered the hallows of St Mary's as a newly baptised soul. Wilt thou chasten me and warn that I should let sleeping fowls lie?'

'Nay, my son,' answered William tranquilly, but with a strange, almost prophetic expression on his face, 'Thou'rt destined to disturb many a dove from his cot, many from their Sabbath's sleep, that they may rather find life and warmth in the day's sun. But beware lest thou fall in deep waters in the doing.'

'Ah, but thou shalt catch me ere I fall, wilt thou not?'

'So I hope. Or peradventure thou shalt cause me to fall also.'

East Ilsley and Beedon Hill were also open to the gospel. After only a week in each place, they established strong groups of followers. Even the priest, a dedicated shepherd with a heart hungry for truth, was easily won over and agreed to read the scriptures in English to his congregation.

'By my fay!' remarked Tom, 'This be no harvest, but rather windfall!'

'Let us give thanks for it then,' William replied. ''Tis the season for these hungry folk. Think not that we shall find all paths to be so plain. But let us go forth into the harvest whilst ripe it be.'

Chapter 12: The forbidden franciscan

The kyng that cometh to mete with the thef and that seyith to him:
"How is hit with the? Whider gost thou? I haue gret pyte of the; I schal
delyure the if thou wilt" — goostely that is the Kyng of Paradys...?

[From "The Weye of Paradys," a Middle English Translation of
"La Voie de Paradis" by 14th Century troubadour, Rutebeuf.]

The monks of the Order of Saint Benedict at the monastery of Saint Cecilia were characterised by an air of aloof other-worldliness, if you disregarded their habitually rotund and well-fed look (and if you disregarded the slightly blurry-eyed euphoria in their faces at Yuletide, Michaelmas and the end of the Lenten season).

An exception to this was Brother Jean-Marie Dupois, an immigrant from a village near Calais.

Thin and wasted, he often wore a haunted expression, more like a lost soul than a monk in comfortable circumstances. This may have been partly due to his dark continental looks, but it was often noted that he would speak little of his past, even to his confessor and spiritual director.

His colleagues looked upon him as a misfit, for his gaunt, ascetic comportment was in stark contrast to their frequent excesses. He was an embarrassment.

Father Abbott, however, thought of him as having political value. Brother Jean-Marie was the epitome of everything the monastery originally stood for. He kept the Rule of St Cecilia's to the letter. He was a serious-minded and learned man, not to mention his palpable piety. So, whenever a model of piety and asceticism was called for, as part of an embassy to a powerful legate for instance, he was the obvious choice. He was also of true Norman stock – a matter of great importance to Father Abbott, a descendant of a noble Norman line himself.

It was a paradox that the local villagers liked him the best of all the brothers. This was in spite of the fact that he was born in Normandy, and in spite of his dark reserve. It had taken some time and patient hard work on his part to gain their confidence.

Soon after joining the monastery as an advanced novice, he had begged leave from Father Abbott to work in the fields with the villagers in times when his monastic duties allowed him. He said it was part of a vow and penance he had imposed upon himself. Looking at him strangely, Father Abbott had given permission, albeit a little reluctantly at first.

Prior Stephen, who disliked and mistrusted the mysterious French brother, expressed his disapproval at such an irregular arrangement.

'O let be, Prior Stephen,' replied the Abbott tolerantly. 'Of these penances he shall grow weary ere long. Oft and lome hath ardent young novices afflicted their souls in like manner, but within a twelvemonth they become even as fat and likerous as thou and I.'

He gave a cynical laugh and added, 'Politic is this also, for lo! The borel villeins and their lords shall behold what holy and pious souls we breed at Saint Cecilia's monastery.'

Yet, in spite of the skepticism of his superiors and the distrust of nearly everyone else at the monastery, Brother Jean-Marie persisted in his practice of assisting the villagers with the seasonal agricultural activities, year in and year out. The farmers especially appreciated it, for he understood farming and worked conscientiously, although he still kept to himself. They soon began to greet him cordially and freely forgave him for being a Frenchman.

The ladies thought his accent and grave Gallic courtesies quite quaint. Some of the younger women were even a little intrigued, but he showed no signs of interest in return.

On the contrary. Once a loose village girl, hoping for a little private transaction, approached him quite brazenly, wearing a low-cut gown. To her chagrin, he gave a strangled cry, followed by an unintelligible string of French words. Covering his face with his ample sleeve, he ran for his life.

Prior Stephen later found him lying on the floor of his cell, sobbing, his bare back covered with whip-wealds.

In spite of his occasional eccentric behaviour, the locals decided he was trustworthy. Some folk even began to confide in him. Some of the younger children were a little nervous of his slightly grim reserve, however, and he had not performed any miracles, so they stopped short of conferring local sainthood upon him.

One particularly fine and windy spring day, Brother Jean-Marie absented himself immediately after morning Lauds. He left the feasting and jesting brothers in the refectory and walked briskly toward the northern gate that faced the village. The porter, accustomed to his regular excursions, opened the single portal without question, and they exchanged courteous but dour greetings.

Once outside, the Frenchman spat silently on the door, then quickly crossed himself as though to cover his gross disrespect. He turned to survey the green valley before him with the village nestled behind the shoulder of the hill and across the river. He took a deep breath and almost smiled.

'*Merci, sacré Saint François!*' he whispered. He almost ran down the road like a prisoner set free. Following directions he had been given the previous day, he crossed the rickety bridge over the mill-stream, climbed vigorously over the lookout and down into the south end of the village to where Master Leonard Carpenter lived and plied his trade.

Leonard looked up from the Prior's chair he was mending and a slow welcoming smile crept across his face.

'How now, Brothey Jommrey! Seekest thou moy guests, then?' He indicated with his mallet the daub-and-thatch cottage which could be seen through the window. 'They be within.'

Being of a taciturn disposition, he returned to his work.

The monk's eyes brightened. He uttered a brief Latin blessing upon his host's house with the sign of the cross, and departed.

Benjamin Abyngdon, an itinerant lay-preacher of a little known order, was cutting up wood outside the door of the cottage. He looked up from his task as the Frenchman approached. His habitual smile broadened into a grin and he threw his axe aside to execute a typical French welcoming gesture.

'Eh! Bong sure, mon amee le bong Frenchman! Common tally view? Say shored, or-sure-dewy, nay surpass?' French had never been Benjamin's strongest subject at Oxford.

The Frenchman, far from being offended, threw his head back and laughed so much, he had to sit down hard on the chopping block. His brethren-monks would not have recognized him.

'*Ciel! Ces Anglais sont trop barbare!*' he declared with joyful Gallic severity. 'I am in *désespoir* that I school thee in *la langage sacré*. The *prononciation*, she is *affreux! Non?*'

Parrying this verbal thrust with a hoot, Benjamin retaliated in kind.

'But thine essay of the fair English tongue wanteth much also, brother. Hence thy yolk of English oxen wist not thy rebuke yestermorn and strayed into the ditch. I des-aspire of thee also.'

Jean-Marie was still chuckling when the mistress of the house emerged from the cottage, drawn by the sound of laughter. Her children peeped curiously from behind her large form, waving a welcome when they recognised their animated visitor.

'How now and art well coome, brothey Jommrey,' said Madame Carpenter affably, wiping her hands on her apron. 'Art uncommon cheerly this morn, forsooth, but so be all as have speech with Master Benjamin. He be born to laugh. But ah! A merry heart be as balm, say the woise. But come ye from this blustious woind else ye catch thoy death. Thou also, Master Benjamin. Father William be within. There be a foine foire a-blazen and good beef brose a-brewen thereon....'

She went on as she ushered her guest inside and bustled about her business with her nonstop cheerful chatter. She was as famous for her hospitality and garrulousness as her husband was for his fine carpentry skills and his taciturnity.

The evening meal had passed and the family had left with Benjamin, visiting neighbours. Father William Thorpe and Brother Jean-Marie were left alone by the fire. There was a meditative silence between them for a while. The monk studied William's profile with a sense of puzzlement.

Why did he like the man so much?

It had nothing to do with his plain but pleasant though slightly melancholic Nordic looks, nor his air of authority. Maybe it was his large hands, calloused with much toil?

Jean-Marie was chagrined at first when he first noticed other clerics labouring in the fields nearby, for he thought he was the only one of his kind. His uniqueness was challenged, and the villagers spoke highly of the strangers, comparing them to his own situation. And when he learned of the nature of the strangers' message from the villagers, he was horrified.

'*Sacré bleu! C'est un erreur* of a sinfulness *plus gross*! This we cannot suffer!'

He stormed off to confront the heretics immediately.

The older villagers nodded wisely as though they already knew the outcome of the conflicting theology.

'Brothey Jommrey' said they,'will set all to roights.'

The reeve, with doleful satisfaction, addressed himself to a band of younger men nearby.

'Mark ye this holy brothey, his demeanour. These vain sayings as these preachers be a-saying o' the free grace o' God be too good for we lickerous sinners. Only the good soul that laboureth to please the Almighty be a-worthy o' heaven's bliss, as Holy Church ever be a-warnen us. Take heed lest ye become wanton for this free grace as that Father William Thorpe be a-speaken of. If good brothey Jommrie sayeth it be not so, then so be it not.'

But many among the younger generation had listened to the young preachers sufficiently to be inspired. They could smell a new breath of freedom in the air and were becoming impatient with what they considered to be the older generation's rigid narrow-mindedness. One young labourer was bold enough to retort.

'If that be sooth, master reeve, then let good brothey Jommrie look to Holy Writ to make it sure!'

Persuasions and threats of hellfire did not deter the strangers from persisting in propagating their supposed heresies. What was even more irritating to the holy brother was that the heretics behaved, mostly, with more graciousness than he did. So he doubled his efforts at proving himself to be on a higher spiritual plane than they, by working harder at his tasks.

But the strangers made it clear that they infinitely preferred to collaborate rather than compete. Especially when they were all suddenly called to assist at rescuing a farmer's best milch cow from drowning in a swamp. All political and theological differences were cast to the winds in such a case – an emergency which only men of the soil could truly appreciate.

Their efforts were accompanied by liberal sprinklings of French oaths from the monk, bovine equivalents from the troubled cow, Latin quotations from Benjamin Abyngdon, crisp directions from William Thorpe, and barely comprehensible expletives from the anxious farmer – not to mention the abundance of mud everywhere. They pulled and heaved together until the poor distressed beast was safe on terra firma where they all collapsed exhausted. They were covered in filth from head to foot.

'*Veii victis!*' panted young Abyngdon with a laugh. 'O that Master Thomas the Plowman were with us. With his might of arm, our task would have been accomplished long since. As the Lullards of Logic Lane, would we not then hymn the victory, thou, he and I?'

'Oh, the saints preserve us!' groaned the exhausted William, who knew what was coming.

Immediately, Benjamin began to sing a popular ballad about a group of young knights of Arthur's court who saved a fair young maiden from a watery death. It was the comparison of the poor cow, a dam of many winters and numerous progeny, to a fair young damsel in distress, which proved the Frenchman's complete undoing. He lay on his back in the mud, shaking and snorting with helpless laughter.

William and Benjamin exchanged grins, knowing that they had won another kind of victory. Still laughing, Jean-Marie staggered to his feet. Cutting short the grateful farmer's thanks, the clerics chatted and laughed all the way to the river to remove the worst of the mud. Theological prejudices rarely stand before mud-covered working men. A bond of camaraderie had been formed from then on.

However, it wasn't that incident alone that had softened the Frenchman toward the strangers. Pacing up and down before the fire at the Carpenter's house, he pondered how it had come about.

'*Pourquoi? Pourquoi? Je me demande!*' he muttered aloud in an intense manner rarely observed by his fellows at the monastery.

Thorpe looked up from the fire and returned the man's intense stare with a hint of a smile in his steady blue eyes.

'And what askest thou of thyself, brother?'

'That I find myself to feel *en rapport* ... what say ye English... er... *un amité*? ... *Non*! ..fellowship with thee. Thou and thy *disciple très méchant*, ye are like unto *les amis de mon jeune age. Mais voila! Un hérétique* art thou ... and an Englishman also. *Quelle dommage!*'

William Thorpe's smile deepened.

'I feel also this ferly *rapport*, my friend. I rejoice that thou hast showed somewhat joy-wit within thee. Yet thou'rt a Romish papelard and a mere Frenchman also, alas! A bowman was my dear departed grandsire, God rest his soul, who fought and died at Poitiers. Verily, from his grave he would weep grievously to behold me this night.'

The Frenchman snorted with amusement again. It suddenly occurred to him that he had relaxed considerably from his harsh, self-imposed regimen – a circumstance he had never allowed to happen at the monastery. Memories of past care-free days with his friends, aptly naming themselves *Les Fils de Vin-Sauvage* – Sons of Wild Wine – had been thrust to the back of his mind until now. Hence, he could feel so much at home – even animated – in the presence of these wayward preachers. He had not realised how much he had missed the mirth, sternly suppressed for so long.

He fell silent, almost broodingly so. Thorpe waited patiently.

It was otherwise certainly an unlikely friendship, for they had argued heatedly, or at least the French brother had, almost from their first meeting. There had been debates on topics ranging through the Virgin Mary's part in redemption, salvation through grace, transubstantiation, the authority of the Bishop of Rome. Throughout their discussions, Jean-Marie developed a profound respect for the other man's honesty, sincerity, unconditional acceptance and scholarship. Even when William had been provoked into unwise retort, he had checked himself and apologised. Yes, that was another quality the Frenchman could add to the list.

' ....*Et l'humilité! C'est énorme .... quel c'est formidable!*' he reflected aloud.

Coming to a decision, he ceased his pacing to and fro and stood before his amiable adversary.

'Art too good a man to perish *en perdition, mon ami. Oui!* Back unto the ways of *sainteté* shall I lead thee.'

William grinned in a rather impious and irreligious manner.

'And wherewithal shalt thou counsel and guide such an heretic as I, O my sainted friend?'

Jean-Marie refused to reply in kind. He sat down opposite the hearth in one of Master Carpenter's well-made chairs. The dark broodiness descended upon his brow again.

'Let us leave *ces plaisanteries, mon ami.* No matter for jest is the holy wrath of *le Bon Dieu*. A secret shall I reveal unto thee *en confidence,* that thou mayest learn thereby. Of this secret ... *Ciel!* ...*Mon Dieu!* If but Prior Stephen, he wisteth of it, I am *hors de concours*. Back to Calais would he send me *sous arrête. Et puis?......*'

His face became even grimmer with dark memories. His eyes glowed with fear. He hesitated, but seeing genuine concern in Thorpe's face, he felt encouraged to continue.

'Dupois, it is not my name *en verité*. Jean-Marie de Montfort was I christened at my birth.'

He waited to see how Thorpe would react.

'De Montfort?' William bent his head in an effort of memory for a brief moment. 'Surely of this name I have heard tell at Oxenford. But stay! Did not my mother speak of it? My memory faileth...'

'Then shall I refresh it, *mon ami*. Frère Jean de Montfort, *mon oncle,* a leader was he *trés grand* of the Franciscans recusants which called of themselves *Les Spirituales....*'

'....That submit not unto the rule of the *Conventuales?*' Thorpe's interest was thoroughly aroused. 'Them that were proscribed and outlawed? Was not de Montfort burnt at the stake that he stood steadfast for that which he believed? A man of renown, full valiant was he, so saith Doctor Wycliffe.'

He stared at the famous friar's nephew in amazement.

'And thou'rt of his blood and kin? Bones of Saint Bernard, man! Wherefore then art thou dwelling as one with them that persecute thee? An heretic bold also art thou, even as I! Wherefore dost thou not also arise 'gainst the tyranny of Rome? Art thou not a man?'

The Frenchman jumped to his feet, almost breathing fire in his outrage and grief.

'*Non! Parbleu!*' he shouted, 'Until his dying day *mon oncle* did give *l'honneur* and obeisance unto the Holy Father, and this also do I vow! But everlasting curses be upon them that opposed themselves 'gainst us in the pontiff's name and sent Jean de Montfort unto his death!'

Grief overwhelmed him. He fell back into the chair and wept.

Many times he had wept in the solitude of his own cell, but this was the first time in many years he had shed tears openly before another man.

'As a father was he unto me,' he sobbed, 'even when *mon père natural*

had fallen into *l'erreur,* and I into gross sin, he took me up as his disciple …
Non! … even as his own son!'

William had risen to his feet, concerned, but sat down slowly again.

'I cry thee pardon, Jean-Marie de Montfort,' he said, subdued and
remorseful. 'I spoke in haste and without truth. I wist not thy torment,
else I would have refrained to touch this wound of soul so gauchely. Yet
I would hear more of thy misfortunes and those of thy kindred. Speak!
Peradventure it shall ease the burden upon thy soul.'

The Frenchman fiercely dashed the tears from his eyes.

'A curse there is upon the great house de Montfort!'

It took some coaxing and patience at first, but finally the whole tragic
tale came tumbling out with many tears and Gallic oaths.

As twins born into a well-connected Norman family, the two brothers,
Jean and Paul de Montfort, had spent most of their youth living riotously.
They were the best of friends – inseparable, even when Paul married.
They were honest men, however, and they began to realise that it was all
an attempt to silence the restlessness that arises from the vast spiritual
vacuum that all experience at least once in their lives. Together, therefore,
they began a long quest for inner peace.

Paul's wife, Marie, was a strong, serious-minded and devout woman,
also of a good family. She patiently endured her husband's excesses for
some years and was relieved when her husband and brother-in-law came to
their senses. She encouraged them in their spiritual quest, even if it meant
separation for a season.

After a number of miscarriages, she had born Jean-Marie. She doted
on him, but to her dismay, he began to show early signs of dissipation, as
his father had. To make matters worse, in his spiritual quest, Paul himself
was showing some interest in a strange sect called the Waldenses.

'*Monsieur, mon mari!*' she remonstrated. 'Is it not enough that Jean-
Paul he pursues *les filles de joie* and spends his nights reveling with *Les fils
du Vin Sauvage*[62]? Why must you also endanger your soul in that you traffic
with *les hérétiques?* Can you not rather follow your brother's calling to the
rule of *Saint François?*'

---

62 "*Vin sauvage*": a fictional drink brewed in secret by French peasants in the forests. The
English equivalent would have been "wood ale."

'Do not distress yourself, *ma chère*,' Paul replied, displaying more concern for her than he had since they were wed. 'A wicked husband and bad father I have been heretofore, but I have found grace and peace with God at last amongst the followers of *le bon Monsieur* Waldo. My brother treads a different path, thinking to earn God's grace. He is a man possessed and will not listen to my counsel, but rails against my newfound faith – and so our paths are sundered. Soon he may see the corruption, even amongst his precious Franciscans and rebel even as I have. But will you not come to hear the words of *le bon Monsieur* Waldo, the preacher? We will bring Jean-Paul with us, and perhaps he will find peace as I have.'

Such was the strength of his wife's Catholic upbringing, she almost violently rejected her husband's offer. He went away sorrowfully to look for his son. Jean-Paul returned home in a drunken state while his father was still looking for him. Alarmed that her husband may take away her darling son and lead him into perdition, she took extreme steps to prevent this. Paul returned late to find all the doors locked against him and the windows shuttered and barred. He wept and pleaded to be let in but she hardened her heart against him. He had no choice but to return to the community that had so readily accepted him and cared for his spiritual well-being, hoping to return and be reconciled with his wife later.

She, however, was convinced he had abandoned them forever, and refused to forgive him. In this, she was encouraged by her brother-in-law, Jean de Montfort, furious at what he perceived as his brother's perfidy and betrayal of the faith.

He himself had indeed discovered the abuses even amongst the Franciscans, even as his brother had predicted. However, refusing to turn to what he was convinced was a heretical cult, he had discovered a group of Franciscan friars who passionately clung to the original rule of Saint Francis. They were a revival sect called the *Spirituales*, who steadfastly refused to follow the modifications, as sanctioned by the church hierarchy, to the original rule of Saint Francis. Inspired by their simple faith and godly lifestyle of evangelical poverty, he whole-heartedly espoused their cause. So much so, he began to be strongly outspoken against corruption of the established *Conventuales,* who followed the new rule allowing the possession of property and riches. He did not care how many influential prelates and clergymen he offended. He soon rose in the ranks of the

Spirituales to be one of the greatest leaders of recusant friars in France's history. But his anger burned also against all other forms of error that he perceived, even in his own brother.

'You have brought curses and judgment upon our house!' he raged at him. He never called him brother again.

Believing that his father had abandoned them, Jean-Paul turned even more to drink to drown his grief and anger. Grief at her husband's perceived betrayal and her son's continued lifestyle affected his mother's health.

Soon after, worse tragedy struck. The church hierarchy sanctioned violent persecution on the Waldenses, and Paul's community was among the first to be targeted. Terrible atrocities were committed in the name of Christ and His church, almost matching those committed on the Cathars many years earlier. Paul himself fell, trying to defend the household that sheltered him. His body was dragged through the streets in dishonour, then thrown into a ditch with other corpses and burnt.

When his wife, suffering from the effects of advanced consumption, heard the news, she was struck with deep remorse and collapsed crying *'Mon mari, mon mari! Ah! Mon Dieu, pardonnez moi!'*

Jean-Paul returned that night, once again in a drunken state, to see his mother on her deathbed, with his uncle in attendance, together with a grim-faced priest muttering the last rites and Monsieur Lenoire *le médicin*, a family friend and the best local physician they could find.

Jean-Paul, his brain befuddled with *le vin sauvage*, scarcely understood what was happening until his strong-minded uncle took hold of him and held his head under a cold water-pump. They both returned to hear the lady's last dying request:

'Jean-Marie, *mon chèr...! mon fils!* Swear to me that you... shall always serve Holy Church ....and the Virgin's grace.'

The shock of seeing his mother in such a state cleared the young man's head even more than the cold water. Her knelt at her side.

'*Oui, Mamman*, I so swear!' he vowed fervently. '*Le Bon Dieu*, He is my witness.'

His mother struggled onto her elbow to tell him something else, although it pained her terribly.

'Jean-Marie!.... Son père est mort, ... Mais il n'est pas...'

But nothing more came, and she collapsed onto her pillow, her life spent. Monsieur Lenoire closed her eyes and pulled the sheet over her. They were never to know what she wanted to say about her husband.

The worthy physician, a long time friend of Paul's who had laboured hard to save the stricken woman, tried to catch Jean-Paul's attention as if to inform him of some important matter. Jean-Paul was too grief-stricken to notice this, and his uncle waved the physician away. So he left, sorrowfully shaking his head.

'*Mamman! Ma mère trés aimée!*' the young man wept bitterly, burying his head upon his mother's pillow. 'We have killed her, my father and I! Oh that I were dead in her place!'

Looking down on his nephew's heaving shoulders, Jean de Montfort felt compassion for his grief.

'It is not for us to determine our fate, *mon gar,* but *le bon Dieu,* only,' he said gently, his hand on the young man's head. 'Nevertheless you may still atone for your sins and those of your father's. Come! Your father is dead, suffering God's judgment, and your mother prayed that I may take care of you. I will be your father hereafter, but you must perform your oath to your sainted mother. You must forsake your former ways.'

The young man jumped to his feet, picked up the rigid hand of his mother, and faced his adopted father.

'If you will lead me, I swear on my mother's dead body to never again to touch *le liqueur,* nor look upon a woman in lust again!'

He had been faithful to his oath from then on, at least, most of the time. He took the habit of the Franciscans, swearing to the same life of evangelical poverty his uncle had, and espousing the same cause his uncle had. He became his uncle's shadow.

He found a measure of balm for his aching heart in working hard at his designated menial and agricultural duties, and even discovered in himself a natural affinity with the soil. He swung the sickle with a will, matched only by his spiritual disciplines of prayer and fasting. His hands grew strong and calloused, his body lean and wasted. He came into full manhood hardened of muscle, but grim of face and thin of frame.

His sadness did not bother his uncle, himself a grim man. He approved and encouraged him, saying 'Many years you will save yourself from *la purgatoire* this way, *mon gar.*'

Not all the young men in his new community adhered as strictly to the Spartan, aesthetic lifestyle the Franciscans *Sprituales* insisted upon. Some grew weary of it, and when their superior's back was turned, there were always some that allowed their eyes to stray toward the village girls, even find opportunities to flirt or snatch a furtive drink.

In the main, Jean-Marie resisted temptation until the day when one lovely young girl managed to seduce him. The pull of his old life was too strong. Guilt-driven religion, he was to discover, cannot truly change a man.

After drowning his guilt and shame in wild wine, he crept back to the community and knelt before his uncle, begging for forgiveness.

'I do not forget my own sinful days *de mon jeunesse, mon gar,*' his mentor said gently but sternly. 'I perform *penance très formidable* to pay for it still, so judgment upon you I will not make. But penance for this sin you must add to what you have vowed. You are of my blood, and one day I wish to pass to you the flame for *l'honneur de le bon Saint François.* The curse it will lift from our house, *peut être.*'

So Jean-Marie gratefully doubled his efforts, beating and starving himself to prove himself worthy of his uncle's mercy and regard. His uncle now took him on his preaching tours as his disciple, much to the younger man's delight. He cheered and stamped with many other disgruntled people as the great Montfort loudly denounced the injustices and abuses of the conventional clergy, in defiance of repeated prohibitions from higher authorities.

The wrath of these clergy had reached boiling point. A convocation was called by the local bishops and well represented by the Franciscan *conventuales.* Montfort and his followers were officially condemned and proscribed. The fear was that the rebel friars would inspire another Jacobin peasant uprising, similar to the one just decades previously which devastated churches, castles and abbeys before it was brutally crushed.

When Montfort heard of his excommunication, he merely laughed, metaphorically snapping his fingers in their face.

'I have long excommunicated them also!' he declared fearlessly. 'We have righteousness as our shield! *Le bon Dieu et le bon Saint François protégez moi!*'

He became even more vocal and condemnatory, gathering more

followers from among the disgruntled populace. Only his adherence to Saint Francis' hatred of violence prevented the movement from active rebellion. Not knowing this, the fearful and infuriated authorities decided that he must be made an example of, to instil the "fear of God" in the common people.

Finally, the storm burst.

Jean-Marie returned from an errand on which he had been sent by his uncle, only to find him being marched off between four soldiers to face the same tribunal he had defied.

Fears for his uncle wrestled with fears for his own safety. Like Saint Peter at the arrest of Jesus, he followed at a distance, but he, as well as the general public, was denied access to the trial.

When it had been noised abroad that Jean de Montfort was in prison, many of the common folk who loved him, as well as his followers, had gathered in protest outside the cathedral where the trial was taking place. But the Bishop of Nice had prepared for this contingency, and a strong deputation of soldiers barred their way to the trial.

If there had been a leader as charismatic as Montfort himself, they may have rioted regardless. Jean-Paul, sensing their mood, took it upon himself to dissuade them.

'*Mais Non, mes amis! Le bon frère* himself would not permit it. Rather he would call us to prayer!'

Nothing, however, could save de Montfort from his martyrdom, not even threats or torture, so he was sentenced to burn in the city square "to cleanse his soul," so they said.

Jean-Marie, horrified at such brutality and devastated at losing even the last of his family so cruelly, cried out for mercy as he watched the wicked flames writhe around his uncle's feet.

Many of de Montfort's bitterest opponents, far from merciful, were present to gleefully witness the spectacle, crying out:

'*Á bas, l'hérétiique*! Let him burn in this life and the next! Amen!'

Even most of his followers had fled in fear at such brutal retribution on their leader. The Franciscan *Spirituales*, as a movement, would never openly rise again.

'*Mon maître! Mon oncle!*' cried Jean-Marie. 'What shall I do without you!'

Through smoke, flame and intense pain, the great man turned to gasp his last words to the last of his family.

'Bear the flame, *mon gar*......even if it be hidden in darkness for a while! .... I pray my soul finds its rest with this my last stand! .... But save yourself! .... Flee! I will not have you share my fate!'

'*Adieu, mon oncle, le plus brave!* I will forget you, never! On my soul I swear I will bear the flame *toujours!*'

The flames had almost engulfed the tormented man, but in the midst of his suffering, he roused himself to one last attempt at speech.

'*Mon gar ... Jean-Marie, bien aimée!... Son père ... Paul de Montfort... n'a pas......!*'

It was too late. With a great cry of pain, Jean de Montfort, leader of the Franciscan *Spirituales*, passed into eternity. His nephew, for the second time, was not to hear the vital news about his father.

In bitterness of soul, he turned on the triumphant clergy and called down curses upon them. This was too much for them, so the soldiers in attendance were called upon to arrest him. Anger turned to fear, and Jean-Marie remembered his uncle's words to flee.

He fled to Calais, his hometown, only to discover that his family name was now anathema throughout France. Changing his name, and disguising himself as a Benedictine monk, he joined the stream of immigrants to England. Many of these immigrants were fleeing the general persecution of heretics. Looking at their hunted and relieved expressions, he realized that they were ordinary folk trying to find a normal life, serving God in the only way they knew.

For the first time, even though they were heretics in his eyes, he felt some sympathy for them – even for his father.

Wandering the English countryside, he obtained what work he could, slowly learning the language. He wandered from monastery to priory. Here he was saddened to discover that a large proportion of clergy were just as corrupt as they were in his homeland.

Finally, he found a place at St Cecilia's in the North of Kent where he felt accepted – if not by the clergy, at least by the villager folk. Here he was able to continue his practice of serving the poor folk in the guise – though partially true – of penances.

* * * * * * *

Jean-Marie concluded his narration, pausing his pacing back and forth, and spread his arms expressively.

'*Et puis … me voici.*'

William Thorpe, moved by the tragic tale, could think of nothing to say at first.

'But whither anon, and what wilt thou do henceforth, Jean-Marie de Montfort? Wilt thou bear this flame in thine heart and in silence for aye?'

'*Je ne sais quoi,*' admitted the Frenchman, resuming his pacing. 'In secret do I serve *le bon Saint François* as *mon maître* he wished.'

Then the pent-up hatred arose within him again.

'But *peut être*, I may raise the standard for the true Franciscans once more, or lead an *armée* to throw down our enemies. *Ces frères et ces* [63] *moines* that dare to call themselves of *l'ordre de Saint François,*' he uttered with contemptuous loathing, ' *Son nom sacré* have they betrayed and soiled by reason of their gross sins and profligacy. And to all this, they have added the murder of *mon maître* and kinsman *très cher.*'

He shook his fist in the direction of the shores of his homeland.

'*Les damnations* be upon their heads ….. May they burn in Hell – *toujours!*'

His diatribe exhausted him, and he sat down cross-legged on the floor.

'*Mais le bon Saint François,* he would forbid it,' he sighed wearily. 'Naught can I do but find peace in serving him *en secrèt.*'

'And hast thou found that which thou seekest, my friend? Hast thou indeed attained unto that peace within?'

'*Mais certainement!*' Jean-Marie dropped his eyes before Thorpe's challenging stare.

William Thorpe arose from his chair by the fire. It was his turn to stride the stage.

'Hearken now unto mine own tale and journey, for my path is not wholly unlike to thine. Furthermore, this is not the first occasion that our families' paths have crossed.'

---

63   monks

Jean-Marie looked up at him, blinking in astonishment.

'*Toujours,* full of enigmas art thou, *monsieur le padré.* But speak!'

Choosing his words carefully, Thorpe opened his own heart and began to share of his own spiritual quest as a young student-cleric, drawing parallels with Jean-Marie's story. His uncles and aunts died in the last big plague, and his father never fully recovered from this loss. He joined the Duke's service and went to the French war, never to return.

His mother, then the only mainstay of his life, gradually died of a wasting disease. She had tried to instil a faith in young William along unorthodox lines, but William was too young and heedless to understand, let alone comply. Finally, she died with a prayer for him on her lips.

Orphaned, remorseful and grief-stricken, he sought solace in a religious life and study – but to no avail. His restlessness and energy urged him to rebel against his self-imposed regimen. Soon he found himself roaming the countryside with the infamous young student-clerics, drinking, whoring and even robbing farms to find the adventures his soul craved. Witnessing a fight to the death between a drunken colleague and an irate farmer made him realise how far he had drifted. He tried to return to his strict lifestyle – again to no avail.

Finally, in desperation, he turned to the only man whom he considered to be truly godly: his professor, Master Smith of Oxford University. It seemed that the quiet man had been expecting him to approach him. After hearing the young man pour out his heart to him, the professor systematically and quietly introduced him to Christ the Saviour. Thorpe realised at last what his mother had tried to teach him.

Standing before Jean-Marie in the carpenter's cottage, Thorpe looked down at him with a glint in his eye, mixed with sadness.

'Knowest thou not what mine own blessed mother said on her deathbed? Thus she spake: "*O bon Dieu, Bon Père celeste.... Regardez mon cher Guillaume, mon fils, en grace...de mon Sauveur Jesu...,*" and so she departed in peace.'

'*En Française?*' gasped Jean-Marie.

'...And of thine own birthplace, even Calais. An *emigrée* was she –

even as thou. And her name, ere she wed my father: Madeleine Lenoire. And her brother? A physician, and long-time friend of thy father.'

Jean-Marie turned pale and trembled. He could not speak.

'Verily, the good Lord hath ordered our steps indeed,' Thorpe continued. 'My sainted mother spake of it once but I wist not of whom she spake until this very night. Her brother was of the disciples of Monsieur Waldo, but he spake of it to none other, save thy father. Thy father came to faith among the Waldenses through him. Monsieur Lenoire beheld not thy father's death, but heard of it of his brethren in the faith. Thy father, *mon ami*, died in great valour, saving my mother from rape and murder when the fury of the dogs of Rome was unleashed upon the people of Waldo. Hence, she alone survived and fled to her brother in Calais, who brought her to England. There she met my father who pitied and loved her, giving her the shelter of his name, a common Sergeant-at-arms though he was. Thus do I stand here before thee, to bring thee tidings of thy father's death.'

There was a long silence. William sat down to await the Frenchman's reaction to these revelations. After a long moment with no response, he became somewhat concerned. He rose again and brought a wooden goblet of ale, wondering if the man would faint. Jean-Marie just sat perfectly still, staring blindly before him.

'Come now, Jean-Marie de Montfort,' said William, offering him the goblet. 'Upon thy name there is great honour. A curse no more doth it bear. For thy father and thine uncle both died for their faith – in great valour and steadfastness.'

'*Pardonnez moi, mon Dieu, pardonnez*,' whispered the Frenchman, the tears flowing at last, '…that I have cursed the name of my father.'

He seized the goblet before him and drank deeply. This was in defiance of his vow to never touch liquor again.

'More also will I say,' continued William, as he smiled and stood up. 'My blessed mother never forgot thy father, and spake of him with full reverence. She also spake of his grief that he could not see his wife, his brother or his son and that he prayed that they may be reconciled.'

Then Jean-Marie gasped as another piece of the puzzle of his family history seemed to fall into place.

'*Les mots*,….. the words on the lips of *mon oncle et Mamman chère*!

With their dying breath, they spake of *mon père...* but accursed death, he hindered their tidings.'

He dropped the goblet and grabbed Williams arm urgently, peering intently into his face.

'*Le bon Dieu*, hath sent thee to reveal to me the truth. This now I know *sans doute*. Tell me, my friend. Speak! Tell me what would they have said, had they lived!'

But William could only shake his head sadly, helplessly.

'I do but shoot in the dark, *mon ami*. Whether I hit the mark or no, I cannot tell. Mayhap thy kinsfolk beheld a little of the peace and joy thy father had found, for so it was my mother's reckoning. Would they have spoken of this with their dying breath? I wist not. But a heedless and redeless young fool was I, and stayed not to learn more. In this, I have failed thee, if God's messenger I am in sooth. But hearkened I enough to know that thy father prayed that his son would find peace with God even as had he. This I know of a certes.'

He let that sink in for a while.

The colour gradually came back into Jean-Marie's face. He arose and poured himself some more ale, then sat down opposite his friend, fixing him with another intense stare.

'*Mon bon papa*, he was a man *plus brave*. This now I see. But *un hérétique* he was still, and so he perished. How can he find this peace if he seeketh not even the grace of *La Marie Sainte? C'est impossible.* My blessed mother, God rest her soul, did make me to take oath ere she died that I should ever seek the grace of the blessed Mother of God. More sainted than ever was I, *ma chère Mamman*. Never shall I forsake this oath.'

He crossed himself again and fingered his rosary, but seeing Thorpe still refrained from following suit, he abandoned his beads and waited for an answer. Thorpe looked at him, considering his reply.

'What sayest thou?' he said slowly. 'Is the blessed virgin more sainted than thy dear departed mother – even wholly without sin?'

'*Tiens!* But of course! From her conception was she kept holy. Else we seek grace through her in vain.'

'Wherefore, then, doth she speak of her need of a saviour?'

'*Comment?? C'est impossible!*' Jean-Marie sat bolt upright, truly alarmed at this. 'Holy Writ, it cannot speak such blasphemy!'

Thorpe calmly reached for his well-thumbed and annotated English New Testament. He found the prophetic song of Mary in the gospel of Luke, when she met Elizabeth, and indicated the passage for his opponent. The single word shone out clearly and irrefutably to Jean-Marie's shocked gaze:

"….and my spirit doth rejoice in God my *Saviour.*"

The Frenchman sat back again, stunned. Had he spent all these years slavishly chasing phantoms?

'Mon Dieu! Non! C'est affreux! This I cannot believe! Is this *un faux traduction, peut être?'*

'A false translation, sayest thou?' retorted William, aroused. 'Then put thou me to the test. Art a learned man, brother. Seek thou then the Latin text in thy libraries and prove it twixt sooth or falsehood, for it is from the selfsame text that Doctor Wycliffe and his translators hath wrought this.'

At that moment, the door opened and Master Abyngdon came bustling in, whistling cheerfully and carrying more firewood. His cheerful spirit (and the cold draught that followed him through the open door) seemed to ease the tension, although Thorpe was slightly annoyed at having their debate interrupted.

'Fermez la porte, s'il vous plait, Monsieur naught-pate, else our guest may take of the ague.'

Jean-Marie laughed, and reaching for his cloak, rose to go.

'Non. I shall depart anon *en paix,* and turn myself again unto mine own ague-ridden quarters. The comforts thereof are greater than thine own, *bien sûr.'*

He gripped the other's hand before he went through the door.

'Au revoir et merci, monsieur l'hérétiique très noble. I will think on these matters, but I am not yet of thy mind. But to speak with thee is of such refreshment to my soul. *A demain?'*

'Yea, return a' the morrow, my splendid papelard French friend. To cross swords with thee hath refreshed my soul also. Are we not soul-brethren? But take this with thee to solace thy solitude in thy cell this night. Fare thee well.'

The door closed. The French friar discovered that he had the English

New Testament in his hands. It was Thorpe's own copy, written with his own firm hand.

Ignoring the cold and slightly blustery wind, he began to read the gospel of Luke as he walked slowly toward his own quarters.

He had much to think about.

Chapter 13: The Fenfolk

*"For if ye forgive to men their sins, [and] your Heavenly Father shall
forgive to you your trespasses. (Forsooth if ye shall forgive to men their
sins, and your Heavenly Father shall forgive to you your sins.)
Soothly if ye forgive not to men [the sins of them], neither
your Father shall forgive to you your sins."*

[Gospel of Matthew, Chapter 6:14, 15. Wycliffe/Purvey translation]

Father John Haswell, one of Wycliffe's "Poor Preachers," was a Norfolkshire
man. For all his sensitivity, scholarship and soft-heartedness, he was as
rugged as the land in which he was raised. He was born on the banks of
the river Ouse in the heart of the Fens.

Now at last he was back in his home county, if only for a brief time,
breathing the sea air with the tang of the distant marshes. He was enjoying
himself immensely, while hard at work repairing a thatched roof for a
widow and her two teenage children.

"All Fensmen," he said, "were cunning of hand to lay reed thatches on
any roof, be it lord's manor or beggar's hovel."

It was not hard to find rooves to mend or thatching to rethatch, for the
sea winds were strong and persistent almost any time of the year.

Lawrence Parsons, lay preacher and Father John's disciple, together
with the two youngsters were carting bunches of dried reeds up the ladder.
Father John was giving Lawrence a lecture, albeit rather breathlessly, on
the history of East Anglia while he skilfully packed the reeds under the
binding.

'...And a-times corsairs would blow in with the east winds.... Then
would my grandsire and many a fensman, yea, even their women and
hardier youths also would take up arms .... be they but staves and clubs,
and stand and fight.... Howsomever, when the might of the raiders was
too great to repel them a' water's edge....'

Father John paused in his labours, laughed and pointed toward Lutton Marsh, shrouded in mist in the distance.

'....Then, God save them, the fenfolk would take refuge in the marshes, and taunted the foe full sore. If the foe they were fool enow to follow and dare the peril of the marshes then perished many in the fell sands, or were marked and slain by the cunning marshmen, or sheriff's bowmen, or even fell prey to marsh wights in the Marshes of the Dead, so 'tis said. The fenfolk knew they every tussock and firm foothold throughout the marshlands, so God preserved them. Surely are the fens both a curse and a blessing sent from the Almighty.'

'Amen,' piously said the youth and his twin sister in chorus as they busily passed up more reeds.

Cedric and Emma Wainthorpe, and their widowed mother, lived in the house under repair. They all stood in awe of these itinerant priests that worked for their living and truly cared for the common folk.

They were among the few of the village that responded to the poor preachers' message, and had been so impressed, they invited them to stay in spite of their very limited resources. Most of the villagers were suspicious of anyone and everyone west of the fens, especially if they advocated new ways of thinking or anything the locals were not accustomed to. Wandering landless labourers seldom came their way, or if they did, they did not stay long. Both the weather and the neighbourhood were rather forbidding.

The villagers were surprised but still suspicious when they discovered that the two preachers didn't come to beg. They warmed a little to Father John when they recognised him as a fensman-born, even though he had acquired considerable Oxford polish and scholarship, which was, they said, "regretterful." But most still took a wait-and-see attitude toward the newcomers, shaking their heads over the Wainthorpes' perilous hospitality toward unknown and untried strangers. The family had a reputation for eccentric behaviour.

The Wainthorpe twins had done their best to mend the roof in the past, but since their father had suddenly disappeared and was never seen again, there were few men to show them the right technique. Most of the neighbours had no time for them, some considering them a family under a curse ever since the disappearance of Cedric Wainthorpe, the elder. The results of the young Wainthorpe's efforts at maintenance were often disastrous, especially during the wild winter and spring storms. They barely made a living from the seashore in the distance. Hence the coming of the two missionaries was, literally, a godsend to them and their mother. Father John decided it was better to do a complete overhaul than maintaining the present state of the roof.

Cedric hauled another armful of reeds from the wagon and carried it over to Lawrence who was descending the ladder. He paused to watch Father John's skill carefully. A thought came to him.

'Father John, Master Lawrence be a-saying yester-nightertale that thou comest o' the line o' the great Hereward the Wake hisself. Be that sooth, Father John?'

'…And hast also cast an haughty Norman lord into his moat,' added Emma with a giggle, coming up with a smaller armload.

Lawrence cleared his throat and hastily went to collect more reeds. Father John, however, threw his head back and laughed.

'Lawrence, thou rogue, fully chastised shouldst thou be that thou'dst deceive a fine pair of younglings for the sake of a geste – or another oyster or five methinks. For shame!'

Emma's face fell, which made John laugh again. He sat down on the rooftop and addressed the disappointed young hero-worshippers below.

'Well, hearken ye then. 'Twas soothly boasted by my father and his kinsfolk upon the strength of their third ale a' Yuletide that the great Hereward was our forebear. But, alas, my son, many and a-many a good fensman hath made of the selfsame boast. But fear not! Ferly words of a seer hath my good mother spoke upon me at my birth, saying: "Surely the spirit of the Wake shall awaken again in thee, my child, and shall arise to once again defy the Norman tyrant." Thus quoth she, God rest her soul. But she spake from the bitterness of her heart, seeking vengeance for the blood of her slain father, my grandsire. But neither God am I, nor King's advocate, that I should avenge ancient wounds nor seek vengeance upon foes long dead. Thus also saith Holy Writ: "We fight not 'gainst flesh and blood, but 'gainst principalities and powers, and spiritual wickedness in high places." Thus do I raise the cry of Hereward: "Awake! Cast off the tyranny of sin and Satanas, the greatest tyrant of all!"'

Cedric digested this for a moment. Anglo-Saxon fervour was pumping too hard in his veins to see it from a spiritual perspective as yet. It inspired another thought.

'But do ye not fight the cautelous Normanish friars and fat monks that came when the Conqueror stole of our lands?'

'Yea, verily!' his sister chimed in eagerly. 'Thus, behold, the spirit o' Hereward hath awoke in thee soothly, Father John.'

'Nay, lad! Nay, thou flightsome lass!' John laughingly protested. 'Forsooth, there be many 'mongst the brethren of all orders that both preach error and seek dishonest gain. 'Gainst these and others in exalted estate in Holy Church hath Doctor Wycliffe raised his voice and wielded his plume. Thus also are we sent, to gainsay these errors and proclaim the truth of salvation in Christ according to the Holy Scriptures. But mark this also: good and godly men have I also met among the orders of the friars that truly seek God with all their hearts, yea, even within the monasteries. Of Norman, Saxon, of Gael and Danish blood, all are these.'

As an example, he indicated Lawrence, standing ready with another armful of reeds, and gave him a wink.

'Behold my good comrade, My Lord Lawrence the Parson, a devout and holy man. Doth he not have Norman blood flowing full pure in his veins?'

Lawrence reddened as two shocked pairs of youthful eyes were turned upon him. He did his best to counter this fall from grace.

'Let not my master deceive you, my friends. A son of the union of a Normanish lord with a common handmaid am I, or so 'tis said. Thus is my boast, if boast it be, as is the blood of the Wake the boast of Father John's.'

The others laughed, and Lawrence, feeling exonerated, passed up his load of reeds to his master, saying with a challenging grin: 'But what of thine exploit of the vanquished Norman lord in his moat, Father John? Was that also but an idle boast?'

Father John, hard at work again, looked over his shoulder with an expression of weary scorn.

"Twere naught but a flightsome young lording, full of bobbance, that boasted himself a hardier man than any common fensman. He would fane sweep me from his drawbridge with his quarterstaff. But mine prevailed.'

The youngsters crowed with triumph on behalf of him and all fenfolk, so he added: 'Twas in my stark youth, ere I felt the call to preach, but the young fool had overmuch wine. Little victory is there of which to boast, my children.'

The conversation passed on to the young folk's circumstances.

Lawrence was interested in the mysterious, so he tentatively broached the subject of their father's disappearance. The youngsters were actually relieved to be able to unburden their grief upon a sympathetic ear.

'Many do be a-speaken o' father a-drinking o' marsh-wine and a-wanderen wood wild i' the marshes,' said Emma soberly.

'Liesings!' cried Cedric angrily 'Father did not so drink!'

'But so 'tis said, natheless,' Emma pursued relentlessly. 'Poor folk are we, Master Lawrence, and grievous hath our father borne it. He spake of the hoard o' the curst corsairs' caverns that be sought by his grandfer. He would dream-speak a' nights of the hoard. A-many said as father be turnen wood-wild and a-drunken.'

'But drink hisself unto the grave and forsake us? Jeffrey's Day, did he! 'Twere by bloody murder, and evermore be I a-sayen so!' countered Cedric hotly, with staunch filial loyalty. His sister sighed and shook her long blond hair sadly. She was the realist of the twins, and was willing to admit the possibility that her father took his own life, or at least suffered a fatal accident as a result of his drinking.

A tentative suggestion by Lawrence that their father may have died through misadventure was scorned and dismissed by the others.

'A canny fensman,' said Father John, 'never doth he perish through mishap.'

There had been floods for two consecutive years that had ruined their crops and salt-pans, the main source of their income, Emma explained. They had been reduced at times to begging from their neighbours. Their father had drunk himself to sleep for weeks, but had pulled himself back from despair and begun again. This was when he began a forlornly hopeful search along the coastline for the legendary pirate's gold, maybe even a trace of King John's hoard, while he caught wild fowl, and gathered oysters, fish, crab and other seafood that at least kept them alive. His neighbours thought his misfortunes had driven him out of his mind.

'A sleeveless quest,' commented Father John, pausing again to listen to the sad tale. 'None have found aught of the crown jewels. And of the corsairs? None have been seen of late for the Black Death slew good and bad men both in my sire's day and their gold would they scarce bury in these sands. Caverns, were there such, have long been devoured by the invading waves. 'Twas said also that ghostly ships full of dead men, slain by the Black Reaper, would drift upon the sea, prey to the sea-fowls, then founder and break asunder upon the rocks as they drifted shoreward....'

'And so hath they gotten o' their just reward,' stated the girl, shuddering at the gruesome vision.

'And so perish himsoever as a-slayen our good father and his grandfer, God rest their souls!' cried the lad bitterly. He fiercely wrenched an armful of reeds free from the cart, then paused, and looked defiantly at his sister.

'And Father be a-sayen oft and lome a' nights afore we be a-bed that he would be a-finden corsair's gold and we be a-thrift again. "An armful o' gold for us all," quod he. I say as he would ha' so done were he not slain o' foul murder. If he find it not, then will I so do! This I sware: His remains will I seek a'til my dying puff! God and the saints be my witness.'

He dumped his armful hardily into Lawrence's waiting arms as though to lay emphasis on his resolve. Father John and Lawrence exchanged looks. Emma cast up her eyes to heaven, but continued her discourse in a tone of tired resignation.

'Thus do we gather whatsoe'er nature do yield o' the sea, and thus do we beg o' the neighbours. They do give but grudgeously, for say they as father were stark wild, and we be a-sufferen judgment for father's sins o' his younger days.'

'Jack mullock!' snapped Cedric.

'Yea, and bravely said, youngling!' agreed Father John, as righteous indignation welled up within him. 'What chinchery is this? Will God visit the sins of the fathers upon the children? Upon the generations of them that hate Him, surely He will. But upon the households of faith and them that love Him will He show mercy. *Thus* saith Holy Writ! Whosoever preacheth such cruel error, to bind the good folk into slavery of fear and dead works ... may he be accursed!'

Father John could not have preached it better and more fervently from a more conventional pulpit. The little congregation below was suitably impressed.

'Wherefore doth not Father Gerard of Bury or Friar Robert so preachen in like manner?' applauded Cedric, his attention fully diverted from his self-proclaimed mission in life. 'O but that I could read o' the blessed book and preach in likeness o' thee, Father!'

The holy wrath faded in Father John's countenance, to be replaced by kindly amusement.

'Come thou then to our reading circle of the Christian Brethren at Bury St Edmond when thou'rt able, Master Cedric, and mayhap Master Scrivener shall so instruct thee thereafter.'

'Sayest thou as days o' weal we shall beholden again, Father John? Words of comfort these be,' said Emma, hope kindling in her breast.

'As thy soul prospereth, so shalt thou be blest in substance and haleness, my child,' John assured her. 'So saith the Apostle John. Truly, many are the afflictions of the righteous, but the Lord delivereth them from them all.'

'O God, make us righteous and so deliver us then!' prayed Emma fervently.

'Amen!' said her brother with equal fervour.

Father John looked down at him with a kindly challenge in his eye.

'Righteousness must first begin with forgiveness, my son. Wilt thou, then, forgive them that slew thy good sire? "….And forgive us our trespassers as we forgive them that trespass 'gainst us…" quoth Our Good Lord Christ.'

Cedric opened his mouth, ready to reject such an unthinkable notion as forgiving his father's murderers. Then, as conviction visibly took hold on him, he stood still with such an expression of consternation that Emma nearly laughed aloud. Lawrence read the situation quickly and clearly and clamped his hand warningly on her shoulder to check her, and she covered her mouth hastily. God alone knew how Cedric might have reacted in his present state of emotional turmoil.

That night at devotions, Lawrence said a special prayer for the family's trials before he went to bed.

Although he was just as compassionate, he was a quieter and more logical thinker than his master, and he tended to express his faith and message in practical ways. Once a carpenter's apprentice, he mended the widow's rickety spinning wheel and earned the lady's undying gratitude.

She was known for her clothes-making skills and had been able to earn a little extra to feed the family until her machine broke down from age and intensive use. Now she was able to finish her homespuns much more efficiently.

However, even after a day's hard labour, Lawrence couldn't sleep. He tossed and turned on his bed of hay and rough cloth as he mulled over the circumstances of the father's disappearance.

He finally fell asleep, but just before daybreak, he had a dream. It was so vivid, however, it could have been a vision.

It seemed as though he stood by the sea at high tide, watching the waters flowing among the salt-marshes as the light of day began to fade. He could hear the cry of the bittern and the whistle of the wind among the rushes.

Suddenly, the idyllic setting was shattered by yells and loud curses, which rose from all around him. A tall man with long blond hair flying in the wind and eyes wild with terror sprang over a nearby sand hill and ran full tilt past him, without even a glance in his direction. He was clutching what appeared to be a heavy bundle. He paused, sobbing and gasping for breath and glanced fearfully behind him, made a sign of the cross and ran on, stumbling a little under the weight of his burden.

His face looked somewhat familiar to Lawrence, but there was little time to speculate, for the hunters soon appeared. They were obviously fierce men, dressed in rough working garments, armed to the teeth, with murder and rage written all over their faces. They leapt up from many directions, looking around for their prey, and seemed not to notice Lawrence at all.

The strange thing was that Lawrence felt neither fear of the ferocious men, nor any sense of urgency of any kind for the poor quarry whose doom was most likely sealed. He felt some sympathy for him, but it was as though he was watching a play unfold. He was not meant to participate in the drama at all – just observe.

The hunters searched around in the mud and sand until a few found footprints and yelled at their comrades in a foreign tongue. They all ran off in the direction of a mist-covered marsh not too far in the distance. Lawrence decided to follow. Louder yells indicated that the fugitive had been sighted.

Lawrence suddenly found himself just outside what appeared to be an entrance of some kind where the darkest and most mysterious part of the distant marshes began. The rushes and coastal vegetation seemed to have increased in size and density, but arched over between two islands almost like the mouth of a cave. There was certainly a cavern-like darkness beyond it. Mists and shadows billowed and blew around him.

The fugitive came staggering and panting up to it and paused again, looking over his shoulder like a hunted deer.

His fears were confirmed.

The islands of mud and sand erupted with hostile men, roaring and spitting their outrage at him. He turned and ran toward the entrance, slipping and falling in the wet earth before he made it. The fall was a fatal mistake. Arrows fell around him, and two found their mark. Crying out and gasping with pain, he plunged into the entrance, refusing to leave his burden behind. Lawrence was only just able to hear the man's agonised utterance before he disappeared.

'The tree… God send I find Saint Aelfrith's tree… God aid me!'

Most of his pursuers did not hesitate to follow, although a little warily. A few hung back, but when verbally chastised by their fellows for doing so, the last shrugged and plunged in.

The scene changed again, and Lawrence found himself standing knee-deep in marshwater before an island, larger than the others, with a solitary tree growing in the middle of it. It was thick and gnarled with age and some of its branches drooped into the brackish waters.

The fugitive had managed to crawl to the foot of the tree, still clutching the heavy leather bag. He was bleeding copiously from his wounds and coughing up blood. Finally, he struggled to a sitting position. With a superhuman effort, he plucked out one arrow from his back and threw it on the ground before leaning back against the tree trunk, exhausted. He dragged the bag onto his knees and looked heavenward. A croaking sound came from his blood-stained lips, then he coughed again and spoke clearly.

'Good Lord Jesu, take Thou my spirit anon… but send Thou my kinlings… for to find this gift when the time be ripe.'

Pondering the dying man's words, Lawrence looked around to see any sign of his pursuers, but the scene changed again, or maybe it moved forward in time. All he could see were dead bodies lying in the mud or floating in the waters. Another remarkable thing that Lawrence noticed in all the bizarre and gruesome scene was that they were facing away from the dying man on the island. Then he noticed that misty, almost human-like figures were hovering nearby. Others seemed to appear out of the waters and the islands like spectres from a bye-gone age. Once again, Lawrence felt no fear, but watched in fascination as they drew closer to the dying man under the tree. They whispered and hissed with as much venom and hatred as the man's pursuers, but with far less volume and far more terror. The dying man shut his eyes and prayed.

Suddenly a light appeared with explosive force next to him. With cries of dread, the ghostly figures took flight before it. It was as though a tall, upright pyre had instantaneously burst into bright blue flames. The clearing was lit up as bright as day. As the light dimmed somewhat, it also took on a human-like shape. Then the light faded completely to reveal a tall, handsome and fully armed warrior, dressed in ancient warrior's attire that Lawrence guessed was those worn by an Anglo-Saxon warrior of high rank. The dying man apparently did not see him, but nonetheless, a smile of relief came over his face. He laid his head back against the tree-trunk and breathed his last.

The warrior was perfectly aware of Lawrence's presence, for he turned toward him and spoke in a clear but distant voice that seemed to come from eternal realms.

'Hail Lawrence Parsons, thou man of God. I was once a hidden guardsman of Thane Aelfrith the Faithful, who died before this tree, defending his folk 'gainst the invading Danes. His time had come for his reward, as it is now the time for this man. Go! Tell the house of Wainthorpe of the things that thou hast seen.'

The scene faded, and Lawrence awoke in darkness. He was trembling with fear and excitement, sensations which were markedly absent during his vision. He lay still as the sensations subsided, wondering whether he should awake the household immediately and tell them. Then he decided that it was best to wait until morning. Weariness finally caught up with him and he fell into a dreamless sleep.

He awoke when the morning had well advanced, still pondering his dream. Had he merely dreamt it or was it really a message from God?

The next thing he noticed was a rather toothsome smell emanating from behind the rough curtain that gave the visitors some sort of privacy. Apparently, Father John had arisen hours before, had sallied forth to the marshes and, with all the skill of an experienced fensman, had caught two magnificent eels.

Madame Wainthorpe was slicing them up, ready to cook them together with a combination of local herbs and turnips in her large pot over a sweet-smelling peat fire. It made Lawrence's mouth water. Putting all heavenly visions aside for the present, he arose and dressed hastily.

'... And no rain through the roof, thanks be to God and thy cunning, father John,' the careworn dame was saying happily. She thoroughly enjoyed the benefits of having men around the house for the first time in years.

Lawrence stepped from behind the curtain just as the twins came bustling through the door with a variety of produce from the sea. They had armfuls of samphire (the asparagus of the sea) as well. They stopped dead and breathed deeply with obvious relish.

'Ha! Marsh-eel such as my father were a-catchen fern ago,' sang Cedric. 'Prithee, Father John, that thou leeren me o' that cunning skill?'

'With a good will, my son. Ye have surely done well also, of the bounty ·of the Wash I see. Samphire as tender as any I gathered in my younger days. A merry feast shall there be this morn.'

He turned to see his disciple emerging from behind the curtain a little sheepishly, and added with a touch of derision:

'....And lo, My Lord Lawrence Parsons hath arisen at last to devour all.'

'And full worthy he be of it, father,' said the widow with a smile, coming to the young preacher's defence, 'for he hath a-mended door, rafter and spinnen-wheel for me. Come ye all to table and feast anon.'

As they ate, Father John noticed that Lawrence was the only one not in a convivial mood, but seemed rather preoccupied. While the others chatted happily, John leaned over and spoke quietly to his disciple.

'Did I offend thee in my japishness, my son? Or did slumber forsake thee a nightertale last?'

'Nay and yea, father,' Lawrence replied, looking up with a weary smile. 'Sleep I do lack, but a little only. Rather do I ponder upon a dream sent from God ...or so it seemeth as a ferly dream. Likened more unto waking life did it seem.'

Lawrence was not normally given to dreams and visions, being a practical young man, so this announcement made Father John stop eating and turn to observe his disciple more closely.

'Describe to me this dream, my son.'

Lawrence did not answer immediately. He first addressed a question to the widow regarding the Tree of Saint Aelfrith.

'Saint Aelfrith's tree?' she answered, surprised. 'Few there be that speak o' that lore. He were a mighty thane, yea, a good man as served good King Edmund, hisself a saint he were, ere the coming o' the Danes. All loved him, for he were piously and openly-handed a' to his folk. When the Danes be come, he fought at Edmund's side, but the foe be too many and too strong. Edmund were captured, but Aelfrith fled with his people to Lutton Marshes for a last stand. Horrorful and bloody slaughter it were, for the Danes be cruel heathen folk then, a-cursen us with their gods. A-many and a-many perished in the sands, but they ceased not a'til all our folk be slain. Aye, our womenfolk and youngerlings among them.'

She sighed. 'They would forsake not the good thane, for so they loved him. Hence, that fell marsh be an accursed place o' dread. It be a-haunted by Swamp-Wights and Marsh-Sprites.'

'Aye!' chimed in Cedric with martial fervour. 'But 'tis said as so many Danes fell a' the marshes, King Alfred o' Wessex were saved to flee and fight again. The Lord o' the Danes fell a'fore Saint Aelfrith's sword, though he were mortal a-wounded hisself. Would that I were there! The Danes would they be as chaff a'fore my sword!'

'But there be much Dane's blood in thy veins, Cedric Wainthorpe,' said his pragmatic sister scornfully.

'Sooth it may be, for Saxon wives they took a-force,' he replied, irritated but undeterred. 'But the Saxons as lived never them forgaven. Fen folk forgive not too easy!'

'Hence the curse of the marshes is kept alive,' commented Father John drily. He let that thought sink in for a moment, then changed the subject.

'Ho, then, Master Lawrence, and what of thy dream? Can it be thou'st beheld Saint Aelfrith's tree?'

Reluctantly, knowing how distressing his message would be for the family, Lawrence told them what he saw in few words as possible. When he described the fugitive the twins both cried out: 'Father??'

'O by the mercies o' God!' cried the widow in grief. 'Say it be not sooth! That my Cedric died a' the hands o' murderous men. Be they the curst corsairs, Master?'

'I know not surely, lady, but they wore rough raiment as for sea-faring. We know not surely if it were thine husband.'

'May their souls rot in hell!' cried young Cedric bitterly. Emma merely wept.

Father John opened his mouth to comment again, but seeing their grief, decided against it. He bade Lawrence continue his story instead.

When Lawrence described the landmarks where the man fled to, the widow's eyes dilated in horror.

'The Marshes o' the Dead!' she cried with dismay. 'Few durst venture thither, and none return that do.'

Cedric, too excited to consider the terror of the marshes, staunchly declared: 'My father did so, and so will I so do!'

'But were it father indeed?' asked Emma anxiously. 'Of what like were he?'

Lawrence did not answer. He was looking carefully at young Cedric's features in his set young face. The bent nose, the same shape of the eyes were there. There was no doubt now, and young Cedric knew it. He stood to his feet, abandoning the last of his breakfast.

'Mother, I must seek him.'

'Nay and nay!' wailed his mother. 'My man be lost to me. Do I lose my son also?'

'I go, mother, whether thou be a-sayen yea or nay.'

His manner was calm and resolute, even though his mother stormed, pleaded, wept and threatened. Emma was silent throughout.

Lawrence told her of the man's dying prayer, and the angelic warrior's command, but even that did not sway their mother.

Finally, pitying the poor widow's distress, Father John intervened.

'Nay then, Madame, be at peace! Dreadless a message it is from heaven that Master Lawrence bringeth. If it be soothly the call of God, Cedric must follow it, and God's arm of strength will protect him. But if thine heart misgiveth thee, then shall I and my good Lawrence be his rearguard.

I have some wit and cunning of the treachery of the marshes. Indeed, my friend must be his guide, for to him was the vision made manifest.'

That relieved the anxious mother's mind considerably, and it never occurred to her that the two preachers may well fail.

'O that I could come also, but my bones be a-waxen old that I durst not face that peril. Nor could I stand afore the evil wights, for a meacock creature I be. Mine Emma and I shall abide hither and pray the Almighty's good aid.'

Emma also stood to her feet resolutely.

'I go with they also, mother. If it be my father, then my duty it be.'

Her mother groaned, but accepted the inevitable.

'Go then, child! Art as headfast and stiffnecked, both, as ever thy father were. Well, these good brethren be as angels o' God, or holy saints, be sure, and will keep ye sure and safe. My blessings and prayers attend ye all, that God send his blessed angels with ye. Go ye, then, ere I change o' mine heart.'

Chapter 14: Mystery in the Marshes

"sed et si ambulavero in valle mortis non timebo malum quoniam tu mecum es virga tua et baculus tuus ipsa consolabuntur me[64]"

[Psalm 22:4 Jerome's Vulgate]

'Whither anon, Lawrence?' Father John shouted above the sound of wind and waves. He turned his back on the sea to shield himself from the chilling onshore winds. 'A sleeveless quest at the westward bounds of the Marshes of the Dead, and this ferly doorway have we not found. We must find what we seek ere the rising of the tide, else it may engulf all.'

Spring was well advancing when the four stood on the shore. The sea winds whipped up the edges of their cloaks. There was a tinge of purple all around them as sea lavender and Aster strove to bring forth their hardy blossoms. A single harrier circled above.

Lawrence was looking in all directions, even scanning the beaches for a sign of the landmarks that appeared so vividly in his dream.

'My memory faileth me, alas!' he confessed. 'Naught save the sea itself beareth likeness to what I beheld in the night. I had hope that the sea would give me counsel, but there is naught. Let us journey inland-ward. Haply a landmark I may see that would aid our quest.'

'For what landmark seekest thou, Master Lawrence?' asked Emma apprehensively. She did not share her brother's enthusiasm for adventure.

'I saw tall reeds in the likeness of a dark doorway, nigh unto a strange and twisted tree, stunted and in likeness even as a dwarf...'

Emma looked up suddenly, alert, her eyes wide with fear and wonder.

'But this tree I ken of right well! It be a step and a-many from hither. The Dwarrow-Tree, so it be named by fenfolk o' the Wash, and they shun it

---

64   "Yea, though I walk through the valley of the shadow of death, I will fear no evil. For Thou art with me. Thy rod and Thy staff they comfort me." Psalm 23 KJV

full barful. Times there were when father would a-show it me as we farmed the salt pans and, quoth he: "Pass yon tree at thy peril! The day I so do, it will be the day I ... die.'"

She gulped and hung her head to hide her tears.

'Wilt thou guide us then, Mistress Emma? Grieve for thy father thou must, but fear not, for God is with us. Death is not our portion on this journey, though perils there may be. We would have forbid thy presence in our fellowship had it not been an errand sent from above.'

Lawrence's bracing but kind words heartened her, so she nodded and led the way. She smiled her thanks as he helped her up the sandy embankment.

'Beware the fell sands!' Father John called out over the sounds of the blustery winds as he and Cedric followed. 'Avoid ye the lower sandy earthen dales and follow rather the hills!'

As they went on, Emma covertly studied Lawrence's profile. It was not often that a rather agreeable, wise, strong and kind young man came her way, let alone walked into the wild with her.

Dick Swain had been the only youth who had shown any interest in her, her modest good looks in his eyes triumphing over the villagers' prejudice against the family. She had welcomed his friendship at first, but when he became very possessive and patronising, she lost interest. It took, however, a well-aimed fist from Cedric on Tom's nose to persuade him to leave her alone. Hence, she found Lawrence's courtesy and considerate manner rather refreshing. She overcame her shyness and began to question him about himself and his remarkable calling.

Even after all the tales of their adventures Father John had enumerated the previous evenings over supper, there was much to tell. Many things had happened since he and Father John set out from Lutterworth, with Doctor Wycliffe's exhortations and benediction ringing in their ears. Some of their adventures were almost as strange as the one they were about to embark upon. He was not troubled by the unknown for, as he said, 'God hath led us into the valley of Death and hath brought us through, times and a-many.'

He spoke frankly about his years as a carpenter's apprentice, then as a frustrated journeyman, dreaming of wealth and honour, and failing that, seeking life's answers. He finally found them when he met Father

John at Oxford. He began his studies there under Father John's aegis, followed by the call to be one of Wycliffe's Poor Preachers. He spoke, not in a boastful spirit, but matter-of-factly about some of their successes and laughed ruefully over their failures as he and Father John went from town to town, village to village.

Emma soon became as fascinated by the man as much as by his story.

'But will ye roam this land and preach the gospel for aye and forever, Master Lawrence?' she asked, after a long pause. 'Will there not be a day thou shalt cease thy wanderings and stay and build thee an abode? Mayhap...that ye marry...and father childlings?'

She blushed deeply, realising that she had betrayed her budding partiality.

He chose to ignore it, however.

'God alone knoweth, Mistress. It shall be many a twelvemonth hence if it must be so. Yea, soothly a-times I have dreamed of riches a-plenty and mine own household, but such is not my season.'

He stopped and looked her straight in the eyes.

'Riches and possessions cannot fill the heart, Mistress Emma. Only the call of God and living in His good grace will suffice. This I have learned through tribulations a-many, though I fall a-dreaming a-times also. But this hath Father John shown me, yea, by his own journey unto full-grown manhood: Seek ye first God's kingdom and His righteousness and all else will follow in His good time. Mind thou this, lady, and thou shalt do well and prosper.'

Emma, turning away to hide her disappointment, nodded reluctantly.

But now was not the time to think of thwarted romantic fancies, for a gust of wind blew the mist aside, and there it was before them – the Dwarrow-tree.

It looked so uncannily human-like, its stunted trunk divided like sturdy legs at the base, its two main boughs reaching upward supporting, or rather grasping at the mass of thick foliage above. A ferociously twisted face-like stump was supported between the boughs, with sunken wooden eye-sockets glowering at them like a hostile gatekeeper, forbidding entry to strangers.

'What pagan abomination is this?' muttered Father John, staring at it with distaste.

What made it even worse for Emma was the strange objects scattered and heaped at the foot of the tree. She ventured to touch one on the ground nearby, wiping the moss and grime off it. She suddenly sprang back in revulsion and horror, making the sign of the cross.

'Bones!'

'Yea! And verily are they of human-kind,' said Lawrence, squatting down to examine them closely with great interest. 'Such I saw in my dream a' nightertale last. A sign is this to me that God guideth our steps.'

'Surely!' agreed Father John as he and Cedric approached. 'Peradventure a mighty battle there was here, even that of which Madam Wainthorpe spake.'

'Aye!' agreed Cedric, excited at the grisly discovery. 'But be this also, mayhap: Folk of old did deem yon tree as be an heathen god, and maketh sacrifice unto he – even human sacrifice.'

Emma shuddered and looked away.

'Hence the curse is first brought upon this place,' John surmised, grimacing at the grotesque tree with distaste. 'Evil there is present. This, I feel in mine own heart.'

Then he added in a loud and defiant voice to anyone in the vicinity, visible or invisible, who could hear:

'For this purpose also hath God sent us hither – to cleanse and to deliver this land of its curse!'

Nothing save the sound of the wind in the rushes answered him. Neither bird nor beast had come near the place for many years.

Lawrence paid more attention to practical detail at that moment than to spiritual warfare. He examined the piles of bones closely.

'Do not wolves and swamp creatures prey upon such, Father John? Yet are there but whole skeletons untouched though they are ancient indeed. Did no man stay or return to give them Christian burial? Yet again do I espy others yonder that are but lately fallen, for the bones are cleaner and bear cloth and skin – a little.'

He rose and walked toward the clearing before the tall, pillar-like rushes that seemed to flank an entrance to a natural passageway of some sort. Corpses, almost fully decomposed, with rusting weapons in hand lay prostrate with their heads facing away from the dark entrance, as though falling in the act of fleeing. There was a trail of them as far as Lawrence's eyes could see into the misty interior.

Traces of clothing, mainly long-lasting leather, still clung to the bones.

'Well-armed, these, but soldiers they are not,' Lawrence noted.

He was about to thrust his way into the passageway when Father John stopped him.

'Stay, my friend. Perils unknown and hidden there may be beyond thy ken. Let the fenfolk lead thee anon. Some cunning do we have of these lands. Mark our footsteps, lest thou fall into the fell sands. Come, Master Cedric! Adventure awaiteth thee within.'

The two fensmen plunged through the rushes, keeping to the side of the natural passageway and watching for other signs of danger. Some of the fallen bodies were almost or semi-submerged in the quicksands and pools that dotted the passageway, giving out a grim warning of other hidden traps.

Emma hesitated, fighting her fears. Lawrence held out his hand.

'Come, Mistress Emma Wainthorpe! The fenfolk must lead.'

Setting her jaw, she gripped his hand and plunged in, racing to get as close to the others as possible.

It was like walking down a long, eerie and windy tunnel with a wall of fog and rushes on each side. Wisps of vapour appeared almost out of nowhere and floated past them. Clouds had gathered above, but no rain fell as yet. All these elements made Emma feel as though she had walked into a gloomy and ghostly trap. She looked anxiously back at the entrance, but that was also shrouded in mist. None of the others appeared perturbed or were too absorbed in their macabre discoveries to notice, so she said nothing.

The macabre signposts of dead bodies continued to guide them for what seemed like an hour. Little was said or heard, save the tramping and squelching of their feet in the mud or sand, and the occasional hiss of the passing wisps of mist. Then the bodies gradually thinned out as they approached a widening area similar to a huge cavern, dimly lit from above.

Lawrence, unmoved by the weird surroundings, stopped to examine a few more of the fallen skeletons and scratched his head. The other three gathered round, questioning.

'Strong and hardy men these were aforetime,' he remarked, somewhat puzzled, 'yet all of stature differing from most fensmen. They all have fallen as if in flight toward yonder passage from whence we came. Fully armed are they all... yet... I see naught of scathe of arrow nor stroke of sword. Not by the hand of men did these fall. Neither were they torn by wild, scavenging beasts. Nor did they all drown in the fell sands. Wherewithal then did they perish? With what weapon were they smitten down? Wherefore....?'

He was interrupted by a slowly rising crescendo of eerie rustling and strange muttering all around them. They had all ignored it at first, thinking it as nothing but the wind among the sparse vegetation or the passing mists. They all froze as the sounds grew louder, coming closer. Emma squeaked something unintelligible and pointed with a shaking finger.

Small but menacing spectral figures appeared vaguely, giving ghostly laughs that echoed uncannily in an environment that dulled any normal echo. The humanlike figures appeared in twos and threes at first, but then seemed to gather in terrifying numbers. Some would creep ever closer to them, then dive or melt back into the mist or marshes, only to reappear closer still. Amongst the muttering, the visitors could hear half-spoken, half-hissing words like 'Death!' or 'Slay them!' An occasional cry was heard, like a wail of despair or a dying man's curse in ages long gone. Emma grabbed Lawrence's hand again.

'Swamp-wights!' cried Cedric with excitement.

'Marsh-sprites!' whispered Emma with fear, and clutched Lawrence's hand even tighter.

Lawrence, however, was looking calmly and expectantly at his master, and with good reason. Father John had learned much since he had left his home in the fens and travelled to Oxford. He gave a laugh of defiance, as was his wont when he faced an impossible situation, and stepped forward.

'Ho!' he called out, taunting the looming apparitions, his hands on his hips. 'Do ye deem yourselves to be the lords of this land then, o little demons?'

At his voice, the ghostly host paused and hissed at him, although some warily half-shrank into the islands. A dark, deep and harsh voice arose from within the host.

'We are the spirits of the dead, ye interlopers. None that dare enter our domain ever return to the land of the living. Your lives are forfeit.'

Even Cedric was now looking nervously at Father John. But the priest seemed to grow in stature as his anger grew.

'Ye are no dead spirits, but mere lying servants of the evil one! Hearken ye then, demon-wights! Henceforth, these lands are yours no longer! Servants of the Lord of all lands and seas are we, even the Lord Christ Jesu! In His Name do we claim these lands for His people's use. What are your names?'

A visible shudder went through the host at the sound of the Name.

'We are called Death and Murder,' came the reluctant reply, as though forced from them, 'but we are many and stronger than thou!'

'What idle boast is this?' Father John laughed louder. 'Stronger than He Who dwelleth within us? O ye pitiful demons of death and murder, I adjure you in the Name of the mighty Lord Jesu Christ to flee this place and that straightway! Begone!..... 'ere the wrath of the Lord of Hosts cometh upon you!'

The ghostly beings, backed away slowly, reluctantly. Those closest to Father John shrank back hastily as he stepped forward again.

Suddenly the wind rose higher, and above it they could hear a mighty thunder of great wings. If they had been birds, they must have been on an enormous scale and in great numbers. Cedric and Emma looked up in wonder, but could see nothing but shifting shapes in the mist. The demon spirits could see them quite clearly, however. They wailed and screeched and fled this way and that, diving into the muddy waters or disappearing into the islands in their disordered retreat.

Soon all traces of evil presence was gone, and even the thunder of the great wings faded into the distance. The young folk blinked as though they had awoken from a bad dream.

'A man full o' faith and power, be thou, Father John,' declared Emma in great awe. 'Be they soothly holy angels that come to our aid? Be ye holy saints, then?'

The fading wrath in Father John's face gave way to sudden merriment.

'Then was Master Ashwardby of Oxenford a mighty apostle! Sayest thou not so, O Saint Lawrence?'

Lawrence chuckled and explained to the youngsters about the unremarkable, dithering and forgetful Oxford professor who had many times cast forth terrible demons from tormented souls. He was numbered among Wycliffe's closest henchmen, and taught the biblical principles and practices of true exorcism to some of Master Smith's disciples, John and Lawrence included. Better known but less affective exorcists had become bitterly jealous and accused him of sorcery.

Cedric, no less awed than his sister, had another thought. He pointed at Father John and cried out: 'Hereward be a-waken!'

John laughed yet again.

'Seest thou sooth at the last, youngling? The Wake himself fought but mere Normans. We fight 'gainst spirits of wickedness in high places. But we fail not, as did the Wake, and he perished. Such is the power and grace in the Name of the good Lord Christ. The blood of Hereward, though it may course within my veins, it availeth me not. The cleansing blood of the Son of God alone can cause such sinners as I to arise and prevail victorious.'

He looked inward toward the darker regions of the marsh, as Cedric digested his words. The wind quietened to a gentle breeze. The mist lifted substantially. Breaks appeared in the clouds, enough for a few rays of sunlight to break through, reminding Father John of his present task.

'A ferly pulpit is this, and we must still look to our quest, comrades. It behooveth us a' the morrow to cut down the abomination that guardeth the gateway to this place, and bury the bones of sacrifice. Else the curse may return.'

He glanced around the immediate surroundings as the light increased, and noticed a larger island in the distance with an unusually large tree growing in the middle of it.

'Do I espy another of these fallen gentry, under the Alder tree yonder?'

They carefully followed him, and found a gnarled, wide-spreading and windswept tree, growing out of a larger island than its fellows surrounding it.

Underneath the boughs, seated as though in peaceful slumber, with its back to the trunk of the tree, sat a larger skeleton, also perfectly intact. Its bony arms tightly clutched a large leather bag which had hardly degenerated at all, resting on its knees. Two half-rotting arrows hung loosely in the dead man's rib-cage, but strangely, from behind, as one that had been struck in the back. Another lay at his feet. There were more broken and dismembered skeletons scattered in a semi-circle. Lawrence noted that the skulls were mostly facing away from the pathetic figure seated before the tree.

'In full likeness to my dream … or nigh unto it!' Lawrence gasped. 'But neither with flesh nor spirit, God rest his soul.'

The young ones crossed themselves, but more out of habit than from conviction.

Father John was rather mystified as he surveyed the whole scene.

'Foes that pursue their quarry full zealous into the marshes, and then perish in the chase, slain by weapons unknown,' he mused aloud. 'Of their prey, if prey he was, he awaiteth them by yonder tree, but they touch him not save by their shafts from afar. Dying, all his flesh is devoured but the bones are not violated by creatures of the swamp, nor do they devour nor scatter of the bones of his fallen foes. The fleshless fallen one before us awaiteth many a twelvemonth for any who mayhap would dare the marshes – for whatsoever purpose? God wot. Dark doings, these. How then read we these riddles?'

Lawrence examined one of the remains nearby, then stooped and pulled something from under its broken skull, washed it in the waters and brought it to John to examine. It looked like a metal collar, though grimed and stained. Parts of it glinted yellow as more pale shafts of sunlight broke through the thinning blanket of hovering mist.

'Gold tainteth but will last longer than iron that rusteth, so say the smiths. Of what handiwork is this? Would fenfolk bear such?'

'Nay!' exclaimed John, as a light dawned. 'My father spoke of such. These the corsairs wore of old whilst a-ravaging of the coasts. Not all that accursed brood is passed, or so it seemeth.'

'Peradventure these are the last of the remnant,' suggested Lawrence. He turned his attention to the lonely skeleton before them, its skull grinning at them in a kind of macabre welcome.

'Let us now seek sooth of him enthroned yonder. What sayest thou, Cedric? Is this he of whom we seek? Is there aught among his apparel, corrupt though it be, wherewith his kindred would ken of? Go forth and fear not! Be strong, for the dead harm thee not. This one would have speech with thee, but not with the words of living tongues.'

Emma, already trembling from the ordeal of the last hour, could not bear the sight of one whose identity she was sure she knew so well, and clung to Lawrence, burying her head in his habit.

Cedric looked questioningly up at Father John and received a nod in reply. Swallowing the nausea that rose in his throat, he approached tentatively. There were only fragments of clothing and flesh on him, and these disintegrated at his touch, but the bony figure kept its place as though it chose not to notice him. Cedric slid his hand along the left radial bone to the hand and found a brass ring.

'The ring!' he cried out hoarsely. 'So did my father wear a' the day he and Mother be a-wedded and ne'er cast he it off.'

A shuddering sob shook Emma's frame, but still she did not look up.

Lawrence did not feel comfortable in his present role.

'Surely, it tryeth thee sorely, lass,' he said awkwardly, 'but be ye strong. It behoveth a fenswoman, yea, Cedric Wainthorpe's daughter to endure hardness, and to prevail. God Almighty shall give thee strength.'

She responded immediately to the challenge, and straightened herself with a determined sniff.

'Aye! So shall I do, God aiding me.'

She set her jaw and joined her brother in his grisly search for clues, although she could not bear to look at the skull as yet. Her attention was caught by the leather bag. It must have been good leather, well treated, for it was about the only fabric that had lasted the years of corruption in that moist environment. Taking a deep breath, she carefully pulled the bag from under the withered arm that held it so tightly. Cedric turned and helped her, for it was heavy. The moment that the bag was free of its dead guardian, the whole skeleton collapsed and fell at their feet, as though it had finally relinquished its charge and could rest in peace.

Startled, they dropped the bag on the ground and the aging leather finally gave way, splitting on one side. Emma shrieked a little and fell on her knees, covering her face again. Out of the broken bag, hard and shiny things fell or rolled onto the soft, muddy earth.

'Coins!' yelled Cedric. 'Gilden and silver, they be! A king's hoard!'

He ran his fingers through them, gasping half in delight and half in dazed wonder. The two men scrambled carefully over to see, but Emma was not interested in forgotten treasure as yet.

'His knife!' she said in a strangled voice. 'Oft and lome would he be a-carven manikins and beasts when a babe I were. His knife it be! O father, forgive me that I be a-doubten o' thee!'

Forgetting her revulsion, she laid her head upon the fallen skeleton and wept.

A knife with a peculiar design on its handle, rusted but still whole, fell out of what was once the right hand. It had been hidden from view by the bag of treasure. Cedric pounced on it.

'Aye! 'Tis the knife, dreadless,' he acknowledged, choking with emotion. 'Ah, God! "An armful o' gold for us all," quod he. But all the treasure I would trade for to bring him back o' the dead.'

Father John looked up from examining a coin.

'Nay, but he surely would wish for thee to take and profit thereof. Be at peace, my son, for thy father would so wish it.'

He turned back and frowned at the coin, holding it at arm's length.

'I wot not what manner of coins these be, for English Marks they are not. Art skilled in coinage, art not, Lawrence? Of what make is this, and from whence?'

'Spanish and French, I ween. Such as were current ten years gone. But mark this, Father, for 'tis of English make.'

He held up a coin, very different from the rest. It was obviously more ancient and corroded, but one could discern the image of a king's head on it. Father John, scraping away more accumulated corrosion, read the inscription engraved around it.

'"*Johannes Rex*"! From King John's lost royal treasures cometh this coin!'

The grief, however, was still too poignant for the brother and sister to fully appreciate their find. They sat in silence by the remains of their father, an arm around each other's shoulder. Cedric fingered the knife glumly.

'I were a' fault,' said Emma brokenly, 'for I believed he had a-drunken hisself unto the grave, as our neighbour-folk said. Soothly, he were slain as thou believed. Thou alone had faith...' She could not go on.

Cedric looked up at the two men who were studying the coins and other jewellery.

'But whence came he by this?' he enquired in perplexity. 'Every stone and cavern do I a-ken of by the sea. And wherefore came he to this accursed place, a-bearen o' this hoard?'

Father John stroked his chin in thought.

'Caverns there were still in thy father's days ere the sea felled them, I deem. Wherefore this place to find refuge? Haply he hoped the foe would not follow for the fear of the Marshes of Death. Peradventure there were both fight and flight ere they drew near to thy father to smite him. But by whom and 'gainst whom, whither and wherefore? For they fall without blows of battle, if the signs lie not. There is much here that I wist not nor understand. What sayest thou, Lawrence? Thine was the vision a' nightertale last.'

Lawrence dropped the coins back into the bag and sat by the tree, staring at the fallen skeleton meditatively. He turned to them with conclusion in his face.

'Thus do I read this enigma, my friends: Corsairs had arisen once again in thy father's time, and return unto these shores, cloaked in darkness. The fenfolk watch for them no longer, deeming them all perished or fled the plagues. Thy father alone, howsomever, kept watch and espied their return. Spake he naught of this?'

'I think not so,' answered Cedric, surprised. 'Had he so spoken of it to mother, she would ha' surely forbid us our forays o' the shore for dread o' them.'

Emma sat up with a gasp. 'And yet there be times late o' nights when I slept not, that he spake in his slumber. "The corsairs!" cried he. "They return! They hide their gold a' shoreward!" I heeded him not, for deemed I that he raved in the wood wildness o' his drunkenness or night visions only. God forgive me that I doubted him.'

'So this we know, then,' Lawrence continued, 'thy father watches, but then the corsairs fail to return. Thus, he seeks for corsair's hoard full diligent, though all other would gainsay him, and he speaks to none of what he had seen, save in his dreams. Then, with his knowledge from watching them in his former watches, he findeth what he seeks. But all is discovered, for by ill-fortune (or haply by the dictates of destiny) the corsairs do return that selfsame hour. Knowing that none escape the vengeance of the corsairs, he fleeth with his hoard unto the only haven he wot of, stark and barful though it be, that his foes may haply fear to

pursue. Unhappily, such is the lust for gold and for blood in them, they
follow him unto their death and his.'

'And by what weapon did they fall?' asked Father John, fascinated, but
with a hint of scepticism. 'Not by the hand of man, sayedst thou?'

'Verily. But mark this: The evil guardians dwelt in these places by
permission of the curse that fell in the days of the abominable sacrifices, and
strengthened their hold when the Thane and all his folk were slaughtered
by the Danes. We, the redeemed, are safe from the hands of the demon
guardians. But men of blood that slay, ravage and steal – are they not fair
prey for them? Mark that they were in rout as they fell. The guardians
could slay with fear alone, methinks.'

'By the Rood, thou hast hit the mark, my friend,' remarked Father
John with another of his laughs. 'Ho! *Captantes capti sumus.*[65] Kind-wit
hast thou in abundance, Lawrence. Yet what of the fallen bold one yonder?
Wherefore did he not fear to enter this guarded realm? Would not the
marsh-sprites devour him also?'

'In my night-vision, I heard him cry out unto the Lord God. Doth it
not say in Holy Writ that "whomsoever calleth upon the Name of the Lord
shall be saved"? Alas that he died of his wounds, but only by the hand of
violent men, for the redeemed are safe from the powers of evil. He hath
found the grace to enter into his heavenly rest. His last prayer ere he died
was that his kin would seek and find him, and claim the gold he guarded
with his last breath.'

No one could doubt Lawrence's reading of the mystery now. The twins
clung to each other and shed more tears of grief for their father, who died
with their well-being as his final thought.

Finally wiping his eyes, Cedric stood up and wrapped the broken bag
of gold in his ragged coat.

'How then shall we use this gold, Father John? Many a neighbour,
would they not surely covet it? Rather would I cast it into the fell sands
than there be a-fighting and a-shedding o' blood over it.'

John heaved himself to his feet with his characteristic laugh and
clamped both his large hands on the youngsters' shoulders.

'Fear not. Come ye with us to Bury-Saint-Edmund a' the morrow.
Thither shall Master Goldsmith give us counsel in this matter, for a man

---

65 Captors have been caught

full trustworthy is he. But now behold! The fortunes of the Wainthorpes have turned at last. Let it be said no longer that they are a family accursed. Ye have wealth abundant and shall be the envy of thy neighbours. But know thee now, Master Cedric Wainthorpe, that to whom much is given, much shall be expected. Use it wisely!'

'But this be full thanks unto thee and Master Lawrence, father,' protested Cedric conscientiously, 'Will ye not take a portion thereof?'

'Nay, lad, but we thank thee of thy generosity. Full thanks rather be rendered unto Almighty God, Who gave thee of His bounty. Poor preachers are we, and so remain while our mission will last, for so is it commanded us of Doctor Wycliffe that we hold nor land nor possessions.'

A quiet sigh of resignation came from Lawrence's direction.

'Natheless,' John continued with a grin, 'speed us on our way and others of the Christian Brethren that pass this way if ye will, and remember the poor, and God in heaven shall reward thee.'

'Ever be ye and all thy brethren welcome, Father, as long as I be master o' household Wainthorpe.' responded Cedric glowingly. He weighed the bag of treasure in his hands soberly, as though newly aware of his new responsibilities.

'Yea, verily and amen,' echoed Emma with slightly less enthusiasm, 'but … will ye depart indeed, brethren? Be there not much to do a' these parts, that thy message ye must preach?'

Her eyes were upon Lawrence as she spoke.

'Alas, but so it must be, Mistress Emma,' he responded with a rueful smile. 'Other realms call us also, and the folk of thy village paid but scant heed to us, though we laboured long amongst them. Hardy are the fenfolk, but oft their hardness doth enter their hearts. Ye of the house of Wainthorpe alone have fully welcomed our message. Natheless, let thy new fortunes be a witness unto them of the grace and bounty of God. Mayhap they will hearken unto thee, their own village-folk.'

She sighed and nodded, but said with quiet conviction, 'So be it, then. And henceforth do I give o' my soul and strength to serve my blessed Saviour and His Kingdom.'

'Bravely spoken, lass!' said Father John approvingly. 'Now must we bury the dead anon with all honour and ceremony due a valiant man, for he gave of his life for thy weal. What sayest thou, Master Wainthorpe?

Shall we return to do the needful, or shall we lay him to rest within the waters of the marsh anon? Thine is the choice.'

Cedric lifted his head, conscious of his new role as head of his house.

'My father hath sat untouched in watch o'er his find for many a winter. We must look to Mother, a-bringen her tidings o' what came to pass. Then return we to cut down the Dwarrow-tree, that pagan abominification, and bury all the dead together in honour, say I.'

Emma was indignant.

'What sayest thou? Bury the slain with his slayers? By the saints! Even our father's murderers? It be an abomination, surelye?'

'Nay, my good sister,' he replied solemnly, looking straight into Father John's eyes as he spoke. 'Almighty God alone be judge o' the quick and the dead. It be our dooty, na'less to forgive our foes, for righteousness beginneth with forgiveness.'

Emma was abashed, and finally nodded in agreement.

A flock of small birds suddenly descended on the Alder tree and began to sing. It was the first time in many years that they, or any creature, had felt welcome there.

Father John laughed yet again.

'Winter is passed! Behold! Spring is come again to these lands!'

He turned and grasped Cedric's hand warmly.

'I foretell that thou shalt be a great man, Master Wainthorpe. The spirit of Hereward hath awoken in thee indeed, and so hath the curse of these marshes been broken, never to rise again. Let us go hence, therefore, and gladden thy mother's heart with these tidings, although it grieve her also.'

Chapter 15: Of Holy Days and Sabbaths

'Ye take keep to days [Ye keep or wait (on) days],
and months, and times, and years.'

(Paul's Epistle to the Galatians 4:10 when he complained of their tendency
back towards religious bondage - Wycliffe/Purvey Translation/Revisions)

William always made a point of attending Mass every Sunday, and resting from their journeys. Tom accepted this at first, but after he had studied the words of Christ in the scriptures concerning Sabbaths and holy days, he began to chafe at these seeming delays. With the exuberance of youth still upon him, he longed to move on to the next harvest of souls, to the next adventure.

One Sunday, after listening to a particularly boring and monotonous rendering of the Latin mass, most of which the parson did not understand himself, he began to fume and fidget. William gave him a warning look, mixed with understanding, so he sighed and settled down.

At the end of the service, Tom was pacing up and down near the graveyard as William held some animated conversation with the parson. When he saw the two priests parting company, apparently on amicable terms, Tom strode impatiently toward his mentor.

'Wherefore do we this, Father William? Witterly and surely, do we not have profit more abundant in our own devotions? Yea and much greater joy?'

'I know it well, my son.'

'Then…would God strike us dead if we eschewed this lifeless office and journeyed onward?' Tom pursued. 'Who would mark our absence?'

'Patience, my son! But thou sayeth sooth also. Yet many hath marked our presence. Oft do parsons themselves also mark of it, and many are the times I have held comely converse with such. If Parson will join our part, we have open doors to the sheepfold for the gospel, and mayhap a ready shepherd to guard our flocks ere we depart.'

Tom acknowledged the force of William's reasoning, so he fell silent, a little ashamed. He himself was so consumed with his own calling to preach and proclaim openly, he often forgot about the quiet word, the empathetic ear that characterised William the Shepherd. His gentle approach often opened many doors that preaching alone could not, and created so many opportunities to share the Gospel.

However, William still saw no reason why they should not travel on saints' days, in spite of local custom. He also pointed out the principle of the Sabbath rest, whatever day it was. So it was agreed: they would rest on the Lord's Day, but travel on saints' days.

(He refrained from telling his restless young companion that he appreciated resting his feet occasionally.)

'And hearken thou to the words of the Mass, and mind thou thy Latin,' he added, always having the last word.

It was St Barnabus' day on the outskirts of Newbury, and it was a delightfully sunny spring day, but the poorer peasant-folk of that area did not appreciate the weather. It had been declared a holy day in honour of the good saint, and folk were commanded not to work, and to attend special masses to seek his blessing.

Farmer Rolf had been taught this tradition from his youth, and he had obediently attended special mass every year, that morning included. Immediately after the service, his wife and children hurried home to prepare 'St Barnabus' Bread,' a traditional meal which they could barely afford. Women, of course, were expected to work regardless of what day it was. He himself decided to go home via his fields, which were crying out to be ploughed for the next sowing.

He sat down on the large stone that marked the corner of his strips, picked a piece of grass and chewed it as he moodily regarded his few acres on which his livelihood depended. He had lost count of the times he had done this on the many saints' days imposed upon him, but today he especially chafed at his forced inaction.

He saw a number of his neighbours gathered in a group and looking anxiously in the direction of their own acres, and turning away again with many sad head-shakings. He would have joined them, but he knew exactly what they were saying, and it made him gloomier still.

The spring thaw had come and they brought the barley harvest in just in time before long periods of rain had set in, making the soil too soggy to plough for the wheat and the rye sowing. Harvest would be late that year and dangerously late if he left it any longer, and this they could ill afford.

Now that the soil had dried sufficiently, he could still do nothing until the morrow. The day before had been the Lord's Sabbath. He was forbidden to work that day even though the sun had shone beckoningly. What if it began to rain again? He looked at the clouds on the horizon and shuddered at the thought. It may be too late to sow then. With a little help, he could do it all in one day.

He remembered that horrible year in his youth during the Great Famine when the unending rains had ruined his father's harvest, and his brothers and sister had nearly all died of starvation. His grandparents did, starving themselves, he suspected, to keep the younger generations alive. He made the sign of the cross and shed a tear. Would he be faced with the same choice for the sake of his little ones?

He mustn't entertain such morbid conjectures, however. Good Saint Barnabus might be told about it by some busybody angel listening in on his thoughts, and then the saint would take offense and refuse to intercede for him.

On more than one occasion, he had been strongly tempted to harness Old Rouncy and work on in the teeth of Holy Church's ban, but he knew it was no use. The saints would bring a curse on him for dishonouring their day as Parson warned him, and his neighbours could not support him however much they sympathised. But yet, what curse could be worse than the inability to pay the rent? The monastery's bailiff was a hard man, and would throw them out in the streets.

Wondering at his own audacity, he muttered the same prayer to Saint Barnabus he had prayed during mass. 'Do not we honour thee enow, blessed Saint Barnabus? O that I could toil this day and give thee thy due still. The greatest of mercies 'twould this be from the good Lord God.'

He opened his eyes and looked up surprised to see two travellers approached from the northern road. They looked like friars at first, but their raiment was unfamiliar. Nor were friars in the habit of journeying on foot, on a saint's day, barefoot and alone through outlaw-infested country.

Normally he ignored friars, hoping that by turning a cold shoulder, they would refrain from begging (or more often, demanding on pain of hellfire) for alms which he could not give. These men were different somehow, and it was not just their apparel and apparent desecration of the saint's day that caught his attention. They looked lean, healthy and strong, wholly different from the pale and often fat friars he did his best to avoid. Their hair was longer than what friars deemed appropriate, one whose hair blended with his beard to form a lion-like mane.

Furthermore, they were smiling. Do holy men smile? Rolf was used to seeing a calculatedly benign, even condescending smirk on the countenances of holy men when they approached him for alms, conveying the impression that their presence was a manifold blessing. The expressions quickly changed when he excused himself on the grounds of his own straightened circumstances. These two men, on the other hand, appeared to be smiling from a spontaneous delight, a spring in their step, looking as though they were ready to make friends with everyone, rather than reading him a stern homily about being in his fields on Saint Barnabus' day.

The two strangers caught his eye and seeing his look of curiosity, approached him.

'I bid thee good den, Master Farmer!' said the young lion cheerily. 'Hath not the good God sent unto us all a right joyous day?'

'Verily,' Rolf answered courteously but unenthusiastically. 'Praise be to God and blessings to ye good brothers. Your pardon I beg. Would that I had aught of almsdeeds for ye both, but I have naught.'

'Alms we take naught of thee, master,' replied the taller stranger. 'We labour with our hands for our faire. All we seek is a bed of straw and a meal.'

Rolf blinked and stared at them, as though he disbelieved his ears.

'What manner of order is this, good friars, that ye beg not, and would work for thy meat and journey on Saint Barnabus' day bare a-foot? I would readily offer ye paid labour, else.'

The taller man gave an impatient sigh and muttered something to the younger man about Devil's holidays, which made him laugh in a very unclerical manner and turn to the farmer with a grin.

'By order of our blessed Saviour, the Lord of the Harvest, do we so come in this manner, master farmer! The good saint Barnabus we honour greatly, but 'tis my belief that he journeyed with Saint Paul even be it an holy day or Sabbath. Did they not, Father William?'

'Witterly so did they, for Paul quoth in his own epistles that 'twas not meet to esteem one day higher than 'tother. Our Lord Jesu Himself did strongly castigate the Pharisees thereto, that they did lay the burden of Sabbath-keeping unfairly on poor men's backs. "The Sabbath was made for man, not man for the Sabbath," quoth He. Truly do we need rest, for so hath God ordained it. But saints' days and other such observances thou shalt find not in Holy Scripture.'

By that time, the other farmers, equally intrigued at the sight of such unlikely-looking holy men, had gathered around to hear what they were saying. They were amazed to hear them quoting from Holy Scriptures, in English. They spoke with such compelling authority and conviction that even the most conservative farmer among them began to wonder if Holy Church had got it wrong.

When the strangers had added that Doctor JohnWycliffe had sent them, their interest was thoroughly aroused. There were both good reports and bad (mainly from the high-ranked clergy) spoken concerning this famous man, but most of the populace agreed that he was a champion of the poorer classes. Upon inquiry, the strangers introduced themselves as William Shephard and Thomas Plowman, members of the Order of Poor Preachers, sent out to preach the gospel according to the scriptures, not according to, as they phrased it, the unholy traditions of men.

The farmers warmed to them immediately. Farmer Rolf even felt it was safe to complain that all the saints' days were all very well for the well-to-do, but the struggling farmers needed all the days they could get to get their work done. The other farmers all rumbled 'Aye!' in a chorus of agreement.

Tom stepped in as inspiration came upon him.

'Hearken unto me then, good sirrahs! Was not good saint Barnabus a kindly and generous man? Even so do we honour him. But if stood he, yea even also the Good Lord Himself, amongst us this day, wrathful would they be that we refrain of our daily tasks but for the sake of his day's observance. Liefer will I, therefore, fear the Lord than neither bishop nor cardinal. Are we not all free men? If ye dare not, then shall I dare the wrath of saint, priest or pope for any man that will hire us and for but a meal and one night's repose. A proud English farmer's son am I!'

With those bold words, he whipped off his outer habit, revealing his work clothes, broad shoulders and muscular arms.

'Show me thy plough and seedbag, Master Farmer. I shall do if thou shalt do not!'

The farmers stood spellbound, looking at each other with eyes shining. They were teetering on the brink of social revolution, civil disobedience – maybe even heresy.

William, stirred by his friend's dramatic gesture, would have followed suit, but their magnificent rebellion was checked by a stern voice that the farmers all dreaded.

'What means this riotous witaldry? Do ye defy the authority of Holy Church?'

The vicar of the parish of Saint Barnabus had approached the group from behind, and heard the last of Tom's fighting words. He was on his way to join Rolf and his family in the Saint Barnabus' day feast, and had brought some vegetables from his garden to help.

Father William Brooks, although once a mere parish clerk, was a good shepherd at heart, but he was caught on the horns of a dilemma. He sympathised with the farmers' plight, being a farmer's son himself. He also took his duties as the local shepherd seriously. He had begged the bishop to give them leave to move some of the saints' days on to Sundays, especially during sowing and harvest, but the bishop had contemptuously spurned his request. However, he would as vigorously defend Holy Church's authority and faithfully remain at his post.

The former rector of Newbury had not been so faithful, and had wandered off, seeking "greener pastures" at Oxford and had finally died in London at the hands of brutal footpads. It was generally agreed that it was the judgment of God, and Father William Brooks, although a mere parish clerk, had carried on in spite of a very meagre wage. He was finally rewarded at the completion of his studies with ordination and the living at Newbury, his hometown. He felt under a strong obligation to the bishop who had used his influence on his behalf.

He approached the strangers belligerently, therefore, ready to defend his flock against any wolfish heretic. He had earned the respect of the people of Newbury, so the farmers immediately, albeit reluctantly, abandoned the idea of defying his authority.

William, however, was not of their number. With a boldness to equal Tom's, but with far more diplomacy, he stepped forward, introduced himself and proceeded to reason with the good man.

Father William Brooks suddenly recognised him from their conversation on the previous day after Mass. He had to admit that this tall man with the lean and kindly face was a profound scholar and he could sense a kinship in him as a true shepherd, and he had faithfully attended mass.

It was not long before he had dropped his defensive stance, and listened to William as it was proved to him, point by point that strict observance of saints' days had no foundation in scripture. The parson was certainly not blind to the faults and corruption of the hierarchy. But he, like many other spiritual shepherds, was left in the dark regarding much of the original teachings of scripture, especially where it challenged the existing supposed spiritual authority of the church.

'But... but... sayest thou that God's Holy Church would deceive her own?'

Even as he said this, the parson knew that he had experienced such deceit first-hand. It had not been easy working as parish clerk to the former rector, an ambitious and arrogant man.

'Doctor John Wycliffe, greatest of theologians in the land, hath spoken boldly of this matter,' William replied mildly. 'Only those that demean themselves worthily of their office are worthy of respect, quoth he. They that use their authority despiteously, though they be high churchmen, even the highest of all though he be, should be stripped of his post. The Doctor would have all clergy tested and proved ere they hold high office. But we speak of Saints' days....'

The farmers settled down to listen intently as William calmly demolished argument after argument put forward. It left the parson looking very thoughtful, but there was still one apparently insuperable barrier. The parson shook his head sadly.

'Then what sayeth the bishop if he heareth of this, our disobedience?'

'Will ye hearken unto the truth of Holy Scripture or unto the traditions of men?' challenged Tom.

There was silence.

'What if the bishop wist not?' said one farmer softly.

Pregnant silence. They all knew the bishop never paid them any heed anyway.

Then before Father William Brooks knew what was happening, farmers were scattering everywhere towards their fields.

'Come thou with me, master lay preacher, proud English farmer's son!' cried Rolf as he ran off to harness Old Rouncy. Tom laughed and followed.

The parson stood rooted on the spot for the moment, bemused. He looked up at William, who was looking at him with a smiling challenge in his eye, mixed with understanding.

Suddenly, Master Brooks let out a great laugh, rolled up his sleeves, tucked up his cassock and marched off to aid the nearest farmer. William stripped off his outer habit to follow suit.

They worked with a will, and soon you could hear Tom's tenor voice carrying for miles as he sang a verse from the Song of the Harvest:

> *'Sing Hey for the oxen, the yoke and the plow!*
> *Sing Ho for the seed o' the corn that ye sow!*
> *Sing Hi for the sun, rain and fresh-melted snow!*
> *There be many a month unto harvest.'*

After two hour's solid work, the children began to arrive, sent out by their mothers to inform the men that the feast was ready. They were astonished to see their fathers working steadily – and on a holy day. They noticed that they were happier than they had been for many a month, as though a weight had been thrown off their shoulders. But the happiest of them all seemed to be Father William Brooks, whose cassock was covered with grime and honest sweat.

He greeted them cheerily.

'Henceforth,' he informed them, 'We shall honour St Barnabus by labouring as hardily as ever he did when he journeyed with the Apostle Paul.'

An idea occurred to him. He motioned the children to gather around.

'Hearken, younglings all! Go ye all unto your mothers and kinsfolk, and bid them bring the feast out to the fields by Donnington's Brook. Say ye that Parson hath so commanded that they enjoy St Barnabus' Day in the sun and free air with their men and their kinsfolk. After the feast, if they will, they shall aid their husbands in the field and sing praises to God for His manifold blessings.'

The idea took well. Soon the dames came forth with their children, carrying St Barnabus' Bread and many other simple and sustaining meats, fruits and vegetables.

A real sense of community began to flow as the men paused in their work, washed their hands in the brook and sat down to eat with their families. The parson prayed a heartfelt blessing on the food, then introduced William and Tom midst a roar of applause from the grateful farmers.

The womenfolk had not had any time to hear why their men had become so cheerful and animated, let alone break a holy day tradition, and they looked in surprise at their husbands.

'Master Thomas!' yelled one lanky young farm worker 'Sing thou the Song o' the Harvest for us all!'

Nothing loath, Tom put down the dennock that Rolf's wife had offered him, quickly slaked his throat with ale and leapt to his feet to oblige them.

His voice soared above the men's as they joined in the chorus, and thunderous applause followed.

Before they could demand another song, he held up his hands for their attention. He had begged the parson's permission to speak to them all, and the parson was now more than happy. That worthy had had plenty of long conversations with William as they laboured together, and had become convinced that the strangers, and their message were sent from God.

This was too good an opportunity for Tom to miss. He mounted a rock as a makeshift pulpit and began by explaining to the womenfolk what had happened that morning. For the benefit of the children, he told the story of how Jesus confounded the Pharisees who were offended at Him healing and doing good on the Sabbath. His highly coloured and comical rendering of the tale drew roars of laughter from everyone. From there it was a short step to preaching the gospel of salvation from dead works and observances, by grace alone, and finding an unfettered relationship with God. He concluded by calling forth any who wished to know more, to speak with William or himself.

Most of the farmers and their families did, considering the state of their soul even more important than the ploughing, although William insisted that they should not waste the day.

'*Carpe diem,*' he said, once all had been said, and eaten. 'Let us make hay while the sun shineth. We shall await ye all a' nightertale to converse further on holy matters.'

Rolf did not mind another hour's delay, for with Tom's aid he was ahead of schedule, having completed one strip already. He and his family were the first to commit their souls to the Lord Jesus as their Saviour directly, rather than through any human intermediary.

Rolf then returned to his plough with a light heart, free from the burden of guilt. He sang as lustily as Tom ever did, if not as tunefully.

The next to make such a total commitment was none other than the parson himself. After this, it became, as Thomas laughingly put it, a 'landslide of souls that falleth into the River of God.'

But William frowned upon this.

'Thou speakest as the Anabaptists would speak. Sufficient heresy do we preach, as Rome would see it. Let us not be heretical as they that would baptize us all again, worthy folk though they may be.'

'I spake but in jest, Father William,' protested Tom, slightly abashed. He would have said more, for he had had occasional interesting discussions with the banned sect back at Oxford. But they were both too busy pastoring enquiring souls to discuss dangerous questions of theology.

The whole day was considered by the community to be a resounding success, and a new tradition was born.

'Henceforth,' proclaimed the parson, 'Let us celebrate the good saints' days on Donnington Brook's banks, if the weather be kindly. But the men shall cease not from their needful toil but to feast with their families if they will.'

It was a tradition that would be followed, at least by Wycliffe's disciples, for many a year.

The pastoring and discipling work continued at the parsonage well into the night, and the evangelists finally tumbled into their beds at the back of the parsonage, exhausted.

The following day, not being a saint's day, found all the farmers hard at work. Clouds were gathering, but those farmers who had followed the new St Barnabus tradition finished their fields well before the afternoon had progressed.

A few farmers from the other side of town who had not received the news of the new tradition until that day, were scandalized. They complained that the great sin of the rebellious farmers had given them an unfair advantage. They expressed their surprise that 'Parson be a-breaken o' Saint Barnabus' Day. Will not the good saint be a-wrathful?' Some even threatened to 'tell all a' the Arch Deacon.'

Things may have gone ill for the parson, but William and Tom forestalled any disaster. They rounded up some of their following of farmers and labourers who had long completed their own tasks, even loading their own ploughs onto carts, and marched in procession through the town centre to where the aggrieved farmers were hard at work, desperately trying to plough at least some of their acreage before the heavens fell upon them.

'The curse o' Saint Barnabus, grievous it shall fall on the backsliders all!' loudly prophesied one to his neighbour as he passed by, ploughing his outermost furrow.

The neighbour said nothing, but sat on the barrier by the main road and watched helplessly. His bullock had gone lame and he couldn't borrow any of his neighbour's beasts, as they were working full stretch already. The farmers who had faithfully obeyed the old tradition refused to associate with the "sons of sin" on the other side of town and refused to humble themselves by asking for help. The man could do nothing but sink into the same quagmire of despair that Rolf had sunk into the previous day.

His forebodings were interrupted by the sound of tramping feet approaching him from the other side of the hill. He was surprised. Was his lordship's men on the march? It sounded more like a market day procession than a band of soldiers sent to raid the neighbouring baron's lands. Besides, the feuding lords had been at peace for decades.

But the faces that first appeared over the brow of the hilly road were not that of men-at-arms. It was the parson himself and Farmer Rolf, with two strange-looking friars. A large following of familiar faces followed, all from the "sinful" side of town and all glowing with goodwill. No sign of Saint Barnabus' curse here, he thought. Behind many were horses and carts and bullocks, all looking as though they meant business – farming business at least.

'How now, Master Ben a' the Woods!' cried Rolf jovially, catching sight of him. 'We come to give thee aid, my Rouncy and I. Be not cast down, man! Hitch up thy plough and we shall till thy lands, thou and I!'

'But…' stammered Farmer Ben, flabbergasted and confused, 'But mine old Barnabus be halt, and thou didst toil Saint Brutus' Day!… Nay!…Say I rather: mine old Brutus be halt o' foot… and didst thou not…?'

'Halt o' foot, be he, thy bullock? Then let him rest. Behold my Rouncy, let him toil in his stead!'

Overwhelmed, Farmer Ben looked helplessly at the parson as Rolf opened the barrier and led his big horse across the field to where the plough stood idle.

'Fear not, Master Woods,' the parson reassured him with a smile he had not smiled for a long, long while. 'A new tradition hath been ordained yestereve, wherewith we honour but the memory of the good Saint, but his day shall not be overly exalted. Thus saith Holy Writ. Fear no curse, for God seeketh to bless, not curse, though even the bishop himself deny it thee.'

Farmer Ben Woods gasped in disbelief.

'But, good Parson, sirrah! Dost thou speak in despite o' Holy Church? Even unto disobeyance?'

'Holy Church, my son, are of they that seek to obey the commands of Holy Writ. They that obey not, and live lives unworthy of their calling, then is their authority forfeit.'

William Shephard, standing next to the parson, smiled to himself. The parson was quoting directly from one of the writings of Wycliffe, raging against the abuse and hypocrisy of many ecclesiastical authorities. The previous night, the parson had sat up late, devouring many of the writings William had brought with him.

When he had been introduced, William gripped the bemused farmer's hand.

'Master Woods, some cunning I have of the healing of the ailments of beasts. Wilt thou lead me to thy poor Brutus? Mayhap I may hasten his restoration.'

Soon William was closely inspecting the swelling on the great bullock's hind foot. An hour later, Brutus was lying at rest, relieved and grateful that the swelling was rapidly diminishing and its fetlock was back in its proper position, with a splint in support. Such modern methods were unknown in those parts, but the farmer could see it had the desired effect.

This was the kind of theology that struggling farmers understood, and it wasn't long before he held up his fist in the direction of the bishop's luxury residence and cried: 'I be Wycliffe's man!'

His neighbours were also changing their tune from curses to blessings as their fellow farmers from the other side of town helped to complete their tasks.

'And timely indeed!' commented Tom, watching the darkening clouds gathering over a deepening dusk. They loaded their wagons in haste before the heavens opened up. They all arrived home in drenching rain, soaked but happy, laden with gifts from the farmers and their wives. Never had there been such a sense of community among the peasant folk of Newbury. Word soon spread to others in the town and beyond about the parson's new stance and the farmer's gesture to their fellows.

Father William Brooks invited William to preach from his own pulpit at Mass the following Lord's Day. The church was packed to overflowing as many from other parishes came to find out more about the amazing events of Saint Barnabus day. The parson was even bold enough to read to the congregation, in English, the scriptures that supported the new tradition. William of course, took up this theme to proclaim his favourite message from the pulpit of seeking a relationship with God rather than fear-filled religious observances.

The day after, Tom preached from the town crier's stand in the town square in the afternoon to possibly the largest crowd that Newbury had ever seen. In this fashion, a large following of disciples were gathered from all walks of life, and they met for readings and prayers at St Barnabus' church.

During their "morning sacrifice" some days after, Tom took a deep breath and let it out again in a sigh of satisfaction. This was as the breath of life to him, but he also felt restlessness in his heart. New harvests called him.

'Methinks 'tis time for the journey onward,' he said. 'What sayest thou, Father William the Wise?'

William thought for a while. He knew in his heart that Tom was right, so he nodded. Father William Brooks was more than capable of caring for this gathering.

'Speak we to the gathering at eventide, and we depart in the morn.'

Then a thought occurred to him.

'God hath spoken of Holy Days and Sabbaths in this place. Can it be that one day we shall find a Sabbath rest of months, nay years from our labours?'

Tom had too much energy and drive in him to appreciate this.

'Come, Father William! Sickerly we shall ceaseless harvest until Doomsday, when the Christ returneth as King. How canst thou speak of such rest?'

William smiled at his friend's unflagging enthusiasm, but it made him feel old.

'And hast thou sown and harvested for aye, without that the land did stand fallow one twelvemonth in three, Master Plowman?'

This was speaking Tom's language and Tom grinned in acknowledgment.

'Thy wisdom doth both silence and chasten me, O wisest of wise. Yet I mark thee well that thou dost plough thine own furrow with vigour like unto mine. Wherefore speakest thou of rest? Art thou so a-wearied?'

''Tis not by might, nor by power, but by the Holy Ghost that I keep step with thine, my friend,' quoted William, laughing, 'else would I have laid me down and died.'

Nonetheless, he looked down at his calloused hands and feet with wonder.

'Slumber hath ne'er been so sweet, and my meat hath not tasted so toothsome ere we began this our task. Many a league hath passed as we tread barefoot on this road, and I have not wearied of it all, nor have we sickened nor taken hurt. Yet mine heart sayeth that there shall be a season of rest 'ere we finish our mission. Whither shall we winter, I wonder?'

'Mayhap that Sabbath be in our hearts, that we find rest in God's will?' suggested Tom.

William sat back and looked at him, a little impressed.

'Soothly said indeed. But there is room for the one and t'other both, methinks. Though a redeless, impious shakebuckler of a lad thou be, there are deep wells of wisdom not yet sounded in thee, my son. Come, let us pray.'

They announced their decision at the gathering that night, much to the grief of the disciples. William spoke at length, strengthening, exhorting and encouraging them.

The parson almost tearfully begged them to stay a while.

'Brethren, ye have ope'd mine eyes even unto new light, such as I ne'er have seen. Will ye leave me bereft of your wisdom? Will ye not feed an hungered soul as I? And fearful am I also, to my shame, alas! I may yet face the wrath of the Archdeacon and My Lord Bishop himself, should they hear of the doings of Saint Barnabus' Day. Not all in Newbury stand with us in this, fearing the wrath of the saint, so they say. Wherewithal shall I speak in my defence, if ye be not at my side?'

William gripped the man's shoulders with his long, strong fingers reassuringly. He knew what it was like to bear responsibility in the face of growing opposition.

'God shall stand with thee, my friend, should it come to this, for He rewardeth them that keep the faith. The way of the cross we must all tread, natheless. Rough and narrow is the way and straightened is the gate unto eternal life. But though we must away to other fields and flocks, God will not have thee bereft of comfort. Let the Word of God be thy guide and solace from henceforth. Silver and gold have I none, but such as I have give I thee.'

He presented the good parson with his last copy of the Epistles of Paul in English. William had frequently resorted to them himself lately, and only had smaller portions left. The parson realised what a sacrifice this was, and was left speechless. No more need he struggle to understand the difficult Latin texts with his limited training.

'A worthy shepherd of the flock art thou, Father William Brooks of Newbury. May the good Lord reward thy faithfulness and steadfastness. This also I beg of thee: If there be any lettered among thy people, pray them that they copy these precious works manifold, that many may read and profit thereby.'

321

The next day they left early accompanied by the prayers, blessings and gifts of the good folk, even from many who were not yet disciples. Newbury folk would never forget them for many generations, especially on Saint Barnabus Day.

Chapter 16: Highclere Skies and Thunderclouds

'Elias was a deadly man like us.
[Elias was a man like to us passible, or able to suffer],
and in prayer he prayed that it should not rain on the earth,
and it rained not three years and six months.'

(Epistle of James 5:17 Wycliffe/Purvey Translation / Revision.)

One of the disciples from Newbury, a merchant who traded in wool, had business at the bishop's manor near Highclere. On hearing that they were leaving on the same day, he accompanied them together with his servant as far as the village. He was glad to have company, especially that of the two men who had made an impact on his life, greater than any others he had ever encountered.

The chapman rode alongside them, marvelling at how they kept up with his horses, on bare feet and without seeming to tire.

Tom was deep in conversation with young Oswald, the servant, who had also become a disciple. Oswald was asking many questions concerning his newfound faith. He dismounted for a while to talk with Tom more easily, but could not keep up the rapid pace that Tom set and was forced to remount.

Observing this, Master Chapman expressed his wonder aloud at the hardihood of the two missionaries, that they had travelled so far, barefoot, and at such a walking pace. William, to whom these observations were made, smiled. He had become so accustomed to their mode of travel that he had not realised how remarkable it would seem to others.

'I had not marked it myself, Master Chapman, 'til yestereve,' he said. 'I deem it to be an especial grace that the good Lord hath given us that we journey thus far without hurt. He hath ever provided our need, and kept us free even of the foot-scathe.'

He stopped momentarily to inspect the thickly calloused soles of his feet. No blisters, scratches or bruises normally suffered from barefoot pilgrimages could be seen at all. And this was a very, very long pilgrimage.

'Did not the children of Israel receive like blessing as they passed through the wilderness?' he pondered out aloud. 'Their shoes perished not – every whit of two score years, methinks.'

'An holy miracle be this!' exclaimed the merchant in awe. 'Are ye holy saints then, Father?'

'God forbid!' laughed William, 'or rather would the Bishop of Rome forbid it. We are but servants of the King of Kings. If we travel afar on affairs of the Kingdom, then the King, He watcheth over us and giveth us the strength needful.'

The leagues flew by and they reached the village of Highclere, stopping to observe the peasant farmers sweating hard over their ploughs. Tom could tell that they too were behind schedule. The recent rain had ceased, but more was threatening in greater measure. They were already trying to plough through wet and sticky soil, and both men and beasts were exhausted.

'Hail and well met, Master Nick Croley!' called the merchant to the nearest farmer who toiled toward them with his plough and ox.

Stopping briefly to chat with the strangers and the merchant, whom he knew well, farmer Nick had a woeful tale to tell.

Not having received the same revelation that the folk in Newbury had concerning Holy Days, many farmers were close to despair. Dutifully observing Saint Barnabus' Day after the last rains, they were well behind schedule in their soil preparation for sowing, and as farmer Rolf of Newbury feared, the rain clouds were gathering again but in greater strength than before. If the heavens opened and plough and beast became bogged, there would be a very limited harvest indeed that year. Sowing in the rain, moreover, often brought on the dreaded Saint Ninian's Blight, where the seed shrivelled in the ground.

Feeling their frustration, Tom kicked savagely at a rock in the road, unaware of the damage it would normally have done to his toes.

'Wherefore did we tarry in Newbury, Father William? We would have proclaimed the gospel of Saint Barnabus here also, else.'

'Times and seasons are in God's hands, my son.' his mentor replied. Nevertheless, he also looked anxiously at the thunderous clouds.

Suddenly, he remembered comments he made on the journey. His heart leapt. Would God really give them another miracle in this desperate situation? Even authority over the elements?

But who was he, a mere man who occasionally struggled to cope with his sinful desires, to command the rains as Elijah the prophet did?

'But stay!' he said aloud to himself, in answer to his thoughts. 'Was Elijah not a man of like passions as we? So quoth the Apostle James.'

Instantly, another scripture dropped into his mind. Faith blazed up in his heart, and he laughed out loud.

'Where is the God of Elijah?' he said aloud, almost as a challenge.

Farmer Nick, in the act of returning to his hopeless task, stopped in his tracks. He turned and gaped. The others stared at William as though he was raving mad.

But William turned and addressed the darkening skies and cried out even louder, conviction adding vibrancy to his normally calm voice and manner.

'Where is the God of Elijah?!'

His outburst took even Tom by surprise. William seemed to have been transformed before them from the kindly and benign shepherd he knew, into a fiery Old Testament prophet. He might have been haranguing the prophets of Baal.

Seeing the confusion on the faces of his companions, William explained, with even a touch of uncharacteristic animation:

'Elijah was a man of like deadly passions as we. Yet prayed he and shut up the heavens that there be no rain. If the King of Kings giveth power unto his messengers, sinners though we be, not even the rains shall hinder us.'

Tom's heart stirred, and he caught the spirit of it immediately.

'Amen, and so be it, Father Elijah!' he cried. 'Let us so pray.'

Nevertheless, their companions were apprehensive.

Had these two men of God taken leave of their senses? Hinder the rains? Was this not presumption? Their tradition and culture dictated that only the holiest of saints were able to command the elements as the Lord did, and William disclaimed any such holiness. Furthermore, as if in defiance of William's faith statement, a few drops of rain began to fall from dark and leaden skies.

William was not daunted.

'Father in heaven, have mercy on thy people!' he cried with his hand and staff raised high. 'Show Thou them Thy power and Thy love, that they may sow and reap in season, and feed their little ones. Thou hast put this spark of faith in mine heart to command the rains. Therefore, in the name of the Lord Jesu, Who commanded the tempest, we say to the clouds: Depart! Cease thou of thy dew and rain not again but according to my word!'

Tom cried out, 'Amen!'

William was immediately conscious of a doubting thought that entered his head.

'What hast thou said, thou japes-head? Thou'rt but a man – and a sinner. Will they not revile thee as a fool?'

He had heard that voice before, and rebuked it. The lesson from little Elspeth of Shipton was not forgotten.

Tom and the other farmer, being men of the soil, were the first to notice the difference. 'The wind! It changeth!' they both cried out.

Sure enough, the rain had stopped, and one minute later, the clouds were rent asunder, and glorious rays of sunshine pierced the darkness and shone all around where they stood. The gap in the clouds widened in an almost perfect circular motion, as though parted by many huge hands. Then the dark clouds appeared to melt away as more and more sunshine flooded through. The farming men had never seen the weather behave like this before. It seemed as though winter had turned to spring in just one moment.

They all fell on their knees and gave audible thanks. Tom's powerful voice arose in song, a psalm he had learnt at Oxford. It echoed across the valley.

'*Caeli enarrant gloriam Dei*! The heavens declare the glory of God!'

Farmer Nick crossed himself and cried out in fear.

'Lord Jesu, forgive Thou my sins! Assoil me, Father! Are ye not holy saints indeed?'

Before William had a chance to refute this, they heard cries of wonder from the neighbouring farms. Neighbouring farmers and labourers, their attention caught by Tom's voice, had noticed the sudden and remarkable change in the dreaded weather. Looking to the skies, the local farmers saw the clouds parting, revealing beams of light illuminating Nick Croley's farm on the hill, and rapidly widening like golden celestial ripples toward the horizon.

Farmers, labourers, and a few women and children came running from all directions. They could see two strangers in clerical garb kneeling there with him, bathed in the heavenly light, hands raised in worship. Farmer Nick was lying face down in the moist earth, sobbing in repentance.

'Saint Barnabus' beard!' whispered one weather-beaten labourer 'Methought friars brought naught but curses!'

'Nay!' replied a young girl, her eyes shining, 'they be holy saints!'

Tom, recognising his cue once again, leapt to his feet and began preaching the gospel.

'Behold!' he concluded. 'The Sun of Righteousness hath risen upon you, bringing healing in His wings!'

Needless to say, the missionaries had a ready harvest of souls that day.

So the local farmers, many with eternity in their hearts and a song on their lips, were able to complete their ploughing and sowing in good time.

Word spread quickly to other villages of the "russet-cloaked friars, miracle-men, holy saints that be a-tamen the storms." And so the harvest of souls continued also into Ashmansworth, Hurstbourne, Enham-Alamein and Tarrant.

They were showered with invitations of hospitality. Many locals were hoping to see more miracles. Some, more interested in seeing the spectacular than hearing the truth, followed expectantly wherever they went, much to William's annoyance and embarrassment. Tom merely laughed at this and lapped up all the attention, the ale, the beer, the good food and even the occasional good bed to sleep in.

Strong disciple groups and reading circles were established throughout that region. Two of the local parsons had caught Father William Brooks' enthusiasm for the new order of things, so William and Tom were able to move on, secure in the knowledge that the flocks would be well cared for.

Andover town was a harder nut to crack.

The enemy of men's souls did not sleep. He had failed to stop the mission through personal temptations and distractions. This time he tried a more direct approach again.

Abbott Roger de Lancey, of the monastery of St Urban, received some slightly disturbing news. Some grey friars had ridden in from Newbury, rather disturbed. It seemed that many of the citizens of Newbury had turned against them.

Abbott Roger shrugged his shoulders at that. There was nothing new in the populace's disgruntlement toward clergy in general – friars and monks in particular. Well, he felt secure enough within his abbey walls, rarely communicated with the common people, and the estates were becoming very profitable indeed. Let the friars beg, borrow and steal their bread, or find rich sponsors as many had done, but it was no concern of his if the people disliked them. He shared the Benedictine order's contempt for grey friars in any case.

Regardless of his personal feelings toward them, it was bad policy (nor did he have the energy) to wrangle with fellow-clergy, and it was supposedly God's business. So he sighed and granted an audience, going so far as to offer them refreshments (not his best wine, of course), smiling upon them with his habitual studied urbanity.

The friars brushed aside the usual niceties and came straight to the point.

'There be renegade priests that have come among the folk, Father Abbot!' said the short, fat friar, his eyes wide with doom. 'They preach damnable heresy – that the Lord Christ alone be the only one to receive confession! They pray not unto Holy Saints, neither observe they the holy saints days... and...' his voice dropped almost to a dread-filled whisper, ' ...they labour for their faire with their very hands!'

This made the abbot choke on his wine more than anything else. It gave him a coughing fit, which made him put down his wine too suddenly, spilling some on his beautiful new gown. Even the suggestion that the regular clergy, especially himself, should have to work to earn a living was Father Abbot's worst nightmare. For this very reason he chose Holy Church for his profession those many years ago.

Observing his reaction with grim satisfaction, the larger friar pushed his cowl away from his bristly-bearded face and thrust his fellow friar aside. He was an angry man. Everyone knew that he still harboured bitter envy and resentment against another colleague who had won the Earl of Winchester's sponsorship over him, even after all his pious cajoling. Now most of the citizens of Newbury no longer kowtowed to him as they once did, thanks to these mysterious heretics who had poisoned their minds. Having to beg for food and shelter from a Benedictine monastery, rather than from the common people, was an added humiliation to him. His hearers were becoming weary of his complaints.

'Father Abbot!' he said grimly, displaying minimal respect in his manner toward ecclesiastical rank, "'Tis said that these sons of deception come hither to spread their abominations! An holy wall o' protection build we around our flocks that they fall not into vile sin as hath the borel-folk in Newbury. The bishop's man will do naught, but Parson Father Gregory stands with us in Andover, though he must needs grutch at the first. His Lordship the Earl also, for we have assoiled him his many sins for naught for this week (though that false friar, his chaplain did slumber at evening confessional). We look to thee that thy mantle be spread over this folk also.'

He stood back and folded his arms, almost as a challenge.

The abbot did not appreciate the arrogance of what he considered as these upstart brothers, but he was forced to admit that there was some danger. He was also of the opinion that it was just a passing fancy, and the common folk could be whipped back into their proper place again when the emergency had passed. An indolent man, he hated having his tranquillity disturbed, but he knew that he could not get back to his wine-tasting until he had satisfied these unwelcome guests before him. He sat back with a sigh of resignation, and wiped the spilt wine from his lap.

'Well, brethren, I shall give thought to't, and shall essay to the full measure of my puissance. May God's will be done in this matter. *Pax vobiscum* and faire ye well.'

On this pious note, he turned away toward his wine collection to indicate that the audience was concluded.

The large, angry brother hovered for a moment like a dark thundercloud. He had looked for more enthusiasm than this and was close to venting his frustration. His companion, though a little disappointed, was basically satisfied that they had fulfilled their mission.

'Our thanks be to thee, and to God, Father Abbot.'

He tugged at his fellow's elbow and said under his breath 'Have done o' thy glumpishesse, Edward! We have done enow anon! The old sloth will speak the matter in chapter and the brothers will do all needfull! Come, avoid!'

He almost dragged him out of the room.

Friar Edward vented his anger at the town square the next day. He thundered the wrath of God and of the Holy Pontiff against all heretics, mean-hearted givers, slothful monks and all sinners in general.

He made the simple folk tremble in their shoes (or bare feet) with warnings of horrible judgment if they lent an ear to any vile heresies that may come their way. The not-so-simple pricked up their ears, and wondered who these heretics may be, but most of these were wise enough not to admit to their curiosity.

Many of the common folk were rather jaded with the corruption and hypocrisy that prevailed amongst the clergy. They remembered the many times when friars had used all sorts of pious-sounding tricks to chisel the hard-earned money out of ordinary citizens. There were whispers of midnight assignations with the bordel women that these supposedly holy men condemned from the pulpit.

The following day, Tom and William addressed a rather unresponsive crowd in the town square. Many in the crowd, obedient to their spiritual guides from long habit, walked away as soon as they realised that these were the men they were warned against. There were even a few hecklers among those who stayed, hoping to gain favour with the saints, angels and maybe even God Himself.

Still, many stayed. These were mainly the curious and the jaded aforementioned. The latter category noted the simple style and appearance of the strange preachers. Peasant folk may have been led by the nose theologically, but most could easily distinguish seasoned workers from soft-bodied parasites. This was fortified by the metaphors that the younger preacher drew from the land.

'By the Saints!' muttered one old labourer, 'Heretics they may be, but they be men, dreadless.'

'Aye!' nodded his neighbour, 'True sons o' the soil. The taller even hath the look o' Saint Francis methinks.'

'Ah!' chimed in his daughter, gazing dreamily at Tom, 'but the young lion-man liketh me well.'

At this stage her father decided to remove her from the vicinity, fearing the wrath of the saints, and angels – or at least that of Parson.

In the end, most of the crowd melted away and only a handful were brave enough to stay and enquire further. The old labourer was among them, but they were among friends.

The two preachers had already won a small following. They had helped out some busy farmers the previous day, and asked for nothing but bed and bread in return. The farmers had realised too late that these hard-working, honest, holy men were the alleged evil deceivers upon whom Friar Edward had poured out his venomous condemnation. Too late, for they had already formed an opinion of them, heretical though that may seem. The contrast between the two parties was so ludicrous, the farmers had laughingly told the two strangers of what had transpired. The farmers were tenants of the monastery estate, and the bailiff had warned them not to have anything to do with the heretics, should they appear. That was the extent to which Father Abbott had bestirred himself in defence of the faith.

William was both amused and saddened by the news that most of the townsfolk were inoculated against their message, but Tom was more sanguine.

'Nay, Father William. Let us pray, then let us preach regardless. Peradventure we shall sow good seed in the hearts of some, that shall bear fruit in later times. But our worthy hosts here can truthfully plead ignorance of even having seen any heretics.'

'Truly, by God!' corroborated one farmer strongly, and laughed. 'There be naught o' heresy-make among us anon, for we hearken only to the holy truth. So will say I should master bailiff ask o' we.'

Hence the nucleus of followers to encourage the two missionaries as they proclaimed the Word of God at St Martin's Square the next day, braving the wrath of the ecclesiastical authorities.

Tom, warned by William of the sensitive nature of the situation, carefully avoided compromising the safety of his friends without compromising his message.

Thus, the small band of disciples grew.

The lack of literate disciples was a problem, for none of the middle classes, and definitely none of the clergy were represented in their small band of followers. Some scriptures could be taught rote of course, and the old labourer, in the manner of most illiterate persons, was especially good at memorising them. But even he had his limits and William refused to move on until they found someone who could read the scriptures to them. So they got down on their knees and prayed.

The answer came next day.

The chapman who had travelled with the preachers to Highclere, together with Oswald his servant, came looking for them. They just happened to be riding along the road to Tarrant village, and Oswald glanced at a group of farmers labouring in the field with Tom and William. He recognised their russet cloaks immediately and called to his master. They were all overjoyed at seeing each other.

'Father William! Master Thomas!' cried the chapman, watching them stride across the field toward them. 'Well met, and praise be to God! All night did I hear a voice in mine heart: "Seek thou the preachers! Seek thou the Wycliffite preachers and cease not a'til thou findest them." Anon I find thee, and I pray thou'lt speak of thy need. Moneys have I in abundance, if that be thy need, for God hath blessed me at every turn. Even in Tarrant village yonder have I found new open doors of trade.'

The farmers came up, wondering who the well-to-do stranger was, and William introduced them all. Without hesitation or any sense of superiority of rank, the chapman invited them all to the local tavern, treating them to a generous meal and drinks at his expense. He seemed to be positively overflowing with goodwill and generosity.

After the meal, he reiterated his offer of funds and immediately drew out a large purse. William waved it away, laughingly overwhelmed by the good man's enthusiasm.

'Out thanks, but give it to folk here that are in great need, good master John. Greater is my need in our midst for the Bread of Life, and one who could dispense it well. For none of these our disciples have the cunning of letters, alas!'

The chapman opened his eyes at that.

'Each sennight do I and Oswald come hither to do trade, thanks be to God's good providence. To read for the circle of brethren in this place? Even as they do in Newbury? 'Twould be an honour of which few could boast!'

'Done!' said William and they clasped hands as though to seal a purchase.

Then his face clouded over a little. He had checked his rapidly diminishing supply of scripture copies that morning. All he had left was his own complete copy of the Wycliffe New Testament, which he was reluctant to part with. There were also some portions of Psalms and Proverbs, which he gave into the chapman's eager hands. It would take a considerable amount of time before Father William of Newbury and his small team of copiers to make another complete New Testament.

Oswald, meanwhile, had been in deep conversation with Tom but overheard the discussion of William's dilemma with his master. He had a bright idea.

'Prithee, master, wilt thou not send me unto Oxenford? For Master Thomas saith that there be a-many and a-many portions of the good Word amongst Doctor Wycliffe's men. I shall have speech with my kinsman there also who laboureth in a doctor's employ.'

In answer, the good merchant handed him the purse with a droll look in his eye.

'Go then, on the morrow at cock-crow, lad. Take the wain and bring back all they can spare. Store thou them in the loft of the warehouse, but tell only the trusty brethren of this. God speed thee. Tarry not, and see that thou waste not my precious gold on drink, else shall I flay thee sore!'

They all toasted Godspeed to Oswald, which made the shy young man blush with pleased embarrassment.

This went well thought William: a good store of scripture at hand should there be the need.

'But wilt thou send him without armed aid, Master John?' Tom was often the practical one. 'Lawlessness groweth apace on many a common of the King's highway twixt hither and Oxenford.'

'Surely and soothly said,' the chapman agreed. 'I will give thought to't. Alas, that all my servants and tradesmen are not free, else I would send them. Men-at-arms are few for the hiring.'

At that point, the old labourer stood forth.

'Thy pardon, master chapman, but prithee sent thou me. Ralph Collard be my name. A man-at-arms in service to My Lord o' Winchester were I, and full cunning with sword and bow be I still, aged though I seem. Dismissed for drunkenness for the grief o' the loss o' my dear wife, but those days be passed. Many here do a-vouch for me as a landless labourer, and full faithful have I been. A servant o' the Blest Saviour be I also. Labour do I seek anon. Send me, master.'

'Forsooth indeed!' exclaimed Tom, delighted at the idea. 'I vouch for his faithfulness also. Strong and full able with bow have I seen of him.'

The chapman glanced in William's direction and received a smile and a nod.

'Oswald, thou shalt have thine armed escort,' said the chapman with a welcoming smile and hand extended to Ralph. 'Take this worthy, equip and attire him as befits a man-at-arms. A week's pay shalt thou also furnish him ere ye depart.'

Early the next day, they all bade farewell and Godspeed to Oswald and his mounted escort. William had written a letter of introduction, requesting more copies of the precious manuscripts, as well as a report to be delivered to Doctor Wycliffe.

Old Ralph had seemed to grow taller now that he had his self-respect once again. He looked every inch an experienced soldier as the party took the road north to Newbury.

'God hath done all things well,' commented William to the chapman. 'Full open-handed art thou also, Master John, that two armed men should be sent. Who is the younger? A might warrior before the Lord doth he seem.'

The chapman turned a puzzled face toward him but it soon changed to wonder.

'I myself hath hired but one soldier, Father William,' he said quietly.

With all their affairs settled at Andover, Tom and William were ready to move on.

Before they left, their farmer host came back from Andover, chuckling, and reported that the grey friars had expressed their satisfaction that all heresy had been stamped out from their midst, and that all appeared to be back to "normal."

'Once again, thou'st driven forth the thundercloud, Father Elijah,' laughed Tom.

'But wilt thou not essay a little more faith of thine own, O mine apprentice?' returned his master in a jovial mood. 'If Elijah had he deadly passions, then 'ware thou mine?'

They moved on the next day with prayers and gifts (and the inevitable tears) from their disciples.

It was not William's passions that caused the next thunderstorm.

Tom had developed a penchant for wild honey. If they noticed an increase in the activity of bees in any forest nearby, Tom took careful note from where it all came. William may mumble his disapproval, but at the next village, when he had the chance, Tom would borrow a smoky, pitch-coated torch and go hunting through the woods for the hive.

The smoke, unfortunately, did not always subdue the affronted insects.

'When wilt thou be done of this tomfoolery, thou great jobbard?' uttered William in mild exasperation, scraping a few stings off Tom's back. 'Will not good village mead suffice thee? At the least shouldst thou eat of the apples of the wild, for they cleanse the mouth that thy teeth be hale and thy speech be clear and sound.'

'But hast thou tasted aught so sweet as the wild wood-mead, Father William?' protested Tom with a grin, totally unrepentant. 'I bring thee some and to spare with the forest berry also, but thou wilt have none. The apple oft and lome is bitter that would put the teeth on edge...'

'...But in the stomach it is sweet,' replied William, shrugging his shoulders in resignation. 'Well, no mortal sin is this, but 'ware that thy teeth be not under siege, and breeched withal.'

His prophecy came true. A week later, William noticed that Tom began to be less than his exuberant self, occasionally sitting with a glum expression, holding his jaw.

In the ancient forest outside Andover, William found Tom sitting cross-legged by a brook, head in his hand, rocking back and forth and groaning.

'The walls are breeched, I deem,' commented William dryly, but not unkindly, leaning on his staff as he bent to study the jaw. 'Show me then thy wounded member. Peradventure find we wood-balm to assuage it.'

Tom reluctantly but obediently opened his mouth and William examined the offending tooth closely.

'Alas and alack, my son, the walls are breeched indeed and the tower shall fall. But then, the house of Samson's captivity slew the foe also.'

Then he struck with his staff, hard and true.

The blow also knocked Tom sideways, and he let out a yell of pain, spitting blood, broken tooth and profanities he had not used for many years. Priding himself on his quick-wittedness, he was not used to being taken by surprise like this, and it infuriated him as much as the pain of the blow. He leapt to his feet and advanced on William, his eyes blazing.

'By the Rood, Father William Shepherd, dost thou not take too much upon thyself? Am I but a beast that thou shouldst so use me?'

He would have wrestled his esteemed mentor to the ground and even thrown him into the stream, such was his anger. The champion wrestler of all Dorsetshire was not to be taken advantage of like this and get away with it.

But instead of taking the expected defensive stance or cowering in fear, William stood patiently, awaiting his fate. He was more intent on wiping the blood off the tip of his staff than the impending danger. He looked up with a slightly wry smile on his lips, not unmixed with understanding.

This made Tom pause, a little perplexed. Incensed as he was, he could not bring himself to do what his natural instinct urged him to do.

'I cry thee pardon that I would mete wood justice upon thy tooth, my son,' said William calmly, as though he was merely commenting on the weather, 'but when the foe hath invaded and is found within the walls, the tower must fall and thou sufferest loss, a little. Shouldst thou not give thanks rather that the battle is won?'

Sheepishly, Tom realised that the ache had gone with the forcible extraction of the tooth, even though his gums smarted somewhat from the blow. His annoyance still lingered, nonetheless. He spat out more blood, stooped and washed his mouth out in the brook, eyeing his master bodingly.

'No gorky lad am I that thou shouldst so smite me without forewarning,

Father. Was I not in thine hands? Trust unwavering gave I thee. Were this a debate of the ring, surely would the Steward of the Fair command that bound thou shouldst be so that I might freely smite thee in return. Such is the Law of the Ring.'

William now felt a little conscience-stricken. Tom had a point.

'So be it, my son. Should mine own teeth suffer a breech also, then likewise shalt thou smite it in return. Tooth for a tooth it shall be. But mind this also: "Let the righteous smite me; it shall be a kindness..."'

In spite of himself, Tom had to laugh.

'A bargain is this? So be it, Father William! Is it not thine both to shepherd the soul and to smite evil, though it be in the mouth of thy disciple. Other towers may fall at thine hand also, but forewarned I must be, for I fear not thy kindly chastening. I have been schooled. Henceforth shall I eschew the sinful honeycomb except that I find the bitter fruit also. Is this not the nature of life's journey?'

'Come then. Forgive the folly of thy master and strike hands. Let us seek the wood-balm herb, thou and I, that the enemy invade not the breech of my making.'

Apart from William wincing a little at Tom's hearty and overwhelming handclasp, their usual amicable relationship was restored.

The thunderstorm had passed.

Chapter 17: Wiltshire Awakes

'And the Word of God waxed,
and the number of the disciples in Jerusalem was much multiplied;
also a much company of priests obeyed to the faith.'

(Deeds of Apostles 6:7 Wycliffe/Purvey Translation)

The bluebells were still blossoming in the Angrove woodland as the two travellers passed through into Wiltshire.

Most of the folk of the towns and villages in the northern parts of Wiltshire welcomed them with open arms as soon as they discovered that they had been sent by Doctor Wycliffe. Many approached them with questions and expressions of support.

The reason for this was that the greatest of Wycliffe's henchmen had been there a number of times, and had made a strong impression. Doctor Nicholas Hereford, Masters John Ashton, Philip Repton, even old Master Robert Winston and John Ashwardby had journeyed through previously and had spread their message through the churches, mainly around the Swindon and Marlborough region. Roger de Morville, Bishop of Salisbury, had welcomed them, honouring them as great scholars at the time.

But something apparently made him change his mind, and they found the doors closed firmly but politely. The message halted its progress before it could be spread south or west of Wiltshire.

When the Archbishop heard that Wycliffe's teaching was gaining popularity in Wiltshire, he sent a stern and explicit directive to Salisbury to ban any Wycliffite Master from preaching in those churches. The bishop of Salisbury obediently sent a civil request to Oxford, asking Doctor Wycliffe that the visits should cease. Wycliffe, reading between the lines, had noted that it was not a hostile demand, but a polite request in compliance with orders from the bishop's superior.

'Roger de Morville is a proud but subtle man, and few know his mind,' he said, discussing the letter with Hereford, Repton and William Shephard one night. 'He was given his bishopric by John of Gaunt himself as reward for service as Chancellor of Lancaster, and full well and faithful performed he his office. And verily, he demeaned himself as bishop right worshipfully, or so it would seem. His predecessor did naught to stem the decadent manner of life of his clergy, and some of the clergy therefore did much evil.'

Master Philip Repton nodded. He had seen some of their doings with his own eyes.

'Rumour have I heard also of the deeds and preaching of John Ball, doctor.'

They all exchanged uneasy glances at this news.

'Too late came de Morville to amend matters,' continued the Doctor. 'Many priests he banished, but others fled the ire of the injured Salisbury folk.'

'Sayest thou that Salisbury is perilous to enter, Doctor?' William asked.

'That I cannot tell, Father William. Haply de Morville hath set all a-right, for he is a man both cunning and politic, but just. Much would I give to know whether he be for us or 'gainst us. Peradventure neither foe, nor friend is he.'

To have him on side once again as a powerful ally, would mean that all southern and western Wiltshire would be open to unhindered preaching of the gospel. William hoped that they could discover if this was so while they were in Wiltshire.

Nonetheless, Tom continually felt the urge in his heart to travel southwest through Wiltshire toward Somerset. They usually resolved any such disagreements with extended prayer.

As Tom prayed earnestly during the next morning's prayers, there came to his mind's eye a circle of huge stones. They faded away to be replaced by a large cathedral with a tall, tall steeple.

'By my faith!' said William, his enthusiasm aroused when Tom described it to him. 'The Henge of Stone and Salisbury cathedral, witterly. It seemeth that I may have speech with Bishop Roger Morville withal if this thy vision is sooth. Make we our course westward unto Amesbury then southward, even to Salisbury. What sayest thou?'

'The Henge of Stone!' said Tom softly, his eyes shining with anticipation. Many legends had been woven around these mysterious edifices, and he had longed to see them for himself. The journey westward could wait for a little.

Passing a few sad and deserted villages along the way, with only a few stray sheep for Tom to preach to, they made good time and distance next day to the village of Ambresbury.

Amesbury, as it is now called, had once been a prosperous small town, clustered about the local Priory of St Melor. This establishment had fluctuated in prosperity as much as the village itself had. Once a well-endowed abbey, it was now a comparatively small double-priory, housing mainly nuns but also about eight brothers under a separate prior, William of Ambresbury.

The occasional conflict was inevitable under this arrangement, and prioress Margery often sat on the bank of the Avon, musing sadly on these.

Margery of Purbrook was a wise woman, and had dealt with these to admiration in the past, and Prior William had been a reasonable man at the beginning of their acquaintance. Over time, it seemed to her that he had become too comfortable with his position, and he could not relate to the spiritual pilgrimage that she was experiencing in her own heart. Their relationship deteriorated to merely civil acquaintances.

She had been a devout woman all her life, and her election to her present position was mainly on the basis of her devotion and charitable works, which were quite considerable and gained renown in ecclesiastical circles. She was almost worshipped by the common folk.

But all her outward works hid a restless heart. She had a longing to draw close to God, but the harder she tried, the further away God seemed to be.

She discovered that five of the priory sister closest to her also confessed to a similar restlessness. She had to find answers for their sakes as well as hers. She began fasting, a practice that had ceased for many years in the priory. It did little more than increase her hunger to find God. Wondering how she dared, she began to question some of the tenets and practices of her ancient order, and even of Holy Church herself.

So she sat that day in her favourite hiding place, the copse of trees by the river, and wept in frustration. Instead of resorting to the set prayers to the blessed virgin and to St Melor that she usually followed so faithfully, which now seemed so powerless, she tried the daring experiment of crying out to God directly from the depths of her heart. She even dared to bypass the set Latin prayers prescribed by her order. The early saints, she reasoned, prayed in their own native Hebrew or Greek.

'O Father that art in heaven. Forgive me if I presume upon Thy grace. Can I not approach Thee for reason of my manifold sins? Did not mine own earthly father love me in despite of mine erring ways? Art Thou not greater, more loving than he? O that I may draw closer unto Thee, but I wot not the way to Thine heart.'

A sob from deep within escaped her.

For a moment, she felt a little comforted, feeling that God had accepted her sincerity and humility. But then, an accusative voice sounded in her mind, invoking all the teaching she had received in her novitiate. What right had she, a sinner, to speak directly to a Holy God? Only through Holy Church, her offices and the holy saints could she ever dare to gain favour with Him. She was in turmoil again.

But that momentary experience of peace had been too much like heaven to be ignored. What was the truth? If only she could read the Holy Scriptures like Prior William had been trained to do (if he ever bothered) to look behind the wonderful stories she had heard of the early disciples. They seemed to have a simple and uncomplicated faith that gave them peace and joy, and sustained them even through torture and death. They did not have all the paraphernalia and ritual that was present in the church of her day.

But she was limited in her Latin, being too busy in her duties to study further and discover their secrets in the Book of books itself. If only she could lay hands even on some of the fragments of the Scriptures she had heard about, translated in the English tongue. But these were extremely rare, and not encouraged by the Archbishop of London.

'What! Translate unto common English? The good year!' he had exclaimed, when it had been suggested to him. 'Shall we throw pearls before swine? Wilt thou take that which is pure and holy and make it common? Jeffrey's Day, by God! If the borel folk do read of it, they shall

341

corrupt and mangle it to their own scathe. Nay! Let but God's Holy Priests interpret Holy Writ, and none other.'

Archbishop Sudbury of Canterbury, lacking the vigour and drive of his colleague, merely nodded in agreement.

Having already become acquainted with the archbishops' arrogance and disregard for the common folk, she felt it was typical of Courtenay to say so, and it did not give her the answers she craved.

She tried her experiment once again. 'Father God. Forgive me. I but seek the Truth,' she whispered aloud. 'Show unto me the way to Thine Heart.'

She was startled and annoyed to hear a fervent 'Amen!' from two male voices nearby.

She stepped out of her retreat in rising wrath, expecting to see two brothers from the priory, disturbing her precious solitude. She had made it clear, even to Prior William that her private times by the river were not to be disturbed.

Instead, she saw two strong, weather-beaten men in russet clerical robes, leaning on their staves, with a look of genuine concern on their faces. It changed to mildly comic apprehension when they saw the expression on her own face.

'Forgive us if we disturb thee of thy devotions, good sister,' said the taller man, who had the kindest face she had ever seen. 'We were but passing when we heard the sound of weeping that came from the trees. We are wont to give aid where're we find need. But I perceive we were in error, and shall leave thee in peace. May God give thee peace indeed.'

They bowed to her and would have passed on, but her annoyance was now displaced by intrigue. She had never seen men of their like before. Friars they may seem from a distance, but there clung about them an air of sincerity, joy and authority that none others had before, and their hearty courtesy totally disarmed her.

'Stay, I pray ye, brethren!' she said as they bowed and turned to go. 'Your pardon for mine ungraciousness at our meeting. Truly, I was in prayer, but its time is now passed. The sisters of St Melor are famed for better hospitality than this.'

She studied them for a moment. 'Prithee, of what order are ye, brethren? Thine habits are beyond my ken. Are ye friars mendicant indeed? There be somewhat of your demeanour that I wist not, but ...' and she nearly said that she rather liked.

The older stranger bowed again and seemed to understand her. He introduced himself as William Shephard, an itinerant priest. His younger colleague (a veritable lion of a man, she thought) cheerily introduced himself as "simple, humble and plain Master Thomas Plowman, lay preacher and obedient servant of the great Father William yonder," and also bowed.

Amused, she introduced herself as the Prioress of the Priory of St Melor, much to the strangers' surprise, for she wore only a simple sister's attire that day. They had heard her devotion and goodness extolled by the folk in the village, and would have liked to meet her. God, once again, had arranged a rendezvous.

'We belong to no order but the rule of Christ, Mother Prioress,' explained William. 'Neither are we mendicant, but is the name of John Wycliffe known unto thee?'

It was indeed, for the Archbishop had straightly forbidden her to read any of his writings, which naturally incited her curiosity. Bishop Roger of Salisbury had secretly given her one of Wycliffe's polemic tracts, but it had fallen accidentally into Prior William's hands and he had burnt it in pious wrath before she had a chance to read it. She had heard rumours that Wycliffe had even authorised and translated portions of scripture into English himself. Was this the hand of God?

'Doctor Wycliffe's men?' she exclaimed, her face lighting up as her yearnings came to the fore again. 'Of he that would translate the Word of God for the common folk? Oh prithee, Father William, hast thou Holy Writ with thee, that is of the English tongue?'

She immediately felt embarrassed. They were strangers after all, however sincere they looked, and she spoke of her longings to no one but her closest sisters.

In answer, William threw down his pack and extracted his last copy of the complete New Testament and handed it to her. Tom gasped in dismay, but held his peace.

'Behold! A gift, with greetings from Doctor Evangelicus, lady,' William said, without flourish.

Speechless, she browsed through the pages of the rapidly copied manuscript.

'The Gospels and Deeds of the Apostles, the Epistles of the Apostles and the Apocalypse!' she breathed ecstatically and she gripped it to her breast and turned tear-filled eyes to heaven.

'I thank Thee! O how could I have doubted Thy goodness?' she whispered.

'Aye! God is good,' said Tom, almost wholeheartedly, then added under his breath, 'and wherewithal shall we find the Word of Life for ourselves, if we have it not?'

William caught the gist of his words, but merely shrugged. It was clear to him that the lady before him had the much greater need.

There was no looking back now for the prioress. Excitedly, she insisted on the two men staying for a while, so that she and her closest sisters could hear their message. She gave them the best guest rooms in the priory, much to Tom's embarrassment.

'Nay, Mother Prioress. We be a charge on no wight. Give us a task that we may earn our meat and shelter o' nights. Or sleep we in the hayloft if need be. So are we content.'

She swept aside their offer with a laugh and a wave of her hand.

'Labour enow there shall be for you, good brethren, if ye will open God's Holy Word unto us. Ye shall have thy meat at my table this night.'

'Yet my fellow speaketh sooth, mother,' William demurred: 'for we are wont to abide with the humble village folk. For such are we, and to such are we sent. To eat with the well-to-do and sleep in the beds of rich guest is not meet for poor preachers, though we give thee thanks. Give us leave to preach at chapel if thine order so alloweth. Yea, speak unto master Parson if thou wilt, that he would give us leave to preach in his pulpit. Else look we to byways and waymeets to preach God's Word.'

The prioress, though amazed at their unique code of practice, was not ready to let them go. Never in all her career had she needed to beg any friars to accept her hospitality. She was convinced that if she let them go, they could easily move on. Perhaps she would never see them again and she would only have the scriptures to help her on her spiritual journey. She was grateful for that, of course, but she somehow knew in her heart that God had sent these men to show her the way to abundant life. They themselves quite obviously possessed it.

So she begged, pleaded and cajoled, but to no avail. It was not until she began to tearfully and honestly describe her own search for God, that William finally relented.

'To such hungry hearts are we sent. Give us the humblest of thy lodgings, lady, and we are content.'

'So be it, Father William, if thou so desire,' responded the prioress, relieved.

By this time, they had reached the gate of the priory.

When they stepped into the courtyard, the guests were impressed. Instead of the opulence and extravagance they expected to see, the found a neat, clean, simply but attractively decorated design. There were flowers and the more attractive herbal shrubs billowing out of the corners, and around the simple but tastefully designed fountain in the centre of the yard. It definitely had the woman's touch, thought William approvingly. Gone were the elaborate, even grotesque carvings and figures, apart from finely carved statues of the boy saint of Brittany, Saint Melor, and one of St Mary. The old Saxon church, what remained of it, was lovingly restored and blended well with the finely cut grey stone. The moss covering the stones seemed to give it that final, homely touch.

'Fair indeed!' commented William, looking around him.

Pleased at the good impression the priory had on at least one of the visitors, Mother Marjory proudly recounted a little of its chequered history, of royal remains and those of Saint Melor himself that were allegedly buried there.

'Come the day that once again it shall be the Abbey of Ambrosius.'

After all the fiery denunciation of expensive Roman edifices by the Wycliffe masters, William and Tom could not bring themselves to say the expected "Amen!" To have expressed their disapproval would not have been well received. William compromised.

'May God bless all His works of mercy, wherever they be.'

Sensing his reserve, the prioress smiled, and added; 'But Prior William would aspire to this more than I.'

They passed by the cloister, beautifully paved, where two elderly sisters paced up and down, busy with their rosaries. They looked up briefly and looked curiously at the strangers as they passed. Seeing the prioress herself with them, they merely bowed their heads in acknowledgement of her rank and returned to their prayers.

In the distance, they heard men's voices chanting. Tom, not as interested in architecture and history as William, lifted his head and listened.

'Mother, I hear but a men's choir. Are not the sisters with them?'

'Matins is long passed, Master Plowman, else they would attend. My sisters do labour in the fields or refectory-kitchens. It is our writ that we do many good works for them that have not.'

'Thy fame is not unknown unto us, good mother,' said William warmly.

'Yea!' echoed Tom, 'thy praises are sung in the village, and few folk are in need.'

He did not mention that this situation actually made the villagers too complacent to look beyond the status quo, and the Wycliffite teaching was of little interest. If the evangelists had not heard Prior Marjory's prayer by the river, they would have passed on, disappointed, without any harvest of souls in Amesbury. Tom was still intrigued by the role of the brothers however.

'But do not likewise the monks of Prior William, mother?'

'Nay. That is not their calling, so saith the prior. Hirelings have they for their fields and such, for Prior William is fully skilled in fiscal affairs. The brothers have holier works than ours. These are especial masses for dear ones' souls that have passed unto purgatory. Or rather, of those that can pay such benefices.'

William noted a tartness in her tone, and smiled wryly.

'And what of the poor that cannot, mother? Will they suffer long in torment until a kindly soul would pay masses, or even indulgences from the pardoners?'

William's sardonic tone in his turn caused the prioress to smile also. She had found a kindred spirit.

'The hardships of the poor are purgatory enow, so 'tis said.'

She stopped in her tracks and looked William in the eye.

'Father William, what saith Holy Writ of these things. Is there purgatory that we face indeed?'

Pleased that she had honest questions about her traditions, William returned her straight gaze.

'Of purgatory itself and masses for moneys, I have seen naught in the Holy Books, lady. Doctor John Wycliffe hath raged 'gainst such Simony oft and oft. Rather doth the Scriptures speak of the free gift of God that is Eternal Life, if we truly seek it.'

'This I truly seek!' she said earnestly, tears starting in her eyes again. 'And that I may find Him, the Heavenly Father. Wilt thou not show me the way, if thou truly knowest this?'

'Come, then good mother. Let us find the chapel, for the guesthouses are not meet for such talk twixt man and woman.'

The church of St Mary and St Melor was a magnificent structure both within and without.

'Beautiful, is this!' breathed William, gazing at the splendid misericords and wood carvings, 'but would cost a mark or many to build it, methinks.'

As they passed through the doors of a quiet room, Tom saw an old, old stone set at the bottom of the wall with faint Latin writing scratched in it.

'"*Gloria….Dei*"' was all he could read. 'Dedicated unto the glory of God is this, mother?'

'In sooth it is. Some say that Ambrosius Aurelius himself did lay this foundation. But whither be the Glory of God? Verily, I have not found it in this place, fair though it be.'

'The Glory of God dwelleth not in temples made with hands, mother.'

William nodded in agreement, but came to the very heart of the matter for Prioress Marjory.

'"Christ in thee, the hope of Glory," quoth the apostle. We have the glory of Lord Christ in our hearts if we come to Him as little children.'

Seated at a small wooden table with the manuscript between them, William was able to show her the difference between trying to earn God's favour and the free grace of a Father Who wanted her to approach His throne as His own daughter.

The idea of the insufficiency of good works was a difficult concept for the prioress to grasp. Good works had been such a large part of her life.

'Then are my works but in vain?' she cried, a little distressed.

'Nay, for God hath seen them. But it is thine heart that He seeketh, not thy good works. Then, with thine heart captured by Him, good works are but fruit of a grateful soul set free by the precious blood of Christ, Who made the way to the Father open unto us. This joy can I and my comrade with me attest to also. Our own works are naught but filthy rags, and cannot win God's good favour. Of what like was thine own father?'

'Perished he did in the Black Plague, alas. But a fine, loving man was he in my girlhood. Wherefore askest thou me this?'

'Did he love you for all thy good works and virtue?'

'Nay!… but sayest thou…?' The light began to dawn.

It took a while, however, and the unfamiliar English passages were at first confusing to one who had been nurtured, and indeed had taught, otherwise for so long.

A beam of sunshine escaped through the rainclouds and pierced a stained glass window high in the wall of that tall room. It shone around her as she knelt and wept with joy, even as she did as a little girl when her earthly father comforted her.

It was evensong for that day, and all the sisters were gathered.

Sister Mary looked up from her rosary to where the prioress was standing. Her superior had appeared to almost dance into the church before them all. Now she was standing, singing the usual chants with an angelic look of joy on her face, and… her hands raised! Was this seemly? It reminded Mary of the first time she had been in love. (But that was in her previous life, before she took her vows.)

She was an ardent soul after all, and it would probably pass. She had tried many religious exercises together, for she too had the same restlessness within. She had confessed it in tears to the prioress herself a while ago, only to discover that she shared it. Four others had also. Since then the "God-seekers" as they secretly called themselves, had tried fasting, ruthless self-denial, even self-flagellation – all to no avail.

Perhaps the prioress had fallen in love? That was unlikely at her age and state of celibacy, but she was flesh and blood after all. The gatekeeper perhaps? Young brother Robert? (although she rather liked him herself) The handsome locksmith? A few feminine roving eyes had followed him in and out of the refectory.

Well, it was none of her business. Mary shrugged and returned to her beads.

At the evening meal, it was even harder to ignore. The prioress insisted on giving thanks this time, but she spoke in English! The older sisters looked up and raised their eyebrows, scandalised.

That was not all. The words she spoke were such an overflowing expression of sincere thankfulness to God for all His blessings, it brought a tear to the eye of more than one sister.

The two novices, not yet schooled in the strict discipline observed at table, sat staring at her with eyes and mouth wide open.

'Be she a-drunken?' one whispered to the other. She was immediately quelled by an icy glare from the novice-mistress nearby.

Immediately after the morning meal, the prioress summoned Sister Mary and the other four whom she knew had been on the same quest for fulfilment. Whatever happened in her office, the other sisters could only speculate. But two of the girls came out of her office hours later with their faces shining like the sun. The other three appeared to be in deep thought, as though they had received the most astonishing news. But they would not speak of it to anyone.

The change in the prioress and the two sisters became the subject of discussion among the sisters for the next seven days at least. They did not recognise her from the kindly but withdrawn figure of authority they had known.

It was not confined to the fields and cloisters of the nuns alone. One of the brothers of the priory soon noticed the effect on the prioress, for he was none other than brother Robert, who often conveyed messages back and forth between the prior and the prioress. He could not help but notice that she now appeared much more cheerful, even happy. This awoke a sleeping giant within his heart, also.

She saw her the following day as she walked out into the sunshine outside the gate and gazed over the great Salisbury plains with a joy he had never seen in her face before.

Overcoming his own shyness, he humbly approached the prioress the next day.

'Mother prioress, I beg leave to speak mine heart,' he said, bowing before her. 'I crave thy pardon upon us that Prior William doth disapprove of thy new piety. This he nameth "mystic mullock of the heresy of the *Spirituales*" which he would distain. He is an orgulous man. Natheless, I also hath an hunger for Truth and the deeper things of God, and would be schooled of thee, if thou wilt.'

The prioress was delighted.

'Brother Robert, ever thou hast a great heart. Come thou unto the nave at St Melor's this eve ere Compline, and hearken to the message that these strangers would give. Prior William shall wist naught of the matter. Mayhap 'twill ease thine heart's ache as it hath mine.'

Such an admission from a superior amazed Brother Lawrence, an earnest young monk who, like the prioress, had also embarked on his vocation to satisfy his inner longings.

He had been shocked to discover the worldly attitude of the other monks there, but had succumbed to the lure of the comforts and even the covert immorality of the other brothers. They had a nominalistic view of their faith, and looked to absolution to ease their conscience.

Well, he had to confess, he enjoyed his post as messenger. He often looked surreptitiously around amongst the sisters for Mary, and exchanged a wink or smile with her on more than one occasion. This did nothing to ease the hunger and longing in his own heart, and he had begun to covertly observe the prioress's own spiritual journey with great interest.

The message of the scriptures, read to him in his mother tongue, was the answer he was craving for. Tom presented the gospel of salvation so powerfully and compellingly, he was readily convinced of its truth. He came to faith through the work of the cross, rather than his own pathetic attempts at righteousness. He never looked back, in spite of the disapproval of his colleagues.

Upon Father William's urgings, he and many of the sisters met privately with the prioress for regular readings and prayer. The prioress had considerable influence, not only in the village, but the outlying hamlets and farms that she occasionally visited. The numbers grew as the prioress spoke to those she knew would be receptive.

It was not until four weeks later that Tom and William finally felt it was time to tear themselves away from their new disciples and move on again, much to the grief of these. The prioress knew that they must go eventually, but it did not make it any easier when they made the announcement.

'Is there naught I can give you to ease your journey, good brethren?' she said with a breaking voice.

'To know that the shepherding of the flock is in thy keeping – that is gift enow for us, dear lady,' responded William, bowing and kissing her hand.

'But stay! There is aught indeed that I can give.'

She skipped away to the next room, leaving the two men a little mystified. Tom started speculating.

'Is it cheese? Nay! 'Tis honeycomb!'

He grinned at William, showing a missing tooth, but William refused to rise to the bait.

The lady returned, carrying a parcel wrapped in beautifully woven cloth.

'My daughters of the God-Seekers have been diligent. Cunning scribes are they.'

William, realising what the package contained, was speechless. Tom had to see for himself.

'By mine holy faith! Five of they! And they almost complete!'

Then he laughed. 'Mine is the folly. A son of the soil am I, and know full well that whatsoever we sow, that also shall we reap – manifold.'

'And many more of these shall there be at need, brethren.'

Before they left the next day, William asked the prioress for information regarding Stonehenge.

'There is great mystery and dark legend that enshrouds these stones, yet I sense that there is destiny for us therein also. Dost thou know naught that would aid us?'

She looked at them strangely and said nothing at first. Pressed, she could not advise them, only stating what the official belief and attitude toward such 'pagan' things was. They seemed to sense that she feared to tell them all she knew.

Gently pressed again, she relented.

Off the record, she had heard whispers of mysterious midnight gatherings at the Henge on midsummer's eve and other times. These folk were hooded and cloaked, bear sprigs of mistletoe and made beautiful music with harp and song, with hands raised as the sun rose. They sang in a strange, poetic language that few could recognise; although the duke's chief minstrel declared it was Welsh, if not elvish. Many locals feared them, thinking these were faerie folk. Others said they were angels, gathered to worship God, for the music was so fair and haunting.

Others had reported similar gatherings at the site of the Henge of Wood, further north. Others had claimed that there had sometimes been dark rituals, even whispering about sightings of trolls and goblins, but feared to say more.

The prioress glanced over her shoulder as though others may hear her, then leaned forward to them and whispered, rather cryptically:

'Look ye for one Merlin ap Dunwal, who names himself also Daniel of Marland, the cowman. But I beg of ye, tell it to no wight. Ye I would trust with this, but none other.' She would say no more.

This obviously intrigued the travellers even more. However, the road called them onward, so the mystery would reveal itself in due time. They waved farewell to the band of disciples gathered at the gate.

'God speed you, and our prayer go with you also,' they all cried.

The travellers new destination: Salisbury.

Chapter 18: The Second Wave Builds

And the church by all Judaea, and Galilee, and Samaria,
had peace, and was edified, and walked in the dread of the
Lord, and was filled with comfort of the Holy Ghost.[66]

[Deeds of the Apostles – Wycliffe translation.]

Doctor Hereford and Masters Parker, Swynderby and Smith walked down the main street of Lutterworth to the church from where the missions were first launched. It was a very important meeting. Possible history-making decisions had to be made.

Master Swynderby, with his usual restless vigour, was holding forth on a matter close to his heart.

'...And though Doctor Evangelicus giveth us not leave the yoke of Rome to cast off, yet none, nor Courtenay, nor Sudbury nor even that Roman Antichrist himself, can hinder God's Work from henceforth. .....'

'Canterbury hath scarce moved 'gainst us, for he heeds us little,' interjected Parker with mild derision, 'and a slothful sluggard is he into the bargain.'

'Oh, let us speak no evil of Sudbury,' said Hereford tolerantly. 'Verily he liveth in lavish wealth, but a gentle man of peace hath he ever been, and thus it worketh mightily in our favour.'

'But and if he were not so,' pursued Swynderby energetically, 'his enmity would be to no avail. Who can stand 'gainst the work of God Almighty? In but three years, I deem, all of England shall have heard the blessed gospel of Christ. Our preachers will disperse multitudes of the good Word in their native tongue. All shall read and turn unto the true faith of Christ, and who shall heed the power of Rome then? These unholy prelates in their palaces of gold, their false authority shall crumble like sand, their riches given unto the poor and great shall be their fall. We shall then raise

---

66   KJV adds: "and multiplied."

up men of true holiness who will lead us back unto the ways of God in its purity and simplicity, as in the days of the blessed apostles.'

Such a rosy picture of the future certainly appealed to them all, but Master Smith and Hereford, who had both been present at the Council of Leicester, exchanged uneasy glances. They had not forgotten the darker forebodings of the Lady Mother's vision, which did not quite match what Swynderby had in mind.

'Well, well,' sighed Master Smith fatalistically. 'Let us rejoice in the seasons of summer and harvest whilst we may. The winter's cold and dark may yet be endured if we have much in store.'

'Ever thou speakest in nyfles, Smith!' responded Swynderby impatiently. 'Who can hinder the work of God, O thou of little faith? No winter shall there be, say I. A wildfire hath been lit in this land, that none can quench. Can the work of God be a-thwarted? Whither thy faith, man?'

Masters Smith and Swynderby, being totally different personalities, often clashed. Smith turned toward his colleague, ready to give him a piece of his mind, but Master Parker held up his hands placatingly.

'Come, come, brethren! To garboil on this matter is needless. Do ye not speak sooth, both, yet in part only? For thus is nature in balance, that many parts labour and strive to make the whole. God omniscient alone seeth the whole. We see through a glass but darkly. In this matter thou seest but dark clouds before us, Smith, and verily we cannot deny the passing of the seasons. But shall the fire of which Swynderby speaketh be quenched?

'Once, in the days of my youth was this, a mighty conflagration did my grandsire build, for a cunning woodsman he was. Slowly did he cover it a-neath the earth as winter came. It smouldered and died not, even in despite of rain and snow. In the advent of spring, it was freed of its tomb, and with the fuelling thereof, it burst into great flame once more. Mark ye also the lessons of history. Pagan Rome could not quench the work of God, though for a season it smouldered a-neath the city within the catacombs, and in the houses and hearts of many. Nor could the fruits of the labours of St Joseph of Arimathea be stayed in this land, though the Caesars did essay so to do years and a-many.'

Smith fell silent, impressed by this wisdom. Hereford turned and smiled at Parker.

'Cunning art thou in the studies of mathematics, the histories and theologies, my friend. A cunning woodsman art thou also.'

'Is it not but logic?' Parker shrugged deprecatingly.

Swynderby was still unconvinced, for he could not rid himself of his passion to see the might of Rome toppled. His vision of the spreading of the gospel even went beyond the shores of England – even to the ends of the earth.

'…..And this blessed consummation shall usher in the Second Advent! The Kingdom Age draweth nigh!' he concluded dramatically, his eyes gleaming with anticipation.

Parker shrugged again, this time with mild scepticism.

'But so quoth many of the church fathers of old. A fair and mighty dream, this, but will it come to pass in our days, deemest thou?'

Their debate continued right up to the very doors of Wycliffe's apartments.

Gerard, Wycliffe's servant and self-styled bodyguard, opened to their knock. He was a large, shaggy-headed and grizzled individual, a soldier honourably discharged from the King's army, after being wounded in the French wars. He was totally devoted to Wycliffe's person and Wycliffe's cause and was a terror to his enemies. He boasted that he could "smell his master's foes two leagues hence." The summoner who first tried to deliver the bishops' summons to Lambeth got short shrift. Gerard, opening the door to him, seemed to know by instinct the nature of that cleric's errand, and simply snarled at him. The summoner gave a cry of fear, backed off and ran for his life. Crossing himself, he swore to the archbishop who despatched him that the man was demon-possessed and barked at him like a dog.

But on this occasion, he knew the visitors well and almost wagged a metaphorical tail in welcome. Even Swynderby, who once thrust past him without the slightest fear, was met with doglike admiration. He had no hard feelings at all after that incident, deeming him to be, "a preacher right valourful." Bowing deeply, he freely acknowledged that 'Master be within,' ushered them into the entrance hall and limped off to inform his master of their arrival.

They had barely hung up their outer coats and hats when Doctor Wycliffe himself approached down the passageway, leaning on the arm of one of his closest friends, fellow translator Doctor Purvey. Accompanying them were two middle-aged but distinguished-looking gentlemen who appeared to be senior clerics. Black haired with dark, flashing eyes, they wore totally unfamiliar habits in the eyes of the English masters. Only Hereford, who had travelled the continent briefly as part of his duties, recognised them as middle European. Wycliffe and Purvey were in the process of bidding them farewell and Godspeed, but stopped when they perceived the masters' arrival.

'Ha! Hereford! Swynderby! Parker and Smith!' barked Wycliffe, who was in an especially good humour. 'In a good hour are ye come! I beg leave to present two strangers to these shores. Far and long have they journeyed, that they may make of our acquaintance and to ask of us a boon.'

Latin was the universal language, so for the strangers sake, Wycliffe made the introductions and explained the situation thus. One of the strangers had a rather difficult name to pronounce, and even Wycliffe himself stumbled over it, in spite of his own European experience. The other was none less than the great Doctor Jerome, a Czech scholar and preacher of great fame.

The two visitors, Wycliffe explained, had come from the great University of Prague, sent by none less than the renowned Doctor Jan Huss. Many on the continent regarded him in a similar light to Wycliffe, either as a dangerous, outspoken heretic or the most brilliant theological mind of his day. The strangers were obviously of the latter opinion, and spoke glowingly of his reforms at Prague.

One of them was clutching two voluminous manuscripts with glee as though he had been presented with the Goose that Lays the Golden Eggs.

'*Gloria in Excelsis Deo!*' he breathed ecstatically, trilling his "R's" and adding many exclamations in his own tongue. Bowing repeatedly to Doctor Wycliffe, he thanked him again and again.

Gerard, little educated, found the combination of Bohemian and Latin too much, so he bowed himself out of their presence and retreated to the comfort of the English-speaking kitchen to fortify himself with a tankard of good English ale.

Seeing the English masters' surprise, Purvey explained that the manuscripts were two copies of Wycliffe's Latin commentaries on the state of affairs in ecclesiastical and temporal politics that John Huss himself longed to see.

'John Huss? The great scholar of fame in Rome's despite?' cried Swynderby, casting a look of vicarious triumph toward his superior and a challenge at Parker. 'Behold, Doctor Evangelicus! Thy fame hath been spread abroad beyond these shores! Even the Bohemians do hear the Word of God!'

Fortunately, the Bohemians did not understand a word of English, otherwise they may have been a little offended. Had Wycliffe not been in a good mood, and the visitors absent, he would have roundly scarified him for his lack of tact.

'We struggle not alone, nor hath God chosen us solely to bear the flame, Swynderby. Much hath come to pass 'mongst our Bohemian brethren that we wist not of. But anon these *clerici nobili*[67] are in haste to be gone, that their barque may not miss the tide. Much speech have we had. Alas, that we could not have all conversed and profited thereby, but they are called to their own duties right speedily. Great is the task before them. God send we meet again, at the least in heaven's paradise.'

So with many a "*Bene vale*[68]" and "*Pax vobiscum*" all around and many more bows, Wycliffe gave a final valedictory benediction. The Bohemians departed on their long journey home to Prague, bearing the manuscripts destined to inspire and encourage the great John Huss and his men. They would need all the encouragement they could get in the days to come.

When the visitors had gone, Wycliffe turned and greeted his colleagues warmly. Last of all, he gripped Hereford's hand.

'Hail, Hereford of Hereford, as thy brethren would call thee! And a chancellor, forsooth. More grey hairs I perceive upon thy brow. Waystract laboureth mightily in thy stead, but I miss thine energy unbounded also. 'Tis many a sennight since I looked upon thy countenance, my friend. What news o' the North West? All's well in thy new post?'

Hereford grinned at the mention of his new nickname.

'Yea, Doctor John. Much to do there is ere I stay mine hand and rest, but this thy summons I could not forego. My lord, the Earl hath granted me leave unto the Lord's Day next. He will take our part methinks, but the

---

67 Noble scholars
68 Similar to "Bon Voyage"

bishop himself loveth me not well. Many a Lord's Day have I proclaimed the gospel and denounced the sins of the high clergy from the pulpit. The bishop he cannot turn his proud back upon me anon, as he hath welcomed me to Herefordshire right royally and would be made to look a fool. It is in my mind that he deemed that my duties would keep me silent, but in vain.'

Even Swynderby laughed at that.

'Ho!' chuckled Purvey, 'he wist not the workhorse thou art, brother Nicolas. Dost thou labour still upon thy translations? Hast thou the Book of Maccabees completed?'

'Nay, but yet a little,' replied Hereford, shaking his head a little ruefully. 'Would that I had William Shephard with me, for few could match his scholarship … but ever did he have an heart for the flock. What news of his mission? Hath he not yet tamed that young knave, Thomas Plowman?'

Amidst the light-hearted camaraderie and exchange of news that ensued, Wycliffe moved them all toward his library, for Hereford's words brought the purpose of this meeting to mind. He called the housekeeper for wine and ushered them in.

The library was spacious and comfortable but not luxurious. With the cool of autumnal evenings upon them, there was a large, aromatic fire crackling in the hearth with early chestnuts roasting on shallow pans. There were hazelnuts, Wycliffe's favourite bannocks, an assortment of local and Devonshire cheeses and a modest range of sweetmeats arrayed on side tables for the guests' refreshment. Still too early for candles, the glow of the fire lit up the golden linings in the great tomes on the bookshelves.

Outside the western window, as if to salute the assembled clerics, the setting sun shone through the foliage of a great ash-grove nearby, turning the leaves of the trees russet and blood red. It was an unusual range of colours, and one of the local wonders that drew many sightseers from the whole shire. Low ground-mist was beginning to gather at the base of the trees. It had been a while since Hereford had sat and admired the "Lollard's grove," as it had been christened by the locals. He fell into a reminiscent reverie of the stirring events before his call to the Northwest. The Summoning Dream, the Council of Leicester at his very own quarters, the earth-shaking prophecies of the Culdees, the resultant commissioning of the chosen clerics and the parting benediction from the great man outside the gate of the church next door.

And now, the purpose of this assembly of so many Wycliffites was to consider the results of all their preparations, the fruit of their labours and whether the sending forth of the Poor Preachers was successful enough to continue. This brought many questions to his mind, and his thoughts returned to the present.

He turned toward the large armchair into which Wycliffe was easing himself. But hardly had he begun to enquire after his health and for other news, when Gerard appeared in the doorway and bowed in more guests. Hereford leapt up and greeted the first arrival with acclaim.

'Master Philip Repton, thou roiling rogue! And Will Sanderly! A merry meeting shall this be indeed.'

Repton came in briskly, as though he had not been in the saddle all day, positively radiating energy. He grasped Hereford's hand and bowed to all and sundry.

'Hail, Christian brethren all! I bring ye fellow labourers from afar.'

A tall figure with burning eyes strode in, a stark contrast to Will Sanderley's unassuming and weary entrance. The presence of the newcomer seemed to fill the room. His voice was like a fanfare.

'Yea! From the far corners of the land are we come, my comrades and I, as an army triumphant.'

'Father Simon Cole an I mistake me not,' Parker murmured to Smith.

Father Edward came in less dramatically, with an arm around Peter's shoulder. He raised a hand in a kind of welcoming salute at Parker, who surged forward to greet him. Few were as like-minded, John Parker had once said, as he and Father Edward, a man of plain truth. In spite of his habit being rather travel-stained and the effects of outdoor living plainly showing on his face, his mind was as clear as ever.

Gerard had to hasten to the door yet again, this time to welcome Father Haswell "the Hardy" and the newly ordained Father Lawrence Parsons. Wycliffe and his masters held the missionaries in such high esteem that they considered the lay-brethren more than ready for full ordination.

Master Parker had asked Lawrence if he would consider a living that had just become vacant. Fully ordained priests were still in short supply ever since the great plague.

Interestingly, the sponsor was sympathetic to Wycliffe's cause, and preferred a "Lollard Priest" to fill the living. He wrote to Master Parker, whom he knew personally, asking whom he would recommend. Parker was convinced that Lawrence was the logical choice when he and Master Waystract interviewed the two missionaries upon their return.

Lawrence had felt a little uncomfortable about it at first, thinking he would be abandoning his friend and companion. John Haswell had announced on his return that he had every intention of continuing his calling as an itinerant preacher, and assumed that Lawrence felt the same. So it was not until Parker explained the benefits of a good living that Lawrence wavered.

'Haven, land and hearth that I my call mine own!' he breathed.

'But what is this?' John Haswell had cried in jovial displeasure. 'Wilt thou no longer toil the King's highway in all tempests, sleep 'mongst the swine, nor face the hoards of Hell with me, thy kind master? What is a mere haven and hearth to all this?'

Lawrence gripped his erstwhile master's hand and replied seriously.

'O my father, fear not for me. If of hearth and haven I shall be a-wearied, then shall I tread that way with thee once more. But ever hath I felt the desire that mine own flock I shouldst care for. An hardy evangel art thou and ever shalt be. It is mine to study, to seek truth and to solve mysteries. But never and never shall I forget the road we have trod together.'

'Well, go to, my son. Thine apprenticeship hast thou truly served and served well. No wonderful thing is this to me that thou wouldst seek thine own flock and pulpit. Thomas Woodward hath prayed that we may take him on our missions, so he shall fill thy shoes full well. Nay! 'Tis a fine thing! 'Tis needful that Wycliffe's men fill these post to watch over our flocks. Alack that there is none to guard our own reading circles. Whither this living that Parker speaks of? Whose is the gift?'

Lawrence grinned and struck the superior attitude of a clergyman of great consequence.

'His Lordship, the Earl of Norfolk the giver ... and the gift: Bury St Edmonds!'

He grinned again at Haswell's delighted reaction.

At that moment the great bell sounded the hour.

'But come! We must away to Lutterworth, for we are summoned thence.'

Thus, they found themselves amongst their fellow missionaries and masters in Wycliffe's library, sharing their stories and being overwhelmed by everyone's good will and welcome.

Next came the great orator himself, Master John Ashton of the Golden Tongue. His voice could be heard above the throng as clear and powerful as Simon Cole's. He came in arm in arm with Master Ashwardby, an ordinary-looking man with a short-sighted and dithering manner. But he was greatly beloved and held in awe by master and student-cleric alike. Many times he had been called upon to cast out demon-goblins or evil in many forms, and had prevailed. Although not as active in the launching of the Poor Preacher missions, he was also known for his hospitality and kindly listening ear. More than once, a troubled or impoverished would-be student had slept on the spare bed in the old master's Oxford apartments. His simple acts of kindness had won over not a few to the message of the gospel.

When John Haswell saw him, he cried out above the clamour of the gathering, pushed his way through and hugged the old man. He had not yet had the chance to tell him of the defeat of the Swamp demons. Even Master Ashwardby himself was impressed.

Lutterworth town had rarely seen such a gathering of dignitaries as more and more horses and carriages crowded the local mews. Wycliffe's large library seemed to be rapidly growing smaller, and Gerard had to race to provide more chairs.

Greetings of all these comrades had barely been done, when four more arrivals were added to the great throng.

Father Richard Brandon came in, conversing animatedly with Master James Crompe, the "master of good rede." Father Richard, not afraid to shed tears when deeply moved, was relating some of his more amazing adventures he experienced on his mission, whilst constantly wiping his eyes. Crompe was so amazed, he was constantly interrupting and peppering him with questions throughout – a practice he normally discouraged in his students.

Richard Brandon had found his adventures wearing on his health, so he was also waiting to find a living wherever Wycliffe's influence was strong.

Next, there was Master Richard Waystract, the master-organiser, who came in with Harold Ravenswood, now also ordained as a priest. Waystract was listening intently to young Father Harold's report on the successes and occasional failures of the master's discipling system: the reading circles.

'Hmm,' commented the master, 'the flocks they shall stay or shall scatter according to the nature of the shepherd that leadeth them, I deem.'

'But must not the sheep themselves also stand together and follow the shepherd in true obeisance?' argued Ravenswood respectfully.

'Truly, my son. If the sheep would stray and flee the flock, a good shepherd he would seek them but may not find. But a shepherd there must be. The reader of the circle, he alone cannot pastor the flock, beyond the reading of the scriptures, save he be called and a-learned in his calling.'

But soon, this discussion was also drowned in the flood of welcoming calls and cheerful chatter.

When the last two guests arrived, one of them laughed as he walked in to the noise of the gathering.

'By the Rood! Do we come to an holy convocation of clergymen or a revelling of monks a' Michaelmas? Or haply the White Bull tavern?'

His companion's reply was lost in the cries of 'William Thorpe hath returned, victorious!' and ''Tis Abyngdon, forsooth! Sing ye for us!' or 'Tell us of the geste of the pardoner!'

Repton had brought back a report of their exploits in the southeast.

Once all the general handshaking, backslapping and welcoming noises had begun to subside, Doctor Wycliffe lifted a questioning eyebrow at Richard Waystract, whose students and servants had organised the whole event.

'Yea, Doctor Evangelicus,' the master responded to the mute question, 'all are accounted for save them of the Southwest Mission. But they are beyond our reach, alas, and feel called onward and southward still, so sayeth Master Repton. He will speak for them, sayeth he.'

Wycliffe sighed and nodded.

'So be it, but 'Tis great loss. Our counsels are lessened without Father William Shephard's wisdom. But tarry we cannot. I shall commence.'

He rose shakily to his feet, and at this signal, all the noise died down and everyone found a seat. The joys of meeting old friends and the sense of expectation was still as intense, but whenever John Wycliffe ever rose to speak, even his gainsayers stopped to listen.

'Brethren and gentlemen,' he began. Then he looked around at all their faces upturned expectantly to his, and he stopped. Each of them had a story of great courage and faithfulness, sometimes in the teeth of stiff opposition, sometimes in the face of great danger. The Poor Preachers themselves certainly looked a little travel-weary, with wear and tear showing on their robes, but the fire and purpose still burned in their eyes, maybe even brighter than before. All the conflict, all the opposition and the scorn, all the struggles with his own physical limitations, all the heartache and heart-searchings he had suffered over this whole enterprise – it had been worth it all. He began again.

'My friends.'

He felt a lump in his throat, and paused again to sip his wine. The gathering stirred and murmured as a wave of supportive emotion swelled through the room and ebbed away. He straightened his back and continued, his voice gaining strength with every sentence.

'What can be said of this day? Nine score and ten months hath passed since I stood upon this my doorstep, and sent forth ye Poor Preachers with our blessing. Ye have returned, save them of the Southern mission who journey onward with a call to other flocks and a greater harvest. We have heard many and a-many tales of thine exploits and there are a-many more yet to tell. But tales enow have we all heard at this time, so that this we may declare: By this emprise a mighty victory hath God wrought in this land! What say you?'

A resounding 'Amen!' came from every throat. They were on their feet, applauding. Smith even fell on his knees and raised his hands in worship. It took a while before they returned to their seats and settled down to allow their host to continue.

'Well, unto God be the glory. But anon we look to that which is to come. The harvest is still great, and the labourers are but few. We must pray the Lord of the Harvest that He may send forth more. Ye, brethren, have been the varward of this army and have proved the faithfulness of God in this. Some of ye have spoken, saying that ye would go forth once more. May the Lord bless your faithfulness and valour. Others have spoken, saying that they are called to other callings. In this there is no shame, for there is a season in all things. Nay, rather is there honour also, for we have need still of clergy in our midst to rise up as master-professors, the flame to ignite 'mongst our rising student-clerics. Shepherds also need we to strengthen our young flocks.'

He bowed toward Lawrence and Richard Brandon as he spoke, who bowed their heads and smiled.

Wycliffe took a deep breath and looked around the room challengingly.

'But whatever be thy calling henceforth, this I ask of all: that thou wouldst tarry at Oxenford and tell the tale of thy journeys, that thou wouldst seek for more labourers...'

He paused again and caught the eye of Richard Waystract.

'Of what number have we 'mongst our graduates that have spoken of their willingness, Waystract?'

'A full multitude, Doctor!' Waystract reported proudly. 'But two score and five we have chosen. Many we have yet to decide thereon.'

This was very encouraging, and generated more wonder and comment from the assembly.

Waystract was a master at recruitment, although he disclaimed this. All he had to do, he said, was speak of the reports that Philip Repton brought back from his wanderings. He had summoned both Masters Smith and Ashwardby to help in the selection process. Many volunteers merely wanted to find adventure and had no idea of the challenges and dangers they faced. Smith and Ashwardby, being men of prayer and spiritual discernment, interviewed each volunteer to discover if they had a real calling or not.

Doctor Wycliffe was visibly impressed and encouraged.

'Two score and five chosen men? Thanks be to God! Much can be done in our land with such. But not all should break fallow earth as have ye, brethren preachers. This therefore I ask of you: 'ere ye return to thy labours, whether evangels or shepherds ye be, take ye some of these new labourers under thine aegis and teach them of the ways of the Poor Preachers. Speak of the lessons ye have learned and snares that were laid for you. Speak of the hunger and thirst of the people and the labour wherewith ye have succoured them. Speak of your victories and even of thy loss a-times. Stay but for a forte' night that we may equip this our new army. Be not deceived, the greatest foe of all doth not sleep, and will destroy this great work if he findeth the means thereof.'

He paused again, knowing how difficult his next request would be. He had discussed it with Waystract and Parker a number of times.

'Mark ye the scriptures that they speak of the Holy Apostles. In twos they were sent forth at the first. But some took other disciples after the Ascension of the risen Lord Christ, when he sent them forth unto all the world to preach the Gospel. We have sent ye forth as companies of two and three, and the older hath instructed the younger, so that the younger hath grown a-pace unto full manhood in his calling. Much need we have of them that have trod the path and fought the fight and won, that they may also raise up disciples. O disciple evangel, thou that art now fully proved, hearken unto me. Not for naught have we ordained thee unto the priesthood. I therefore also ask thou of this: Seek thou the face of God, that thou mayest leave the service of thy master heretofore, and take rather thine own disciple. When it is settled within thy soul, speak thou unto Master Waystract that thou mayest find thy disciple from they that are willing. The elder I also pray, that thou mayest find a new disciple from among these two score and five to take upon the way with thee. Such is our great need, brethren, but I command no man in this.'

He waited for this to sink in. Many of the returned missionaries looked a little disconsolate at this request, for they were hoping to continue with the same team as they had started with. Young father Peter, who felt uncomfortable at his recent promotion, looked at Father Edward in alarm. Edward whispered reassuringly.

'Thou'rt no more a youth, my son. So hath Simon spoken of thee also. Thine own victories thou'st wrought in God's strength. But still a shepherd thou art and will ever be. It is no shame if thou'lt seek thine own flock. Mind thee of the youth, Master Lawrence Martinhoe in Lincoln also. He may yet come unto Oxenford and look to thee to guide his steps in ministry as he hath done aforetime.'

Peter nodded, partially reassured. He had a decision to make.

'Speak thy mind, brethren.' commanded Wycliffe. 'What is thy thought in this matter, for I wist that conflict rageth within the soul of some at this my request.'

After some quiet discussions and whisperings, Harold Ravenswood rose to his feet. His earnest young face was set, although a little pale.

'Doctor Evangelicus. I must perforce seek a new way-fellow as my master aileth and cannot journey. But an evangelist am I, and will go forth upon whatever mission He sendeth me. I will take a disciple with me. May God give me grace.'

He sat down to the sound of supportive applause.

'A fine lad, that,' Hereford whispered to Waystract, 'yet no longer a lad.'

In contrast, Benjamin Abingdon sprang to his feet.

'My erstwhile way-fellow would welcome my departure, I deem, good Doctor, so I must needs also seek a new companion. But may he be of sober mind that may keep my steps from the nearest tavern of the town. But ever are my feet fated to wander.'

Laughter greeted this light-hearted response. It was felt to be typical of him to announce his decision in such a ribald manner. William Thorpe protested and wondered aloud about who was going to take Benjamin's place to lighten his darker moods.

Parker leaned over to Father Edward and murmured "Tis my belief yon Abyngdon shall lie jesting upon his deathbed.'

William Thorpe himself stood to his feet. The slightly grim, set look of his mouth in contrast to his friend's light-heartedness.

'Good Doctor Evangelicus, I bring tidings both good and less-so, but that I have had speech with thee on these matters a sennight gone.'

Wycliffe's countenance became sad and careworn, and others present looked at each other concerned. Even Benjamin's face fell momentarily.

'Say on, Father William,' Wycliffe said steadily, 'for not all here present have heard of the affairs in Kent.'

The tale of the amazing conversion of the pardoner and the other stirring events at Faversham. When he spoke of the ban placed upon all Wycliffites (supposedly in league with the rebel-priest, John Ball) a heavy sigh and murmur could be heard amongst the assembly.

'A grievous blow, this' the Doctor commented aloud. 'Ever hath Satanus sought to hinder us in our mission. Wherefore gain we tidings of the disciples of Faversham anon, if none return to Faversham unmarked?'

At this point, Master Philip Repton arose, his clear voice and cheerful energy cutting through the general despondency in the room like a knife.

'Thy pardon, good Doctor, but one hath done so! My face is known in Kent, but not so is that of Will Sanderley, though he goeth thither in other guise. Speak, Master Will! Tell thy tale.'

He waved his hand toward Will Sanderley who struggled painfully to his feet, wincing a little.

'A worn and weary errand am I, good Doctor, good brethren, for three days have I endured in the saddle. Nor have I the buttocks of iron that my master possesseth. But good tidings I bear natheless. In the guise of an humble scrivener, I sought out the disciples at Feaversham. All is well.'

He turned and grinned at William Thorpe.

'The former pardoner of which thou spake hath truly become as father and shepherd of the flock. Jacob of the one-eye also. A mighty evangelist is he, but netteth his catch one-a-one but yet a-many. The Guild Hall cannot hold all the multitude, and the big master-fisher hath taken some to a farmer's barn without the city of Canterbury itself. Even his lordship's husbandman hath become as one of us, and some of his lordship's servants also. Holy Church and the Sheriff consider us of none account, thus do we grow unhindered. Unrest groweth, alas, with the broilings of John Ball and Wat Tyler. Many folk have turned to the counsels of hate and may take up arms if this poll tax be enforced. But many also will hear the gospel and find hope.'

Benjamin laughed with delight as the assembly applauded once again.

'Thanks be to God!' cried William Thorpe, somewhat overcome. 'Our defeat hath turned unto victory at the last! My thanks to thee, good Will, and blessings be upon thy pate. Wilt thou also go to them again and bring them scriptures translated?'

'Such is mine errand a' Monday next, brother if my back faileth me not,' replied the slightly reluctant secret-agent with a weary nod. 'I drive a wain of turnips with the Word of Life sown amongst them, to be delivered to Master Jacob.'

Doctor Wycliffe, invigorated by this news, stood up again.

'God moveth in mysterious ways His wonders to perform, forsooth! The affairs of Kent go on well, although thought must be given to the feeding of such a flock. But praise be to God! Is there others of ye, brethren preachers that would speak of your intentions?'

Peter shyly stood to his feet.

'Good Doctor, much I have learned of my travels with my brethren beside me. Yet it is mine to pastor the flock. Much thought have I given to them that are called to ministry, for such an one was I. Many a young cleric have I seen that have fallen into the snare of the evil one, yea, even within the walls of Oxenford. If a living there is none, then suffer me to stay at Oxenford that I may give aid to the souls of these, that they hear the true Gospel and join the Christian Brethren.'

At that point, Master Crompe started, nudged Waystract's arm and jumped to his feet.

'May God be praised! Such a need I have seen also, and have oft spoken of this. I also have need of an intern for Master Adam hath fallen gravely ill of the ague, and is passed away unto his reward. If it pleaseth thee, good Doctor, I shall take this good man, priest though he be. Shepherds of his like are hard to come by.'

The expression on Peter's face was enough to confirm to all that he accepted Crompe's generous offer.

'So be it!' smiled Wycliffe. 'Though for Master Adam we grieve, yet God hath turned evil unto His good purpose. Anon have all the disciples spoken and decided their fate, but what of their masters? Speak, brethren!'

John Haswell the Hardy stood to his feet.

'Mine intent is no secret, Doctor Evangelicus, as is that of Lawrence, my fellow-priest. The length and breadth of England I would walk to preach the gospel. Give me a disciple as hardy and of like forbearance t'ward his master as had Lawrence Parsons, and we shall shake the very gates of Hell!'

He sat down to thunderous applause and cries of 'Hail, Hereward the Hardy!' and 'Awake!'

Father Simon, after being advised by Edward to keep his speech short, sprang to his feet. The room seemed to shrink even further.

'It hath ever been my wont' he declared with a sweeping glance around the room, 'to stride the world as a king's mimer and player would stride the stage. But my brethren and way-fellows have schooled me a little, I pray God, that I may walk more humbly before him. Yet the drama of life groweth a-pace and the clamour of the players of evil must be silenced by the voice of Truth. Short indeed is our span of life and much is there to be performed to advance the Kingdom of Heaven. Let us continue, then, to bring this miracle-play of the Gospel to the people that they may believe; that they may also walk the stage themselves to declare God's truth thereon. But I must desist, lest I weary your ears. Give me a disciple with a mind as scholarly as Edward's, and an heart as warmful as Peter's and all England shall hearken to the orator and not be turned away.'

Loud applause and some laughing comments followed. Master Ashton's voice rose above all.

'Yea, surely, Simon thou'rt not destined to preach from one pulpit alone! Only the streets and fields are pulpits full worthy for thine oratory. Go forth, man, go forth!'

Edward also rose and spoke simply.

'I also will preach the Word of Life, although it is mine more to teach the principles of Holy Writ than to sound the evangel's trumpet. I have not Simon's great gift for this. If the evangels amongst us will lead, then I will follow in their footsteps that our new followers may be grounded in Truth to make them strong. What sayest thou, good Doctor?'

This made sense to all, and Wycliffe and Waystract exchanged nods. Parker applauded loudly.

'Let it be so according to thy word, Father Edward,' approved the Doctor, adding reflectively, 'O that we had more teachers that rightly divide the Word of Truth. Prophets also, as thou art Master Smith. To this we must give more thought a' the morrow. Have all spoken? Father Richard Brandon I excuse for his vocation is sure, and a good living Waystract hath planned for thee. With the Southwest mission in full flight, every tale is told anon.'

He stood up straighter than before, and everyone in the room instinctively stood to their feet as he pronounced a benediction.

'Christian brethren! Whatever be thy calling, go forth!'

'Amen!' they cried as one voice.

Glossary

Accesse	Fever
Accidie	Slothfulness, laziness
Aforetime	Before
Alaunts	Hunting-dogs. Also a derogatory term for attendant men-at-arms
Almoner	Distributer of alms to the poor
Anon	Now
Assart	Land cleared of trees for agricultural purposes
Assoil	Absolve
Astringer	A keeper of the falcons
Awehape	Amazed
Barful	Dangerous
Bestadance	Circumstances
Bobance	Boasting, pride, self-consequence
Borel	Common, uneducated
Bretheling	Sycophant
Brose	Broth, soup
Cautelous	Deceitful, cunning
Chapman	Merchant
Chincherous	Tight fisted
Covertise	Covertousness, greed
Despiteously	Spitefully
Devoir (Norman)	Duty
Dreadless	Without a doubt
En assuivant (Norman French)	In pursuit. A hunting term.
En foison (Norman)	In abundance, liberally

Enow	Enough
Eschew	Refuse, reject, avoid
Even-Christians	Fellow-men
Favel	Flattery
Ferly	Strange
Fern ago	A long time ago
Fetchings	Crafty schemes
Fey, Fay	Faith (not to be confused with fey-madness.)
Flightsome	Aggressive, pugnacious
Fliting	Strife, contention
Forestraught	Extremely worried
Frape	Crowd, pack, usually in mischief or riot
Gainbite	Remorse, guilt
Garboil	Trouble, unrest, brawl
Gigelot	Wencher, adulterer, strumpet
Glosery	Flattery
Gokey	Foolish
Grutch	Grouch, complain
Guerdon	Reward, spoils of war
Handfast	Betrothed
Headfast	Stubborn
Hie (verb)	Send, travel
Hurling	Fighting
Indurate	Obstinate
Jack-eater	Braggart
Jack-raking	Drudgery
Janglery	Jesting
Jape	Joke
Jeffrey's Day	Never
Jobbard	Idiot. (An affectionately derogatory term.)
Kennel-hoves	Slums
Kennels	Street guttering
Kind-wit	Common-sense

Lachesse	Carelessness, negligence
Lavender	Washer woman
Lewed, lewd	Uneducated, ignorant, low-class, vulgar
Lief	Love, preference
Liesings	Lies
Likerousness	Lust, licenteousness
Limiter	Friars limited to begging in a defined region
List, listeth (verb)	Desires, wishes
Losel	A failure, a worthless person
Lout	Bow obsequiously
Lurdan	A demeaning term
Malapert	Insolent, presumptuous, impudent
Mawtrews	Pounded meat
Mell	Meddle
Miscreant	Malefactor, wrong-doer
Mullock	Rubbish
Mumpish	Grumpy, depressed
Natheless	Nonetheless
Nightertale	Night-time
Nithing	Disgraced or cowardly person
Nyfles	Silly stories
Not a whit	Not at all, nothing
Obdurate	Stubborn, unrepentant
Oft and lome	Time and time again
Orgulous	Proud, pompous
Papelard	Popish, overly-pious
Puissant	High-ranking, of great importance
Reck (verb)	Care
Recusant	Rebellious, heretical
Rede	Counsel, advise
Roiling (verb)	Roving about, wandering
Ruth	Mercy, pity
Sand-blind	Half blind, obtuse

Scathe	Hurt, wound
Sely	Happy, carefree, innocent, simple
Sennight	One week
Shamefast	Humble, modest
Shapster	Cutter of cloth or garments
Shendful	Shameful
Shent	Ruined
Sickerly	Surely, doubtlessly
Shakebuckler	A reckless dare-devil
Simony	Dishonest gain through false piety e.g. Indulgences
Sins Seven	The Seven Deadly Sins
Sleeveless	Useless, pointless
Soothsaw	A truth, a sooth-saying
Stint	Cease
Suckfist	Idiot. A derogatory term.
Thrall	Slave
Three-so-much	Thrice, three times
Thrift	Prosperity
Tregatour	Illusionist, magician
Vavasour	Feudal lord
Vaward	Vanguard
Ventosity	Colic
Void, avoid	Dismount, remove
Wain	Wagon
Want-wit	Nit-wit
Wereguild	Reward. Sometimes loot from battle.
Wherewithal	How
Whirlicote	Horse-drawn vehicle
Whither away	Where are you going?
Wist (verb)	Know, understand, be aware of
Witaldry	Stupidity, folly
Witterly	Assuredly

Wolfshead	Outcast, a derogatory term
Wont	Custom, habit
Wood (adjective)	Mad, wild
Wot (verb)	Know
Wynd	Wind
Yellowbeak	Youth, youngster, immature young man